GUS

& HIS GANG

Chris Blain

GUS

& HIS GANG

Translation by Alexis Siegel

:01

First Second

NEW YORK & LONDON

CONTENTS

NATALIE

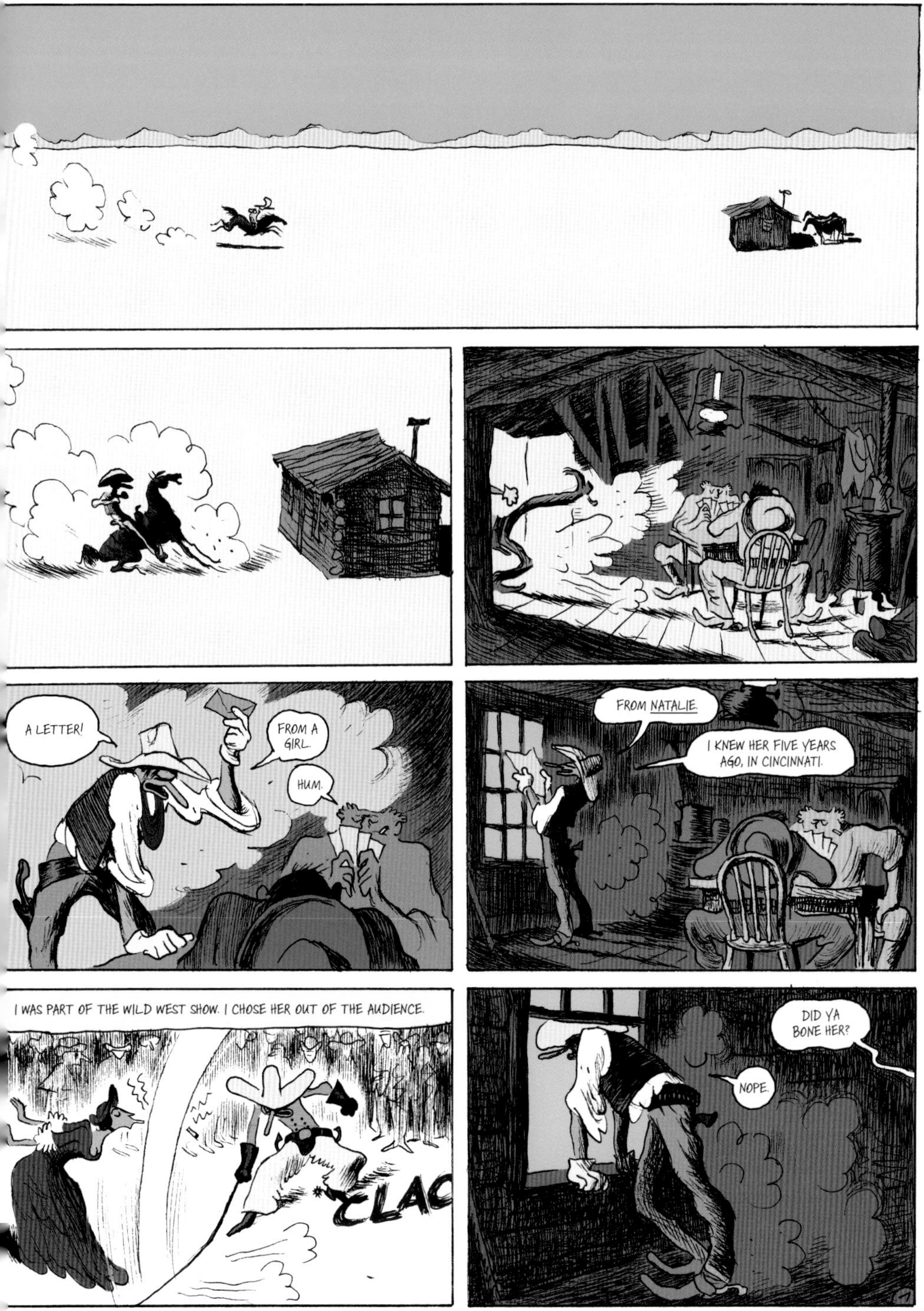
A LETTER!
FROM A GIRL.
HUM.
FROM NATALIE.
I KNEW HER FIVE YEARS AGO, IN CINCINNATI.
I WAS PART OF THE WILD WEST SHOW. I CHOSE HER OUT OF THE AUDIENCE.
CLAC
DID YA BONE HER?
NOPE.

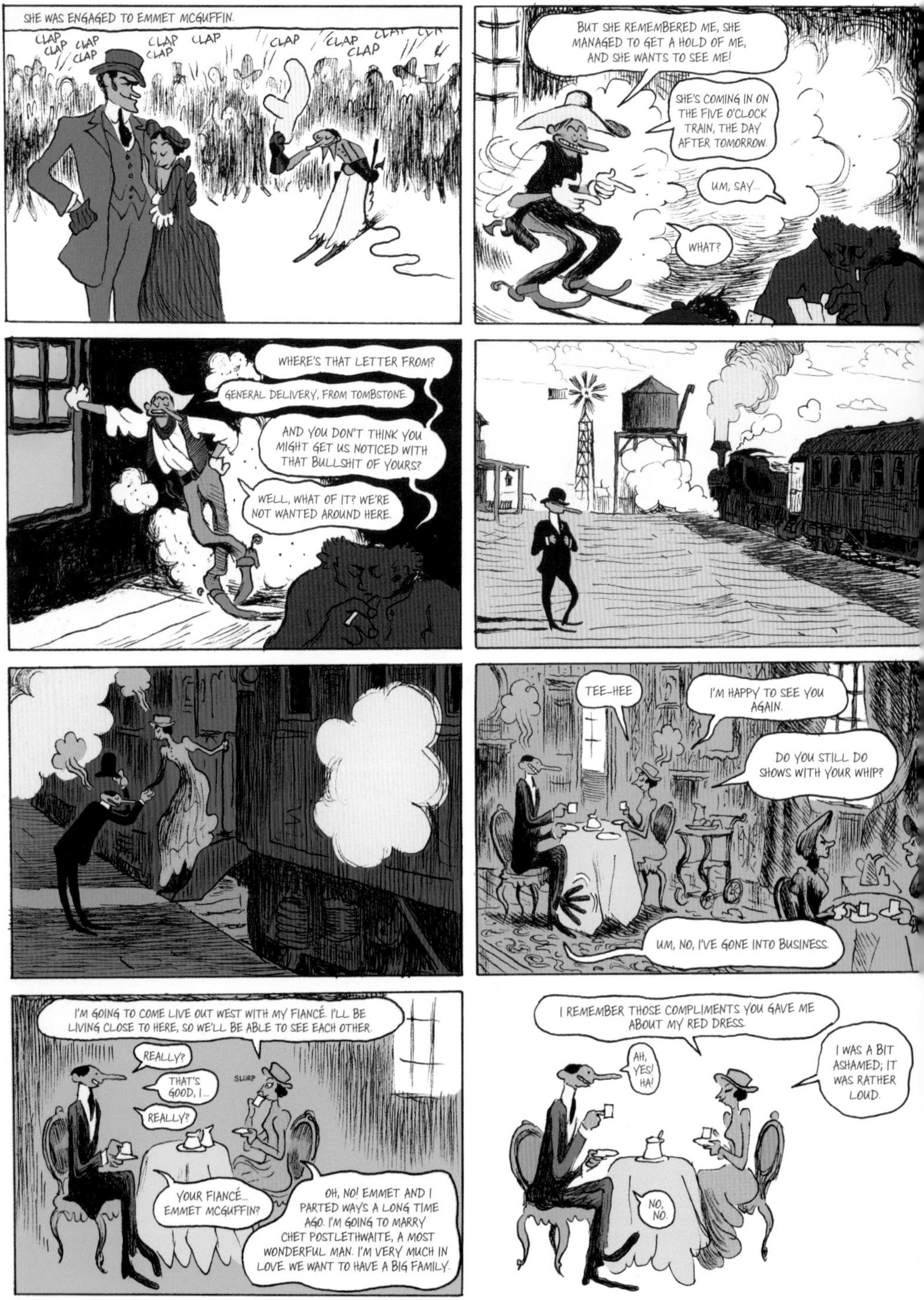
SHE WAS ENGAGED TO EMMET MCGUFFIN.
CLAP CLAP CLAP CLAP CLAP CLAP CLAP CLAP CLAP CLAP
BUT SHE REMEMBERED ME, SHE MANAGED TO GET A HOLD OF ME, AND SHE WANTS TO SEE ME!
SHE'S COMING IN ON THE FIVE O'CLOCK TRAIN, THE DAY AFTER TOMORROW.
UM, SAY...
WHAT?
WHERE'S THAT LETTER FROM?
GENERAL DELIVERY, FROM TOMBSTONE.
AND YOU DON'T THINK YOU MIGHT GET US NOTICED WITH THAT BULLSHIT OF YOURS?
WELL, WHAT OF IT? WE'RE NOT WANTED AROUND HERE.
TEE-HEE
I'M HAPPY TO SEE YOU AGAIN.
DO YOU STILL DO SHOWS WITH YOUR WHIP?
UM, NO, I'VE GONE INTO BUSINESS.
I'M GOING TO COME LIVE OUT WEST WITH MY FIANCÉ. I'LL BE LIVING CLOSE TO HERE, SO WE'LL BE ABLE TO SEE EACH OTHER.
REALLY?
THAT'S GOOD, I...
SLURP
REALLY?
YOUR FIANCÉ... EMMET MCGUFFIN?
OH, NO! EMMET AND I PARTED WAYS A LONG TIME AGO. I'M GOING TO MARRY CHET POSTLETHWAITE, A MOST WONDERFUL MAN. I'M VERY MUCH IN LOVE. WE WANT TO HAVE A BIG FAMILY.
I REMEMBER THOSE COMPLIMENTS YOU GAVE ME ABOUT MY RED DRESS.
AH, YES! HA!
I WAS A BIT ASHAMED; IT WAS RATHER LOUD.
NO, NO.

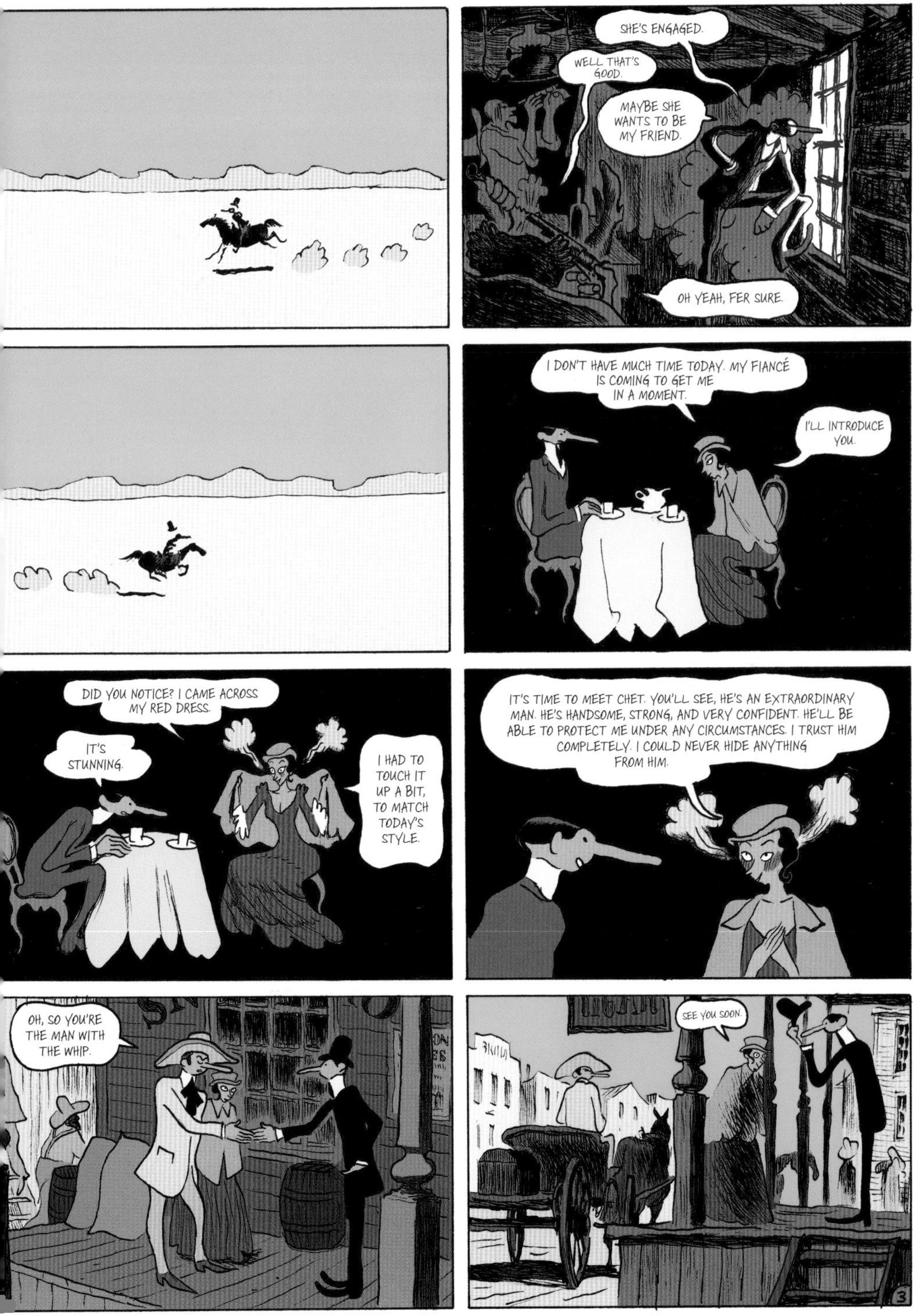
SHE'S ENGAGED.
WELL THAT'S GOOD.
MAYBE SHE WANTS TO BE MY FRIEND.
OH YEAH, FER SURE.
I DON'T HAVE MUCH TIME TODAY. MY FIANCÉ IS COMING TO GET ME IN A MOMENT.
I'LL INTRODUCE YOU.
DID YOU NOTICE? I CAME ACROSS MY RED DRESS.
IT'S STUNNING.
I HAD TO TOUCH IT UP A BIT, TO MATCH TODAY'S STYLE.
IT'S TIME TO MEET CHET. YOU'LL SEE, HE'S AN EXTRAORDINARY MAN. HE'S HANDSOME, STRONG, AND VERY CONFIDENT. HE'LL BE ABLE TO PROTECT ME UNDER ANY CIRCUMSTANCES. I TRUST HIM COMPLETELY. I COULD NEVER HIDE ANYTHING FROM HIM.
OH, SO YOU'RE THE MAN WITH THE WHIP.
SEE YOU SOON.
3

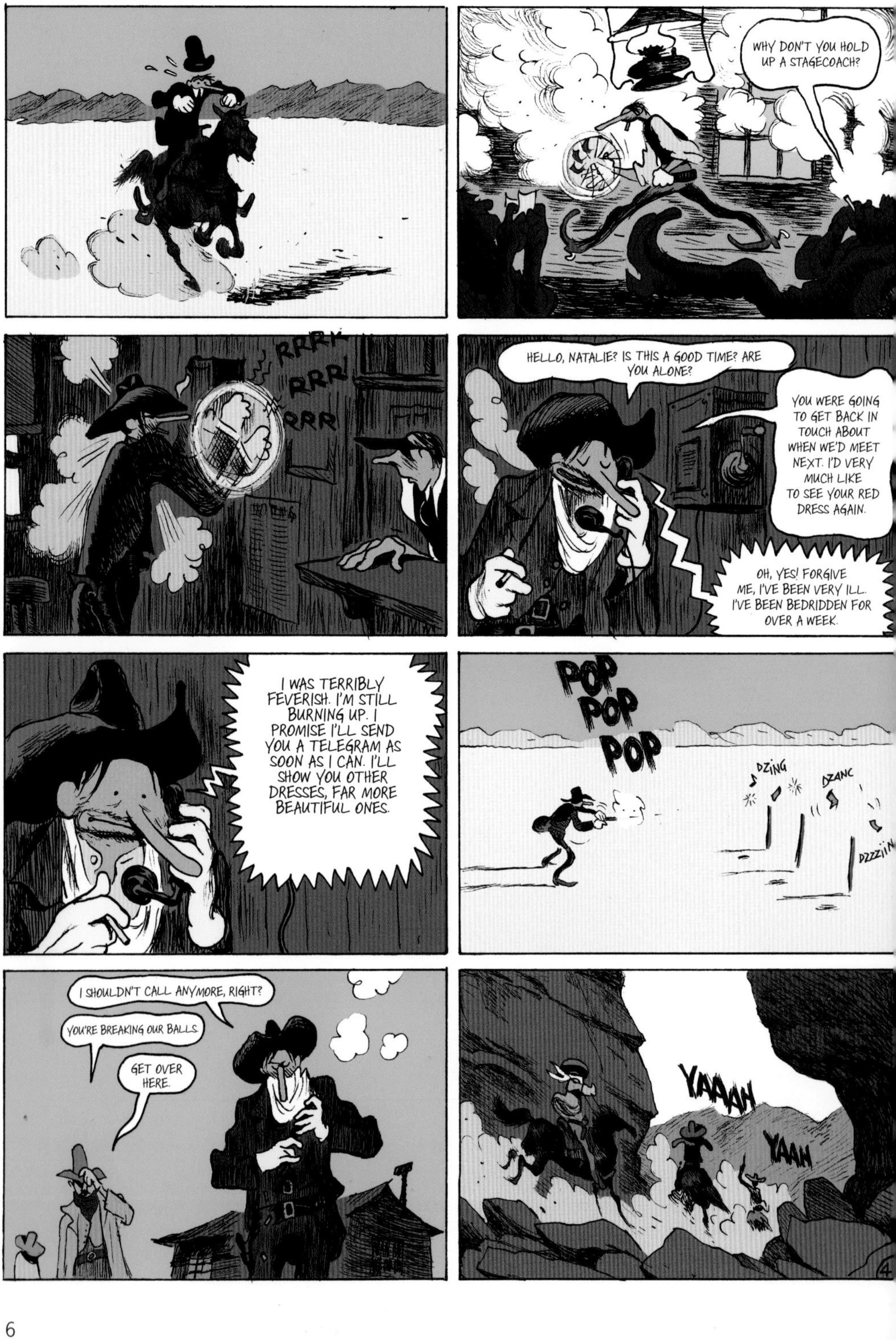
WHY DON'T YOU HOLD UP A STAGECOACH?
RRRK
RRR
RRR
HELLO, NATALIE? IS THIS A GOOD TIME? ARE YOU ALONE?
YOU WERE GOING TO GET BACK IN TOUCH ABOUT WHEN WE'D MEET NEXT. I'D VERY MUCH LIKE TO SEE YOUR RED DRESS AGAIN.
OH, YES! FORGIVE ME, I'VE BEEN VERY ILL. I'VE BEEN BEDRIDDEN FOR OVER A WEEK.
I WAS TERRIBLY FEVERISH. I'M STILL BURNING UP. I PROMISE I'LL SEND YOU A TELEGRAM AS SOON AS I CAN. I'LL SHOW YOU OTHER DRESSES, FAR MORE BEAUTIFUL ONES.
POP
POP
POP
DZING
DZANC
I SHOULDN'T CALL ANYMORE, RIGHT?
YOU'RE BREAKING OUR BALLS.
GET OVER HERE.
YAAAH
YAAN

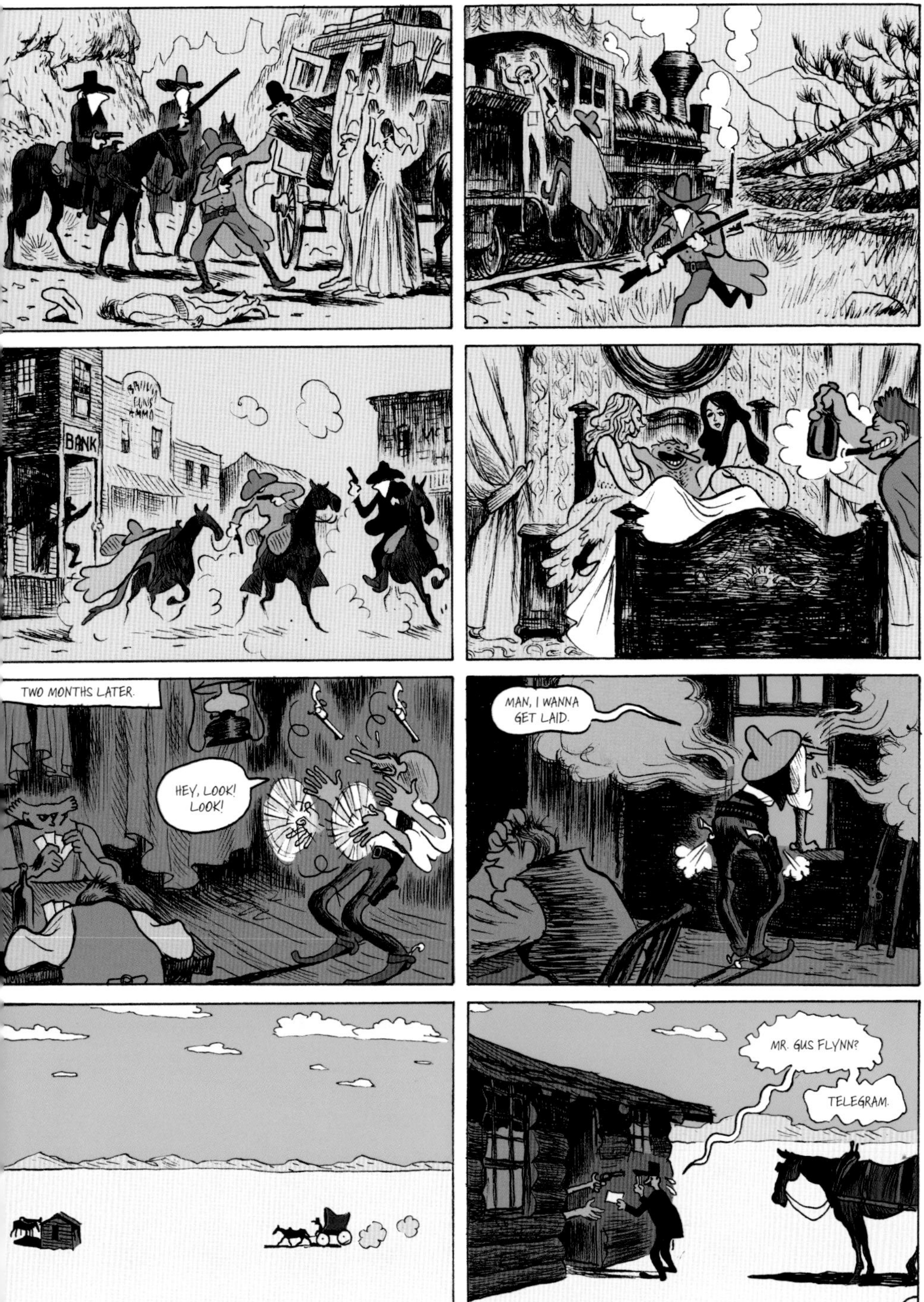
BANK
TWO MONTHS LATER.
HEY, LOOK! LOOK!
MAN, I WANNA GET LAID.
MR. GUS FLYNN?
TELEGRAM.
5

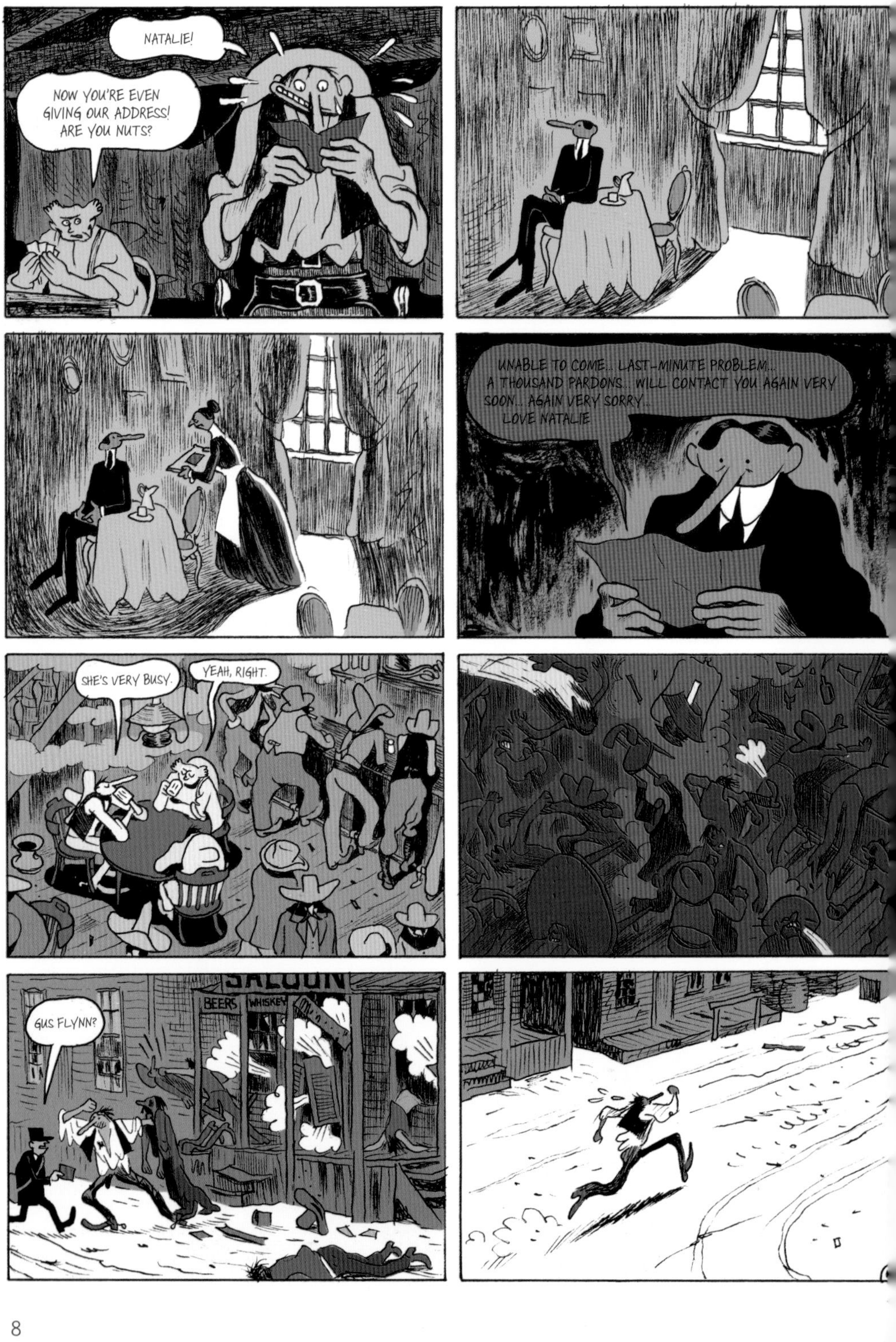
NATALIE!
NOW YOU'RE EVEN GIVING OUR ADDRESS! ARE YOU NUTS?
UNABLE TO COME... LAST-MINUTE PROBLEM... A THOUSAND PARDONS... WILL CONTACT YOU AGAIN VERY SOON... AGAIN VERY SORRY... LOVE NATALIE
SHE'S VERY BUSY.
YEAH, RIGHT.
SALOON
BEERS
WHISKEY
GUS FLYNN?

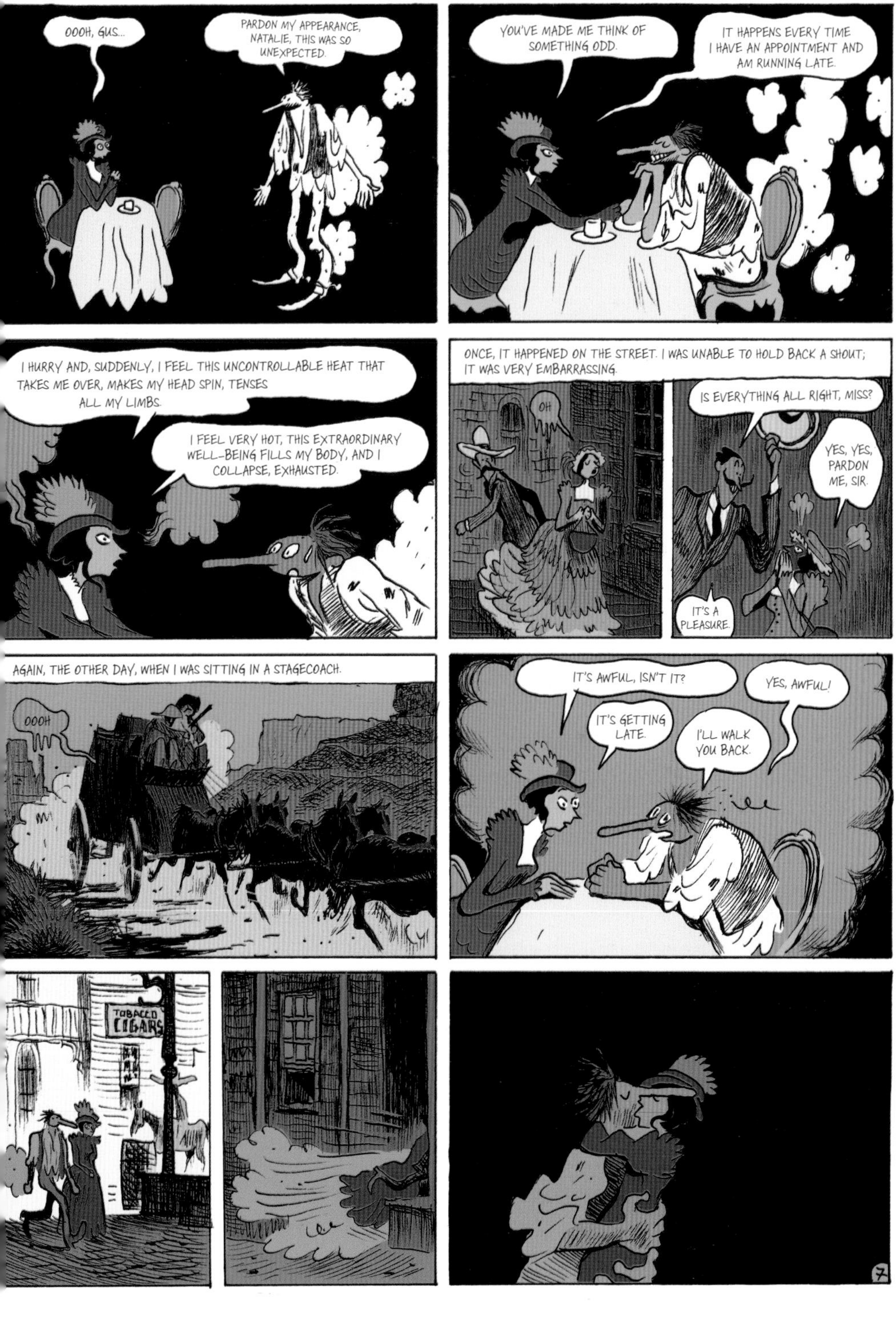
OOOH, GUS...
PARDON MY APPEARANCE, NATALIE, THIS WAS SO UNEXPECTED.
YOU'VE MADE ME THINK OF SOMETHING ODD.
IT HAPPENS EVERY TIME I HAVE AN APPOINTMENT AND AM RUNNING LATE.
I HURRY AND, SUDDENLY, I FEEL THIS UNCONTROLLABLE HEAT THAT TAKES ME OVER, MAKES MY HEAD SPIN, TENSES ALL MY LIMBS.
I FEEL VERY HOT, THIS EXTRAORDINARY WELL-BEING FILLS MY BODY, AND I COLLAPSE, EXHAUSTED.
ONCE, IT HAPPENED ON THE STREET. I WAS UNABLE TO HOLD BACK A SHOUT; IT WAS VERY EMBARRASSING.
OH
IS EVERYTHING ALL RIGHT, MISS?
YES, YES, PARDON ME, SIR.
IT'S A PLEASURE.
AGAIN, THE OTHER DAY, WHEN I WAS SITTING IN A STAGECOACH.
OOOH
IT'S AWFUL, ISN'T IT?
YES, AWFUL!
IT'S GETTING LATE.
I'LL WALK YOU BACK.
TOBACCO CIGARS
7

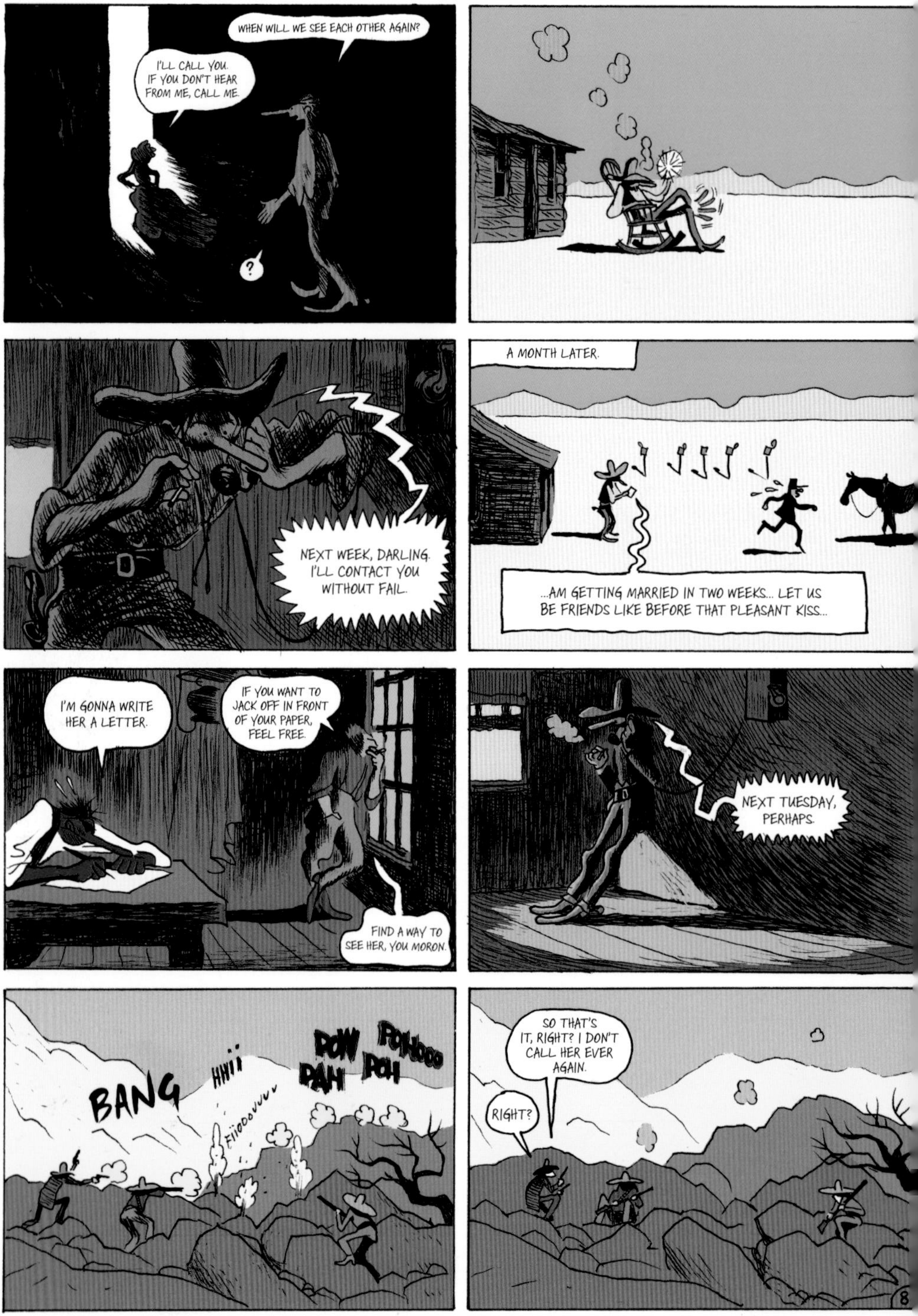
WHEN WILL WE SEE EACH OTHER AGAIN?
I'LL CALL YOU. IF YOU DON'T HEAR FROM ME, CALL ME.
?
NEXT WEEK, DARLING. I'LL CONTACT YOU WITHOUT FAIL.
A MONTH LATER.
...AM GETTING MARRIED IN TWO WEEKS... LET US BE FRIENDS LIKE BEFORE THAT PLEASANT KISS...
I'M GONNA WRITE HER A LETTER.
IF YOU WANT TO JACK OFF IN FRONT OF YOUR PAPER, FEEL FREE.
FIND A WAY TO SEE HER, YOU MORON.
NEXT TUESDAY, PERHAPS.
BANG
HHIÏ
FIIOOUUUU
POW
PAH
POHOOO
POH
SO THAT'S IT, RIGHT? I DON'T CALL HER EVER AGAIN.
RIGHT?
8

christopheblain septembre 2004

GUS, CLEM, GRATT

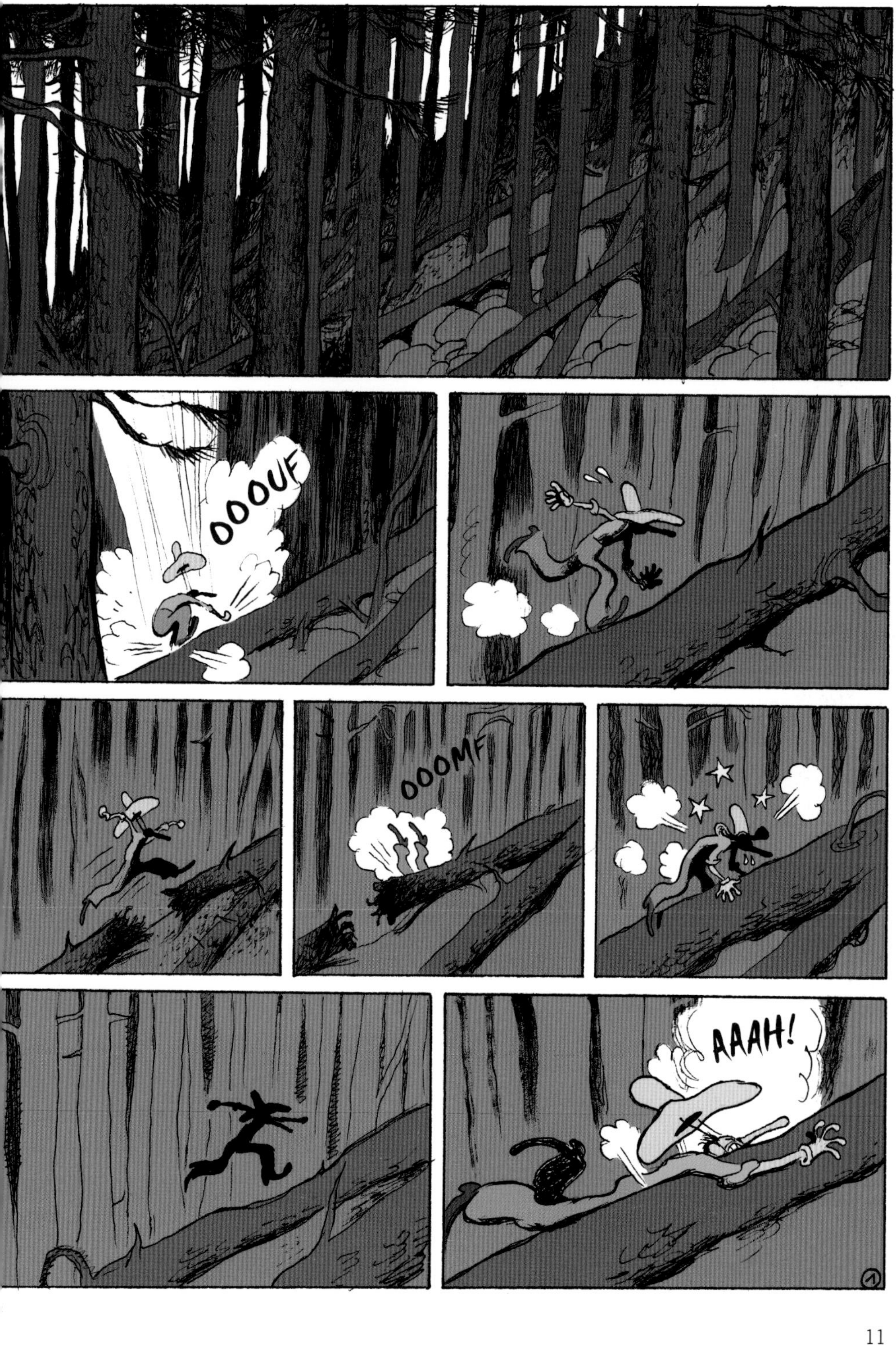
OOOUF
OOOMF
AAAH!

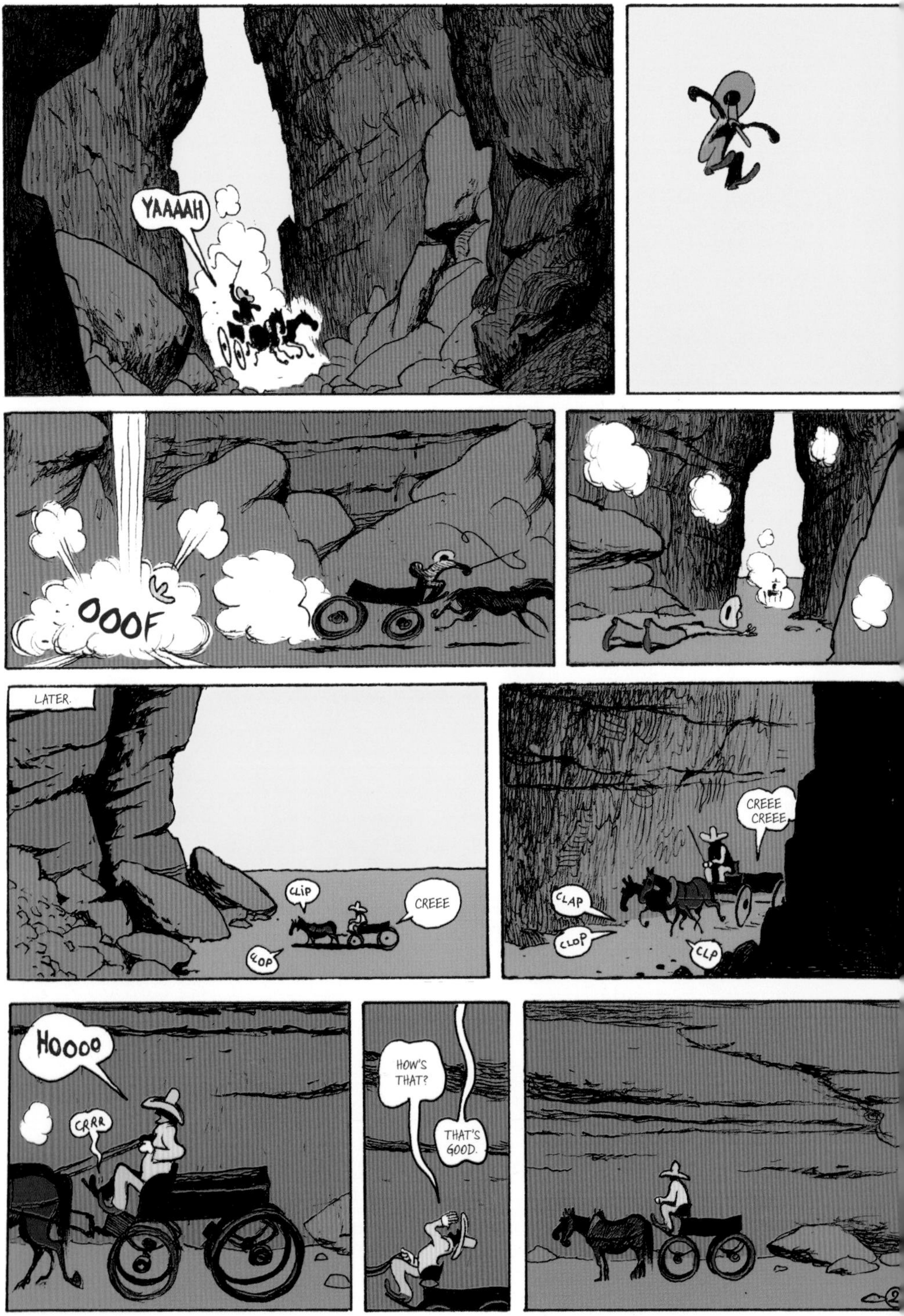
YAAAAH
OOOF
LATER.
CLIP
CREEE
CLOP
CREEE CREEE
CLAP
CLOP
CLP
HOOOO
CRRR
HOW'S THAT?
THAT'S GOOD.

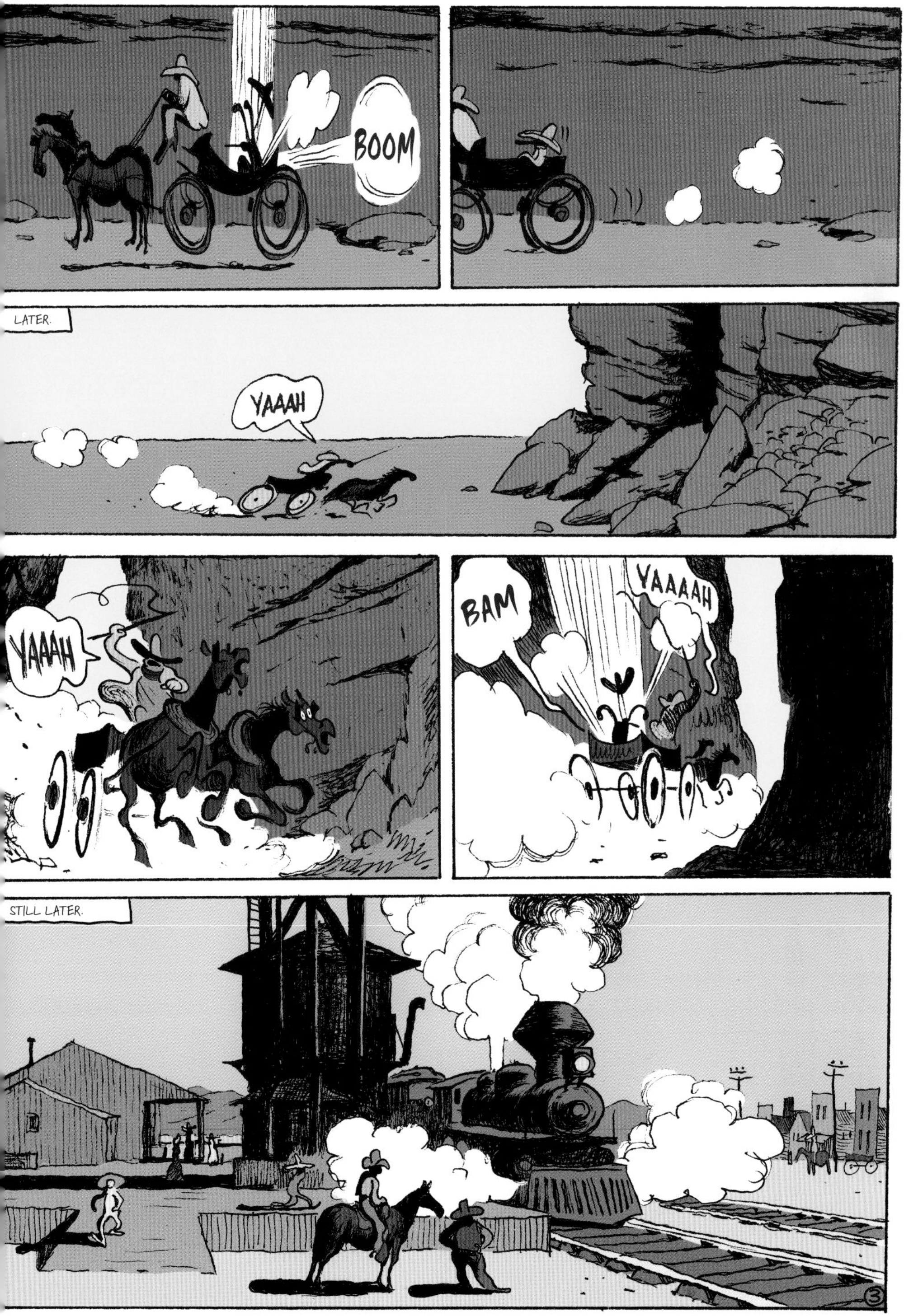
BOOM
LATER.
YAAAH
YAAAH
BAM
YAAAAH
STILL LATER.
3

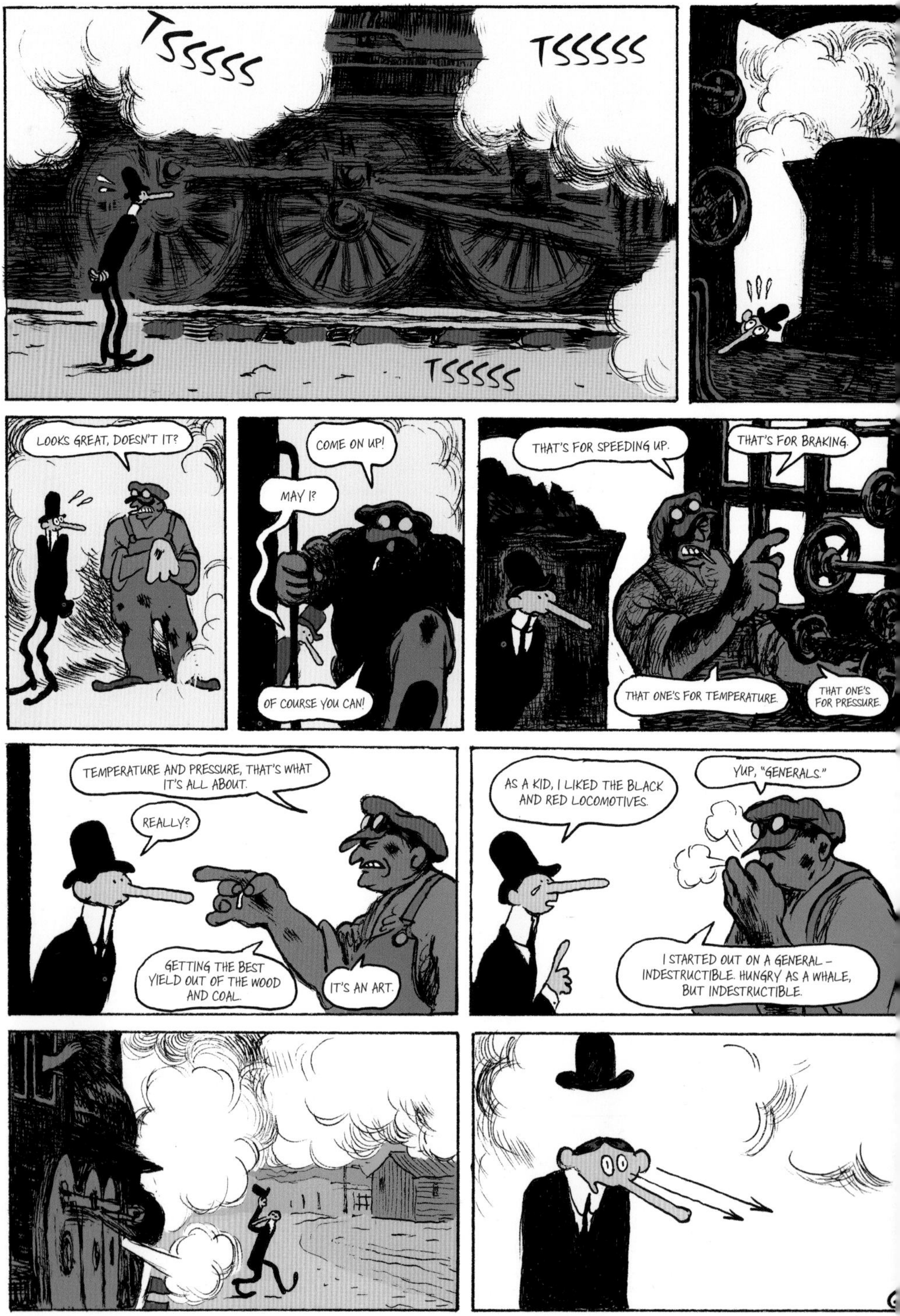
TSSSSS
TSSSSS
TSSSSS
LOOKS GREAT, DOESN'T IT?
COME ON UP!
MAY I?
OF COURSE YOU CAN!
THAT'S FOR SPEEDING UP.
THAT'S FOR BRAKING.
THAT ONE'S FOR TEMPERATURE.
THAT ONE'S FOR PRESSURE.
TEMPERATURE AND PRESSURE, THAT'S WHAT IT'S ALL ABOUT.
REALLY?
GETTING THE BEST YIELD OUT OF THE WOOD AND COAL.
IT'S AN ART.
AS A KID, I LIKED THE BLACK AND RED LOCOMOTIVES.
YUP, "GENERALS."
I STARTED OUT ON A GENERAL – INDESTRUCTIBLE. HUNGRY AS A WHALE, BUT INDESTRUCTIBLE.

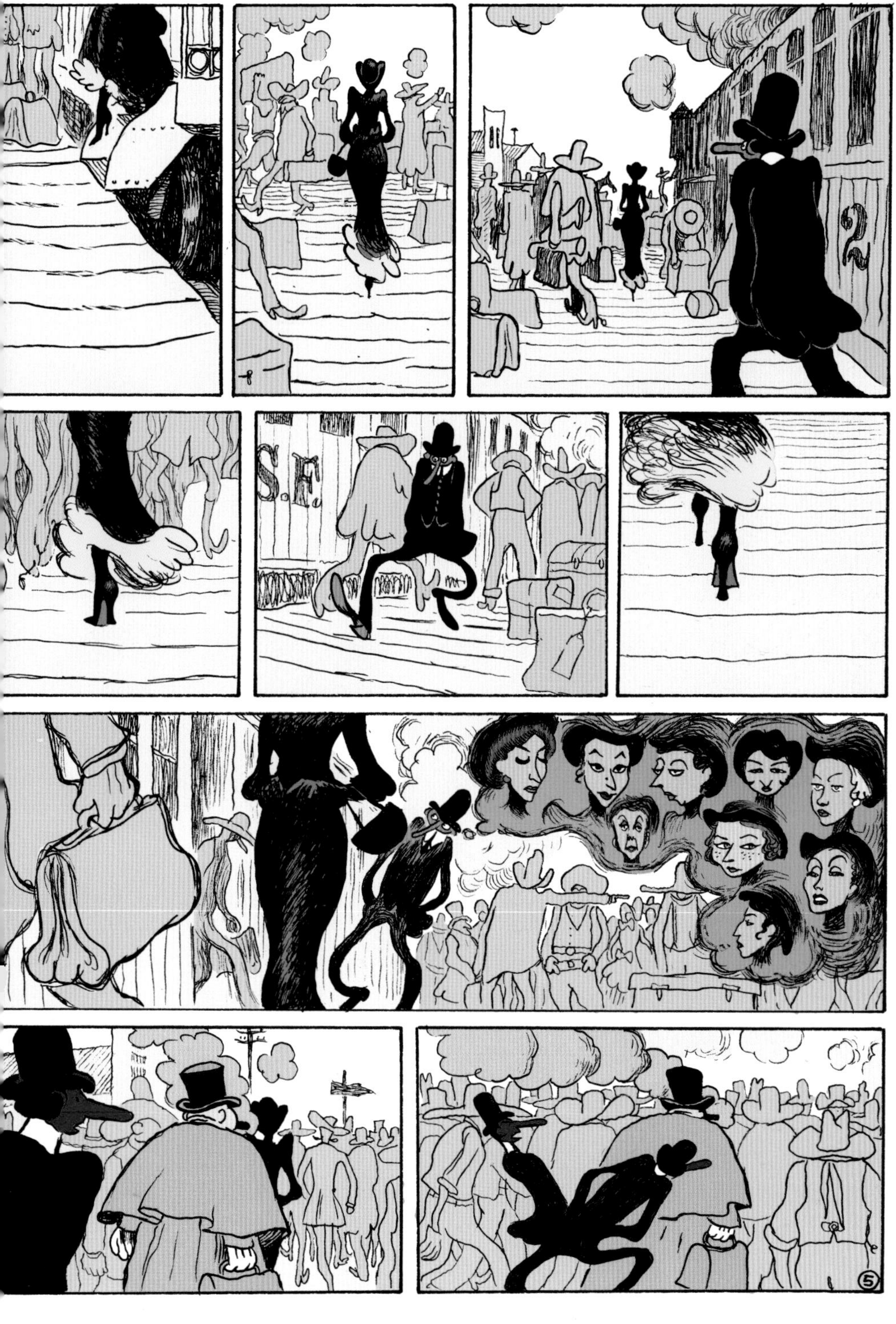
S.F.

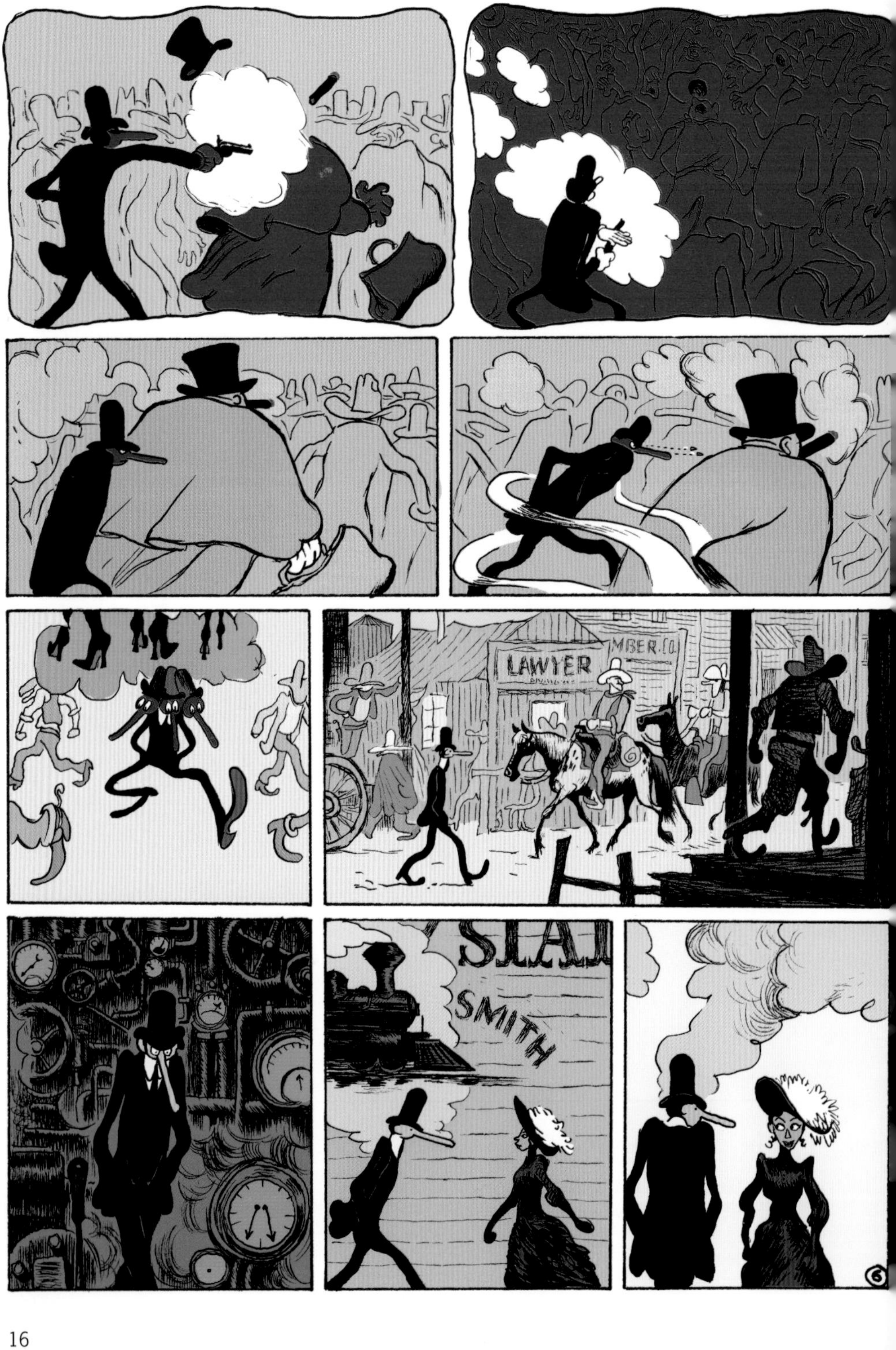
LAWYER
MBER.CO.
SMITH
6

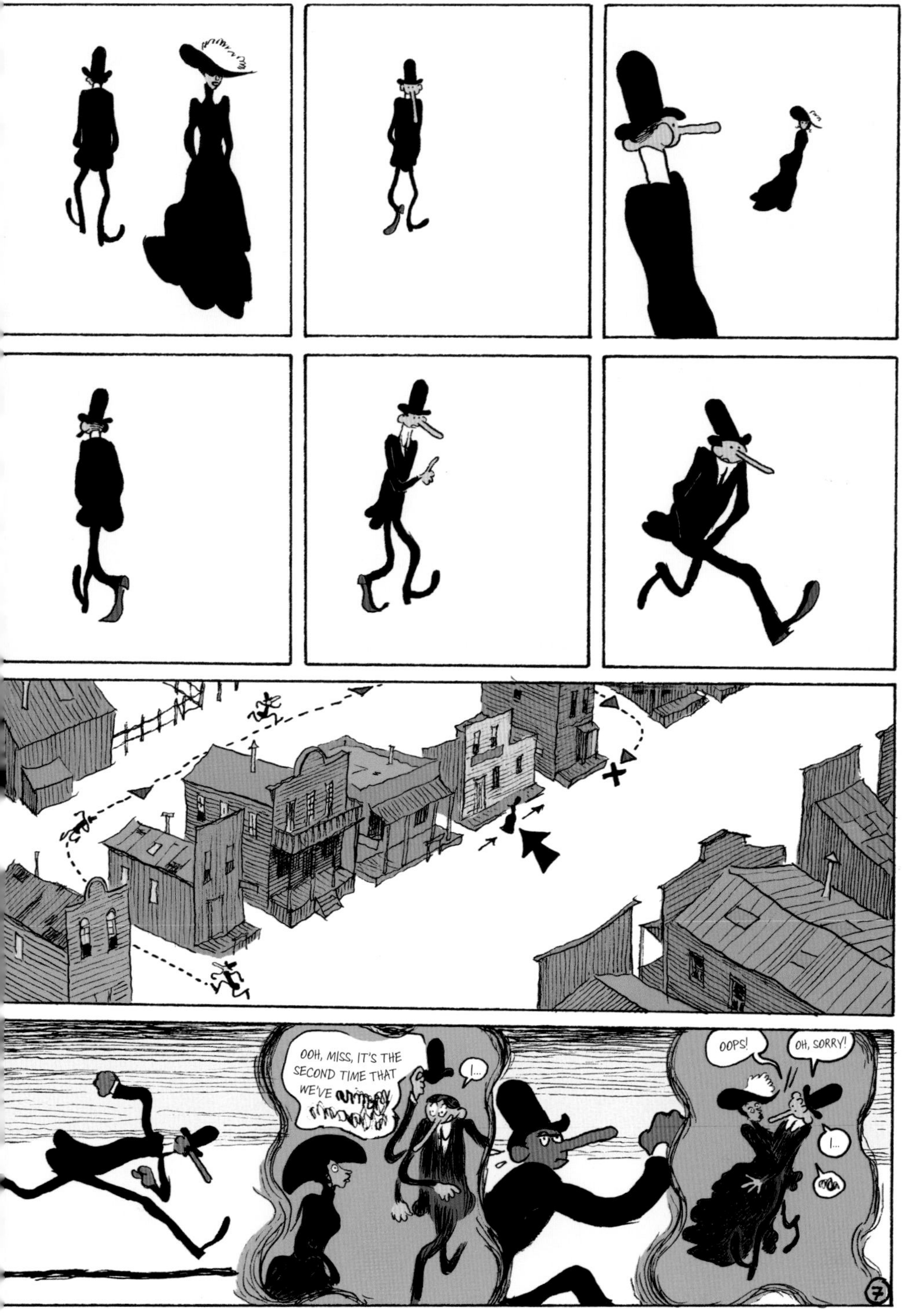
OOH, MISS, IT'S THE SECOND TIME THAT WE'VE
I...
OOPS!
OH, SORRY!
I...

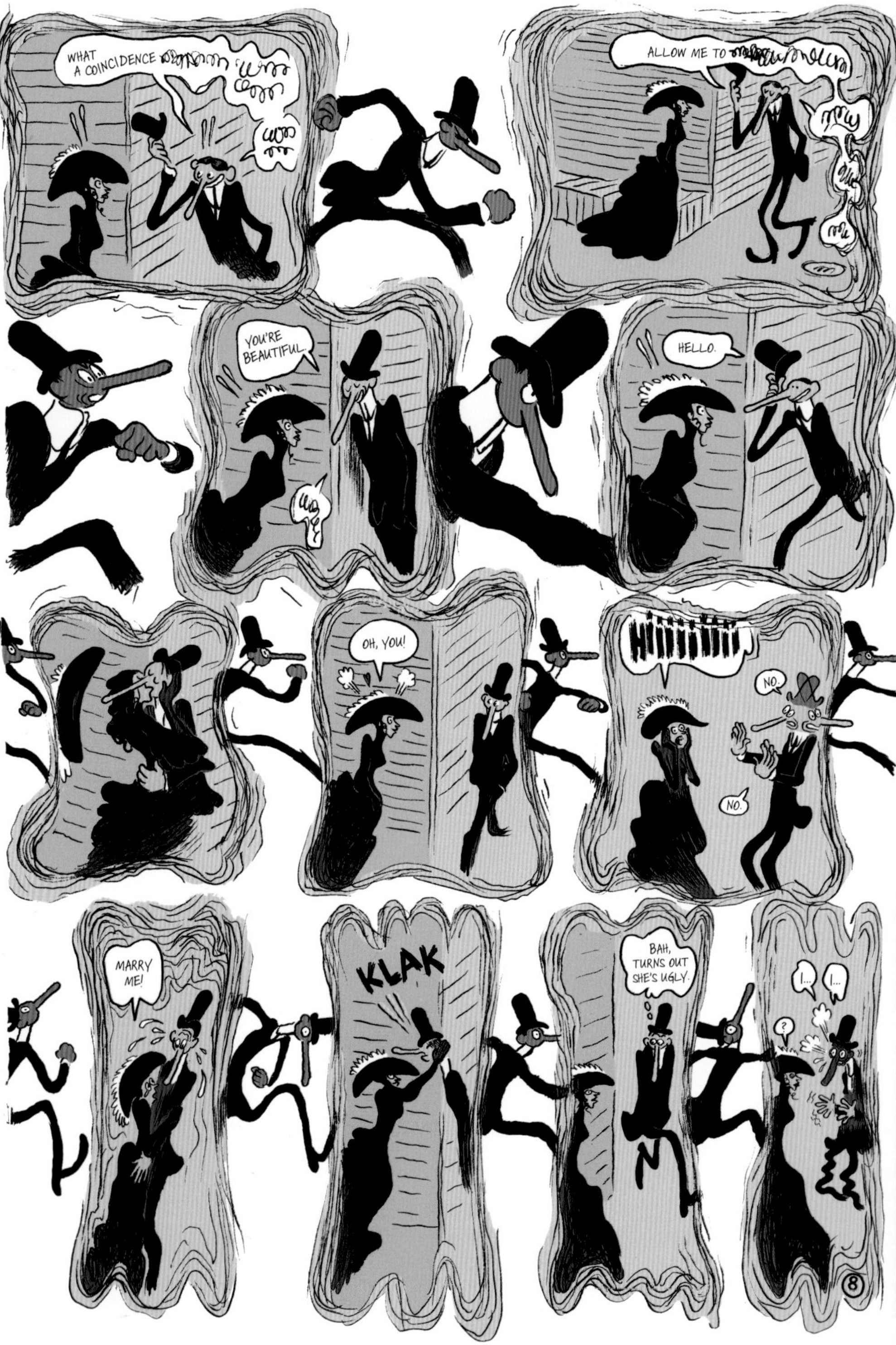
WHAT A COINCIDENCE
ALLOW ME TO
YOU'RE BEAUTIFUL.
HELLO.
OH, YOU!
NO.
NO.
MARRY ME!
KLAK
BAH, TURNS OUT SHE'S UGLY.
I...
I...
?
8

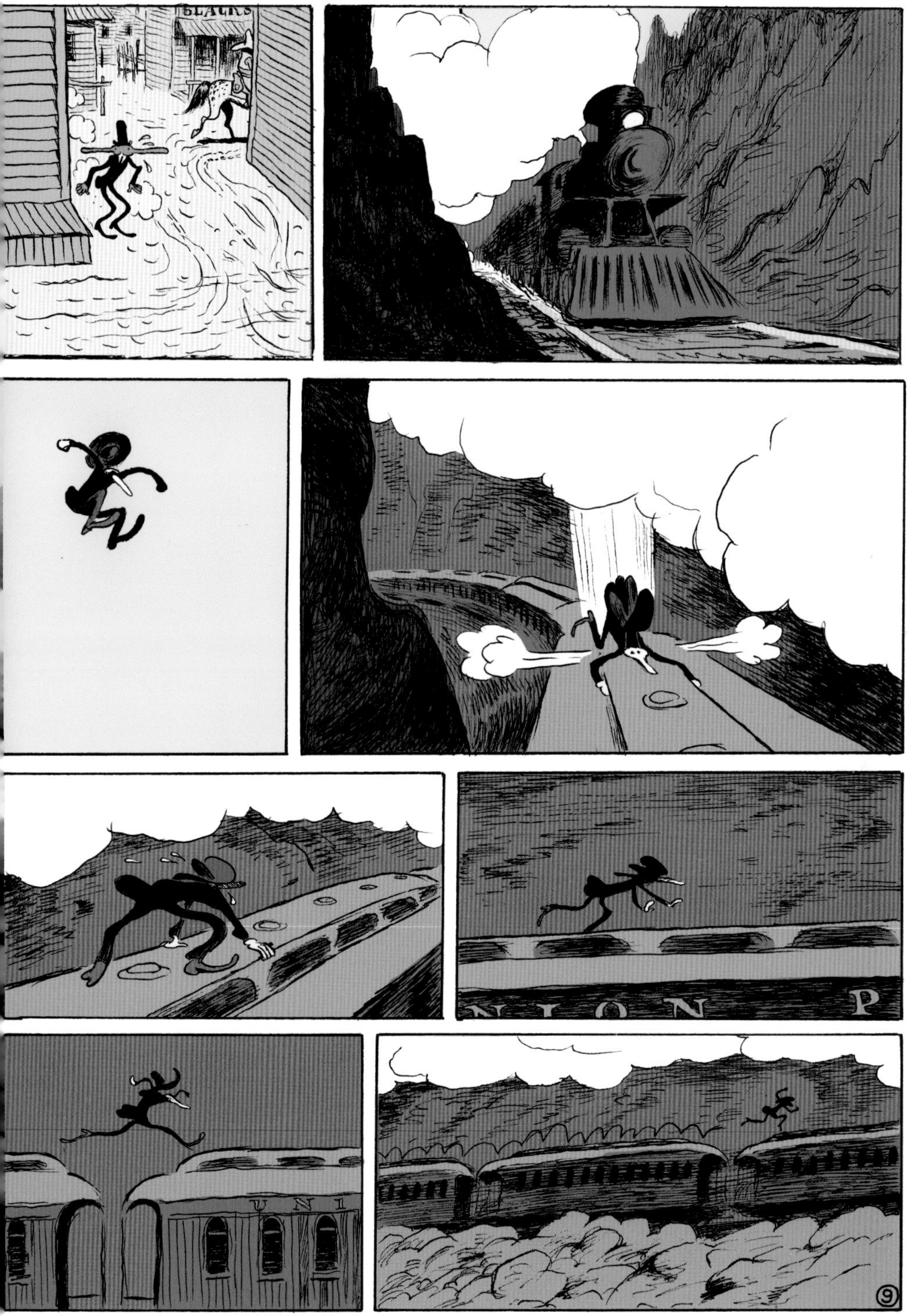
BLACKS
NION P
UNI
9

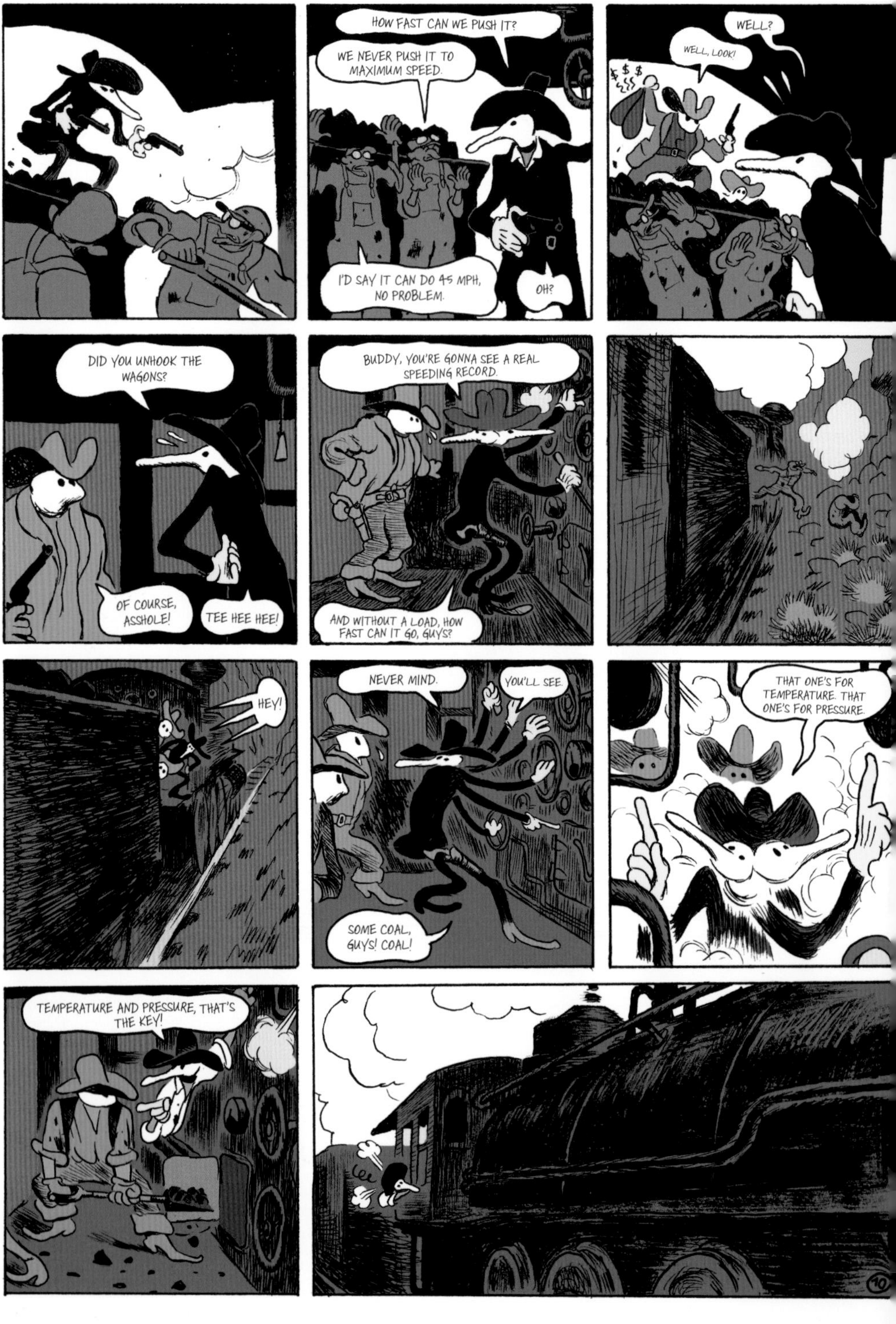
HOW FAST CAN WE PUSH IT?
WE NEVER PUSH IT TO MAXIMUM SPEED.
I'D SAY IT CAN DO 45 MPH, NO PROBLEM.
OH?
WELL?
WELL, LOOK!
DID YOU UNHOOK THE WAGONS?
OF COURSE, ASSHOLE!
TEE HEE HEE!
BUDDY, YOU'RE GONNA SEE A REAL SPEEDING RECORD.
AND WITHOUT A LOAD, HOW FAST CAN IT GO, GUYS?
HEY!
NEVER MIND.
YOU'LL SEE.
SOME COAL, GUYS! COAL!
THAT ONE'S FOR TEMPERATURE. THAT ONE'S FOR PRESSURE.
TEMPERATURE AND PRESSURE, THAT'S THE KEY!
10

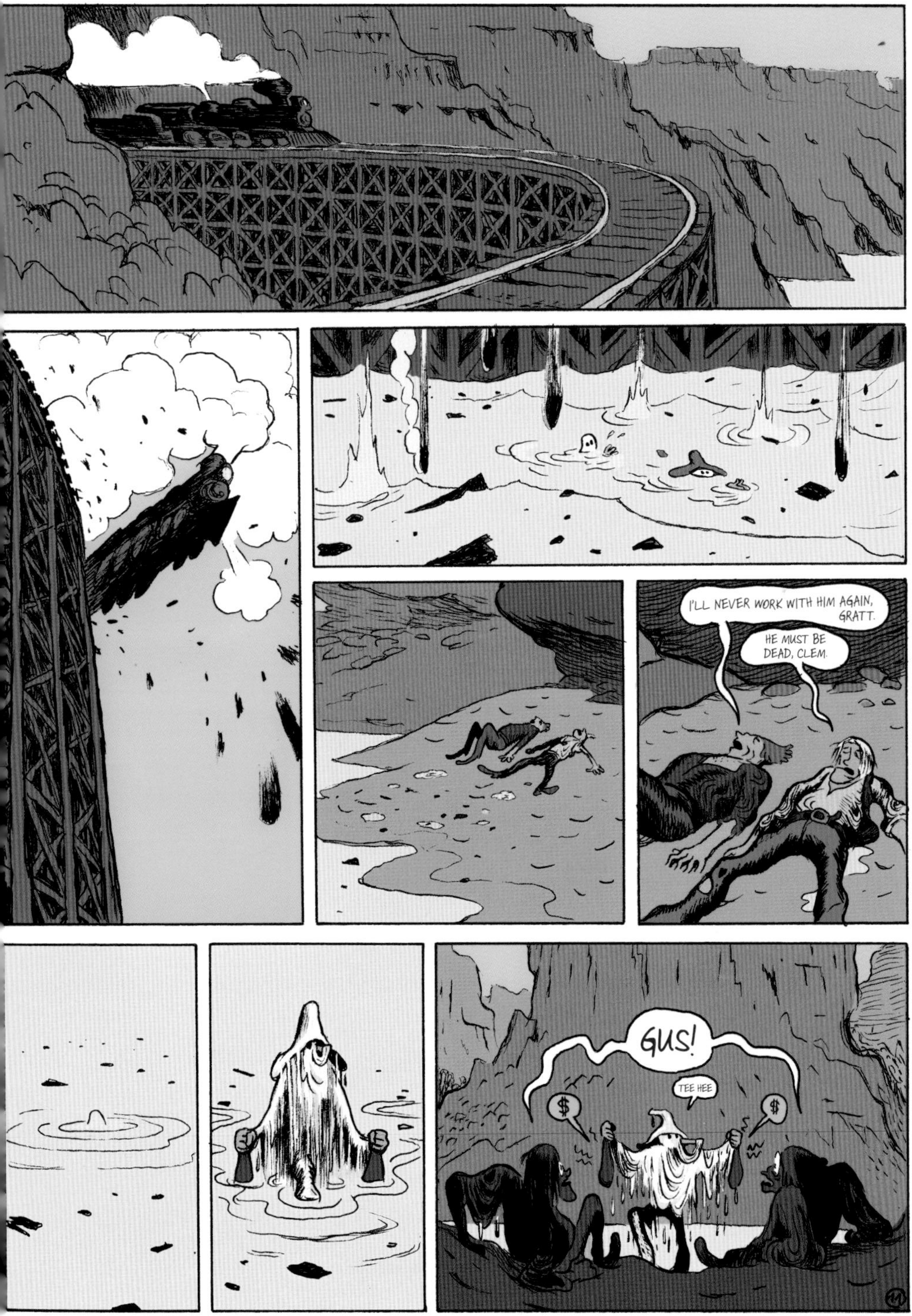
I'LL NEVER WORK WITH HIM AGAIN, GRATT.
HE MUST BE DEAD, CLEM.
GUS!
TEE HEE
$
$
11

christopheblain mai 2005

EL DORADO

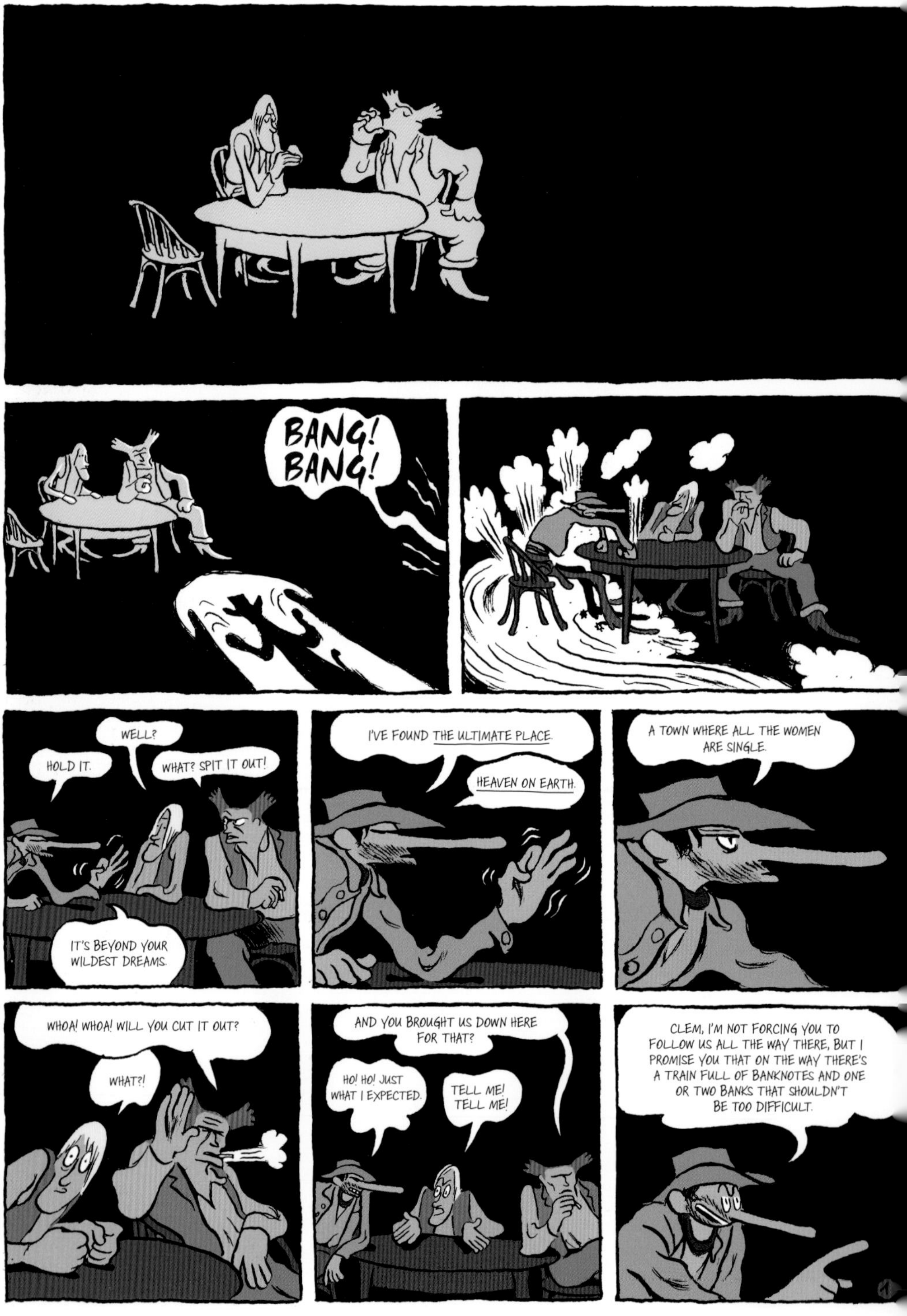

BANG! BANG!
HOLD IT.
WELL?
WHAT? SPIT IT OUT!
IT'S BEYOND YOUR WILDEST DREAMS.
I'VE FOUND THE ULTIMATE PLACE.
HEAVEN ON EARTH.
A TOWN WHERE ALL THE WOMEN ARE SINGLE.
WHOA! WHOA! WILL YOU CUT IT OUT?
WHAT?!
AND YOU BROUGHT US DOWN HERE FOR THAT?
HO! HO! JUST WHAT I EXPECTED.
TELL ME! TELL ME!
CLEM, I'M NOT FORCING YOU TO FOLLOW US ALL THE WAY THERE, BUT I PROMISE YOU THAT ON THE WAY THERE'S A TRAIN FULL OF BANKNOTES AND ONE OR TWO BANKS THAT SHOULDN'T BE TOO DIFFICULT.

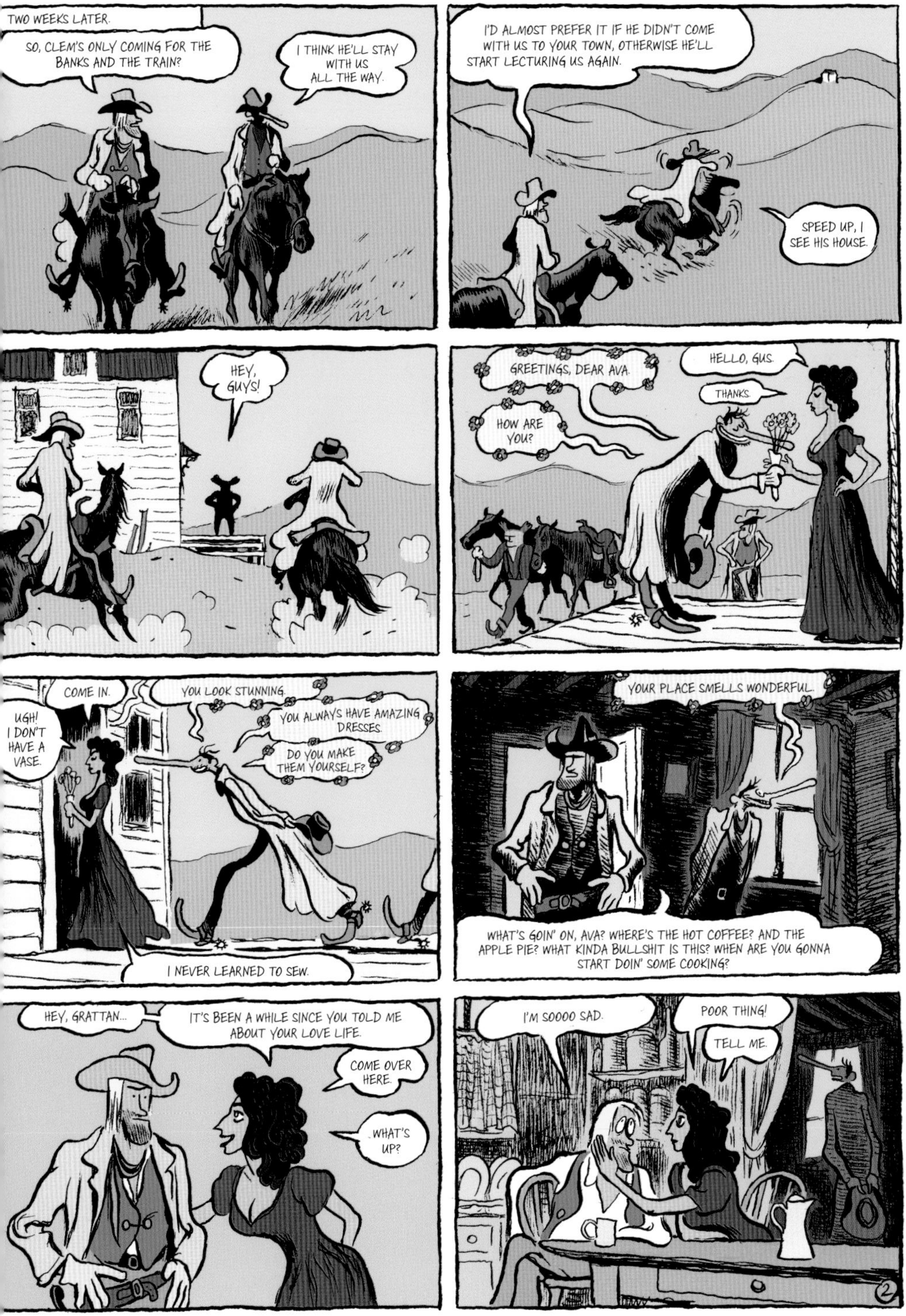
TWO WEEKS LATER.
SO, CLEM'S ONLY COMING FOR THE BANKS AND THE TRAIN?
I THINK HE'LL STAY WITH US ALL THE WAY.
I'D ALMOST PREFER IT IF HE DIDN'T COME WITH US TO YOUR TOWN, OTHERWISE HE'LL START LECTURING US AGAIN.
SPEED UP, I SEE HIS HOUSE.
HEY, GUYS!
GREETINGS, DEAR AVA.
HOW ARE YOU?
HELLO, GUS.
THANKS.
COME IN.
UGH! I DON'T HAVE A VASE.
YOU LOOK STUNNING.
YOU ALWAYS HAVE AMAZING DRESSES.
DO YOU MAKE THEM YOURSELF?
I NEVER LEARNED TO SEW.
YOUR PLACE SMELLS WONDERFUL.
WHAT'S GOIN' ON, AVA? WHERE'S THE HOT COFFEE? AND THE APPLE PIE? WHAT KINDA BULLSHIT IS THIS? WHEN ARE YOU GONNA START DOIN' SOME COOKING?
HEY, GRATTAN...
IT'S BEEN A WHILE SINCE YOU TOLD ME ABOUT YOUR LOVE LIFE.
COME OVER HERE.
WHAT'S UP?
I'M SOOOO SAD.
POOR THING!
TELL ME.
2

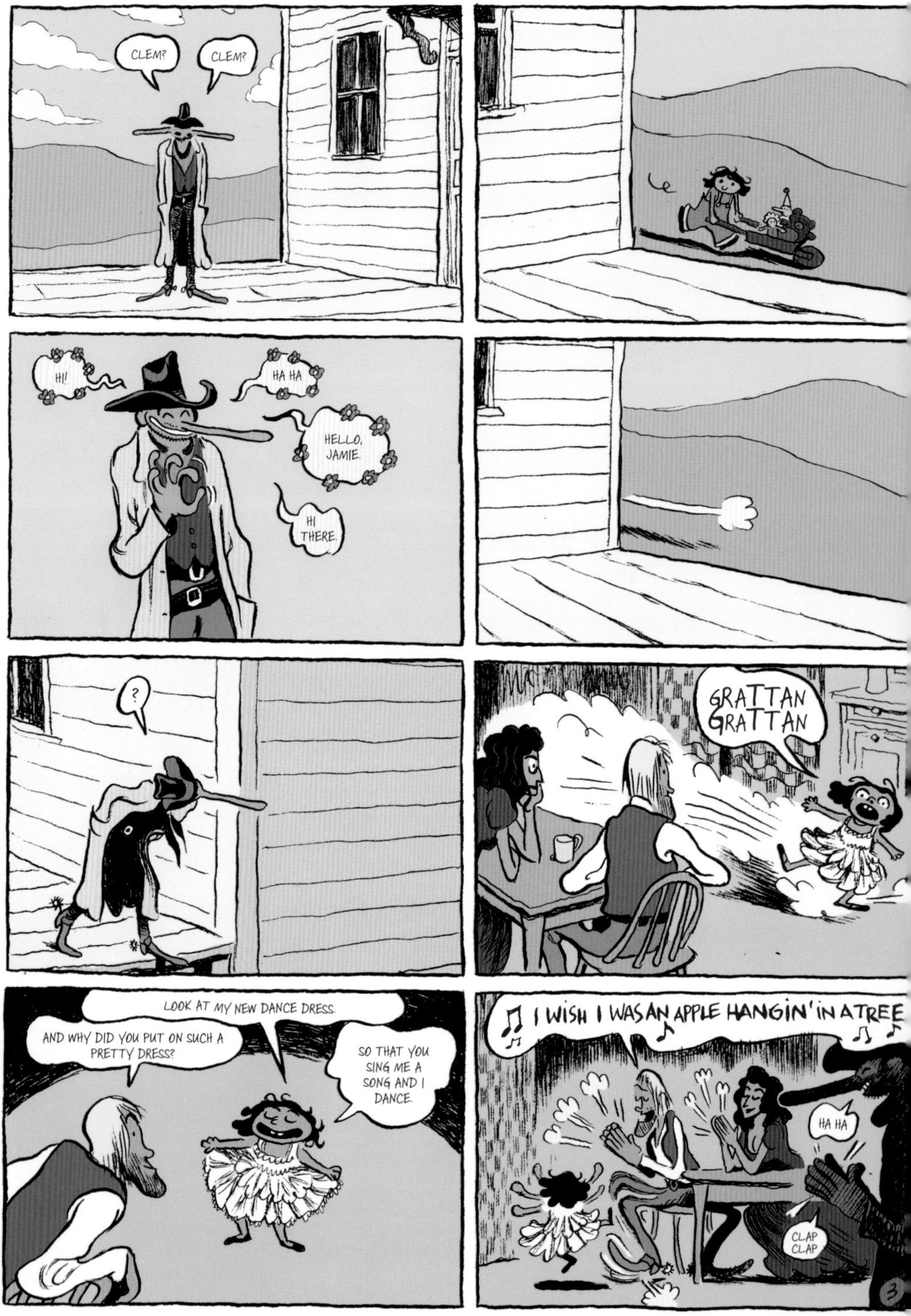
CLEM?
CLEM?
HI!
HA HA
HELLO, JAMIE.
HI THERE.
?
GRATTAN GRATTAN
LOOK AT MY NEW DANCE DRESS.
AND WHY DID YOU PUT ON SUCH A PRETTY DRESS?
SO THAT YOU SING ME A SONG AND I DANCE.
I WISH I WAS AN APPLE HANGIN' IN A TREE
HA HA
CLAP CLAP

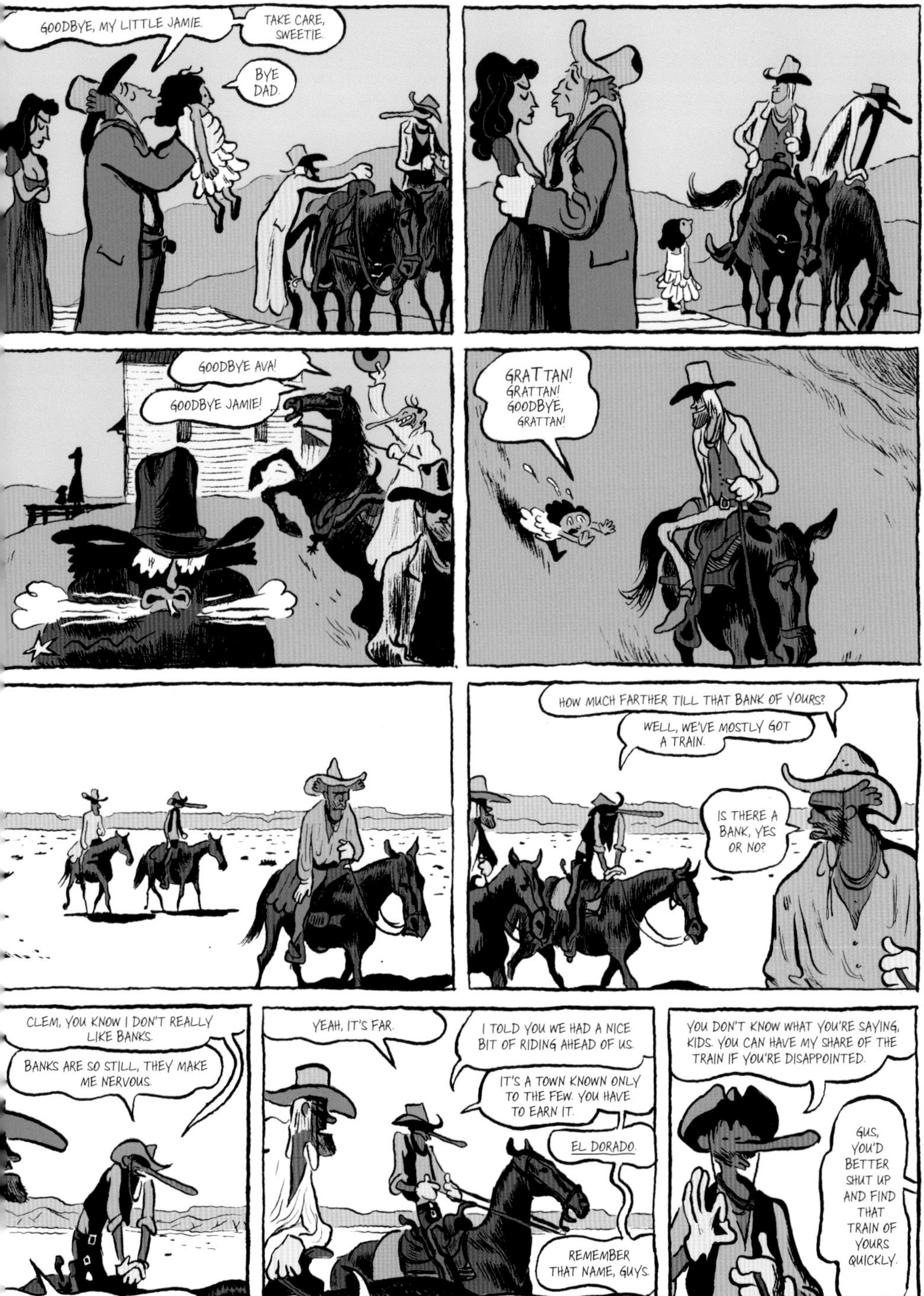
GOODBYE, MY LITTLE JAMIE.
TAKE CARE, SWEETIE.
BYE DAD.
GOODBYE AVA!
GOODBYE JAMIE!
GRATTAN! GRATTAN! GOODBYE, GRATTAN!
HOW MUCH FARTHER TILL THAT BANK OF YOURS?
WELL, WE'VE MOSTLY GOT A TRAIN.
IS THERE A BANK, YES OR NO?
CLEM, YOU KNOW I DON'T REALLY LIKE BANKS.
BANKS ARE SO STILL, THEY MAKE ME NERVOUS.
AND YOUR TOWN? IS IT FAR?
YEAH, IT'S FAR.
I TOLD YOU WE HAD A NICE BIT OF RIDING AHEAD OF US.
IT'S A TOWN KNOWN ONLY TO THE FEW. YOU HAVE TO EARN IT.
EL DORADO.
REMEMBER THAT NAME, GUYS.
I DON'T KNOW, GUS. KINDA LOOKS LIKE YOU'RE OVERPLAYING YOUR HAND.
YOU DON'T KNOW WHAT YOU'RE SAYING, KIDS. YOU CAN HAVE MY SHARE OF THE TRAIN IF YOU'RE DISAPPOINTED.
GUS, YOU'D BETTER SHUT UP AND FIND THAT TRAIN OF YOURS QUICKLY.
4

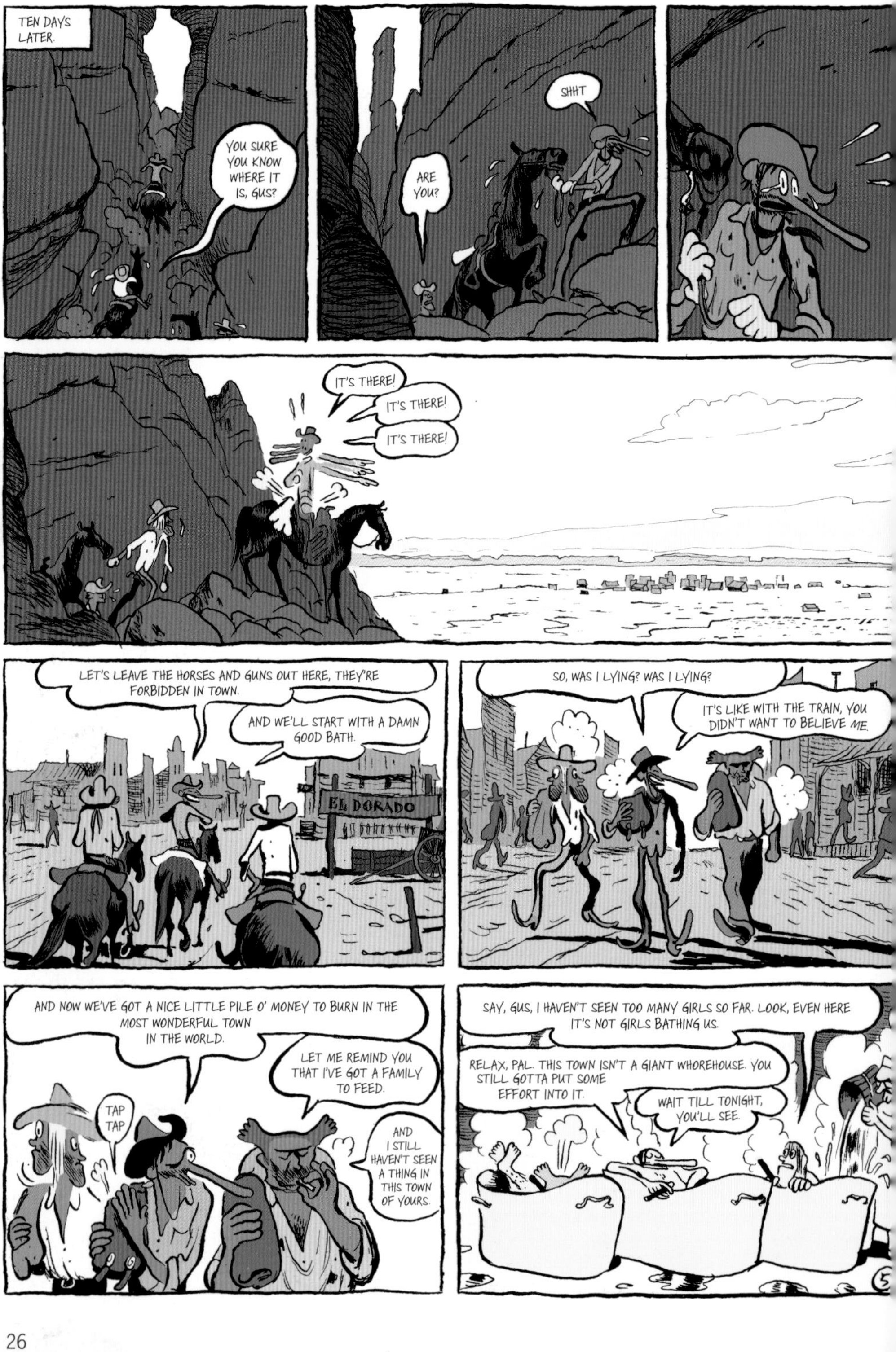
TEN DAYS LATER.
YOU SURE YOU KNOW WHERE IT IS, GUS?
ARE YOU?
SHHT
IT'S THERE!
IT'S THERE!
IT'S THERE!
LET'S LEAVE THE HORSES AND GUNS OUT HERE, THEY'RE FORBIDDEN IN TOWN.
AND WE'LL START WITH A DAMN GOOD BATH.
EL DORADO
SO, WAS I LYING? WAS I LYING?
IT'S LIKE WITH THE TRAIN, YOU DIDN'T WANT TO BELIEVE ME.
AND NOW WE'VE GOT A NICE LITTLE PILE O' MONEY TO BURN IN THE MOST WONDERFUL TOWN IN THE WORLD.
TAP TAP
LET ME REMIND YOU THAT I'VE GOT A FAMILY TO FEED.
AND I STILL HAVEN'T SEEN A THING IN THIS TOWN OF YOURS.
SAY, GUS, I HAVEN'T SEEN TOO MANY GIRLS SO FAR. LOOK, EVEN HERE IT'S NOT GIRLS BATHING US.
RELAX, PAL. THIS TOWN ISN'T A GIANT WHOREHOUSE. YOU STILL GOTTA PUT SOME EFFORT INTO IT.
WAIT TILL TONIGHT, YOU'LL SEE.
5

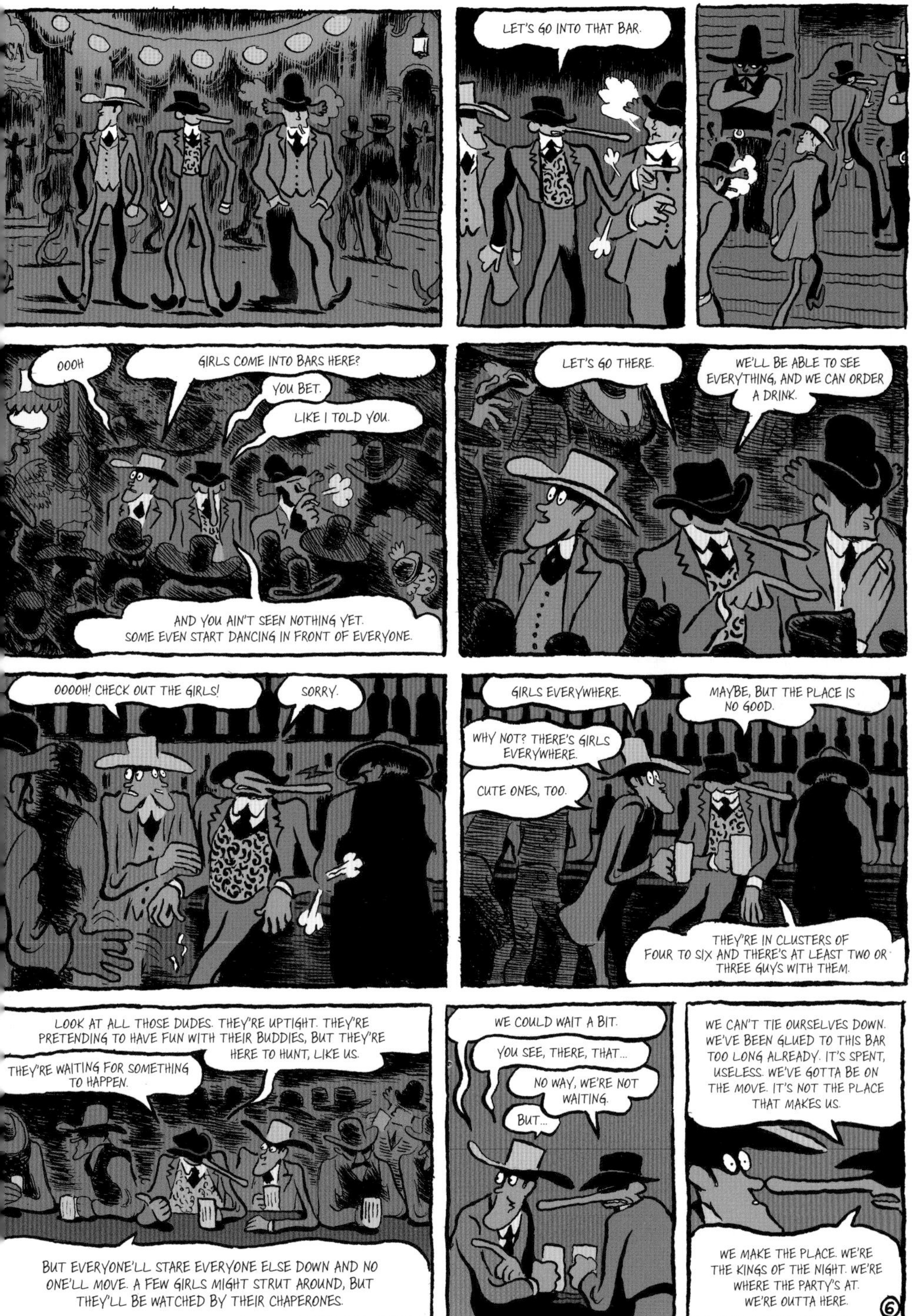
LET'S GO INTO THAT BAR.
OOOH
GIRLS COME INTO BARS HERE?
YOU BET.
LIKE I TOLD YOU.
AND YOU AIN'T SEEN NOTHING YET. SOME EVEN START DANCING IN FRONT OF EVERYONE.
LET'S GO THERE.
WE'LL BE ABLE TO SEE EVERYTHING, AND WE CAN ORDER A DRINK.
OOOOH! CHECK OUT THE GIRLS!
SORRY.
GIRLS EVERYWHERE.
MAYBE, BUT THE PLACE IS NO GOOD.
WHY NOT? THERE'S GIRLS EVERYWHERE.
CUTE ONES, TOO.
THEY'RE IN CLUSTERS OF FOUR TO SIX AND THERE'S AT LEAST TWO OR THREE GUYS WITH THEM.
LOOK AT ALL THOSE DUDES. THEY'RE UPTIGHT. THEY'RE PRETENDING TO HAVE FUN WITH THEIR BUDDIES, BUT THEY'RE HERE TO HUNT, LIKE US.
THEY'RE WAITING FOR SOMETHING TO HAPPEN.
BUT EVERYONE'LL STARE EVERYONE ELSE DOWN AND NO ONE'LL MOVE. A FEW GIRLS MIGHT STRUT AROUND, BUT THEY'LL BE WATCHED BY THEIR CHAPERONES.
WE COULD WAIT A BIT.
YOU SEE, THERE, THAT...
NO WAY, WE'RE NOT WAITING.
BUT...
WE CAN'T TIE OURSELVES DOWN. WE'VE BEEN GLUED TO THIS BAR TOO LONG ALREADY. IT'S SPENT, USELESS. WE'VE GOTTA BE ON THE MOVE. IT'S NOT THE PLACE THAT MAKES US.
WE MAKE THE PLACE. WE'RE THE KINGS OF THE NIGHT. WE'RE WHERE THE PARTY'S AT. WE'RE OUTTA HERE.
6

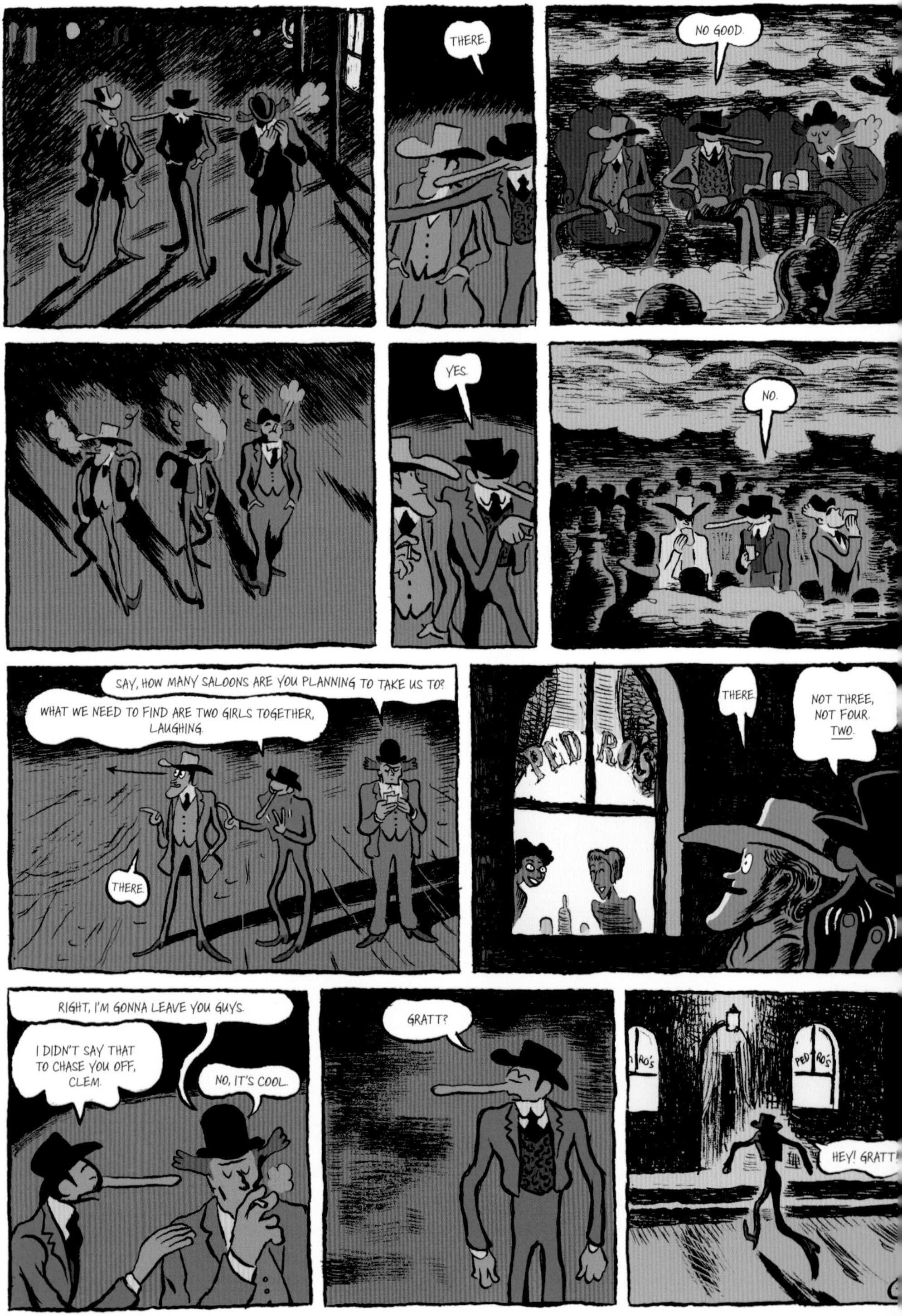
THERE.
NO GOOD.
YES.
NO.
SAY, HOW MANY SALOONS ARE YOU PLANNING TO TAKE US TO?
WHAT WE NEED TO FIND ARE TWO GIRLS TOGETHER, LAUGHING.
THERE.
PED RO'S
THERE.
NOT THREE, NOT FOUR. TWO.
RIGHT, I'M GONNA LEAVE YOU GUYS.
I DIDN'T SAY THAT TO CHASE YOU OFF, CLEM.
NO, IT'S COOL.
GRATT?
RO'S
PED RO'S
HEY! GRATT!

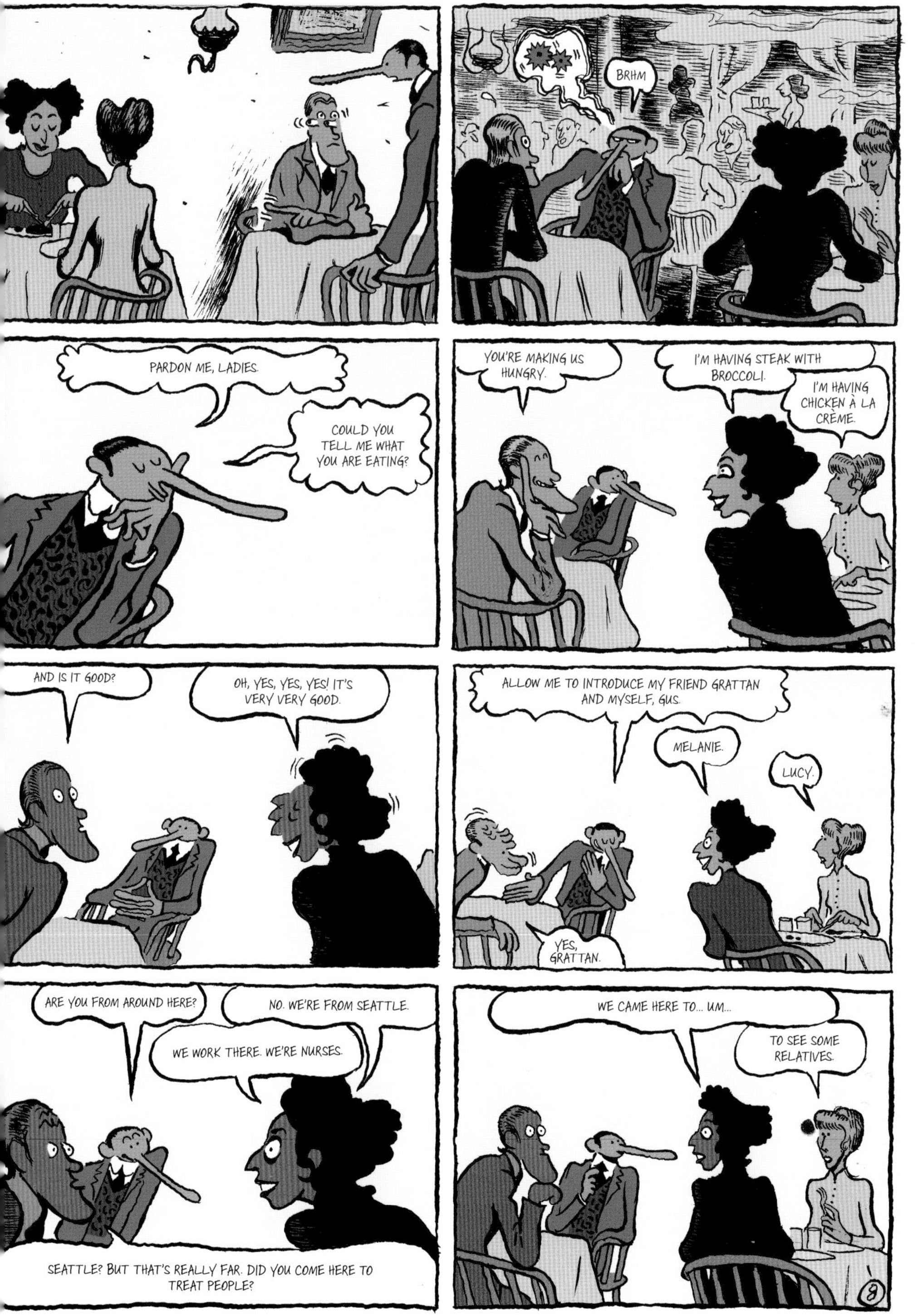
BRHM
PARDON ME, LADIES.
COULD YOU TELL ME WHAT YOU ARE EATING?
YOU'RE MAKING US HUNGRY.
I'M HAVING STEAK WITH BROCCOLI.
I'M HAVING CHICKEN À LA CRÈME.
AND IS IT GOOD?
OH, YES, YES, YES! IT'S VERY VERY GOOD.
ALLOW ME TO INTRODUCE MY FRIEND GRATTAN AND MYSELF, GUS.
MELANIE.
LUCY.
YES, GRATTAN.
ARE YOU FROM AROUND HERE?
NO. WE'RE FROM SEATTLE.
WE WORK THERE. WE'RE NURSES.
SEATTLE? BUT THAT'S REALLY FAR. DID YOU COME HERE TO TREAT PEOPLE?
WE CAME HERE TO... UM...
TO SEE SOME RELATIVES.
8

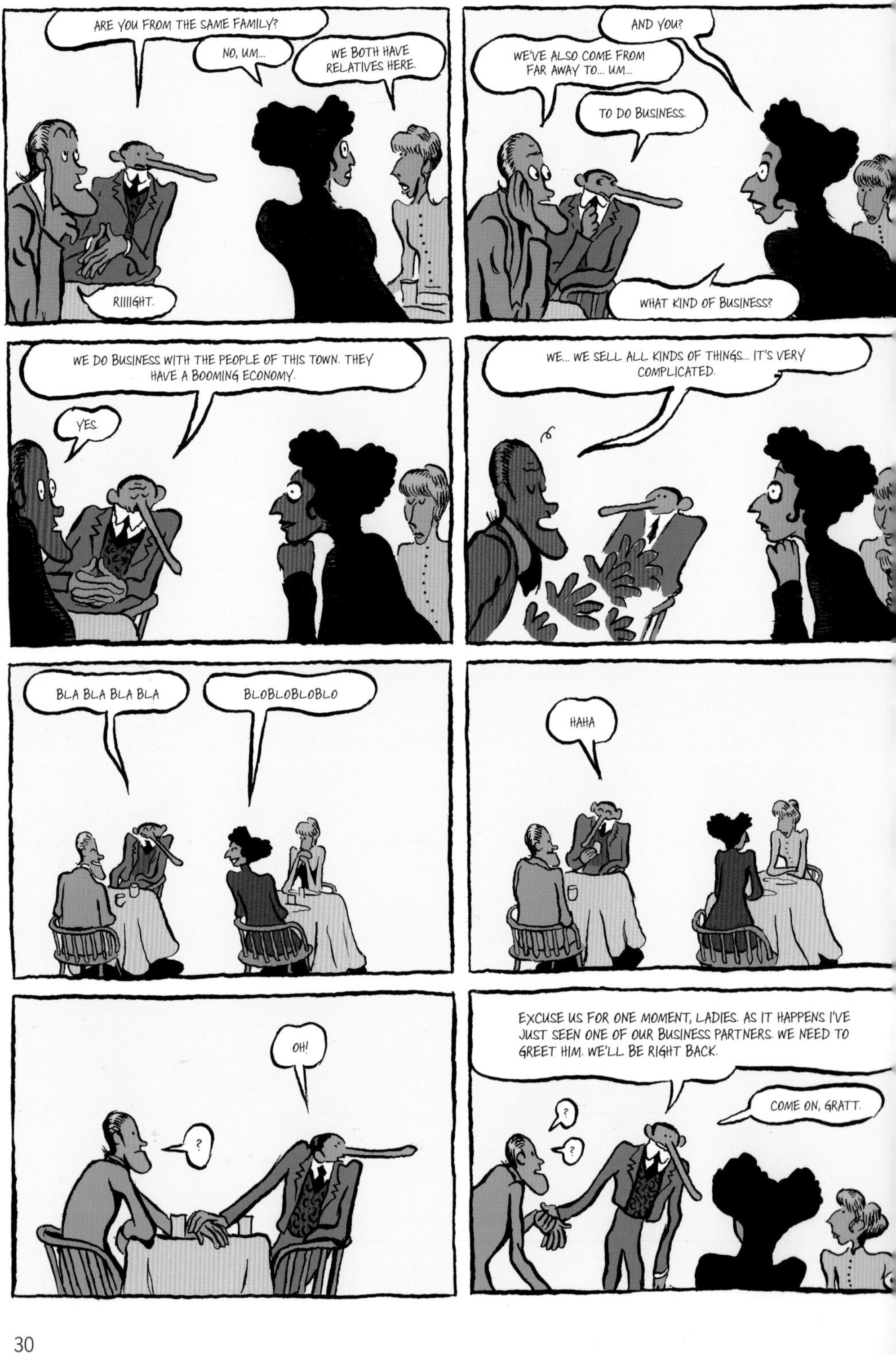
ARE YOU FROM THE SAME FAMILY?
NO, UM...
WE BOTH HAVE RELATIVES HERE.
RIIIIGHT.
AND YOU?
WE'VE ALSO COME FROM FAR AWAY TO... UM...
TO DO BUSINESS.
WHAT KIND OF BUSINESS?
WE DO BUSINESS WITH THE PEOPLE OF THIS TOWN. THEY HAVE A BOOMING ECONOMY.
YES.
WE... WE SELL ALL KINDS OF THINGS... IT'S VERY COMPLICATED.
BLA BLA BLA BLA
BLOBLOBLOBLO
HAHA
OH!
?
EXCUSE US FOR ONE MOMENT, LADIES. AS IT HAPPENS I'VE JUST SEEN ONE OF OUR BUSINESS PARTNERS. WE NEED TO GREET HIM. WE'LL BE RIGHT BACK.
?
?
COME ON, GRATT.

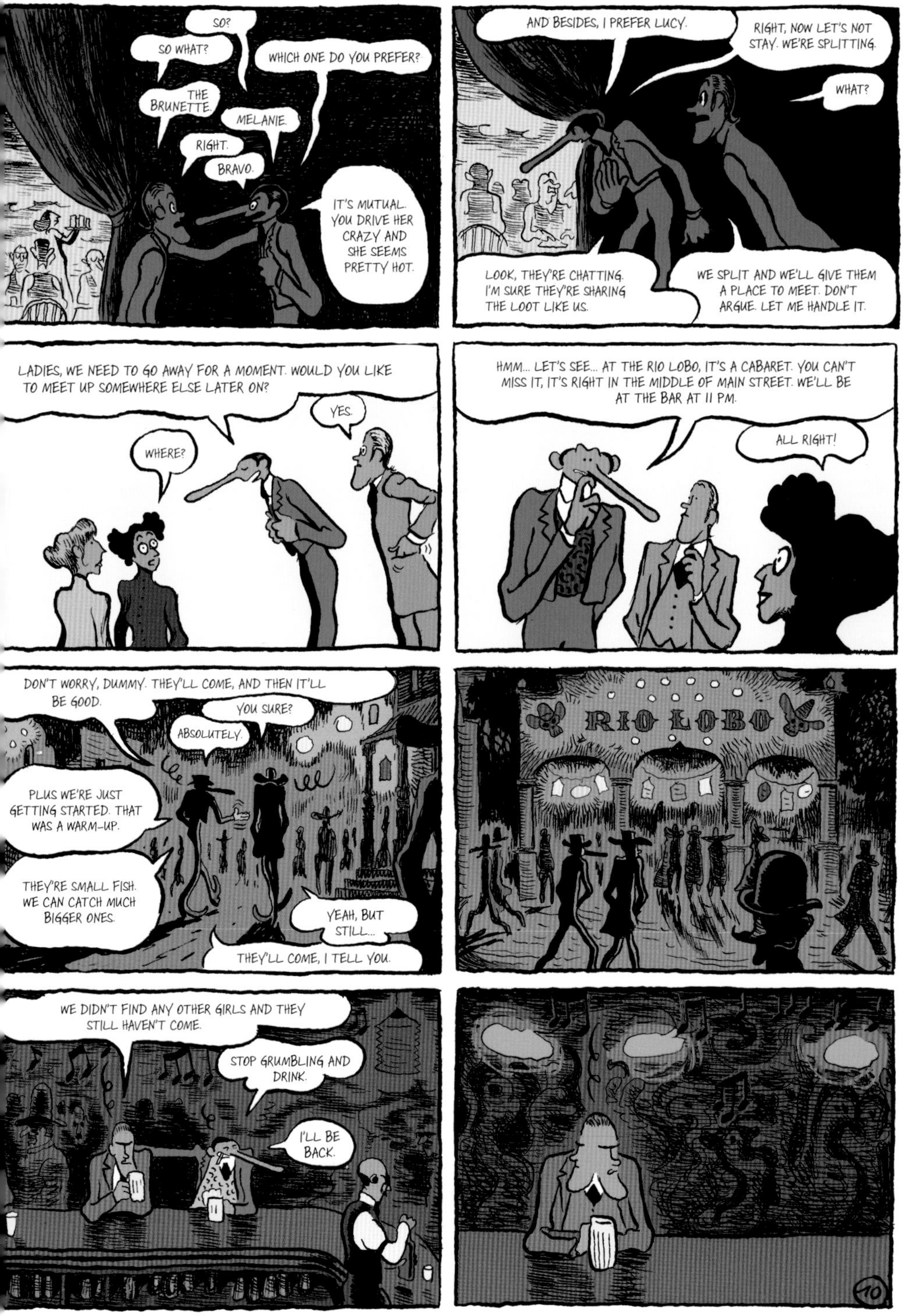
SO?
SO WHAT?
WHICH ONE DO YOU PREFER?
THE BRUNETTE.
MELANIE.
RIGHT.
BRAVO.
IT'S MUTUAL. YOU DRIVE HER CRAZY AND SHE SEEMS PRETTY HOT.
AND BESIDES, I PREFER LUCY.
RIGHT, NOW LET'S NOT STAY. WE'RE SPLITTING.
WHAT?
LOOK, THEY'RE CHATTING. I'M SURE THEY'RE SHARING THE LOOT LIKE US.
WE SPLIT AND WE'LL GIVE THEM A PLACE TO MEET. DON'T ARGUE. LET ME HANDLE IT.
LADIES, WE NEED TO GO AWAY FOR A MOMENT. WOULD YOU LIKE TO MEET UP SOMEWHERE ELSE LATER ON?
YES.
WHERE?
HMM... LET'S SEE... AT THE RIO LOBO, IT'S A CABARET. YOU CAN'T MISS IT, IT'S RIGHT IN THE MIDDLE OF MAIN STREET. WE'LL BE AT THE BAR AT 11 PM.
ALL RIGHT!
DON'T WORRY, DUMMY. THEY'LL COME, AND THEN IT'LL BE GOOD.
YOU SURE?
ABSOLUTELY.
PLUS WE'RE JUST GETTING STARTED. THAT WAS A WARM-UP.
THEY'RE SMALL FISH. WE CAN CATCH MUCH BIGGER ONES.
YEAH, BUT STILL...
THEY'LL COME, I TELL YOU.
RIO LOBO
WE DIDN'T FIND ANY OTHER GIRLS AND THEY STILL HAVEN'T COME.
STOP GRUMBLING AND DRINK.
I'LL BE BACK.
10

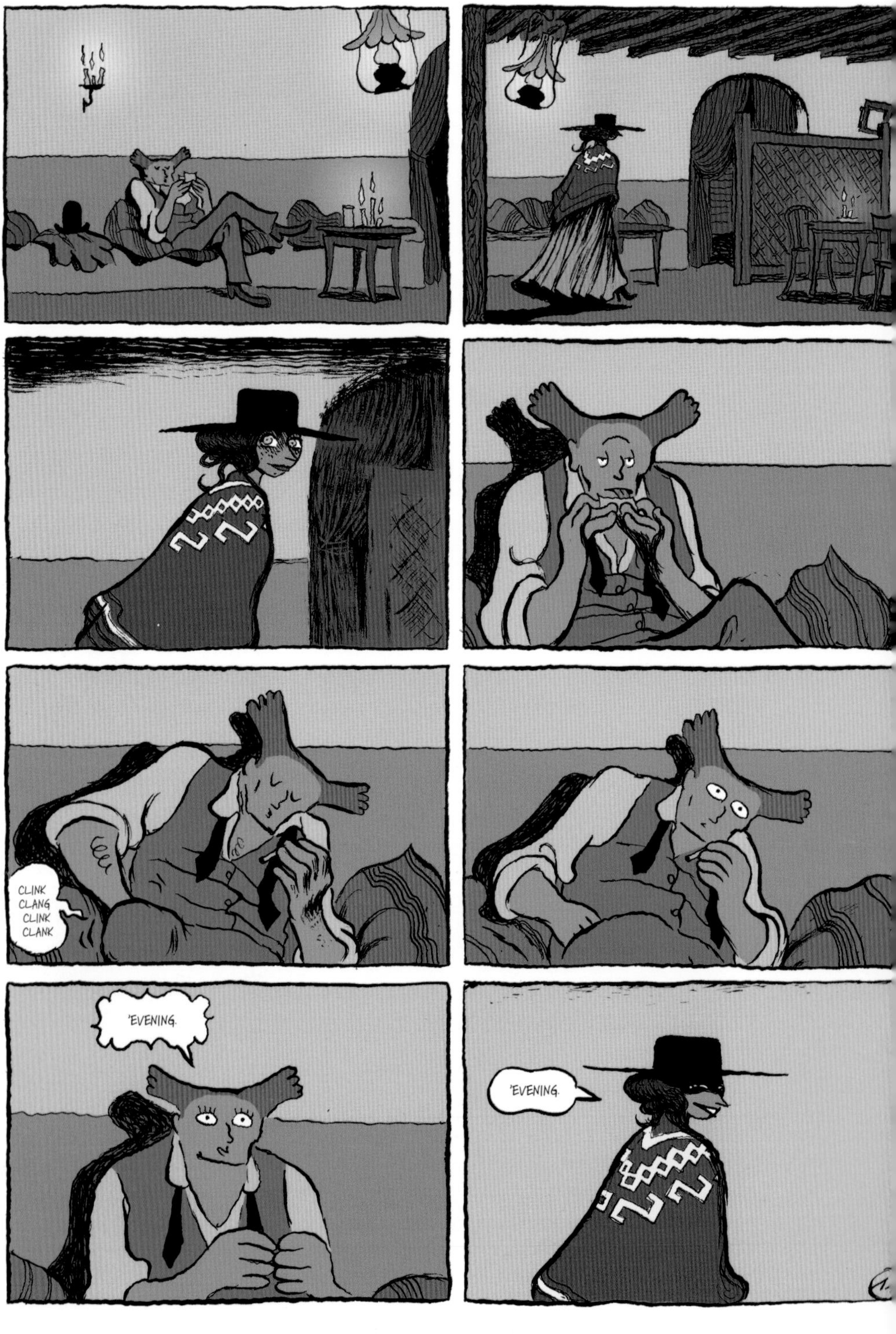
CLINK
CLANG
CLINK
CLANK
'EVENING.
'EVENING.

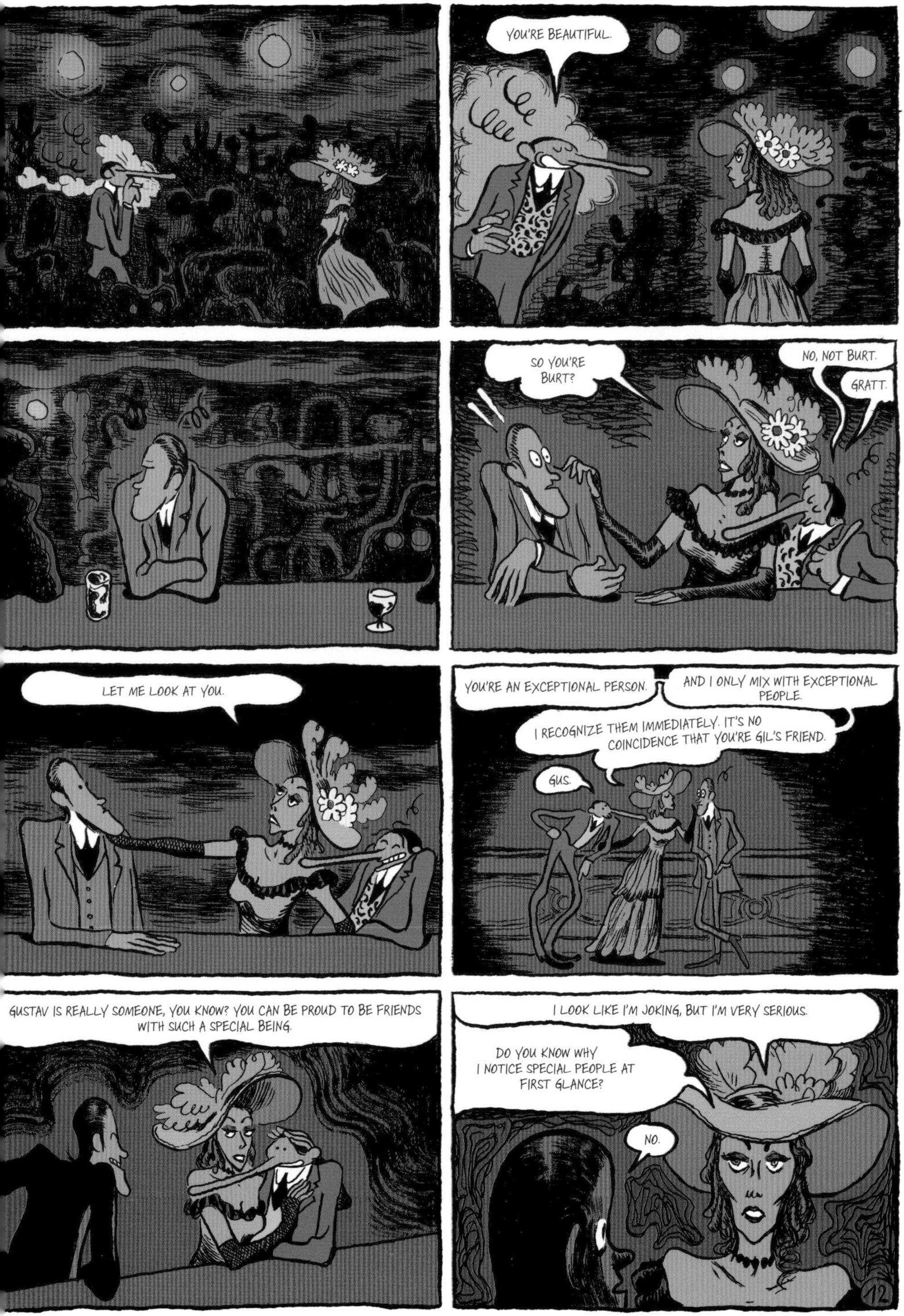
YOU'RE BEAUTIFUL.
SO YOU'RE BURT?
NO, NOT BURT.
GRATT.
LET ME LOOK AT YOU.
YOU'RE AN EXCEPTIONAL PERSON.
AND I ONLY MIX WITH EXCEPTIONAL PEOPLE.
I RECOGNIZE THEM IMMEDIATELY. IT'S NO COINCIDENCE THAT YOU'RE GIL'S FRIEND.
GUS.
GUSTAV IS REALLY SOMEONE, YOU KNOW? YOU CAN BE PROUD TO BE FRIENDS WITH SUCH A SPECIAL BEING.
I LOOK LIKE I'M JOKING, BUT I'M VERY SERIOUS.
DO YOU KNOW WHY I NOTICE SPECIAL PEOPLE AT FIRST GLANCE?
NO.
12

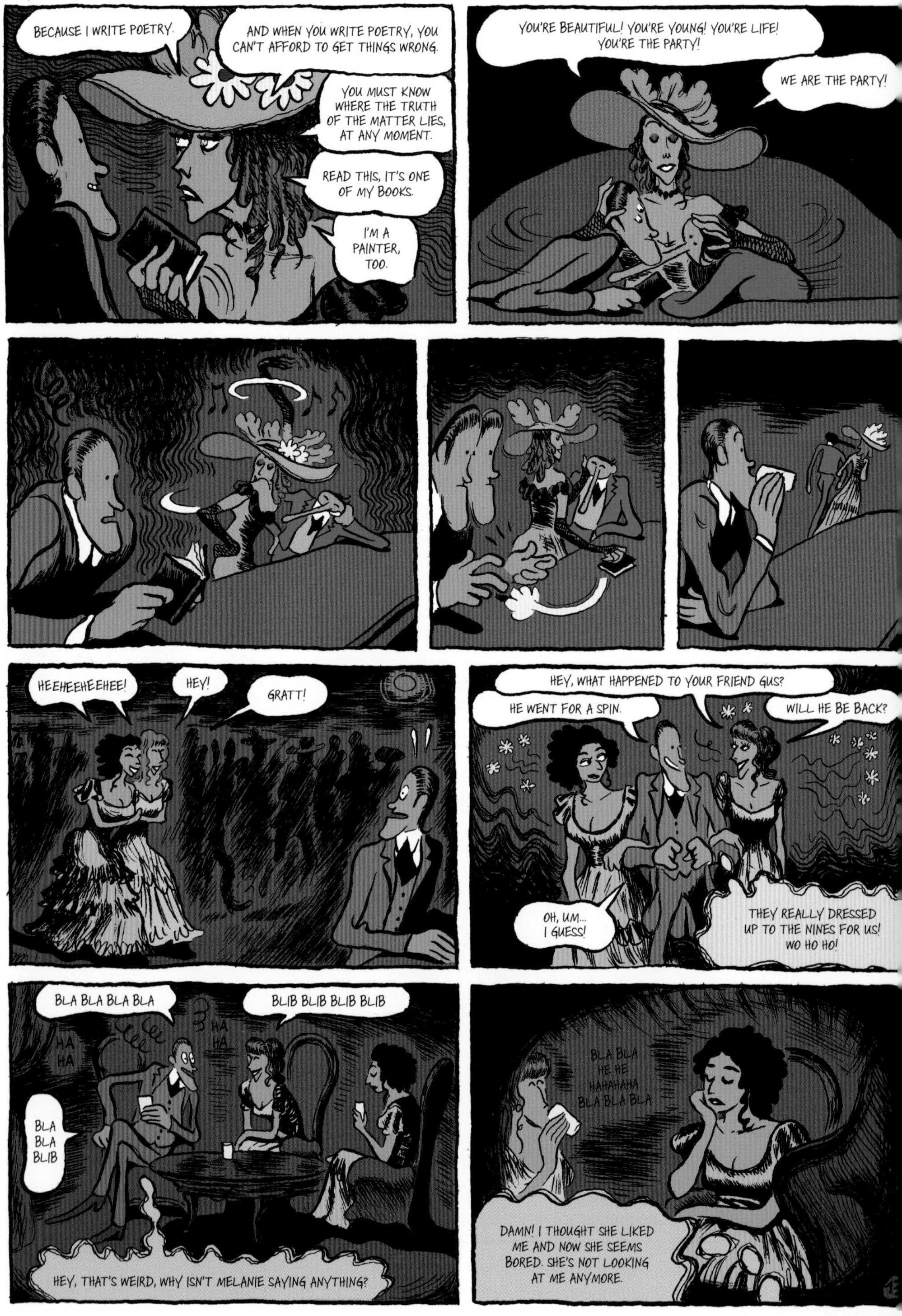
BECAUSE I WRITE POETRY.
AND WHEN YOU WRITE POETRY, YOU CAN'T AFFORD TO GET THINGS WRONG.
YOU MUST KNOW WHERE THE TRUTH OF THE MATTER LIES, AT ANY MOMENT.
READ THIS, IT'S ONE OF MY BOOKS.
I'M A PAINTER, TOO.
YOU'RE BEAUTIFUL! YOU'RE YOUNG! YOU'RE LIFE! YOU'RE THE PARTY!
WE ARE THE PARTY!
HEEHEEHEEHEE!
HEY!
GRATT!
HEY, WHAT HAPPENED TO YOUR FRIEND GUS?
HE WENT FOR A SPIN.
WILL HE BE BACK?
OH, UM... I GUESS!
THEY REALLY DRESSED UP TO THE NINES FOR US! WO HO HO!
BLA BLA BLA BLA
BLIB BLIB BLIB BLIB
HA HA
HA HA
BLA BLA BLIB
HEY, THAT'S WEIRD, WHY ISN'T MELANIE SAYING ANYTHING?
BLA BLA HE HE HAHAHAHA BLA BLA BLA
DAMN! I THOUGHT SHE LIKED ME AND NOW SHE SEEMS BORED. SHE'S NOT LOOKING AT ME ANYMORE.

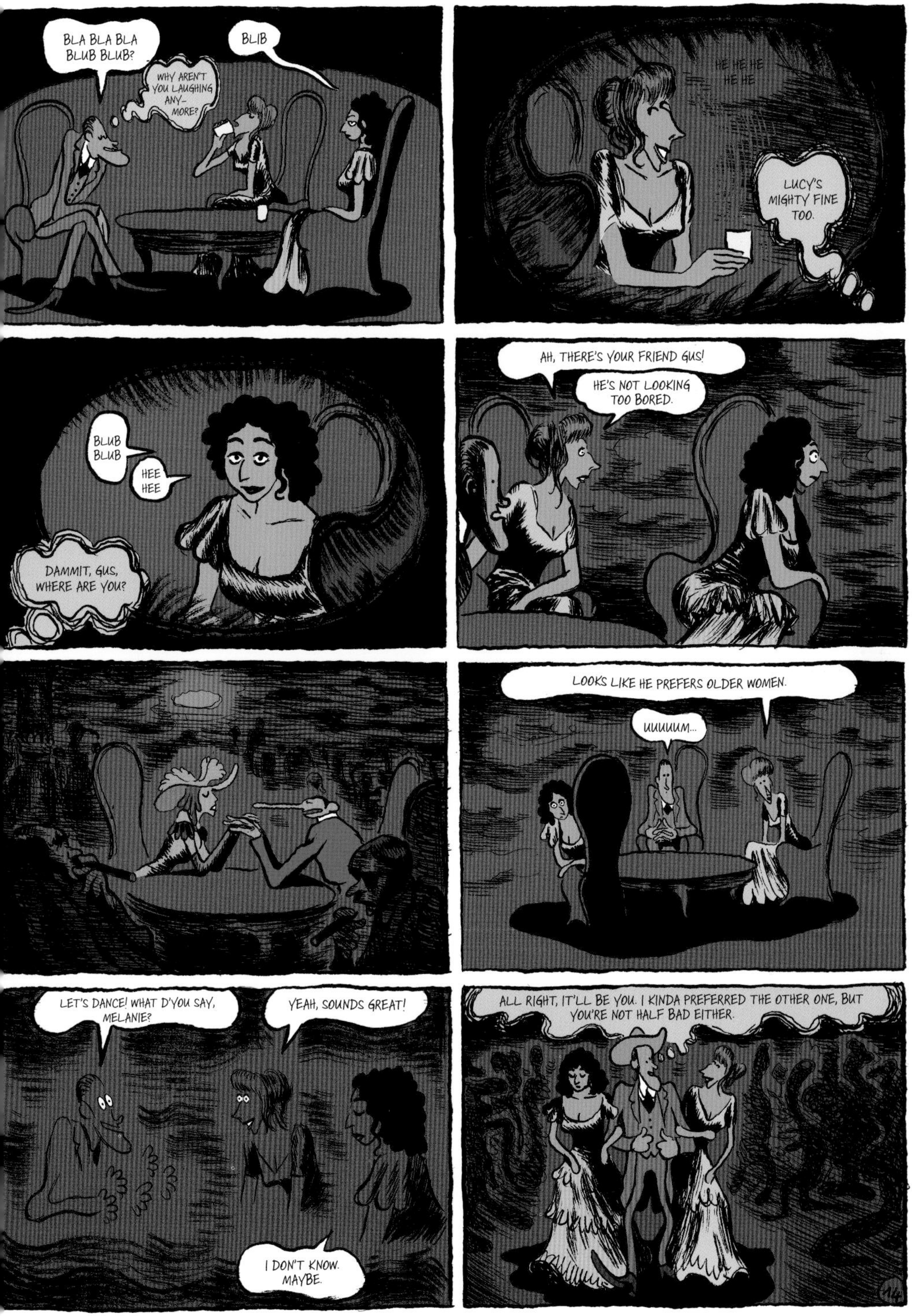

BLA BLA BLA BLUB BLUB?
WHY AREN'T YOU LAUGHING ANY-MORE?
BLIB
HE HE HE HE HE
LUCY'S MIGHTY FINE TOO.
BLUB BLUB
HEE HEE
DAMMIT, GUS, WHERE ARE YOU?
AH, THERE'S YOUR FRIEND GUS!
HE'S NOT LOOKING TOO BORED.
LOOKS LIKE HE PREFERS OLDER WOMEN.
UUUUUM...
LET'S DANCE! WHAT D'YOU SAY, MELANIE?
YEAH, SOUNDS GREAT!
I DON'T KNOW. MAYBE.
ALL RIGHT, IT'LL BE YOU. I KINDA PREFERRED THE OTHER ONE, BUT YOU'RE NOT HALF BAD EITHER.
14

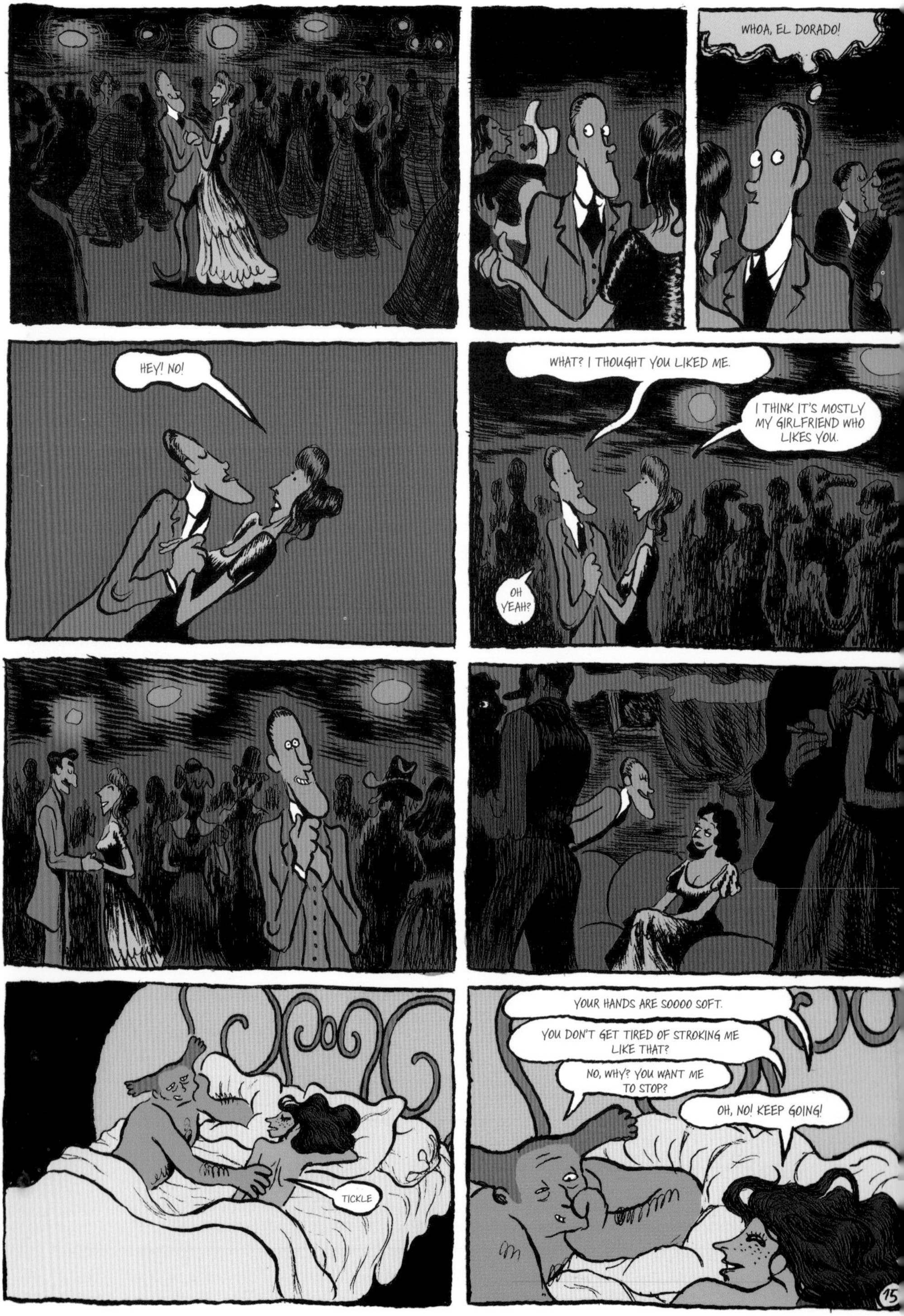

WHOA, EL DORADO!
HEY! NO!
WHAT? I THOUGHT YOU LIKED ME.
I THINK IT'S MOSTLY MY GIRLFRIEND WHO LIKES YOU.
OH YEAH?
TICKLE
YOUR HANDS ARE SOOOO SOFT.
YOU DON'T GET TIRED OF STROKING ME LIKE THAT?
NO, WHY? YOU WANT ME TO STOP?
OH, NO! KEEP GOING!
15

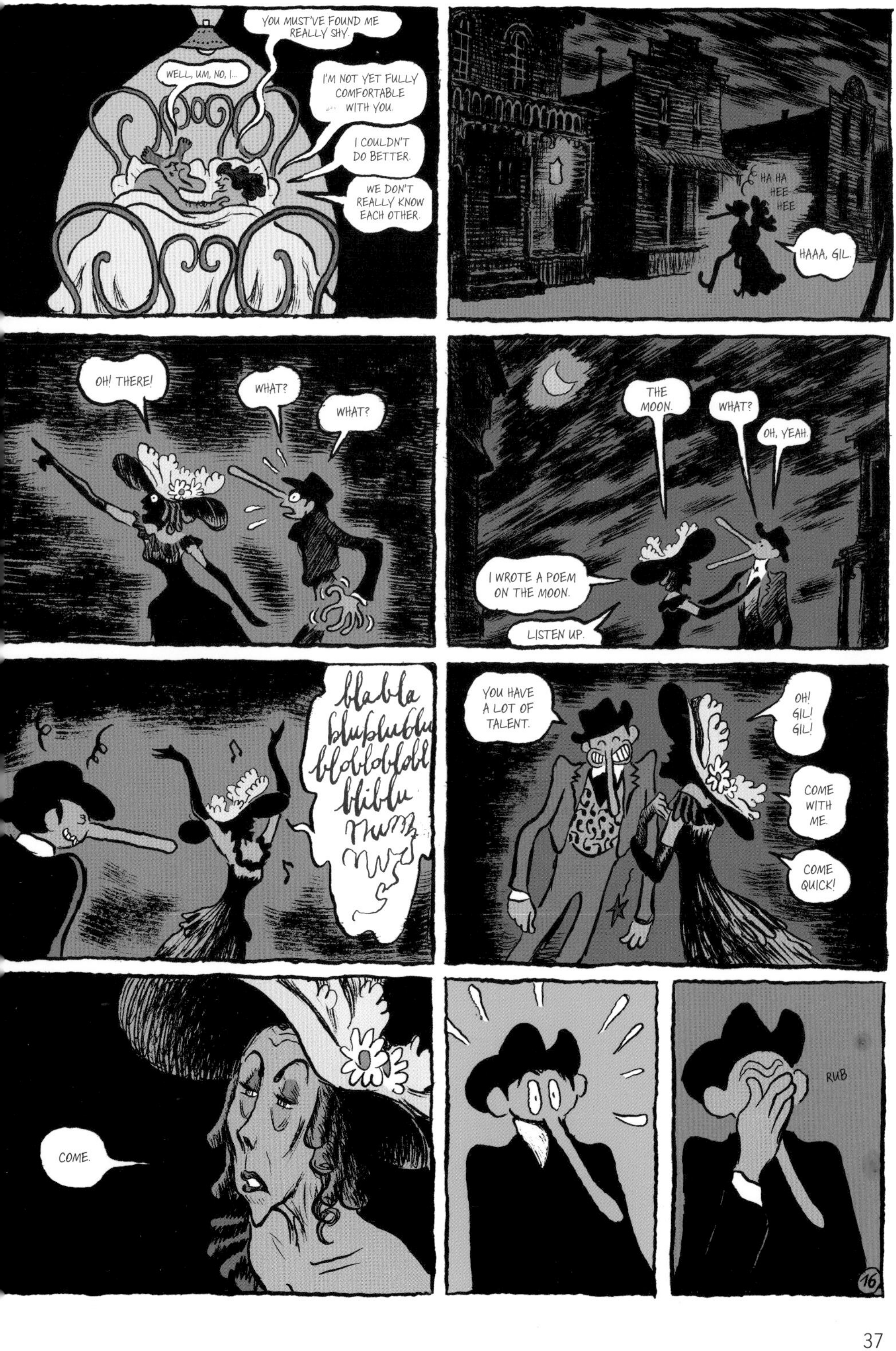
YOU MUST'VE FOUND ME REALLY SHY.
WELL, UM, NO, I...
I'M NOT YET FULLY COMFORTABLE WITH YOU.
I COULDN'T DO BETTER.
WE DON'T REALLY KNOW EACH OTHER.
HA HA HEE HEE
HAAA, GIL.
OH! THERE!
WHAT?
WHAT?
THE MOON.
WHAT?
OH, YEAH.
I WROTE A POEM ON THE MOON.
LISTEN UP.
blabla
blublublu
blobloblobl
bliblu
YOU HAVE A LOT OF TALENT.
OH! GIL! GIL!
COME WITH ME.
COME QUICK!
COME.
RUB
16

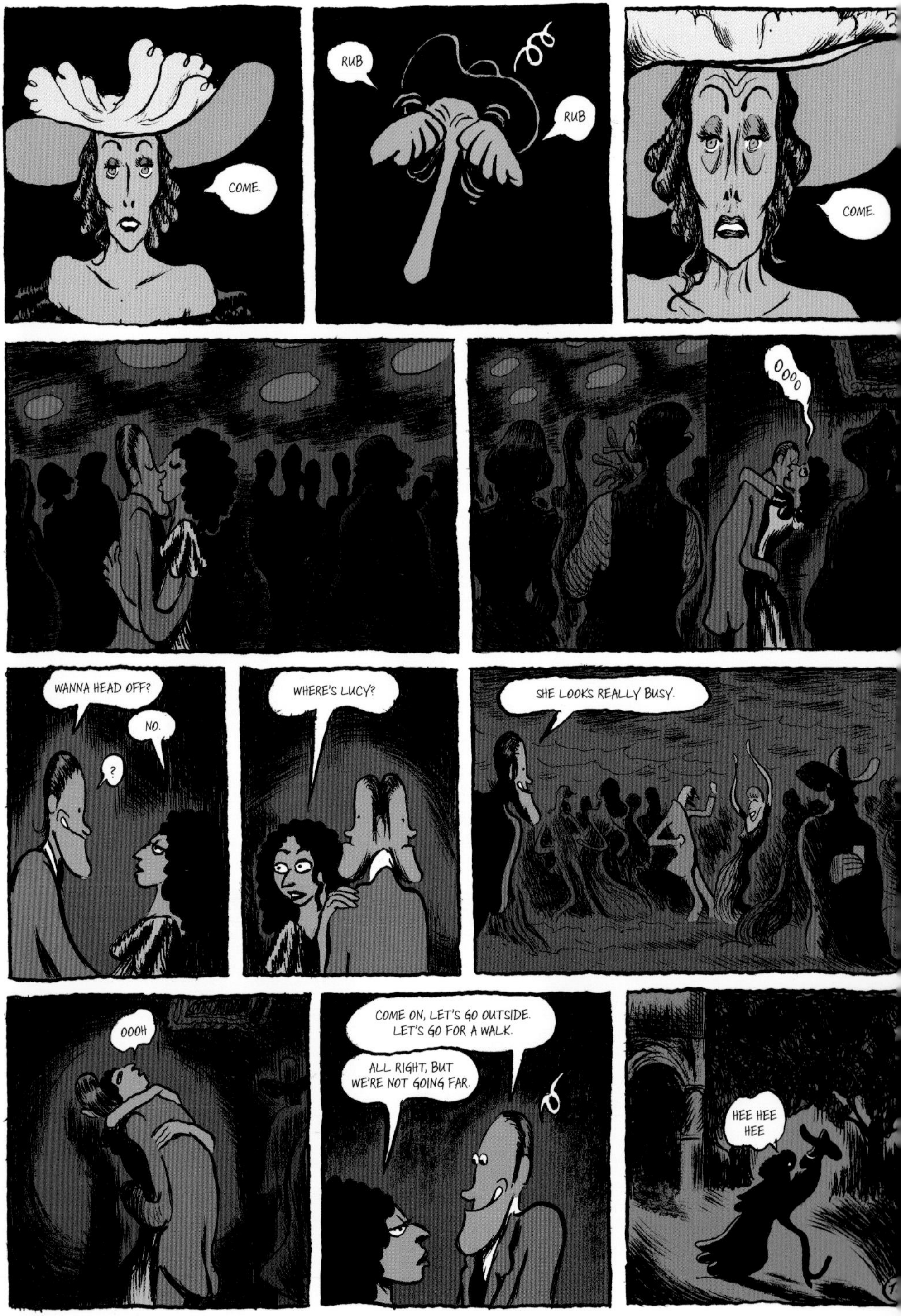
COME.
RUB
RUB
COME.
OOOO
WANNA HEAD OFF?
NO.
?
WHERE'S LUCY?
SHE LOOKS REALLY BUSY.
OOOH
COME ON, LET'S GO OUTSIDE. LET'S GO FOR A WALK.
ALL RIGHT, BUT WE'RE NOT GOING FAR.
HEE HEE HEE

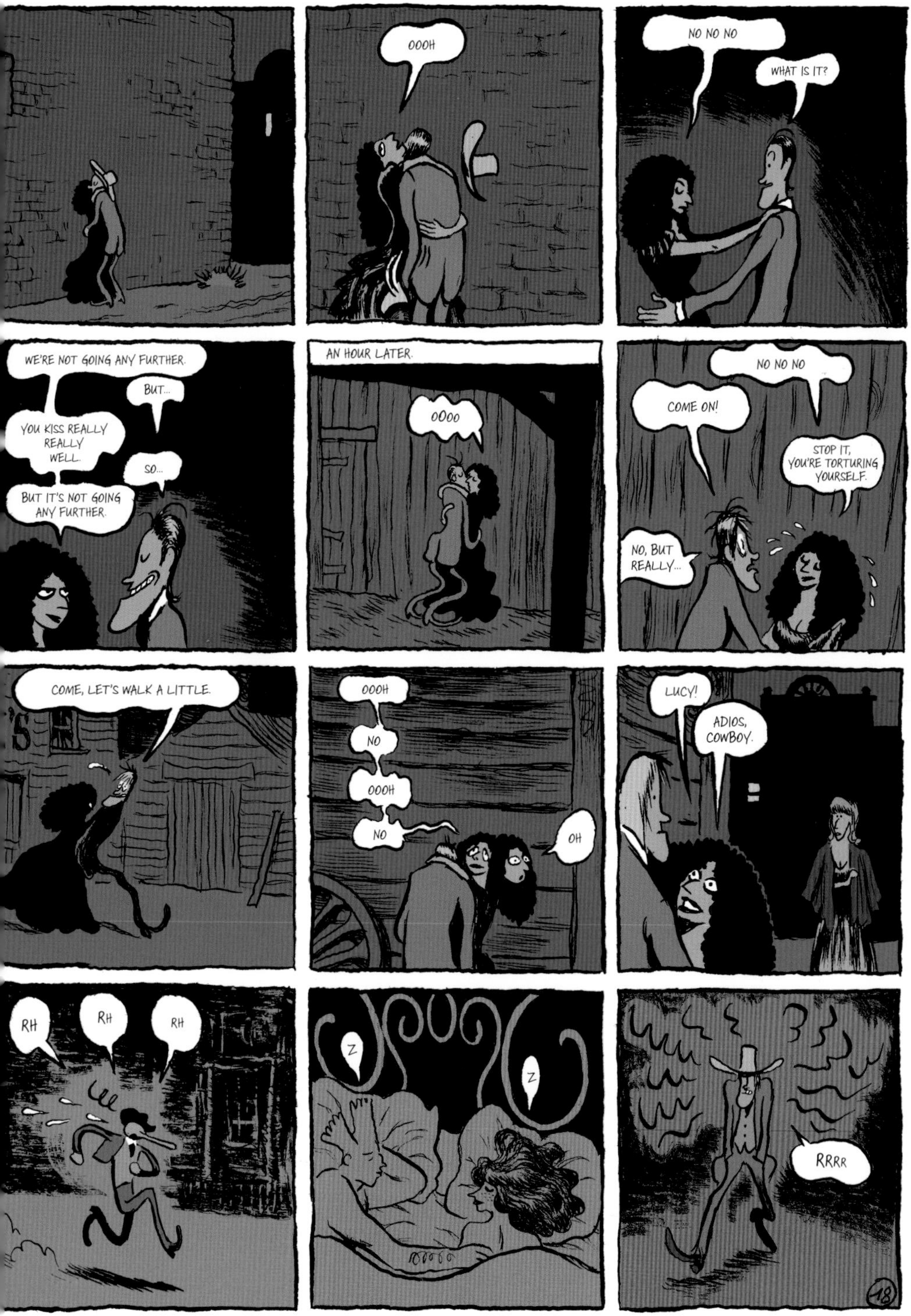
OOOH
NO NO NO
WHAT IS IT?
WE'RE NOT GOING ANY FURTHER.
BUT...
YOU KISS REALLY REALLY WELL.
SO...
BUT IT'S NOT GOING ANY FURTHER.
AN HOUR LATER.
OOoo
NO NO NO
COME ON!
STOP IT, YOU'RE TORTURING YOURSELF.
NO, BUT REALLY...
COME, LET'S WALK A LITTLE.
OOOH
NO
OOOH
NO
OH
LUCY!
ADIOS, COWBOY.
RH
RH
RH
Z
Z
RRRR
18

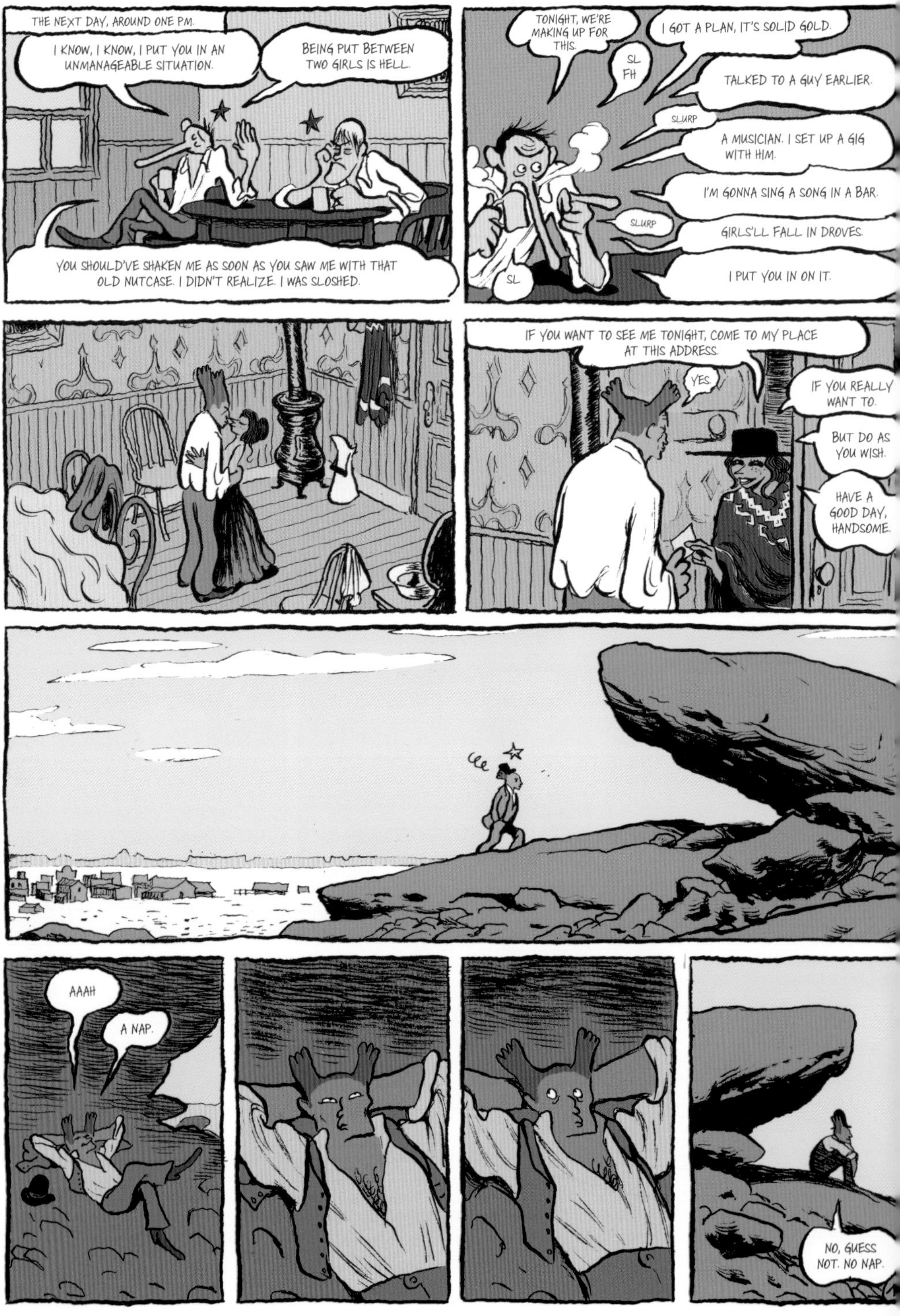
THE NEXT DAY, AROUND ONE P.M.
I KNOW, I KNOW, I PUT YOU IN AN UNMANAGEABLE SITUATION.
BEING PUT BETWEEN TWO GIRLS IS HELL.
YOU SHOULD'VE SHAKEN ME AS SOON AS YOU SAW ME WITH THAT OLD NUTCASE. I DIDN'T REALIZE. I WAS SLOSHED.
TONIGHT, WE'RE MAKING UP FOR THIS.
SL FH
I GOT A PLAN, IT'S SOLID GOLD.
TALKED TO A GUY EARLIER.
SLURP
A MUSICIAN. I SET UP A GIG WITH HIM.
I'M GONNA SING A SONG IN A BAR.
SLURP
GIRLS'LL FALL IN DROVES.
SL
I PUT YOU IN ON IT.
IF YOU WANT TO SEE ME TONIGHT, COME TO MY PLACE AT THIS ADDRESS.
YES.
IF YOU REALLY WANT TO.
BUT DO AS YOU WISH.
HAVE A GOOD DAY, HANDSOME.
AAAH
A NAP.
NO, GUESS NOT. NO NAP.

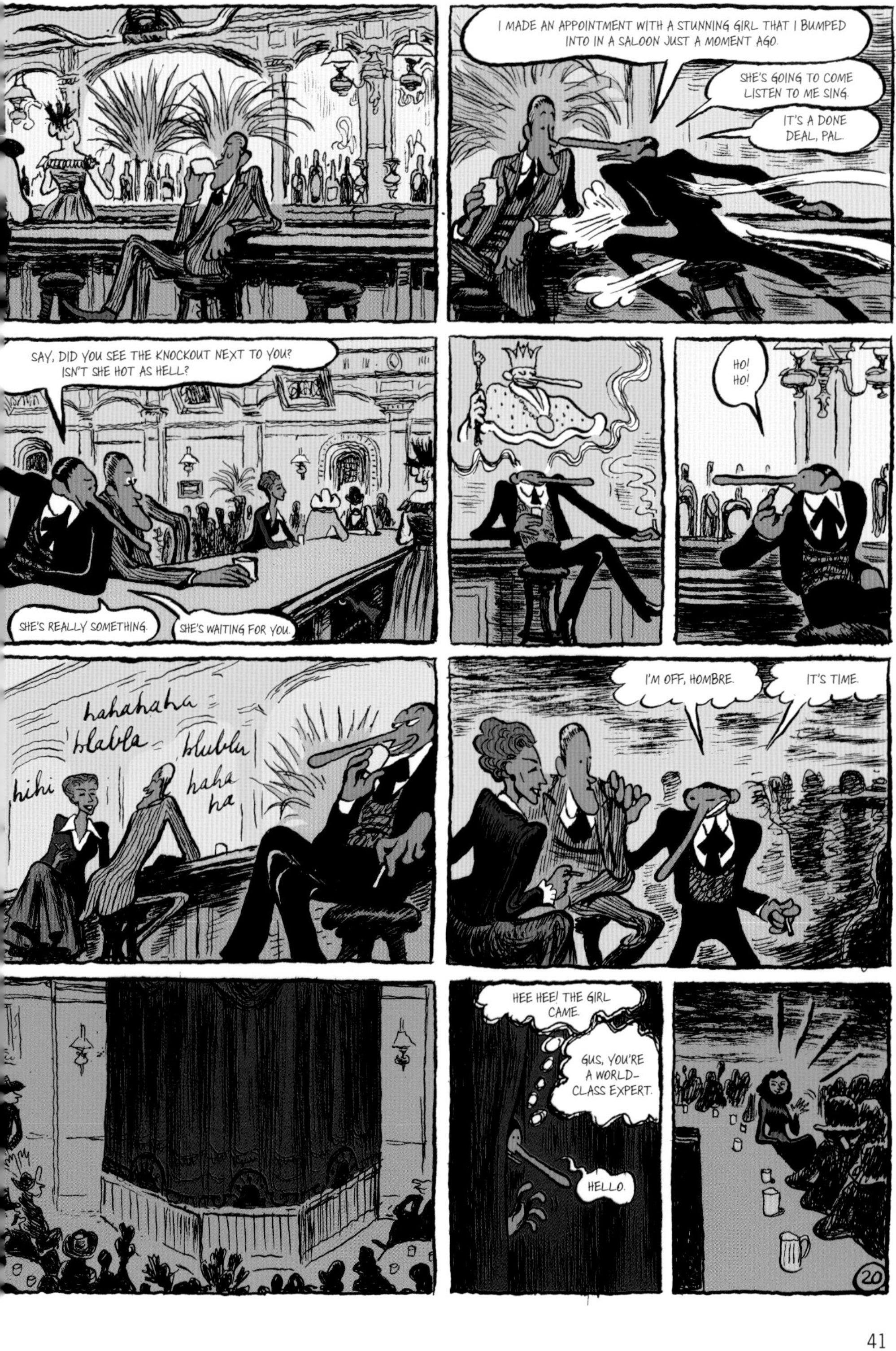
I MADE AN APPOINTMENT WITH A STUNNING GIRL THAT I BUMPED INTO IN A SALOON JUST A MOMENT AGO.
SHE'S GOING TO COME LISTEN TO ME SING.
IT'S A DONE DEAL, PAL.
SAY, DID YOU SEE THE KNOCKOUT NEXT TO YOU? ISN'T SHE HOT AS HELL?
SHE'S REALLY SOMETHING.
SHE'S WAITING FOR YOU.
HO! HO!
hahahaha
blabla
blublu
hihi
haha ha
I'M OFF, HOMBRE.
IT'S TIME.
HEE HEE! THE GIRL CAME.
GUS, YOU'RE A WORLD-CLASS EXPERT.
HELLO.
20

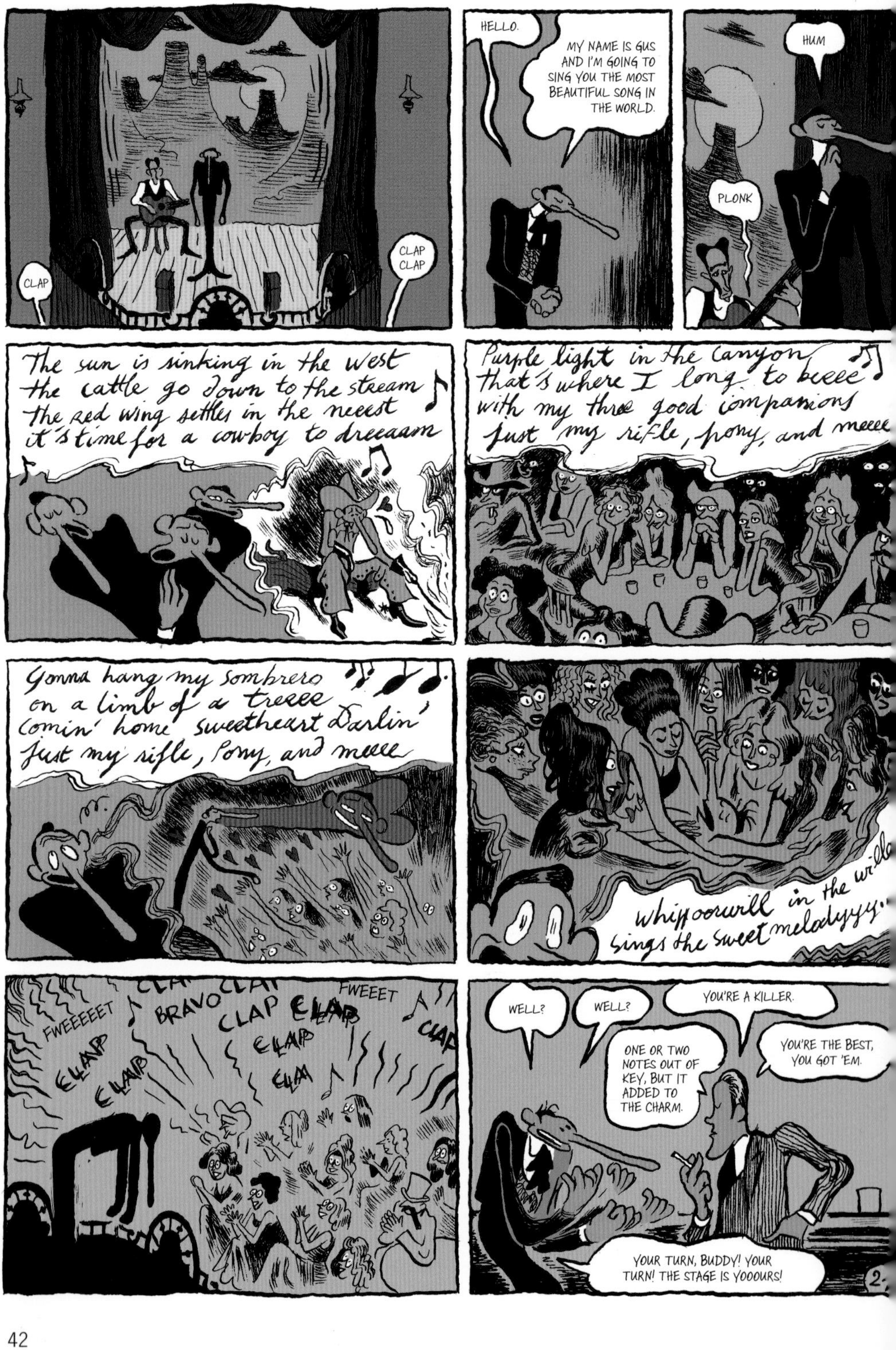
CLAP
CLAP
CLAP
HELLO.
MY NAME IS GUS AND I'M GOING TO SING YOU THE MOST BEAUTIFUL SONG IN THE WORLD.
HUM
PLONK
The sun is sinking in the west
the cattle go down to the steeam
the red wing settles in the neeest
it's time for a cowboy to dreeaam
Purple light in the canyon
that's where I long to beeee
with my three good companions
just my rifle, pony, and meeee
Gonna hang my sombrero
on a limb of a treeee
comin' home sweetheart Darlin'
just my rifle, pony, and meeee
whippoorwill in the wil
sings the sweet melodyyy..
FWEEEEET
CLAP
BRAVO
CLAP
CLAP
FWEEET
CLAP
CLAP
CLAP
CLAP
CLAP
CLAP
CLAP
WELL?
WELL?
YOU'RE A KILLER.
ONE OR TWO NOTES OUT OF KEY, BUT IT ADDED TO THE CHARM.
YOU'RE THE BEST, YOU GOT 'EM.
YOUR TURN, BUDDY! YOUR TURN! THE STAGE IS YOOOURS!

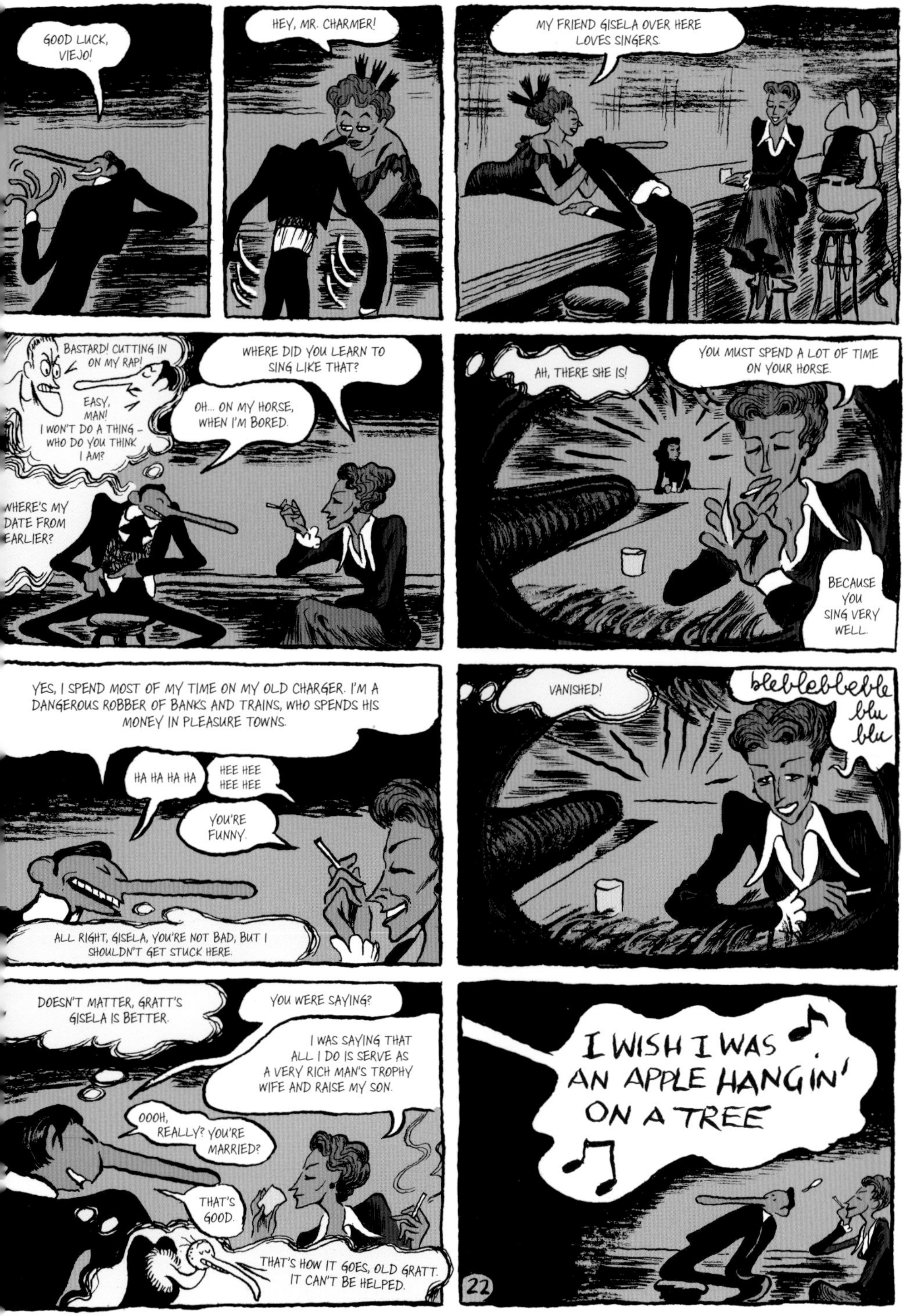
GOOD LUCK, VIEJO!
HEY, MR. CHARMER!
MY FRIEND GISELA OVER HERE LOVES SINGERS.
BASTARD! CUTTING IN ON MY RAP!
EASY, MAN! I WON'T DO A THING – WHO DO YOU THINK I AM?
WHERE'S MY DATE FROM EARLIER?
WHERE DID YOU LEARN TO SING LIKE THAT?
OH... ON MY HORSE, WHEN I'M BORED.
AH, THERE SHE IS!
YOU MUST SPEND A LOT OF TIME ON YOUR HORSE.
BECAUSE YOU SING VERY WELL.
YES, I SPEND MOST OF MY TIME ON MY OLD CHARGER. I'M A DANGEROUS ROBBER OF BANKS AND TRAINS, WHO SPENDS HIS MONEY IN PLEASURE TOWNS.
HA HA HA HA
HEE HEE HEE HEE
YOU'RE FUNNY.
ALL RIGHT, GISELA, YOU'RE NOT BAD, BUT I SHOULDN'T GET STUCK HERE.
VANISHED!
bleblebbeble blu blu
DOESN'T MATTER, GRATT'S GISELA IS BETTER.
YOU WERE SAYING?
I WAS SAYING THAT ALL I DO IS SERVE AS A VERY RICH MAN'S TROPHY WIFE AND RAISE MY SON.
OOOH, REALLY? YOU'RE MARRIED?
THAT'S GOOD.
THAT'S HOW IT GOES, OLD GRATT. IT CAN'T BE HELPED.
22
I WISH I WAS AN APPLE HANGIN' ON A TREE

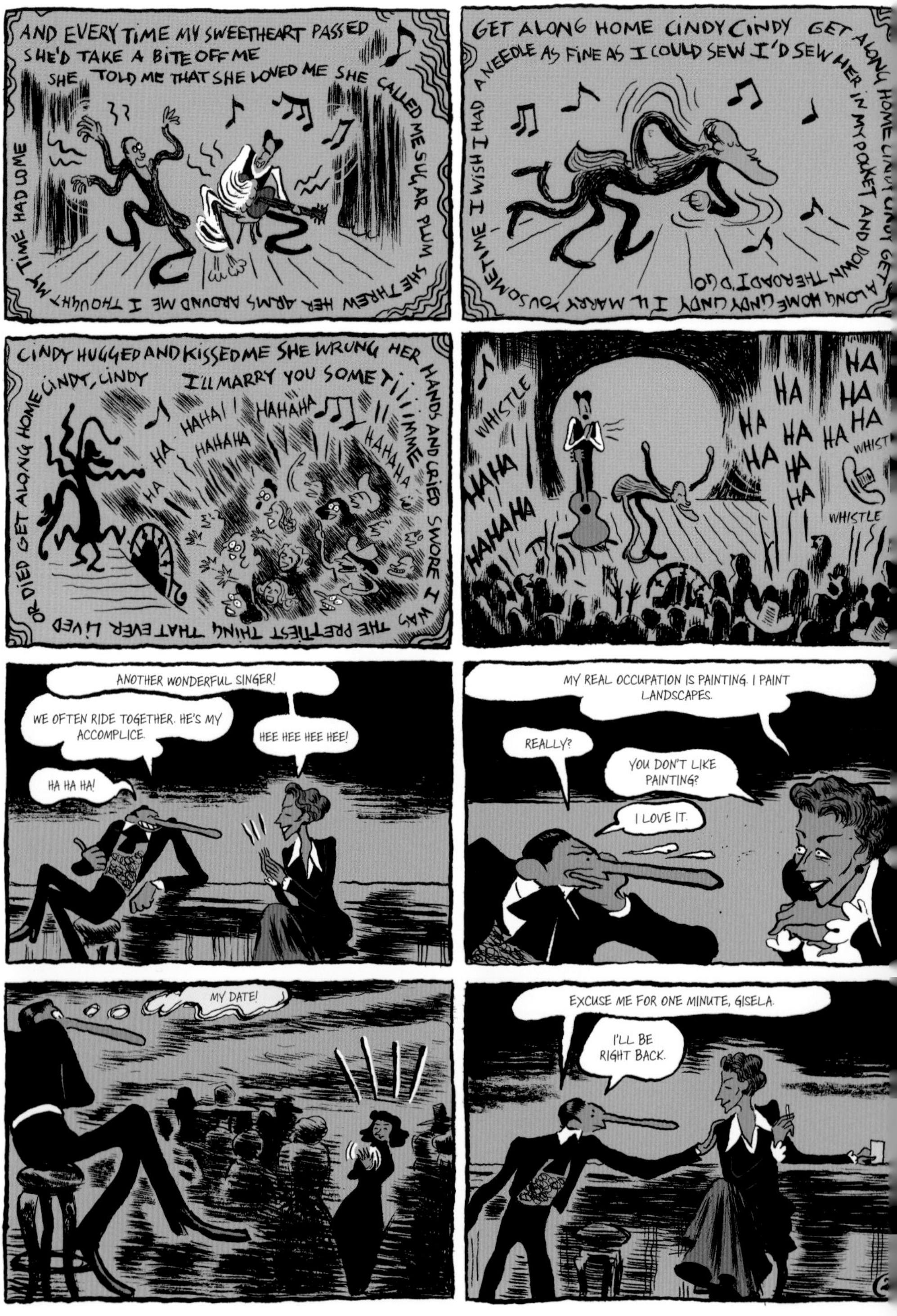
AND EVERY TIME MY SWEETHEART PASSED
SHE'D TAKE A BITE OFF ME
SHE TOLD ME THAT SHE LOVED ME SHE CALLED ME SUGAR PLUM SHE THREW HER ARMS AROUND ME I THOUGHT MY TIME HAD COME
GET ALONG HOME CINDY CINDY GET ALONG HOME CINDY CINDY GET ALONG HOME CINDY CINDY I'LL MARRY YOU SOMETIME I WISH I HAD A NEEDLE AS FINE AS I COULD SEW I'D SEW HER IN MY POCKET AND DOWN THE ROAD I'D GO
CINDY HUGGED AND KISSED ME SHE WRUNG HER HANDS AND CRIED SWORE I WAS THE PRETTIEST THING THAT EVER LIVED OR DIED GET ALONG HOME CINDY, CINDY
I'LL MARRY YOU SOMETIME
HA HA HAHA! HAHAHA HAHAHA HAHAHA
WHISTLE
HAHA
HAHAHA
HA HA HA HA HA HA HA HA HA HA HA
WHISTLE
WHISTLE
ANOTHER WONDERFUL SINGER!
WE OFTEN RIDE TOGETHER. HE'S MY ACCOMPLICE.
HEE HEE HEE HEE!
HA HA HA!
MY REAL OCCUPATION IS PAINTING. I PAINT LANDSCAPES.
REALLY?
YOU DON'T LIKE PAINTING?
I LOVE IT.
MY DATE!
EXCUSE ME FOR ONE MINUTE, GISELA.
I'LL BE RIGHT BACK.

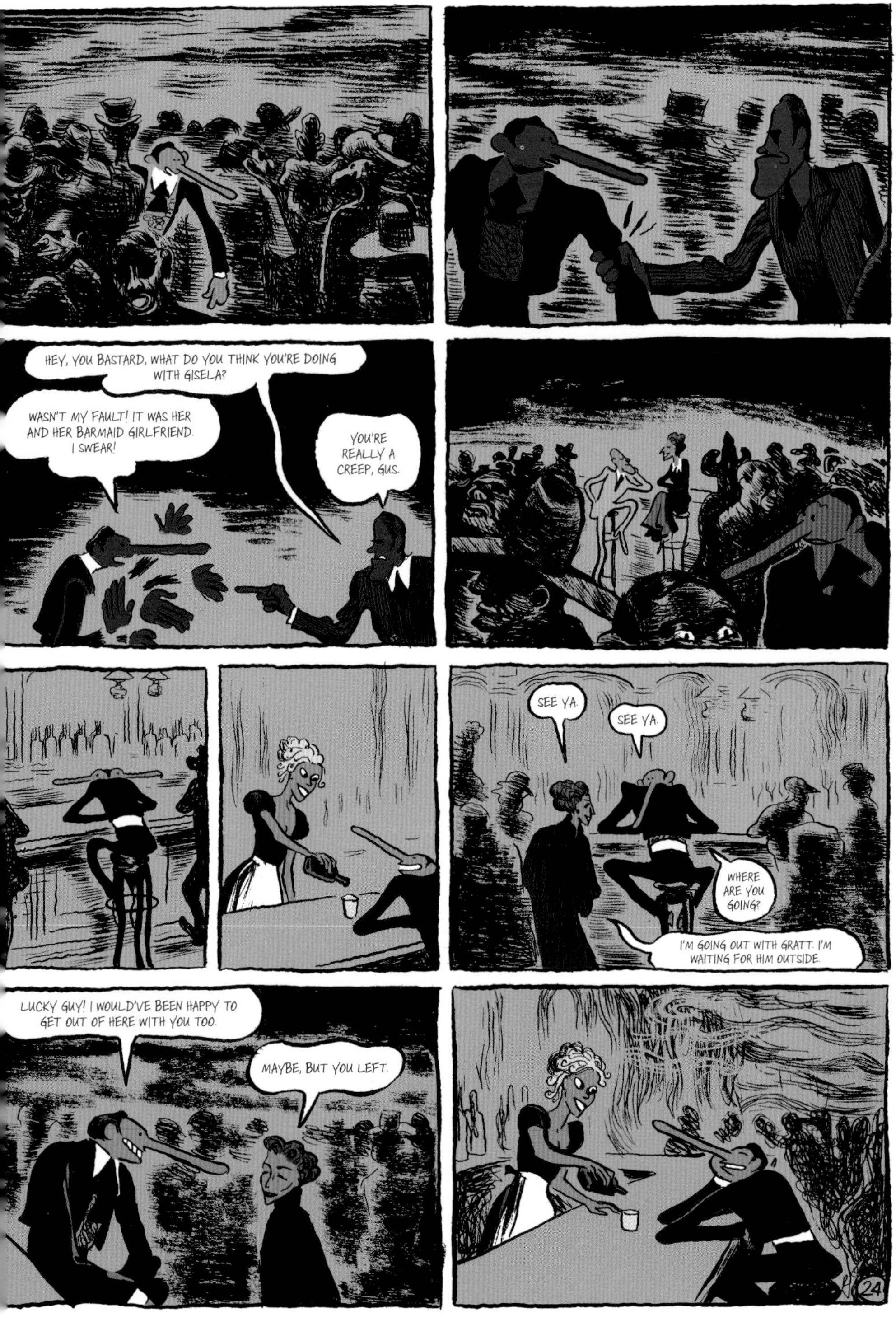
HEY, YOU BASTARD, WHAT DO YOU THINK YOU'RE DOING WITH GISELA?
WASN'T MY FAULT! IT WAS HER AND HER BARMAID GIRLFRIEND. I SWEAR!
YOU'RE REALLY A CREEP, GUS.
SEE YA.
SEE YA.
WHERE ARE YOU GOING?
I'M GOING OUT WITH GRATT. I'M WAITING FOR HIM OUTSIDE.
LUCKY GUY! I WOULD'VE BEEN HAPPY TO GET OUT OF HERE WITH YOU TOO.
MAYBE, BUT YOU LEFT.
24

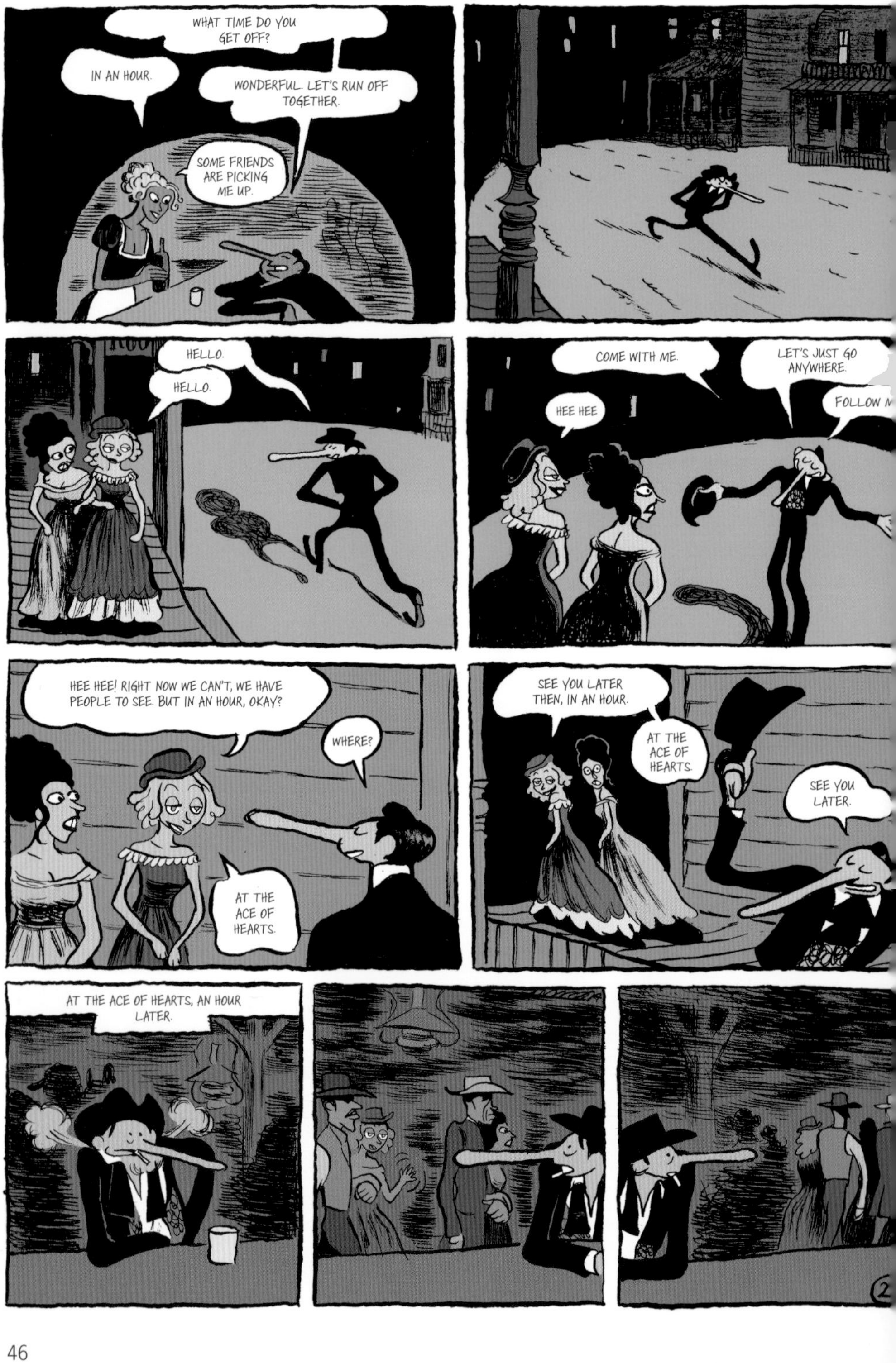
WHAT TIME DO YOU GET OFF?
IN AN HOUR.
WONDERFUL. LET'S RUN OFF TOGETHER.
SOME FRIENDS ARE PICKING ME UP.
HELLO.
HELLO.
COME WITH ME.
HEE HEE
LET'S JUST GO ANYWHERE.
FOLLOW M
HEE HEE! RIGHT NOW WE CAN'T, WE HAVE PEOPLE TO SEE. BUT IN AN HOUR, OKAY?
WHERE?
AT THE ACE OF HEARTS.
SEE YOU LATER THEN, IN AN HOUR.
AT THE ACE OF HEARTS.
SEE YOU LATER.
AT THE ACE OF HEARTS, AN HOUR LATER.

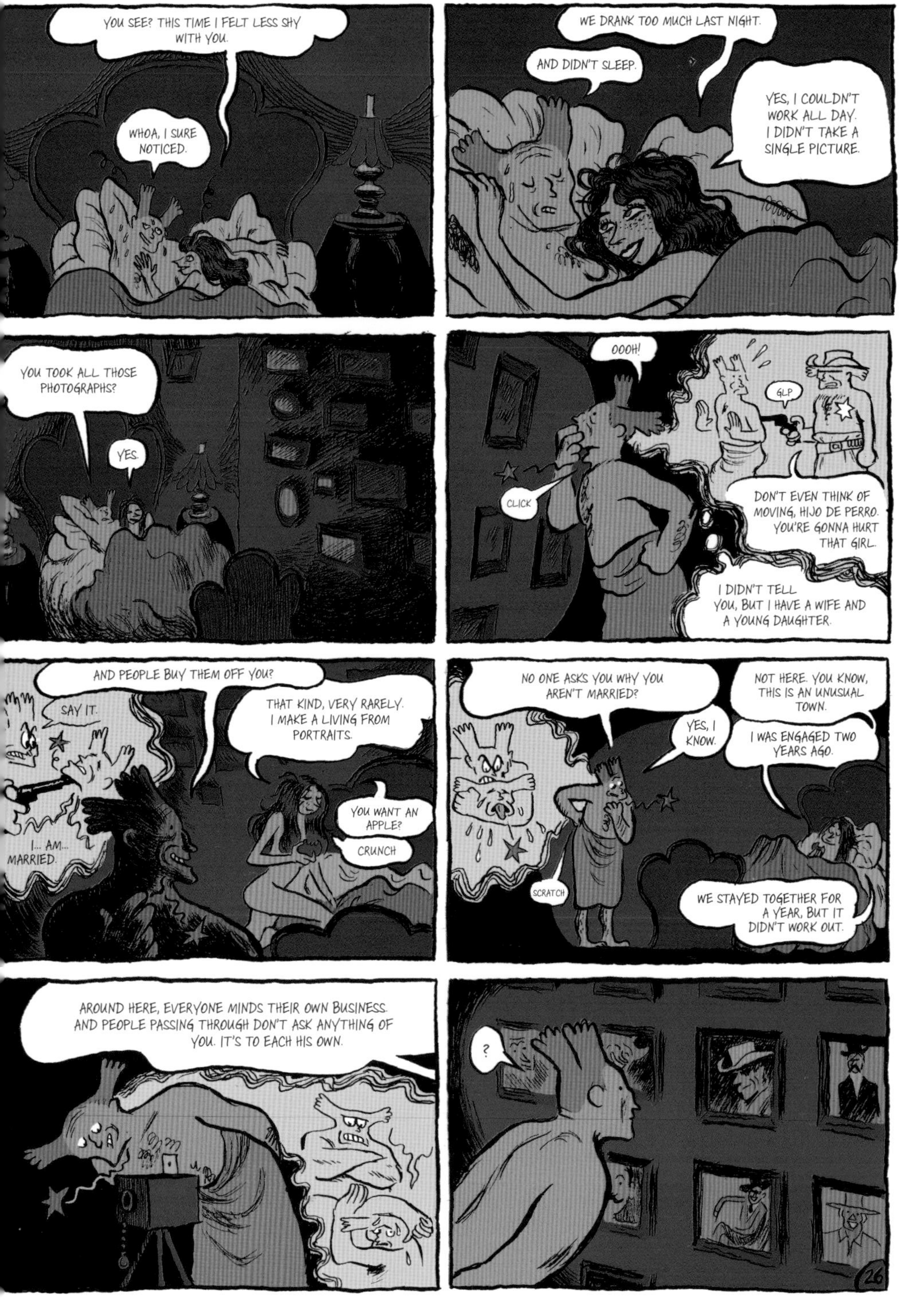

YOU SEE? THIS TIME I FELT LESS SHY WITH YOU.
WHOA, I SURE NOTICED.
WE DRANK TOO MUCH LAST NIGHT.
AND DIDN'T SLEEP.
YES, I COULDN'T WORK ALL DAY. I DIDN'T TAKE A SINGLE PICTURE.
YOU TOOK ALL THOSE PHOTOGRAPHS?
YES.
OOOH!
GLP
CLICK
DON'T EVEN THINK OF MOVING, HIJO DE PERRO. YOU'RE GONNA HURT THAT GIRL.
I DIDN'T TELL YOU, BUT I HAVE A WIFE AND A YOUNG DAUGHTER.
AND PEOPLE BUY THEM OFF YOU?
SAY IT.
THAT KIND, VERY RARELY. I MAKE A LIVING FROM PORTRAITS.
I... AM... MARRIED.
YOU WANT AN APPLE?
CRUNCH
NO ONE ASKS YOU WHY YOU AREN'T MARRIED?
YES, I KNOW.
NOT HERE. YOU KNOW, THIS IS AN UNUSUAL TOWN.
I WAS ENGAGED TWO YEARS AGO.
SCRATCH
WE STAYED TOGETHER FOR A YEAR, BUT IT DIDN'T WORK OUT.
AROUND HERE, EVERYONE MINDS THEIR OWN BUSINESS. AND PEOPLE PASSING THROUGH DON'T ASK ANYTHING OF YOU. IT'S TO EACH HIS OWN.
?
26

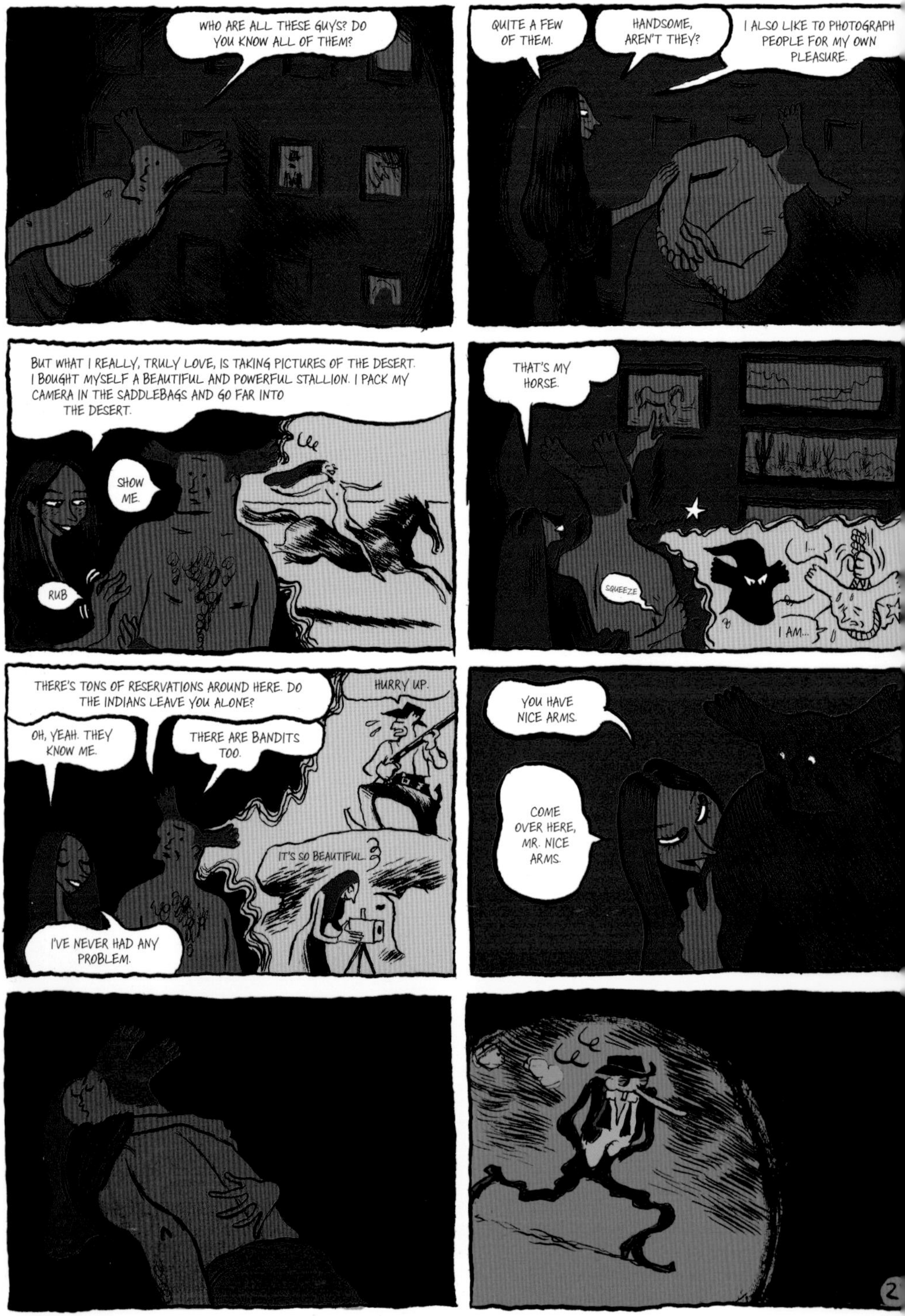
WHO ARE ALL THESE GUYS? DO YOU KNOW ALL OF THEM?
QUITE A FEW OF THEM.
HANDSOME, AREN'T THEY?
I ALSO LIKE TO PHOTOGRAPH PEOPLE FOR MY OWN PLEASURE.
BUT WHAT I REALLY, TRULY LOVE, IS TAKING PICTURES OF THE DESERT. I BOUGHT MYSELF A BEAUTIFUL AND POWERFUL STALLION. I PACK MY CAMERA IN THE SADDLEBAGS AND GO FAR INTO THE DESERT.
SHOW ME.
RUB
THAT'S MY HORSE.
SQUEEZE
I...
I AM...
THERE'S TONS OF RESERVATIONS AROUND HERE. DO THE INDIANS LEAVE YOU ALONE?
OH, YEAH. THEY KNOW ME.
THERE ARE BANDITS TOO.
HURRY UP.
IT'S SO BEAUTIFUL.
I'VE NEVER HAD ANY PROBLEM.
YOU HAVE NICE ARMS.
COME OVER HERE, MR. NICE ARMS.

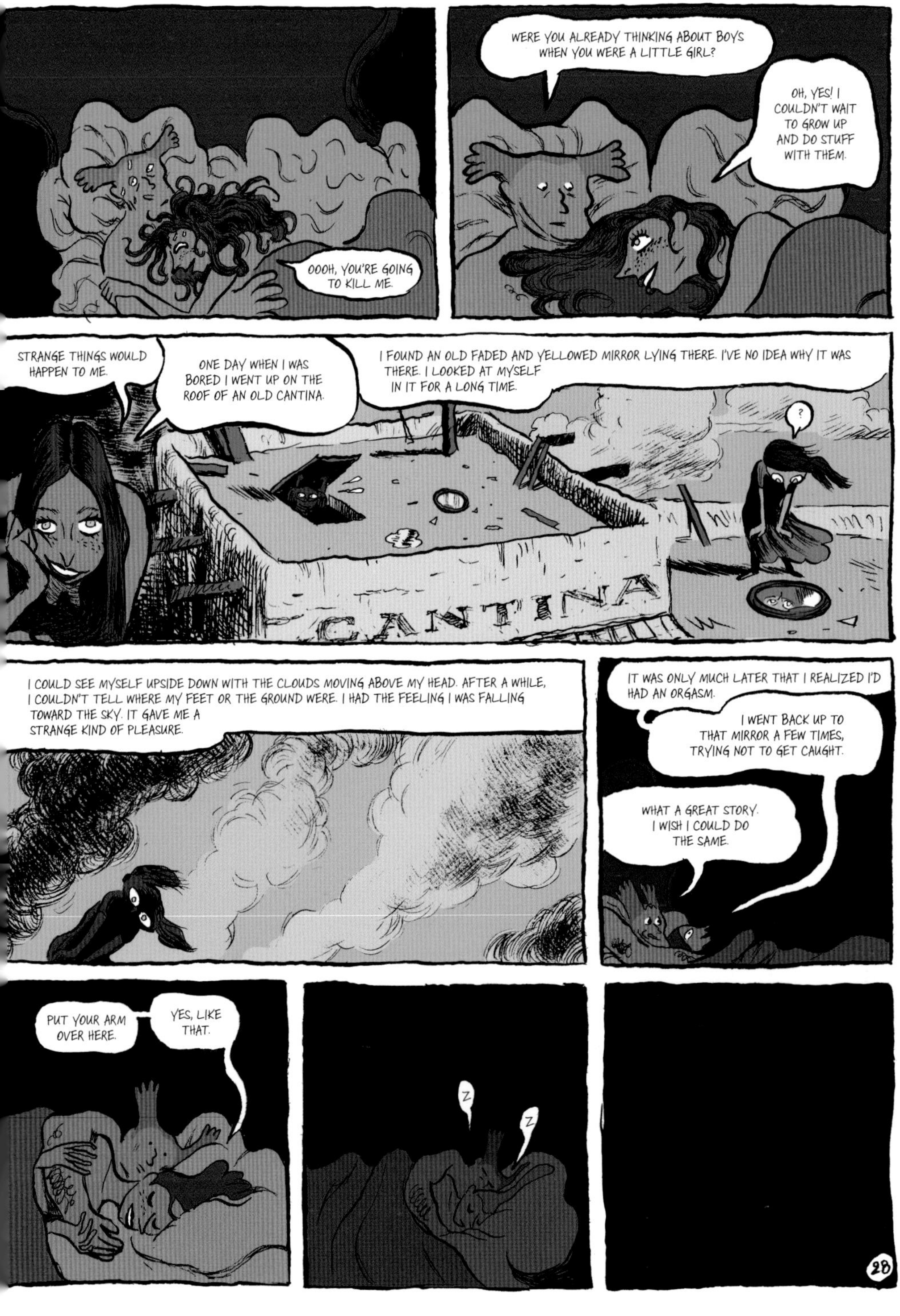
OOOH, YOU'RE GOING TO KILL ME.
WERE YOU ALREADY THINKING ABOUT BOYS WHEN YOU WERE A LITTLE GIRL?
OH, YES! I COULDN'T WAIT TO GROW UP AND DO STUFF WITH THEM.
STRANGE THINGS WOULD HAPPEN TO ME.
ONE DAY WHEN I WAS BORED I WENT UP ON THE ROOF OF AN OLD CANTINA.
I FOUND AN OLD FADED AND YELLOWED MIRROR LYING THERE. I'VE NO IDEA WHY IT WAS THERE. I LOOKED AT MYSELF IN IT FOR A LONG TIME.
?
CANTINA
I COULD SEE MYSELF UPSIDE DOWN WITH THE CLOUDS MOVING ABOVE MY HEAD. AFTER A WHILE, I COULDN'T TELL WHERE MY FEET OR THE GROUND WERE. I HAD THE FEELING I WAS FALLING TOWARD THE SKY. IT GAVE ME A STRANGE KIND OF PLEASURE.
IT WAS ONLY MUCH LATER THAT I REALIZED I'D HAD AN ORGASM.
I WENT BACK UP TO THAT MIRROR A FEW TIMES, TRYING NOT TO GET CAUGHT.
WHAT A GREAT STORY. I WISH I COULD DO THE SAME.
PUT YOUR ARM OVER HERE.
YES, LIKE THAT.
Z
Z
28

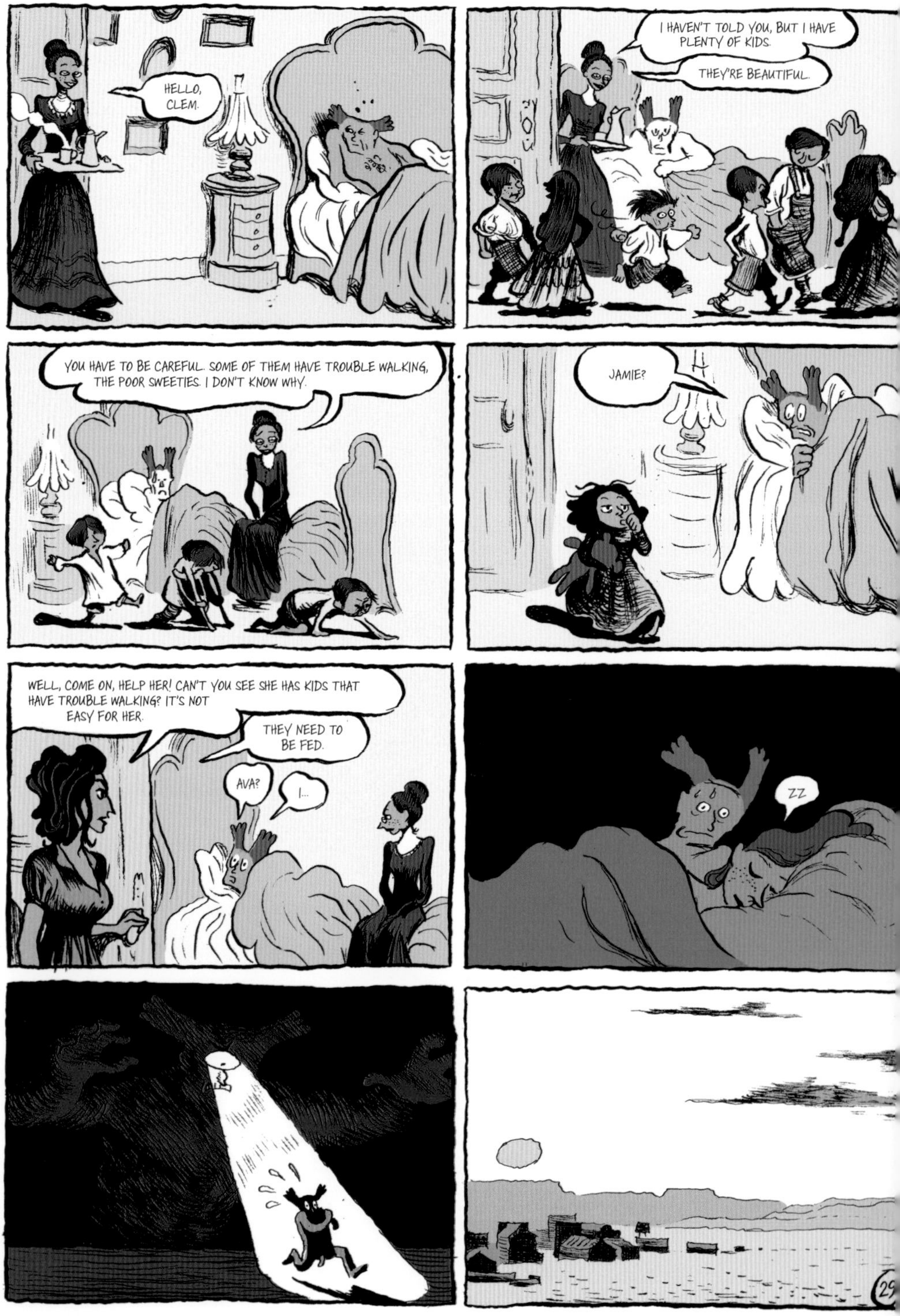
HELLO, CLEM.
I HAVEN'T TOLD YOU, BUT I HAVE PLENTY OF KIDS.
THEY'RE BEAUTIFUL.
YOU HAVE TO BE CAREFUL. SOME OF THEM HAVE TROUBLE WALKING, THE POOR SWEETIES. I DON'T KNOW WHY.
JAMIE?
WELL, COME ON, HELP HER! CAN'T YOU SEE SHE HAS KIDS THAT HAVE TROUBLE WALKING? IT'S NOT EASY FOR HER.
THEY NEED TO BE FED.
AVA?
I...
ZZ
29

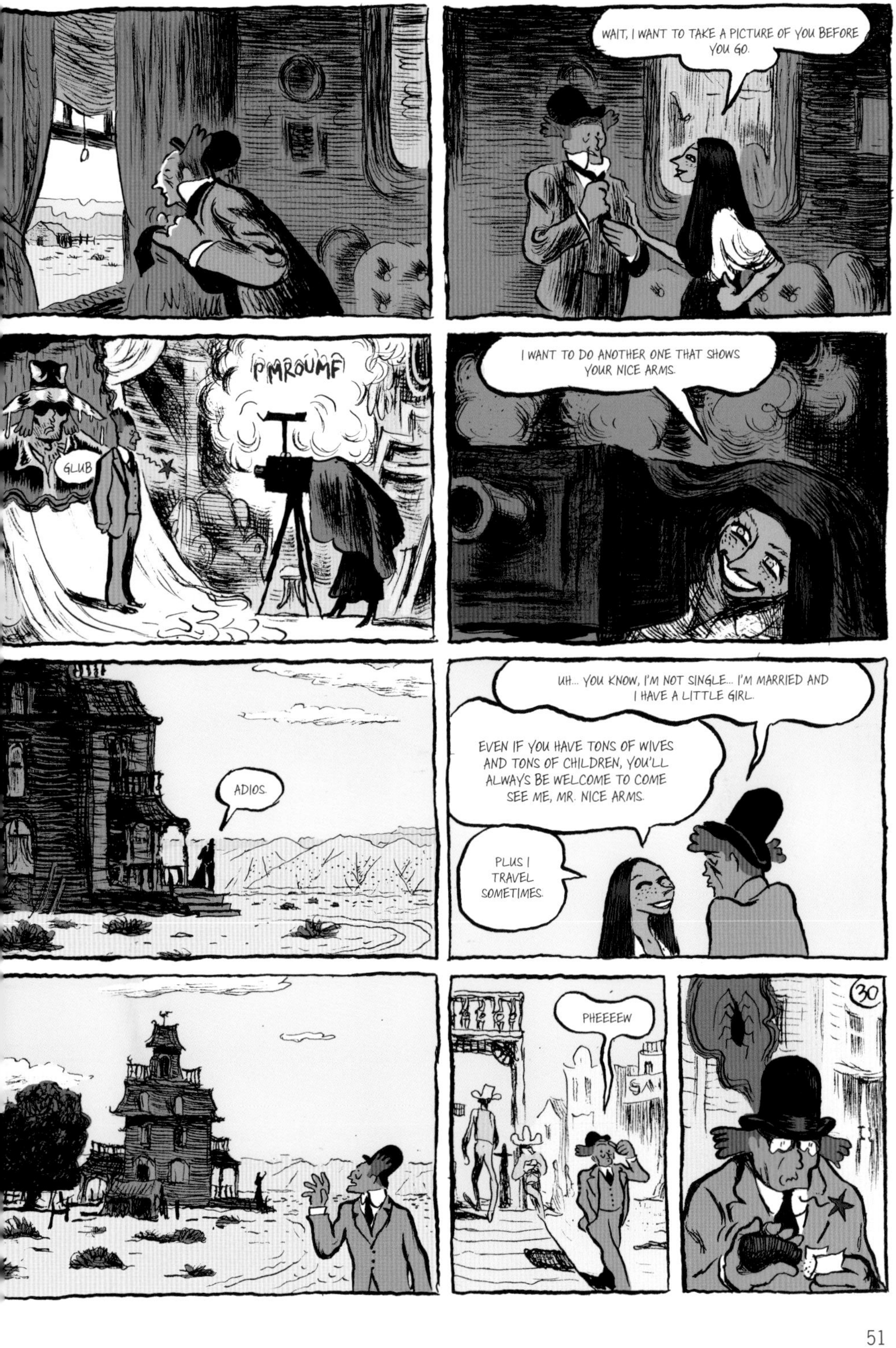
WAIT, I WANT TO TAKE A PICTURE OF YOU BEFORE YOU GO.
P'MROUMF
GLUB
I WANT TO DO ANOTHER ONE THAT SHOWS YOUR NICE ARMS.
ADIOS.
UH... YOU KNOW, I'M NOT SINGLE... I'M MARRIED AND I HAVE A LITTLE GIRL.
EVEN IF YOU HAVE TONS OF WIVES AND TONS OF CHILDREN, YOU'LL ALWAYS BE WELCOME TO COME SEE ME, MR. NICE ARMS.
PLUS I TRAVEL SOMETIMES.
PHEEEEW
30

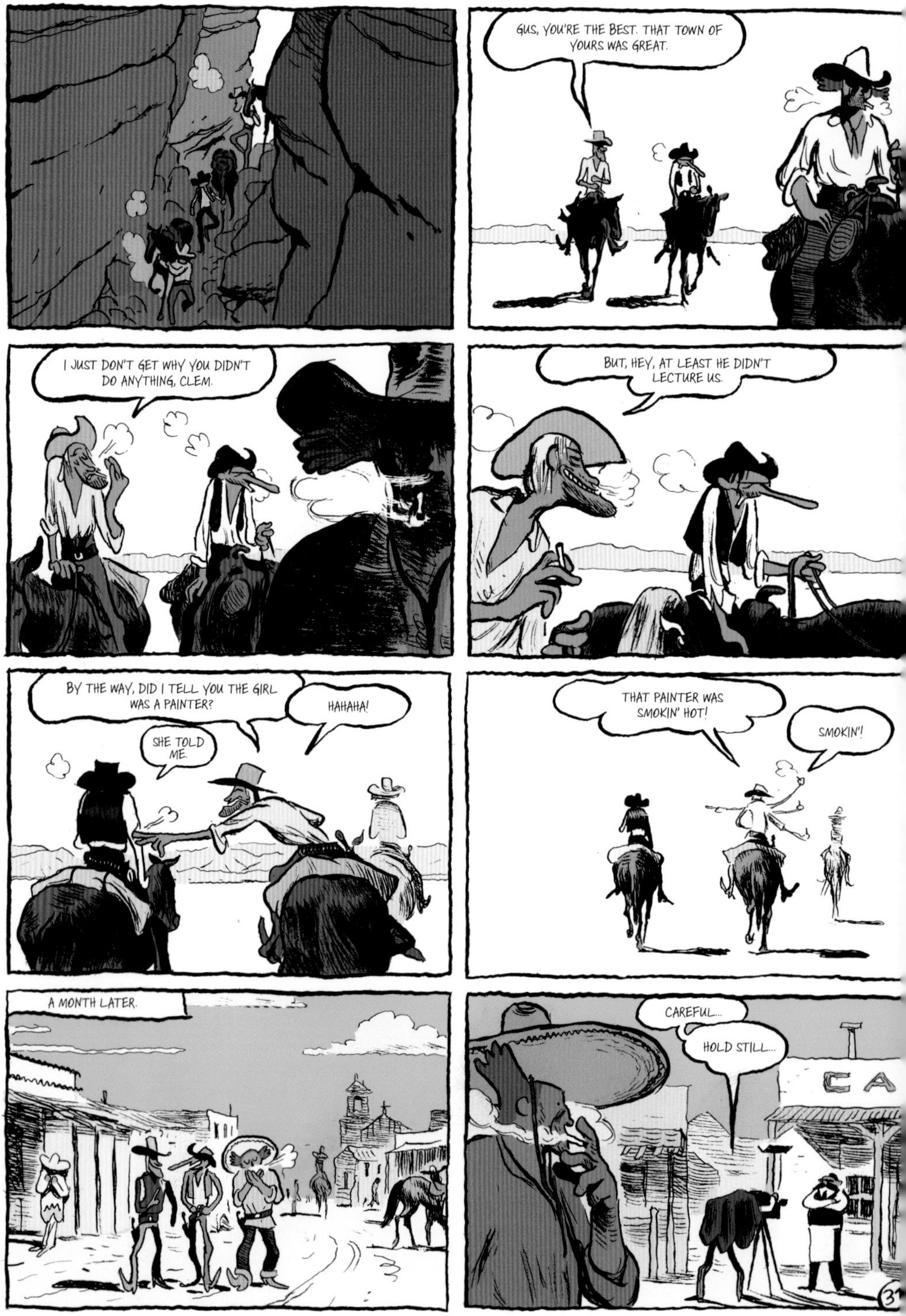
GUS, YOU'RE THE BEST. THAT TOWN OF YOURS WAS GREAT.
I JUST DON'T GET WHY YOU DIDN'T DO ANYTHING, CLEM.
BUT, HEY, AT LEAST HE DIDN'T LECTURE US.
BY THE WAY, DID I TELL YOU THE GIRL WAS A PAINTER?
SHE TOLD ME.
HAHAHA!
THAT PAINTER WAS SMOKIN' HOT!
SMOKIN'!
A MONTH LATER.
CAREFUL...
HOLD STILL...
CA

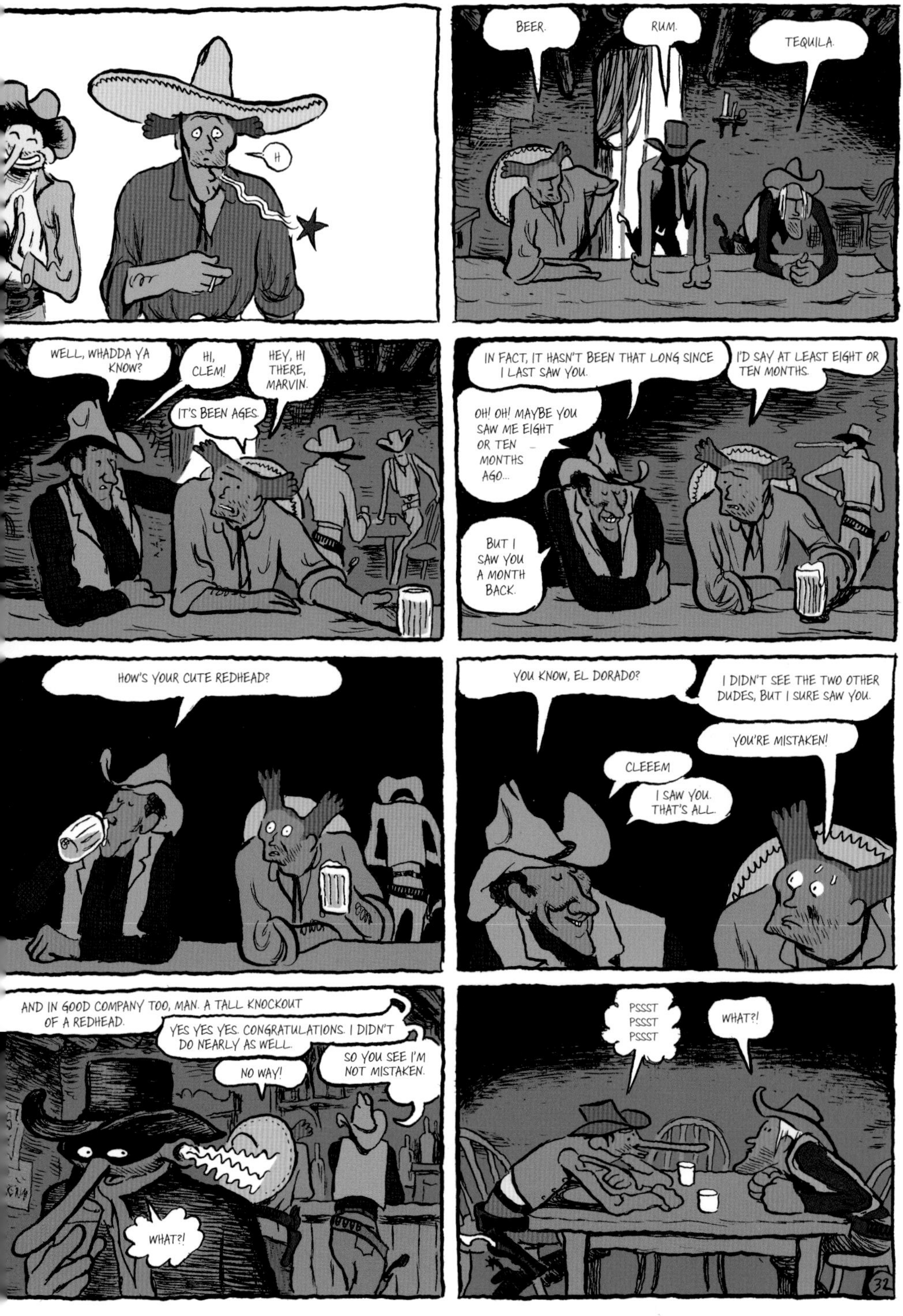
H
BEER.
RUM.
TEQUILA.
WELL, WHADDA YA KNOW?
HI, CLEM!
HEY, HI THERE, MARVIN.
IT'S BEEN AGES.
IN FACT, IT HASN'T BEEN THAT LONG SINCE I LAST SAW YOU.
I'D SAY AT LEAST EIGHT OR TEN MONTHS.
OH! OH! MAYBE YOU SAW ME EIGHT OR TEN MONTHS AGO...
BUT I SAW YOU A MONTH BACK.
HOW'S YOUR CUTE REDHEAD?
YOU KNOW, EL DORADO?
I DIDN'T SEE THE TWO OTHER DUDES, BUT I SURE SAW YOU.
YOU'RE MISTAKEN!
CLEEEM
I SAW YOU. THAT'S ALL.
AND IN GOOD COMPANY TOO, MAN. A TALL KNOCKOUT OF A REDHEAD.
YES YES YES. CONGRATULATIONS. I DIDN'T DO NEARLY AS WELL.
NO WAY!
SO YOU SEE I'M NOT MISTAKEN.
WHAT?!
PSSST PSSST PSSST
WHAT?!
32

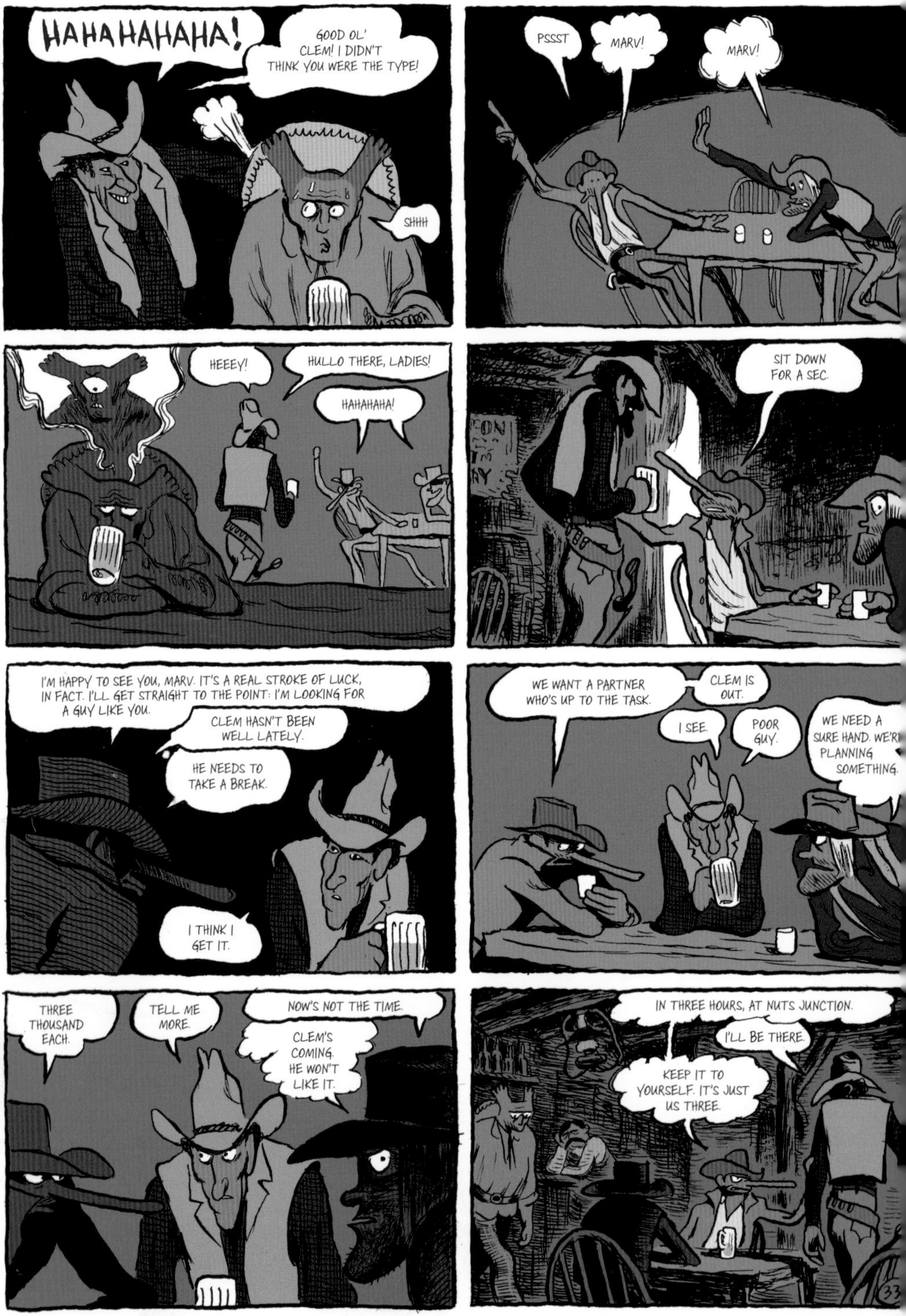
HAHAHAHAHA!
GOOD OL' CLEM! I DIDN'T THINK YOU WERE THE TYPE!
SHHH
PSSST
MARV!
MARV!
HEEEY!
HULLO THERE, LADIES!
HAHAHAHA!
SIT DOWN FOR A SEC.
I'M HAPPY TO SEE YOU, MARV. IT'S A REAL STROKE OF LUCK, IN FACT. I'LL GET STRAIGHT TO THE POINT: I'M LOOKING FOR A GUY LIKE YOU.
CLEM HASN'T BEEN WELL LATELY.
HE NEEDS TO TAKE A BREAK.
I THINK I GET IT.
WE WANT A PARTNER WHO'S UP TO THE TASK.
CLEM IS OUT.
I SEE.
POOR GUY.
WE NEED A SURE HAND. WE'RE PLANNING SOMETHING.
THREE THOUSAND EACH.
TELL ME MORE.
NOW'S NOT THE TIME.
CLEM'S COMING. HE WON'T LIKE IT.
IN THREE HOURS, AT NUTS JUNCTION.
I'LL BE THERE.
KEEP IT TO YOURSELF. IT'S JUST US THREE.

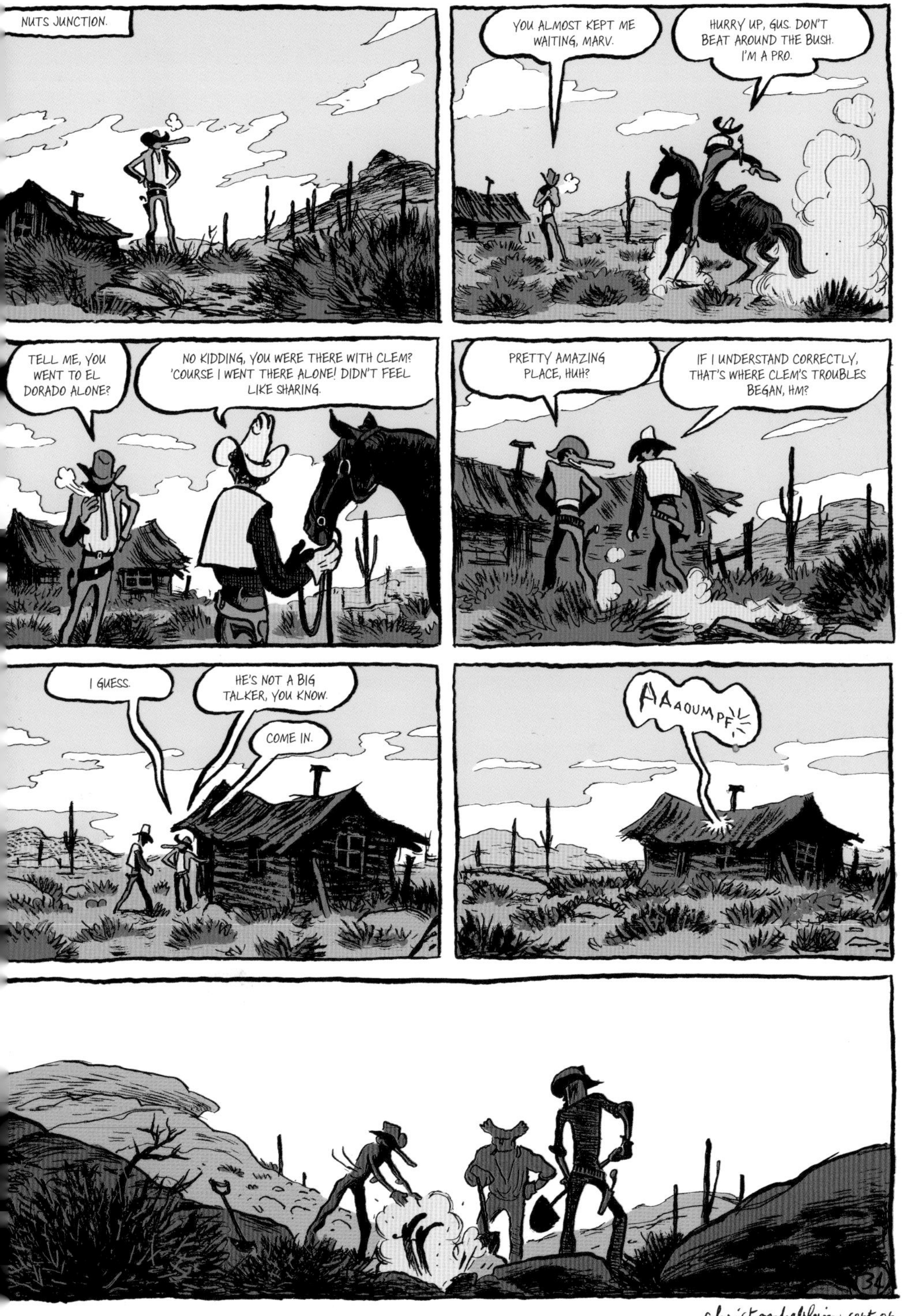
NUTS JUNCTION.
YOU ALMOST KEPT ME WAITING, MARV.
HURRY UP, GUS. DON'T BEAT AROUND THE BUSH. I'M A PRO.
TELL ME, YOU WENT TO EL DORADO ALONE?
NO KIDDING, YOU WERE THERE WITH CLEM? 'COURSE I WENT THERE ALONE! DIDN'T FEEL LIKE SHARING.
PRETTY AMAZING PLACE, HUH?
IF I UNDERSTAND CORRECTLY, THAT'S WHERE CLEM'S TROUBLES BEGAN, HM?
I GUESS.
HE'S NOT A BIG TALKER, YOU KNOW.
COME IN.
AAAOUMPF
34

christopheblain sept 06

LINDA MC CORMICK

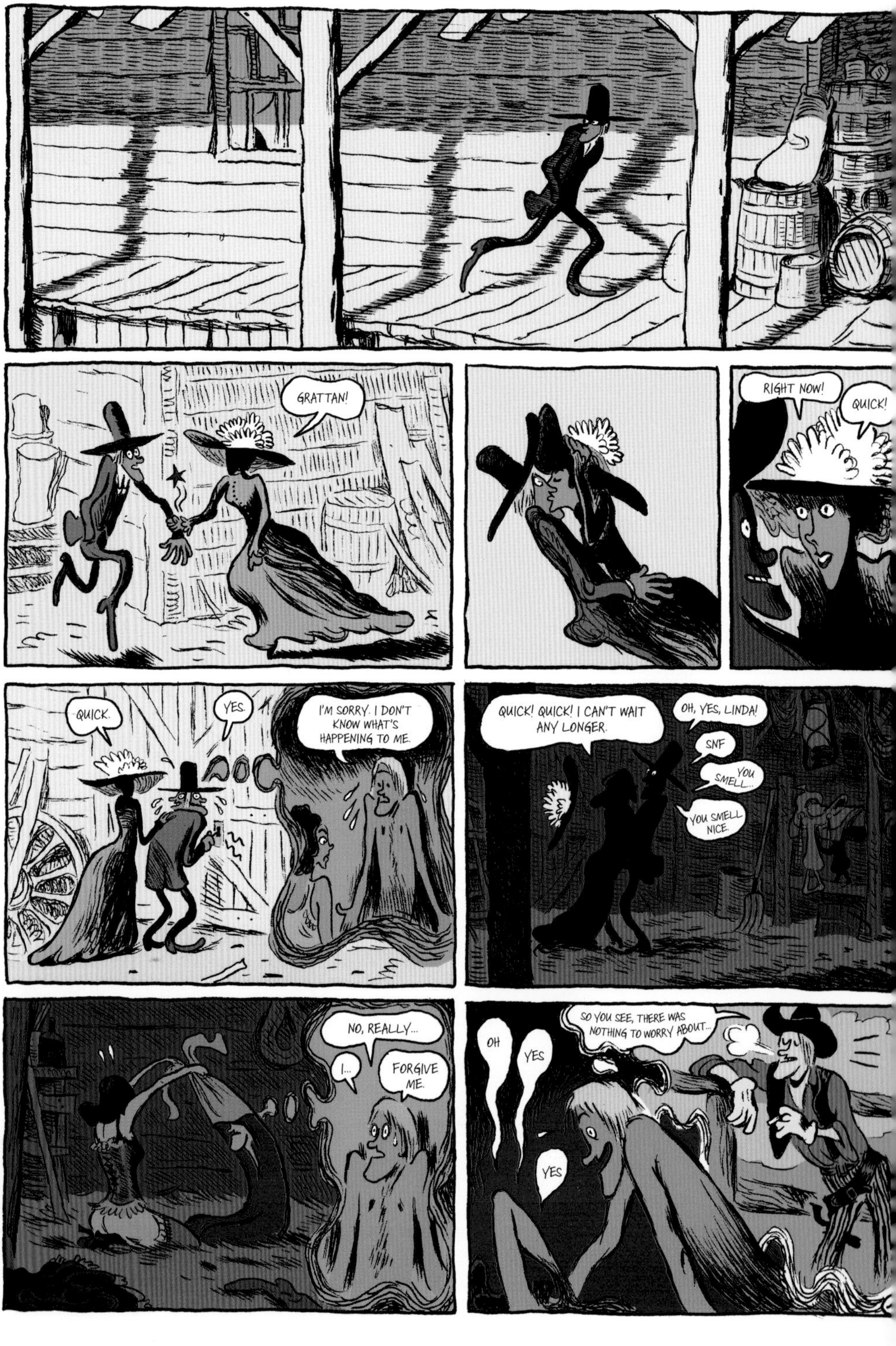
GRATTAN!
RIGHT NOW!
QUICK!
QUICK.
YES.
I'M SORRY. I DON'T KNOW WHAT'S HAPPENING TO ME.
QUICK! QUICK! I CAN'T WAIT ANY LONGER.
OH, YES, LINDA!
SNF
YOU SMELL...
YOU SMELL NICE.
NO, REALLY...
I...
FORGIVE ME.
OH
YES
YES
SO YOU SEE, THERE WAS NOTHING TO WORRY ABOUT...

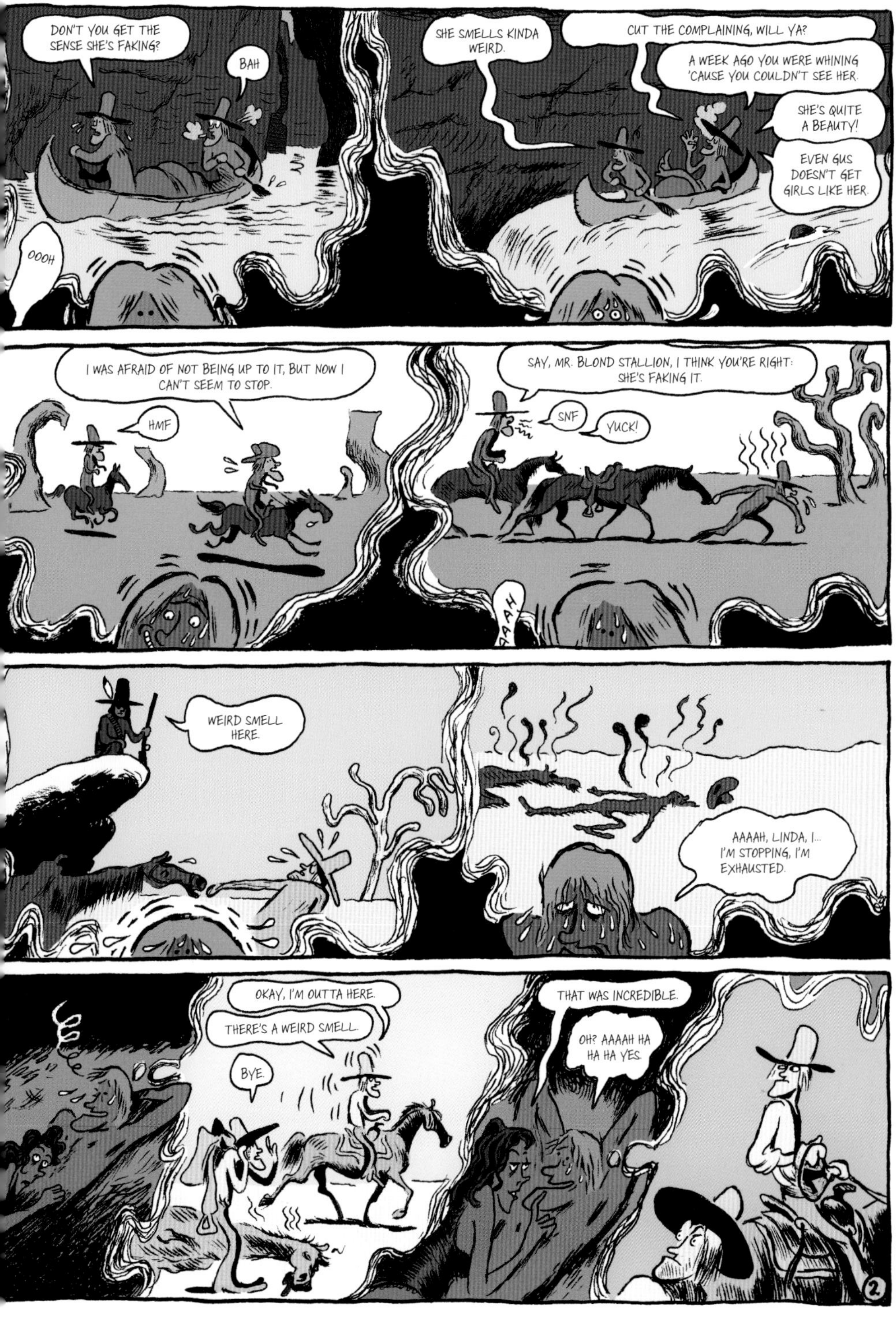
DON'T YOU GET THE SENSE SHE'S FAKING?
BAH
OOOH
SHE SMELLS KINDA WEIRD.
CUT THE COMPLAINING, WILL YA?
A WEEK AGO YOU WERE WHINING 'CAUSE YOU COULDN'T SEE HER.
SHE'S QUITE A BEAUTY!
EVEN GUS DOESN'T GET GIRLS LIKE HER.
I WAS AFRAID OF NOT BEING UP TO IT, BUT NOW I CAN'T SEEM TO STOP.
HMF
SAY, MR. BLOND STALLION, I THINK YOU'RE RIGHT: SHE'S FAKING IT.
SNF
YUCK!
AAAH
WEIRD SMELL HERE.
AAAAH, LINDA, I... I'M STOPPING, I'M EXHAUSTED.
OKAY, I'M OUTTA HERE.
THERE'S A WEIRD SMELL.
BYE.
THAT WAS INCREDIBLE.
OH? AAAAH HA HA HA YES.
2

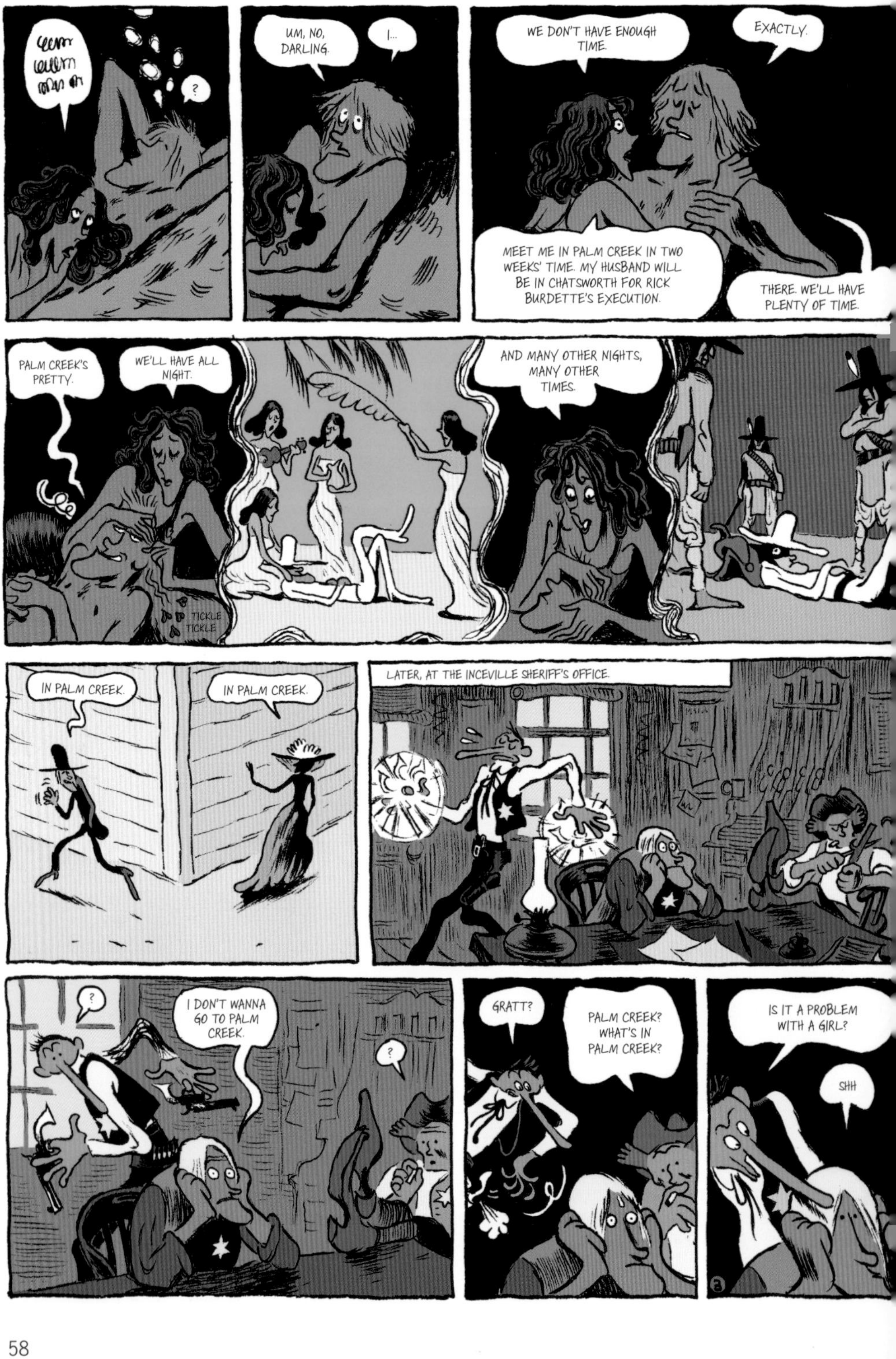
?
UM, NO, DARLING.
I...
WE DON'T HAVE ENOUGH TIME.
EXACTLY.
MEET ME IN PALM CREEK IN TWO WEEKS' TIME. MY HUSBAND WILL BE IN CHATSWORTH FOR RICK BURDETTE'S EXECUTION.
THERE. WE'LL HAVE PLENTY OF TIME.
PALM CREEK'S PRETTY.
WE'LL HAVE ALL NIGHT.
TICKLE TICKLE
AND MANY OTHER NIGHTS, MANY OTHER TIMES.
IN PALM CREEK.
IN PALM CREEK.
LATER, AT THE INCEVILLE SHERIFF'S OFFICE.
?
I DON'T WANNA GO TO PALM CREEK.
?
GRATT?
PALM CREEK? WHAT'S IN PALM CREEK?
IS IT A PROBLEM WITH A GIRL?
SHH

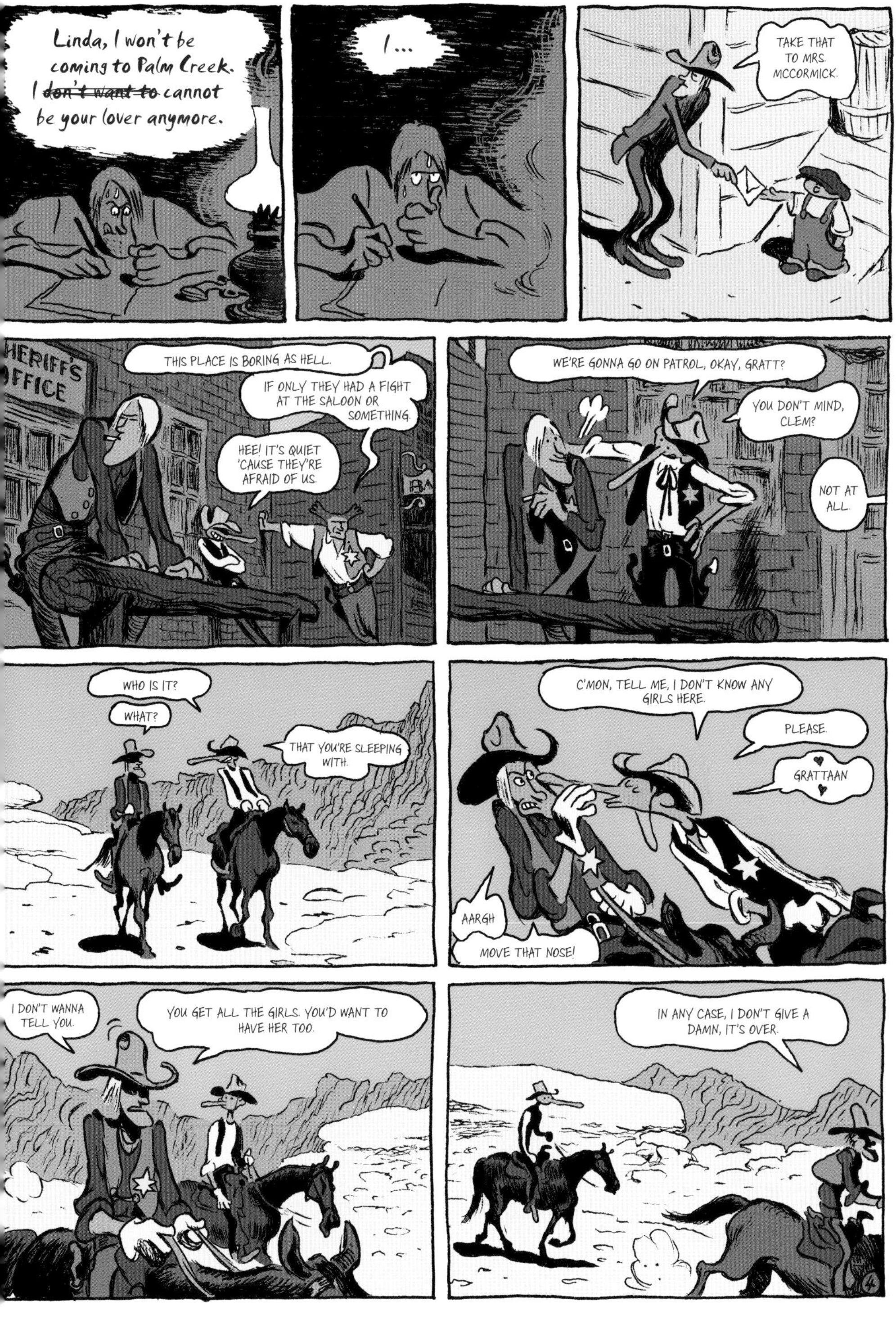
Linda, I won't be coming to Palm Creek. I ~~don't want to~~ cannot be your lover anymore.
I...
TAKE THAT TO MRS. MCCORMICK.
HERIFF'S OFFICE
THIS PLACE IS BORING AS HELL.
IF ONLY THEY HAD A FIGHT AT THE SALOON OR SOMETHING.
HEE! IT'S QUIET 'CAUSE THEY'RE AFRAID OF US.
WE'RE GONNA GO ON PATROL, OKAY, GRATT?
YOU DON'T MIND, CLEM?
NOT AT ALL.
WHO IS IT?
WHAT?
THAT YOU'RE SLEEPING WITH.
C'MON, TELL ME, I DON'T KNOW ANY GIRLS HERE.
PLEASE.
GRATTAAN
AARGH
MOVE THAT NOSE!
I DON'T WANNA TELL YOU.
YOU GET ALL THE GIRLS. YOU'D WANT TO HAVE HER TOO.
IN ANY CASE, I DON'T GIVE A DAMN, IT'S OVER.
4

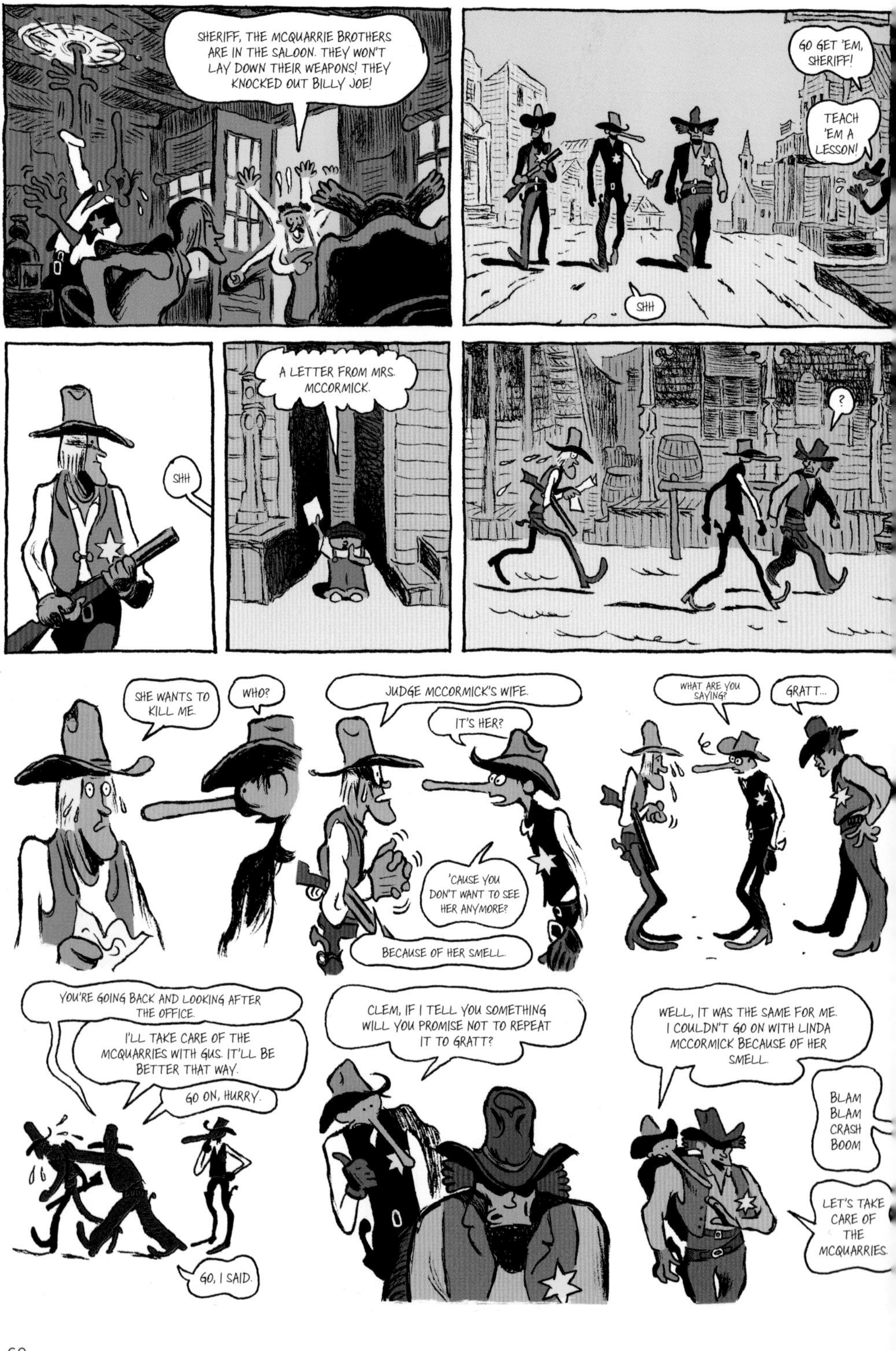
SHERIFF, THE MCQUARRIE BROTHERS ARE IN THE SALOON. THEY WON'T LAY DOWN THEIR WEAPONS! THEY KNOCKED OUT BILLY JOE!
GO GET 'EM, SHERIFF!
TEACH 'EM A LESSON!
SHH
SHH
A LETTER FROM MRS. MCCORMICK.
?
SHE WANTS TO KILL ME.
WHO?
JUDGE MCCORMICK'S WIFE.
IT'S HER?
'CAUSE YOU DON'T WANT TO SEE HER ANYMORE?
BECAUSE OF HER SMELL.
WHAT ARE YOU SAYING?
GRATT...
YOU'RE GOING BACK AND LOOKING AFTER THE OFFICE.
I'LL TAKE CARE OF THE MCQUARRIES WITH GUS. IT'LL BE BETTER THAT WAY.
GO ON, HURRY.
GO, I SAID.
CLEM, IF I TELL YOU SOMETHING WILL YOU PROMISE NOT TO REPEAT IT TO GRATT?
WELL, IT WAS THE SAME FOR ME. I COULDN'T GO ON WITH LINDA MCCORMICK BECAUSE OF HER SMELL.
BLAM BLAM CRASH BOOM
LET'S TAKE CARE OF THE MCQUARRIES.

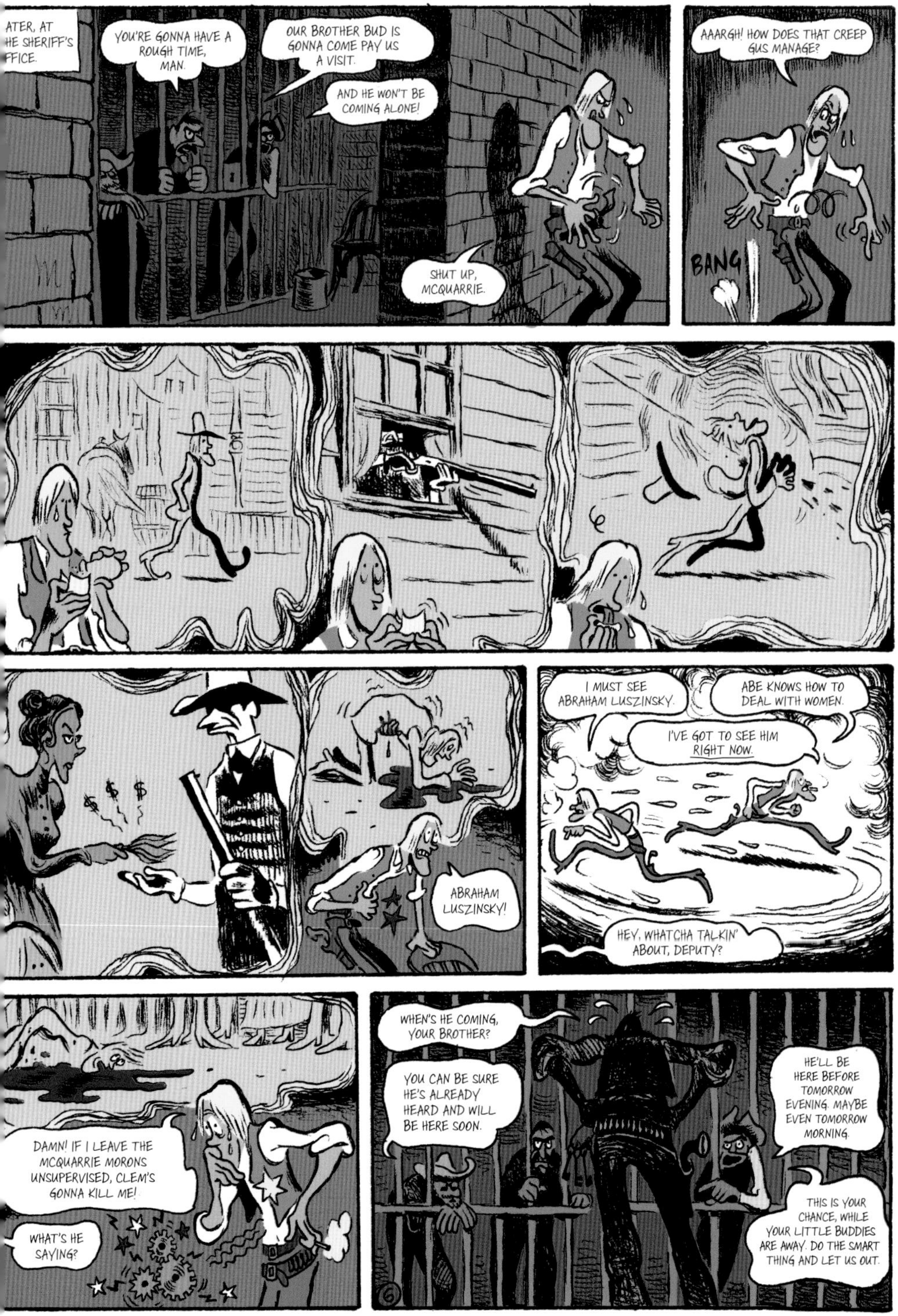

ATER, AT
HE SHERIFF'S
FFICE.
YOU'RE GONNA HAVE A ROUGH TIME, MAN.
OUR BROTHER BUD IS GONNA COME PAY US A VISIT.
AND HE WON'T BE COMING ALONE!
SHUT UP, MCQUARRIE.
AAARGH! HOW DOES THAT CREEP GUS MANAGE?
BANG
ABRAHAM LUSZINSKY!
I MUST SEE ABRAHAM LUSZINSKY.
ABE KNOWS HOW TO DEAL WITH WOMEN.
I'VE GOT TO SEE HIM RIGHT NOW.
HEY, WHATCHA TALKIN' ABOUT, DEPUTY?
DAMN! IF I LEAVE THE MCQUARRIE MORONS UNSUPERVISED, CLEM'S GONNA KILL ME!
WHAT'S HE SAYING?
WHEN'S HE COMING, YOUR BROTHER?
YOU CAN BE SURE HE'S ALREADY HEARD AND WILL BE HERE SOON.
HE'LL BE HERE BEFORE TOMORROW EVENING. MAYBE EVEN TOMORROW MORNING.
THIS IS YOUR CHANCE, WHILE YOUR LITTLE BUDDIES ARE AWAY. DO THE SMART THING AND LET US OUT.

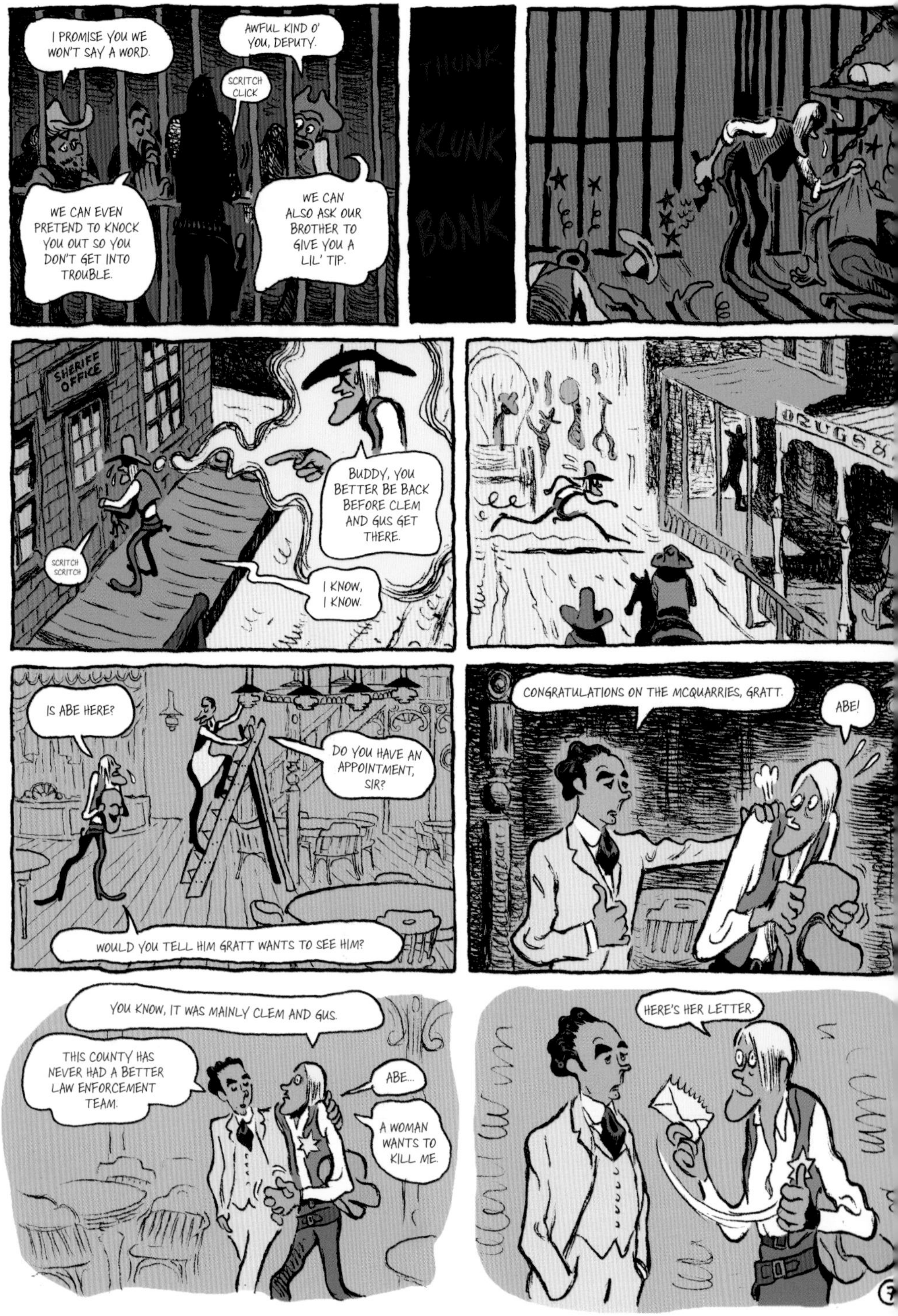

I PROMISE YOU WE WON'T SAY A WORD.
AWFUL KIND O' YOU, DEPUTY.
SCRITCH CLICK
WE CAN EVEN PRETEND TO KNOCK YOU OUT SO YOU DON'T GET INTO TROUBLE.
WE CAN ALSO ASK OUR BROTHER TO GIVE YOU A LIL' TIP.
THUNK
KLUNK
BONK
SHERIFF OFFICE
BUDDY, YOU BETTER BE BACK BEFORE CLEM AND GUS GET THERE.
SCRITCH SCRITCH
I KNOW, I KNOW.
IS ABE HERE?
DO YOU HAVE AN APPOINTMENT, SIR?
WOULD YOU TELL HIM GRATT WANTS TO SEE HIM?
CONGRATULATIONS ON THE MCQUARRIES, GRATT.
ABE!
YOU KNOW, IT WAS MAINLY CLEM AND GUS.
THIS COUNTY HAS NEVER HAD A BETTER LAW ENFORCEMENT TEAM.
ABE...
A WOMAN WANTS TO KILL ME.
HERE'S HER LETTER.

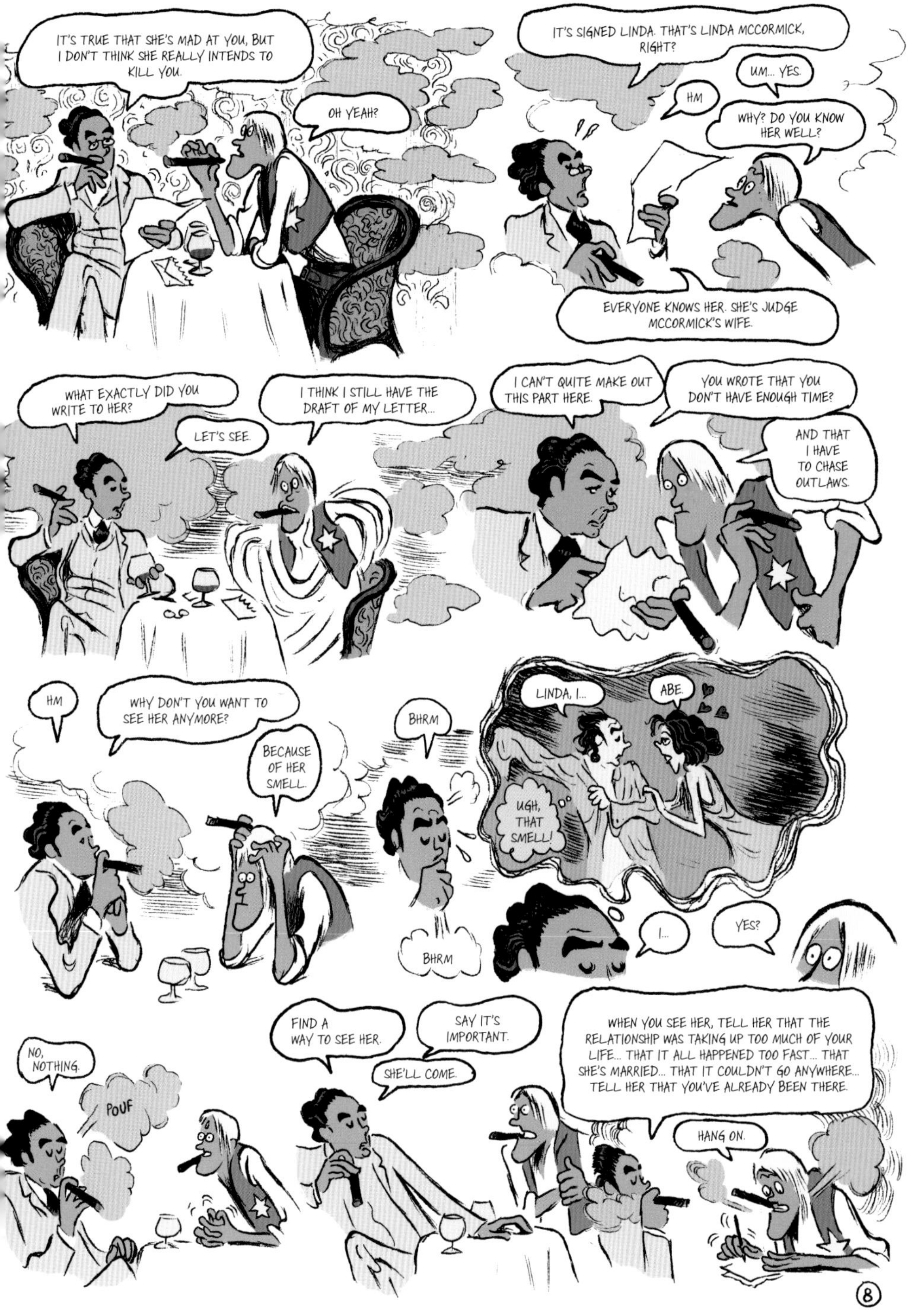
IT'S TRUE THAT SHE'S MAD AT YOU, BUT I DON'T THINK SHE REALLY INTENDS TO KILL YOU.
OH YEAH?
IT'S SIGNED LINDA. THAT'S LINDA MCCORMICK, RIGHT?
HM
UM... YES.
WHY? DO YOU KNOW HER WELL?
EVERYONE KNOWS HER. SHE'S JUDGE MCCORMICK'S WIFE.
WHAT EXACTLY DID YOU WRITE TO HER?
LET'S SEE.
I THINK I STILL HAVE THE DRAFT OF MY LETTER...
I CAN'T QUITE MAKE OUT THIS PART HERE.
YOU WROTE THAT YOU DON'T HAVE ENOUGH TIME?
AND THAT I HAVE TO CHASE OUTLAWS.
HM
WHY DON'T YOU WANT TO SEE HER ANYMORE?
BECAUSE OF HER SMELL.
BHRM
BHRM
LINDA, I...
ABE.
UGH, THAT SMELL!
I...
YES?
NO, NOTHING.
POUF
FIND A WAY TO SEE HER.
SAY IT'S IMPORTANT.
SHE'LL COME.
WHEN YOU SEE HER, TELL HER THAT THE RELATIONSHIP WAS TAKING UP TOO MUCH OF YOUR LIFE... THAT IT ALL HAPPENED TOO FAST... THAT SHE'S MARRIED... THAT IT COULDN'T GO ANYWHERE... TELL HER THAT YOU'VE ALREADY BEEN THERE.
HANG ON.
8

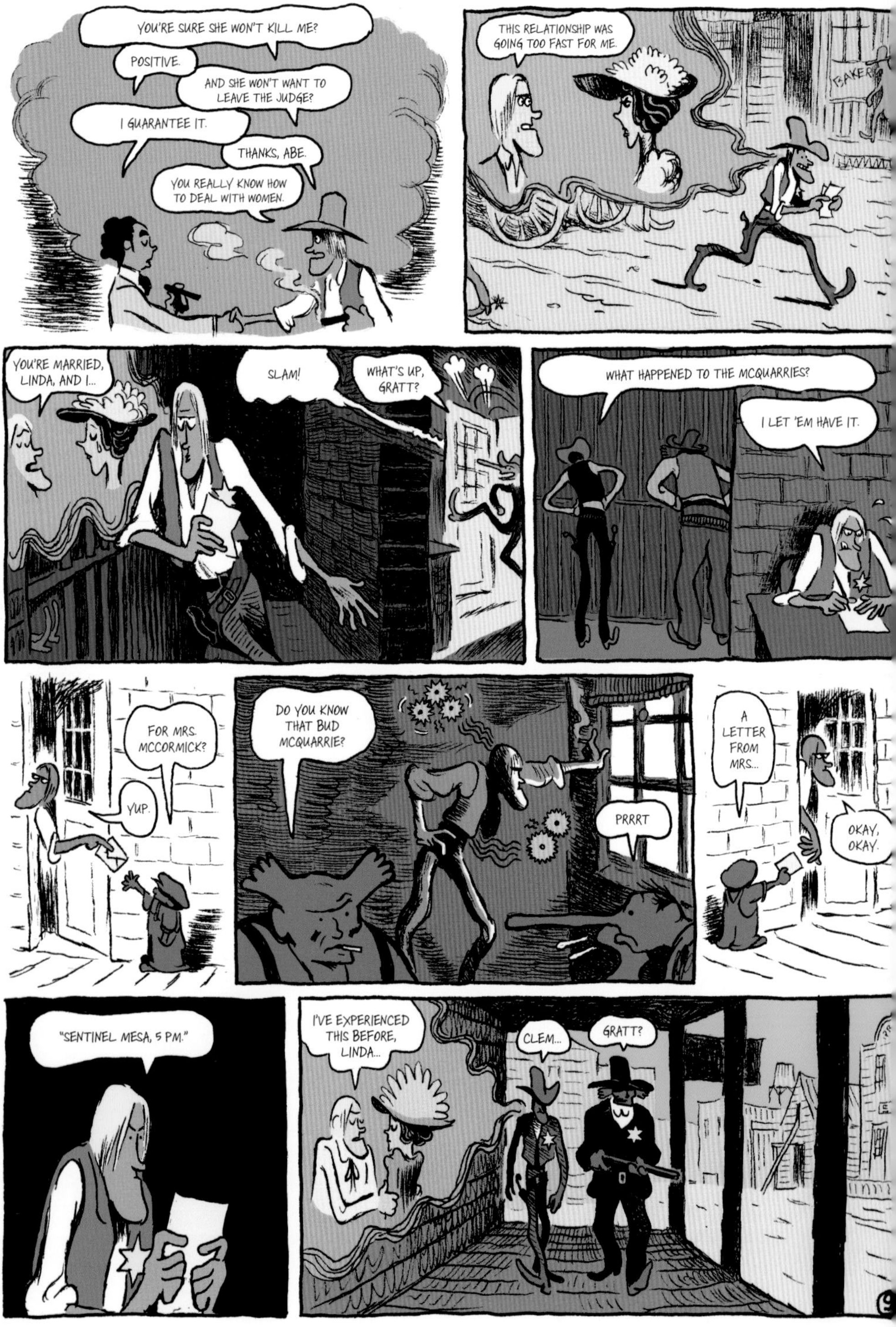
YOU'RE SURE SHE WON'T KILL ME?
POSITIVE.
AND SHE WON'T WANT TO LEAVE THE JUDGE?
I GUARANTEE IT.
THANKS, ABE.
YOU REALLY KNOW HOW TO DEAL WITH WOMEN.
THIS RELATIONSHIP WAS GOING TOO FAST FOR ME.
BAKER
YOU'RE MARRIED, LINDA, AND I...
SLAM!
WHAT'S UP, GRATT?
WHAT HAPPENED TO THE MCQUARRIES?
I LET 'EM HAVE IT.
FOR MRS. MCCORMICK?
YUP.
DO YOU KNOW THAT BUD MCQUARRIE?
PRRRT
A LETTER FROM MRS...
OKAY, OKAY.
"SENTINEL MESA, 5 P.M."
I'VE EXPERIENCED THIS BEFORE, LINDA...
CLEM...
GRATT?

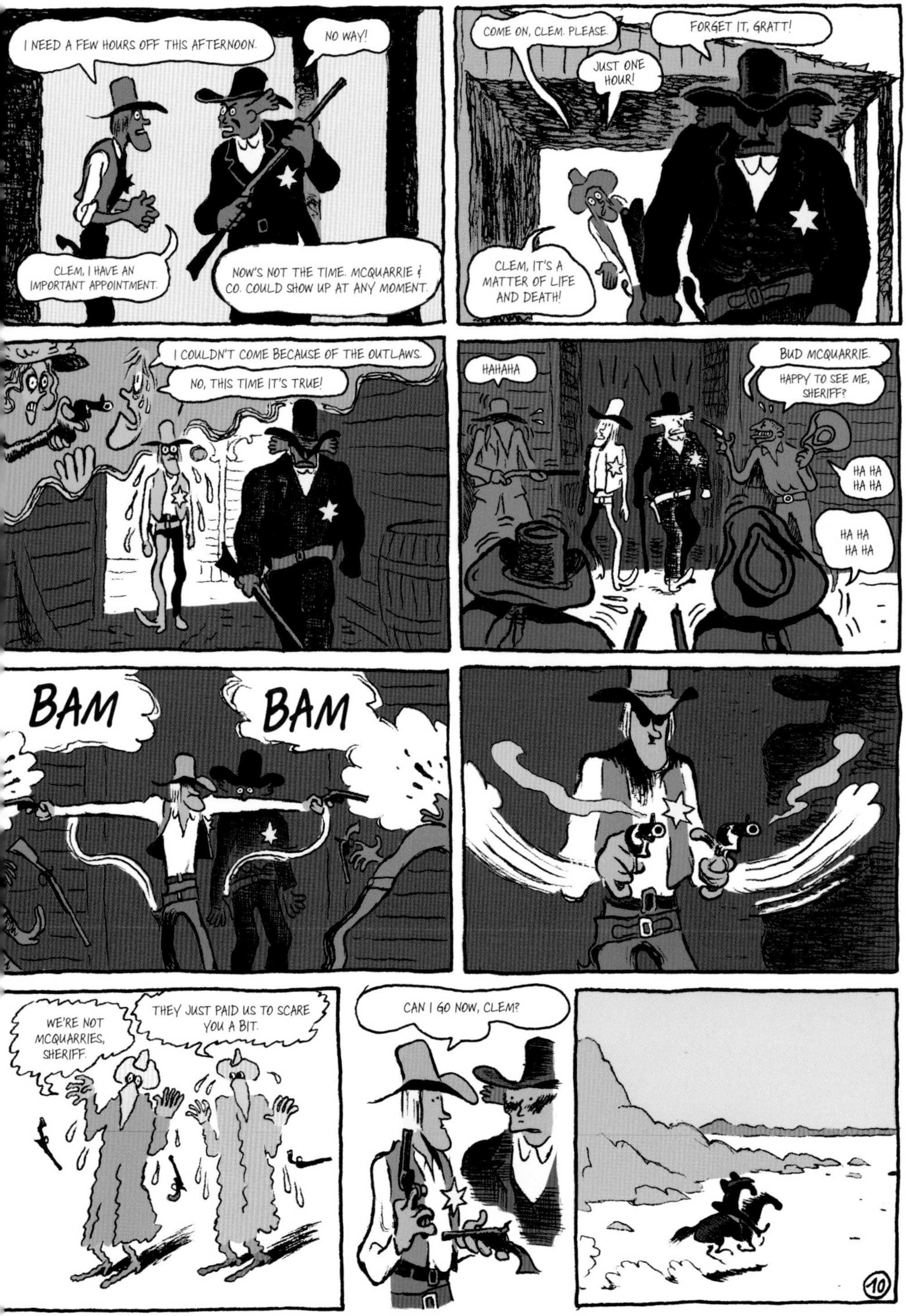
I NEED A FEW HOURS OFF THIS AFTERNOON.
NO WAY!
CLEM, I HAVE AN IMPORTANT APPOINTMENT.
NOW'S NOT THE TIME. MCQUARRIE & CO. COULD SHOW UP AT ANY MOMENT.
COME ON, CLEM. PLEASE.
JUST ONE HOUR!
FORGET IT, GRATT!
CLEM, IT'S A MATTER OF LIFE AND DEATH!
I COULDN'T COME BECAUSE OF THE OUTLAWS.
NO, THIS TIME IT'S TRUE!
HAHAHA
BUD MCQUARRIE.
HAPPY TO SEE ME, SHERIFF?
HA HA HA HA
HA HA HA HA
BAM
BAM
WE'RE NOT MCQUARRIES, SHERIFF.
THEY JUST PAID US TO SCARE YOU A BIT.
CAN I GO NOW, CLEM?
10

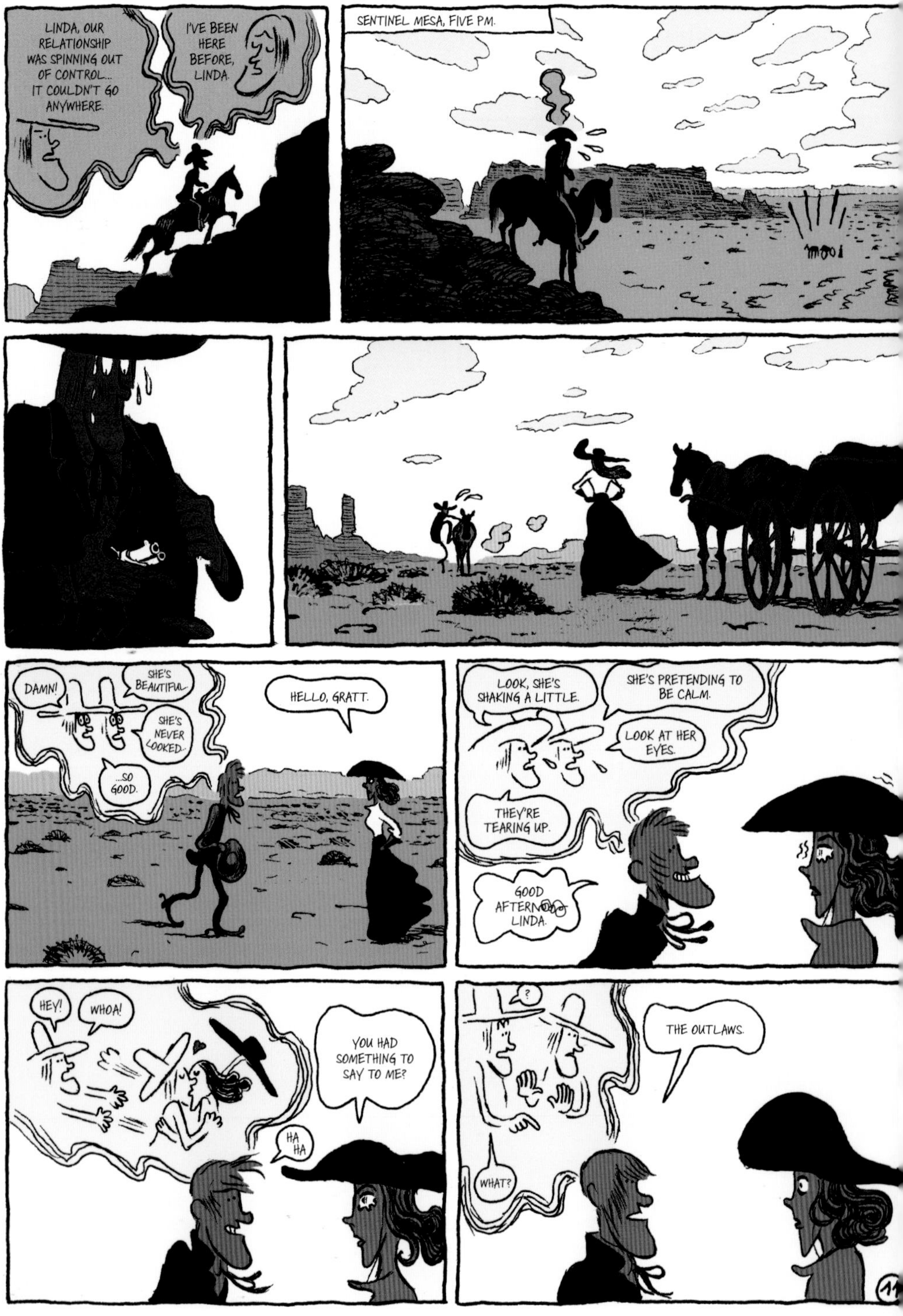
LINDA, OUR RELATIONSHIP WAS SPINNING OUT OF CONTROL... IT COULDN'T GO ANYWHERE.
I'VE BEEN HERE BEFORE, LINDA.
SENTINEL MESA, FIVE P.M.
DAMN!
SHE'S BEAUTIFUL.
SHE'S NEVER LOOKED...
...SO GOOD.
HELLO, GRATT.
LOOK, SHE'S SHAKING A LITTLE.
SHE'S PRETENDING TO BE CALM.
LOOK AT HER EYES.
THEY'RE TEARING UP.
GOOD AFTERNOOO LINDA.
HEY!
WHOA!
YOU HAD SOMETHING TO SAY TO ME?
HA HA
?
WHAT?
THE OUTLAWS.

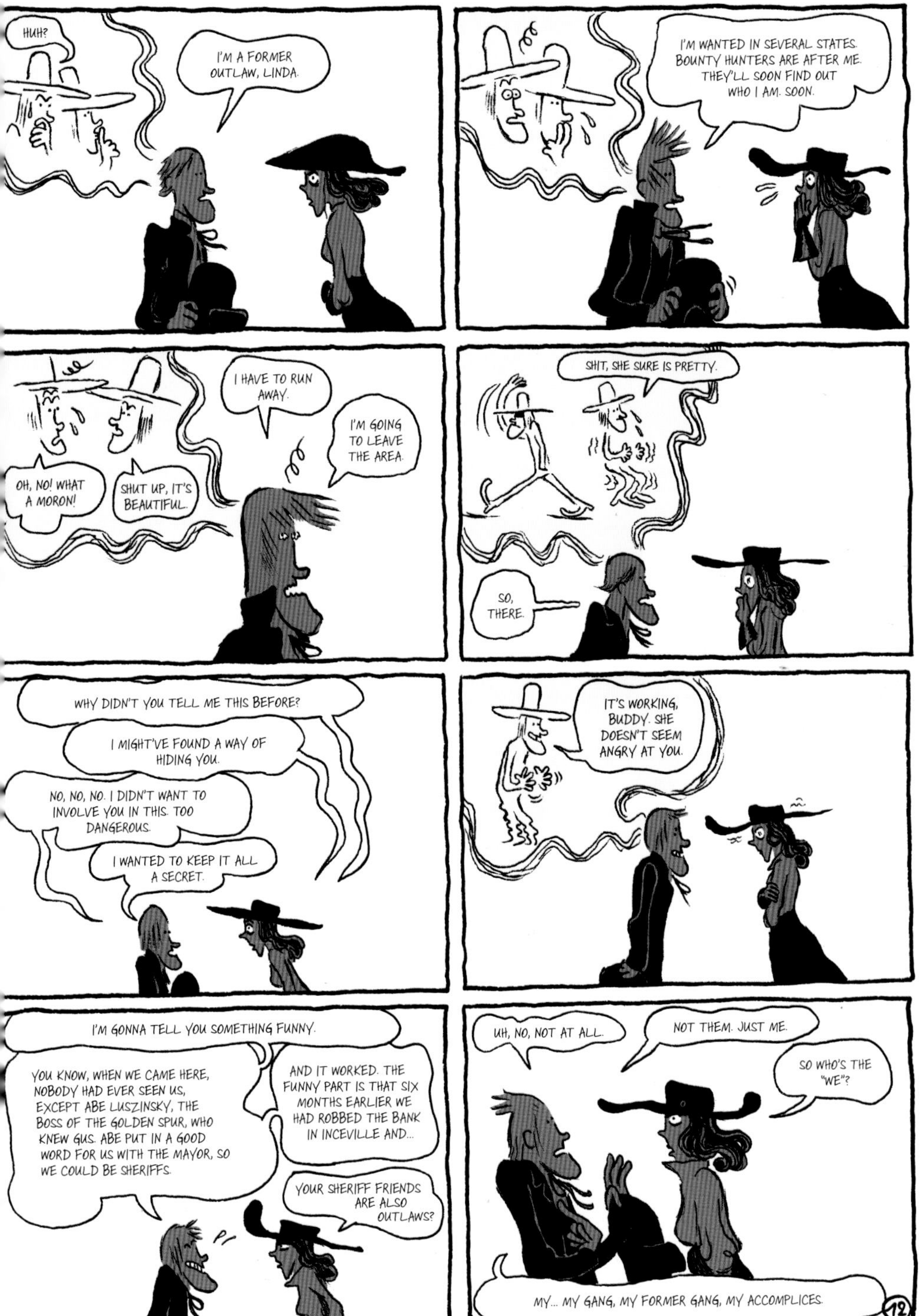
HUH?
I'M A FORMER OUTLAW, LINDA.
I'M WANTED IN SEVERAL STATES. BOUNTY HUNTERS ARE AFTER ME. THEY'LL SOON FIND OUT WHO I AM. SOON.
I HAVE TO RUN AWAY.
I'M GOING TO LEAVE THE AREA.
OH, NO! WHAT A MORON!
SHUT UP, IT'S BEAUTIFUL.
SHIT, SHE SURE IS PRETTY.
SO, THERE.
WHY DIDN'T YOU TELL ME THIS BEFORE?
I MIGHT'VE FOUND A WAY OF HIDING YOU.
NO, NO, NO. I DIDN'T WANT TO INVOLVE YOU IN THIS. TOO DANGEROUS.
I WANTED TO KEEP IT ALL A SECRET.
IT'S WORKING, BUDDY. SHE DOESN'T SEEM ANGRY AT YOU.
I'M GONNA TELL YOU SOMETHING FUNNY.
YOU KNOW, WHEN WE CAME HERE, NOBODY HAD EVER SEEN US, EXCEPT ABE LUSZINSKY, THE BOSS OF THE GOLDEN SPUR, WHO KNEW GUS. ABE PUT IN A GOOD WORD FOR US WITH THE MAYOR, SO WE COULD BE SHERIFFS.
AND IT WORKED. THE FUNNY PART IS THAT SIX MONTHS EARLIER WE HAD ROBBED THE BANK IN INCEVILLE AND...
YOUR SHERIFF FRIENDS ARE ALSO OUTLAWS?
UH, NO, NOT AT ALL.
NOT THEM. JUST ME.
SO WHO'S THE "WE"?
MY... MY GANG, MY FORMER GANG, MY ACCOMPLICES.
12

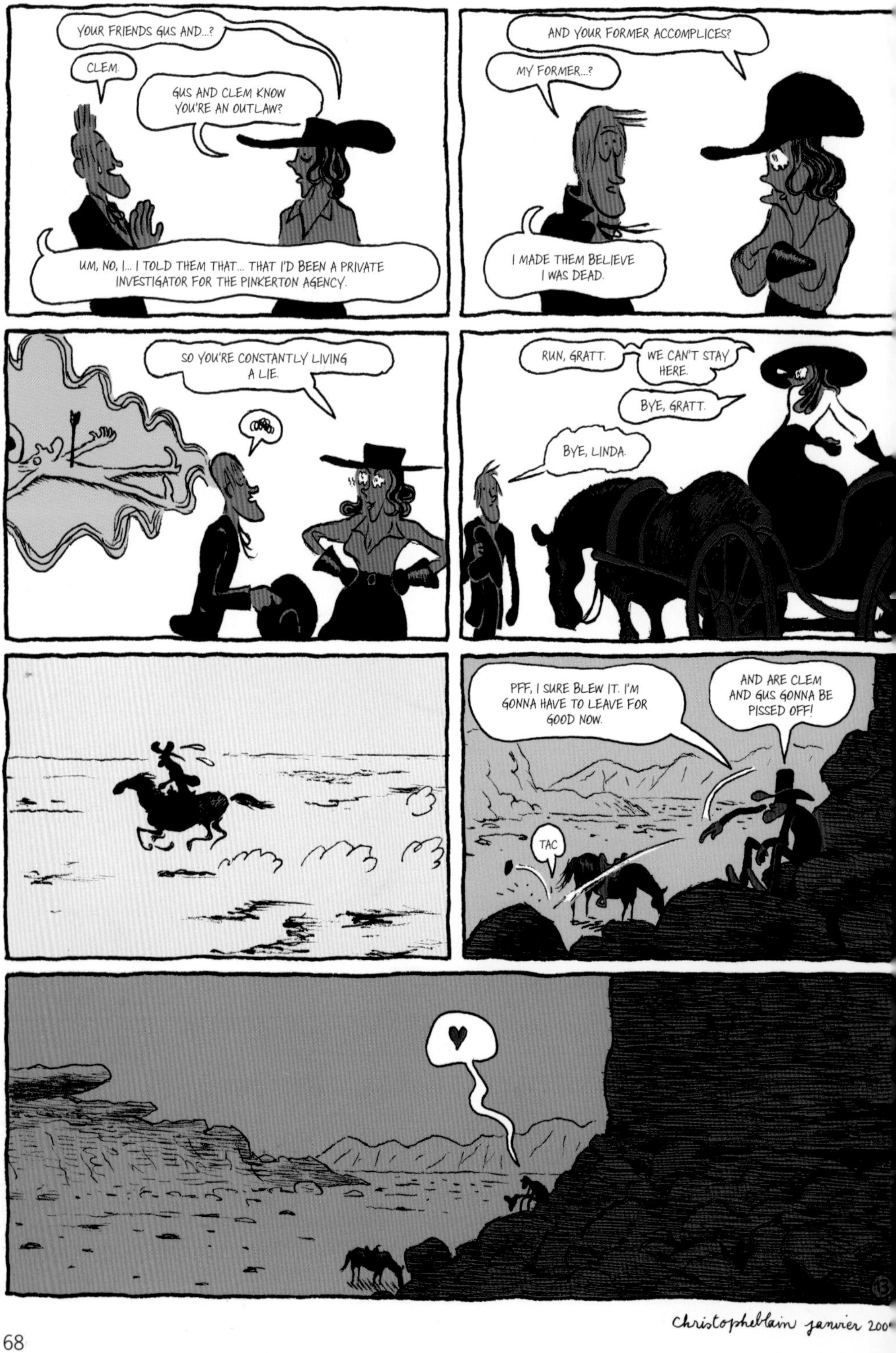
YOUR FRIENDS GUS AND...?
CLEM.
GUS AND CLEM KNOW YOU'RE AN OUTLAW?
UM, NO, I... I TOLD THEM THAT... THAT I'D BEEN A PRIVATE INVESTIGATOR FOR THE PINKERTON AGENCY.
AND YOUR FORMER ACCOMPLICES?
MY FORMER...?
I MADE THEM BELIEVE I WAS DEAD.
SO YOU'RE CONSTANTLY LIVING A LIE.
RUN, GRATT.
WE CAN'T STAY HERE.
BYE, GRATT.
BYE, LINDA.
PFF, I SURE BLEW IT. I'M GONNA HAVE TO LEAVE FOR GOOD NOW.
AND ARE CLEM AND GUS GONNA BE PISSED OFF!
TAC
Christopheblain janvier 200

ISABELLA

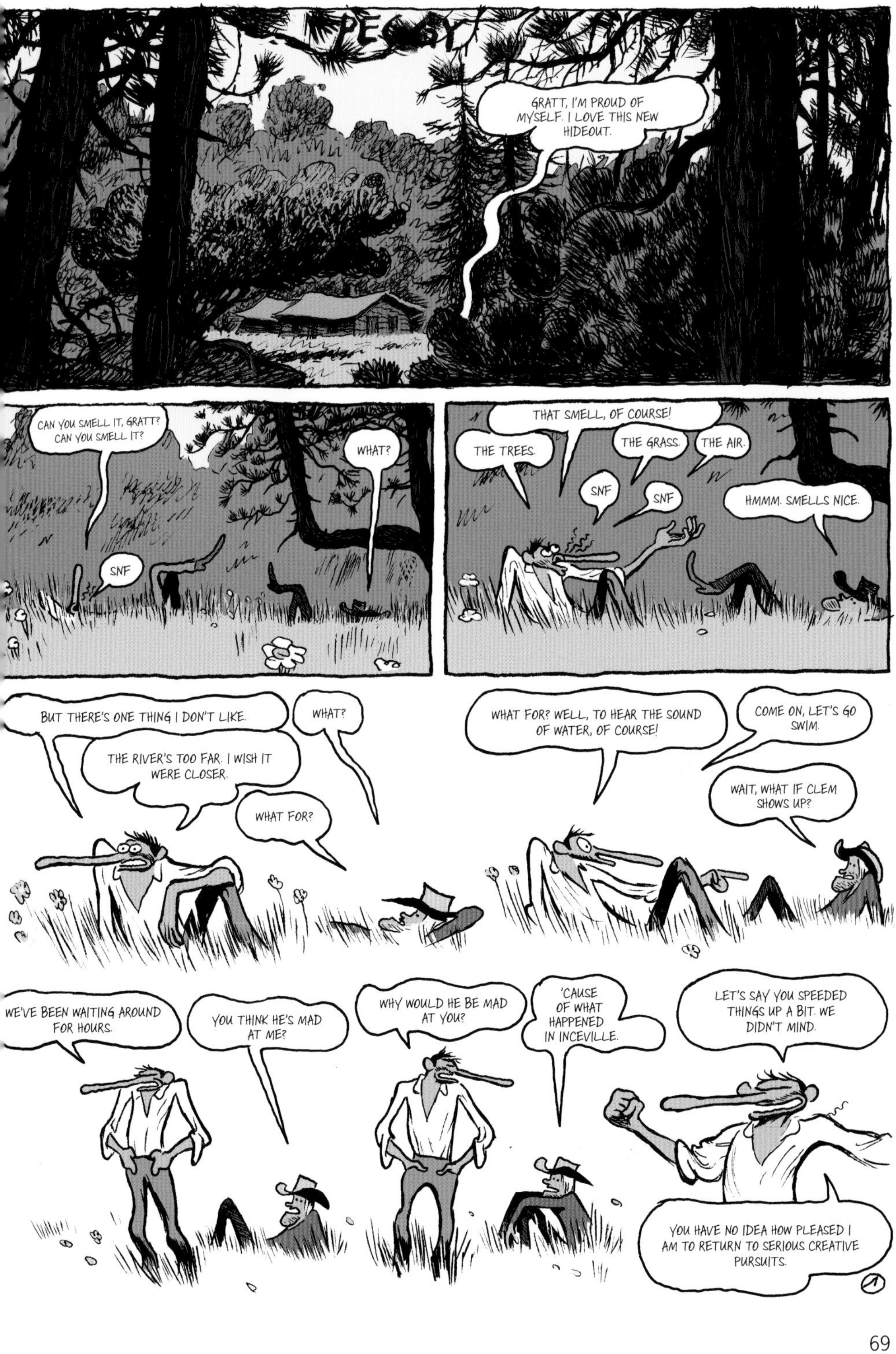

PEGGY
GRATT, I'M PROUD OF MYSELF. I LOVE THIS NEW HIDEOUT.
CAN YOU SMELL IT, GRATT? CAN YOU SMELL IT?
SNF
WHAT?
THAT SMELL, OF COURSE!
THE TREES.
THE GRASS.
THE AIR.
SNF
SNF
HMMM. SMELLS NICE.
BUT THERE'S ONE THING I DON'T LIKE.
WHAT?
THE RIVER'S TOO FAR. I WISH IT WERE CLOSER.
WHAT FOR?
WHAT FOR? WELL, TO HEAR THE SOUND OF WATER, OF COURSE!
COME ON, LET'S GO SWIM.
WAIT, WHAT IF CLEM SHOWS UP?
WE'VE BEEN WAITING AROUND FOR HOURS.
YOU THINK HE'S MAD AT ME?
WHY WOULD HE BE MAD AT YOU?
'CAUSE OF WHAT HAPPENED IN INCEVILLE.
LET'S SAY YOU SPEEDED THINGS UP A BIT. WE DIDN'T MIND.
YOU HAVE NO IDEA HOW PLEASED I AM TO RETURN TO SERIOUS CREATIVE PURSUITS.

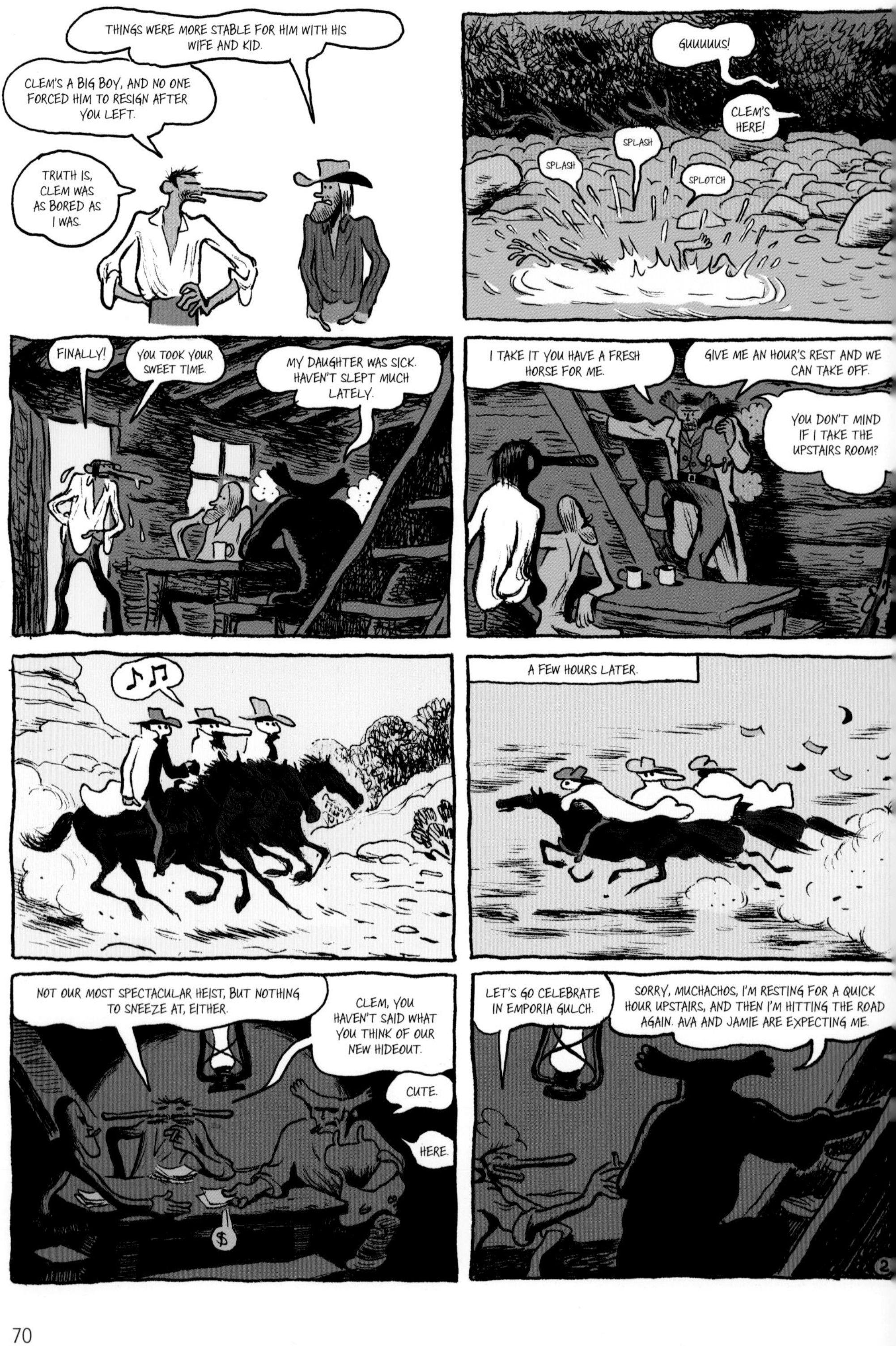
THINGS WERE MORE STABLE FOR HIM WITH HIS WIFE AND KID.
CLEM'S A BIG BOY, AND NO ONE FORCED HIM TO RESIGN AFTER YOU LEFT.
TRUTH IS, CLEM WAS AS BORED AS I WAS.
GUUUUUS!
CLEM'S HERE!
SPLASH
SPLASH
SPLOTCH
FINALLY!
YOU TOOK YOUR SWEET TIME.
MY DAUGHTER WAS SICK. HAVEN'T SLEPT MUCH LATELY.
I TAKE IT YOU HAVE A FRESH HORSE FOR ME.
GIVE ME AN HOUR'S REST AND WE CAN TAKE OFF.
YOU DON'T MIND IF I TAKE THE UPSTAIRS ROOM?
A FEW HOURS LATER.
NOT OUR MOST SPECTACULAR HEIST, BUT NOTHING TO SNEEZE AT, EITHER.
CLEM, YOU HAVEN'T SAID WHAT YOU THINK OF OUR NEW HIDEOUT.
CUTE.
HERE.
$
LET'S GO CELEBRATE IN EMPORIA GULCH.
SORRY, MUCHACHOS, I'M RESTING FOR A QUICK HOUR UPSTAIRS, AND THEN I'M HITTING THE ROAD AGAIN. AVA AND JAMIE ARE EXPECTING ME.

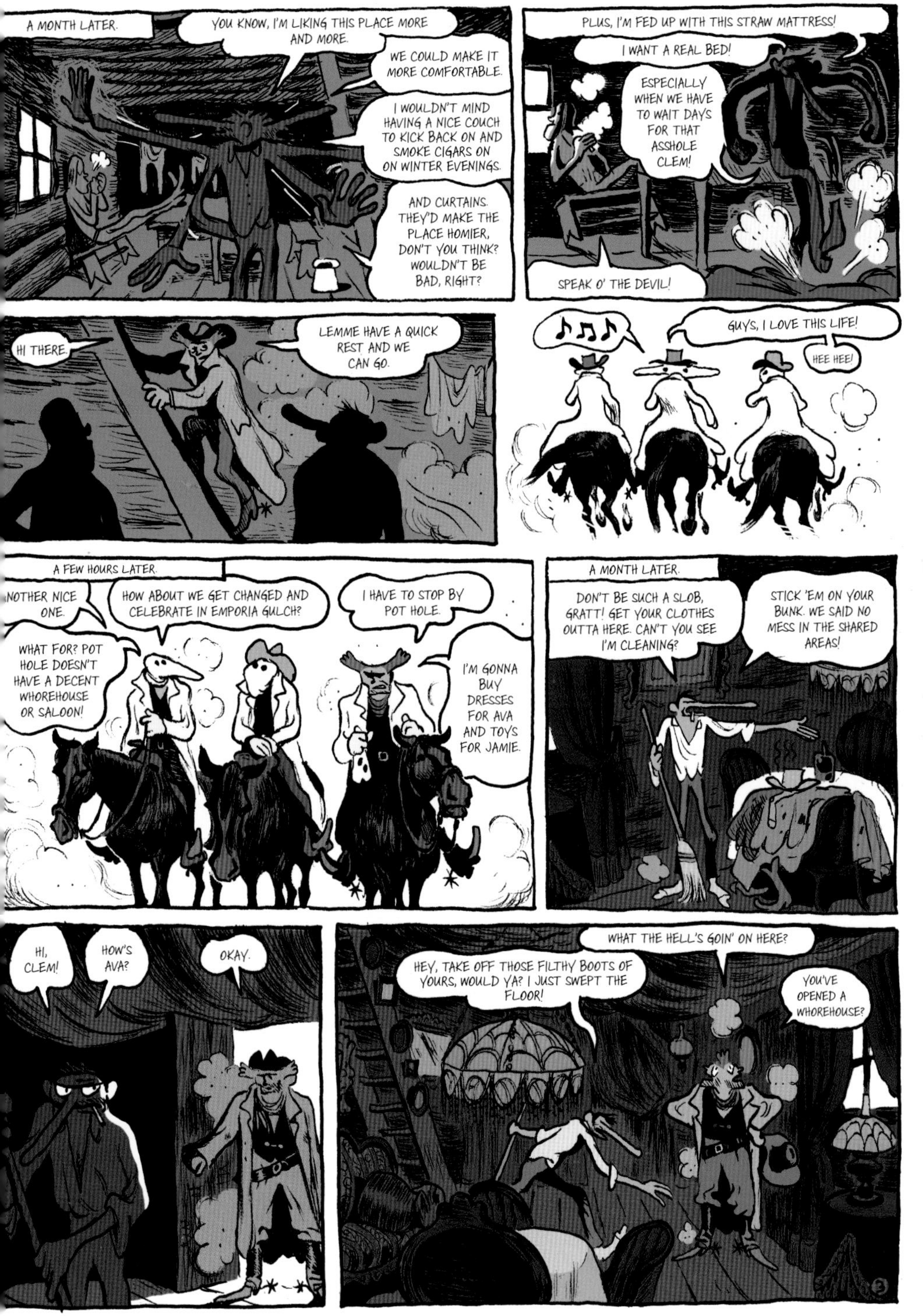
A MONTH LATER.
YOU KNOW, I'M LIKING THIS PLACE MORE AND MORE.
WE COULD MAKE IT MORE COMFORTABLE.
I WOULDN'T MIND HAVING A NICE COUCH TO KICK BACK ON AND SMOKE CIGARS ON ON WINTER EVENINGS.
AND CURTAINS. THEY'D MAKE THE PLACE HOMIER, DON'T YOU THINK? WOULDN'T BE BAD, RIGHT?
PLUS, I'M FED UP WITH THIS STRAW MATTRESS!
I WANT A REAL BED!
ESPECIALLY WHEN WE HAVE TO WAIT DAYS FOR THAT ASSHOLE CLEM!
SPEAK O' THE DEVIL!
HI THERE.
LEMME HAVE A QUICK REST AND WE CAN GO.
♪♫♪
GUYS, I LOVE THIS LIFE!
HEE HEE!
A FEW HOURS LATER.
NOTHER NICE ONE.
HOW ABOUT WE GET CHANGED AND CELEBRATE IN EMPORIA GULCH?
I HAVE TO STOP BY POT HOLE.
WHAT FOR? POT HOLE DOESN'T HAVE A DECENT WHOREHOUSE OR SALOON!
I'M GONNA BUY DRESSES FOR AVA AND TOYS FOR JAMIE.
A MONTH LATER.
DON'T BE SUCH A SLOB, GRATT! GET YOUR CLOTHES OUTTA HERE. CAN'T YOU SEE I'M CLEANING?
STICK 'EM ON YOUR BUNK. WE SAID NO MESS IN THE SHARED AREAS!
HI, CLEM!
HOW'S AVA?
OKAY.
WHAT THE HELL'S GOIN' ON HERE?
HEY, TAKE OFF THOSE FILTHY BOOTS OF YOURS, WOULD YA? I JUST SWEPT THE FLOOR!
YOU'VE OPENED A WHOREHOUSE?

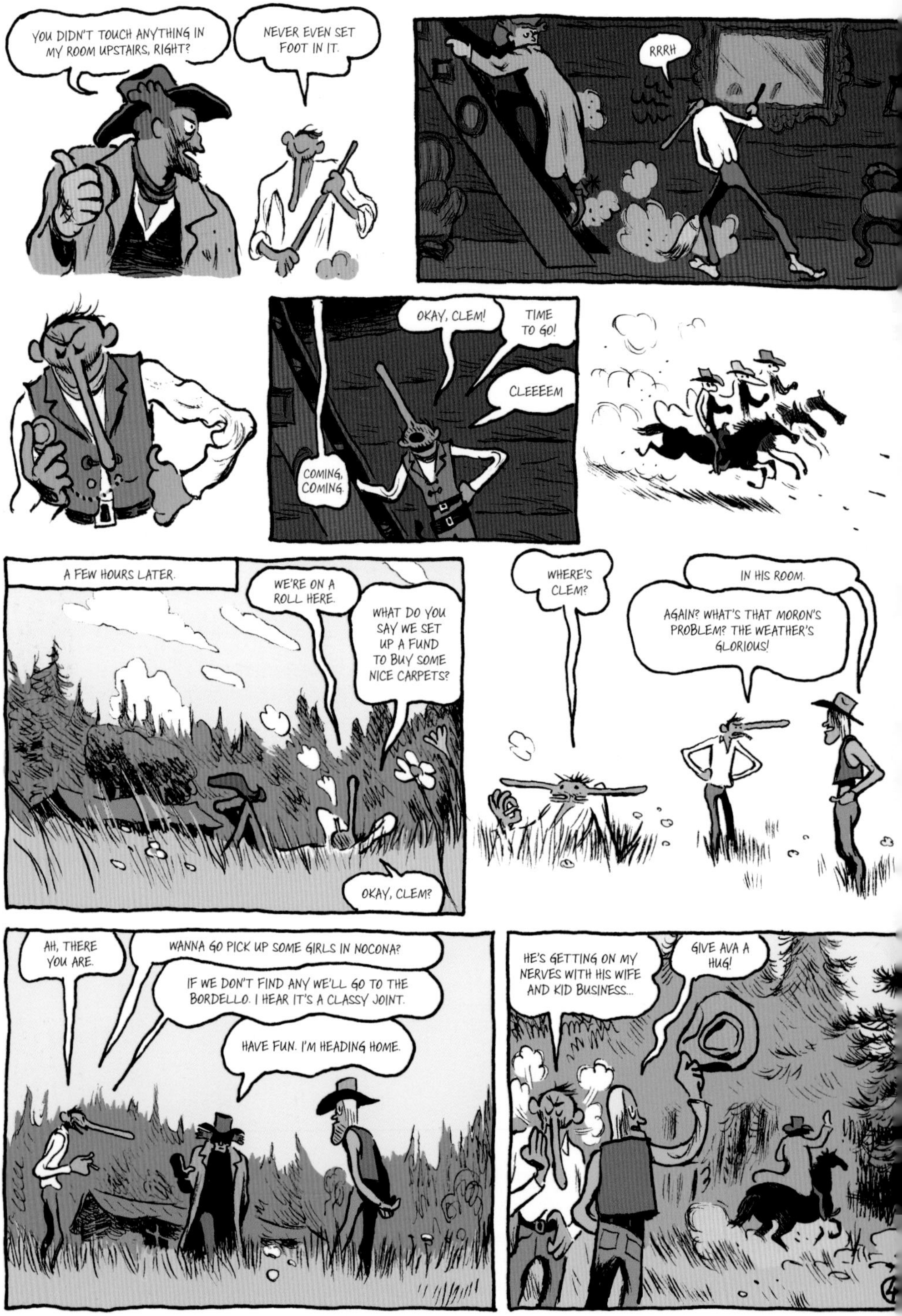
YOU DIDN'T TOUCH ANYTHING IN MY ROOM UPSTAIRS, RIGHT?
NEVER EVEN SET FOOT IN IT.
RRRH
OKAY, CLEM!
TIME TO GO!
CLEEEEM
COMING, COMING.
A FEW HOURS LATER.
WE'RE ON A ROLL HERE.
WHAT DO YOU SAY WE SET UP A FUND TO BUY SOME NICE CARPETS?
OKAY, CLEM?
WHERE'S CLEM?
IN HIS ROOM.
AGAIN? WHAT'S THAT MORON'S PROBLEM? THE WEATHER'S GLORIOUS!
AH, THERE YOU ARE.
WANNA GO PICK UP SOME GIRLS IN NOCONA?
IF WE DON'T FIND ANY WE'LL GO TO THE BORDELLO. I HEAR IT'S A CLASSY JOINT.
HAVE FUN. I'M HEADING HOME.
HE'S GETTING ON MY NERVES WITH HIS WIFE AND KID BUSINESS...
GIVE AVA A HUG!

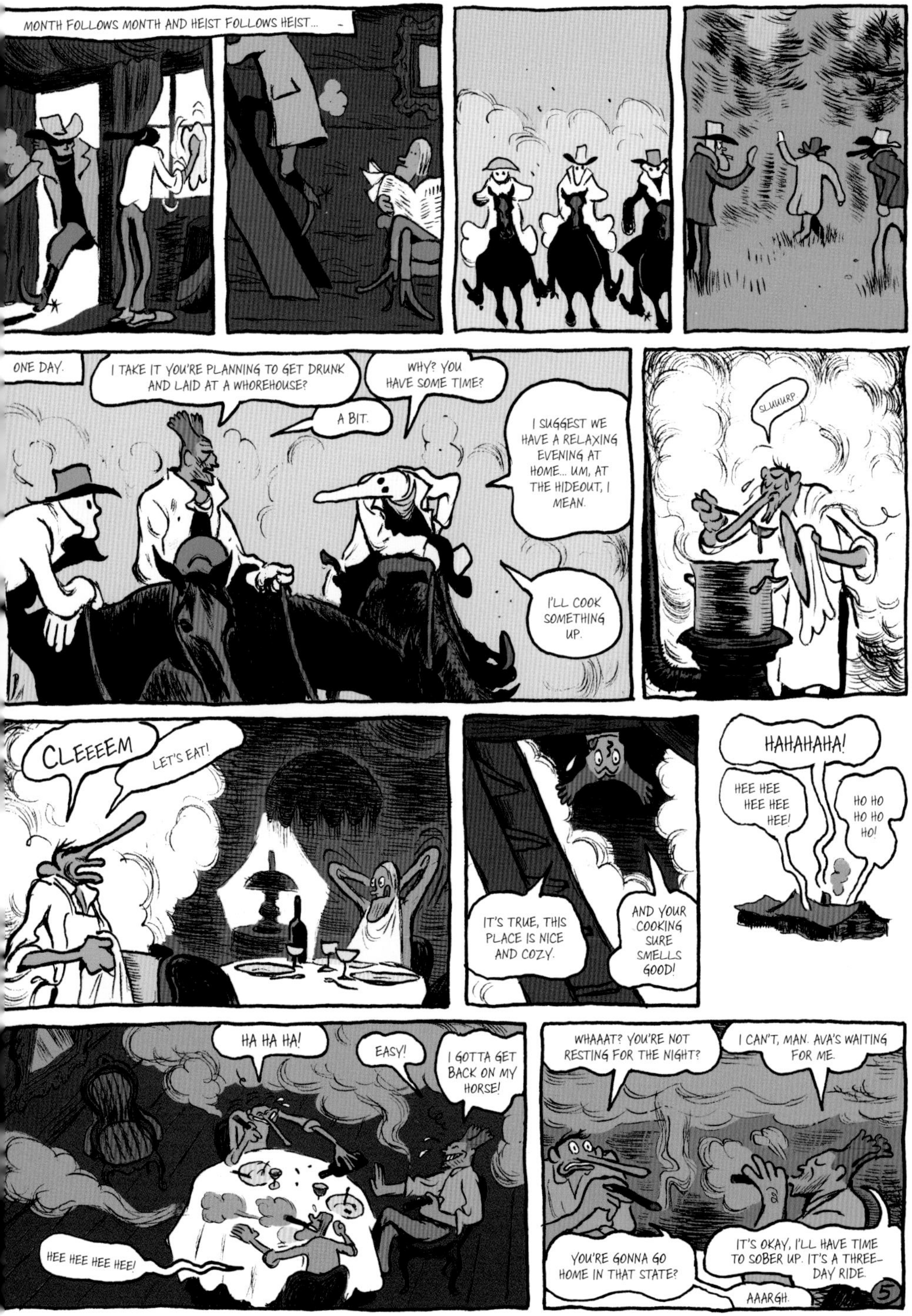
MONTH FOLLOWS MONTH AND HEIST FOLLOWS HEIST...
ONE DAY.
I TAKE IT YOU'RE PLANNING TO GET DRUNK AND LAID AT A WHOREHOUSE?
WHY? YOU HAVE SOME TIME?
A BIT.
I SUGGEST WE HAVE A RELAXING EVENING AT HOME... UM, AT THE HIDEOUT, I MEAN.
I'LL COOK SOMETHING UP.
SLUUURP.
CLEEEEM
LET'S EAT!
IT'S TRUE, THIS PLACE IS NICE AND COZY.
AND YOUR COOKING SURE SMELLS GOOD!
HAHAHAHA!
HEE HEE HEE HEE HEE!
HO HO HO HO HO!
HA HA HA!
EASY!
I GOTTA GET BACK ON MY HORSE!
HEE HEE HEE HEE!
WHAAAT? YOU'RE NOT RESTING FOR THE NIGHT?
I CAN'T, MAN. AVA'S WAITING FOR ME.
YOU'RE GONNA GO HOME IN THAT STATE?
IT'S OKAY, I'LL HAVE TIME TO SOBER UP. IT'S A THREE-DAY RIDE.
AAARGH.
5

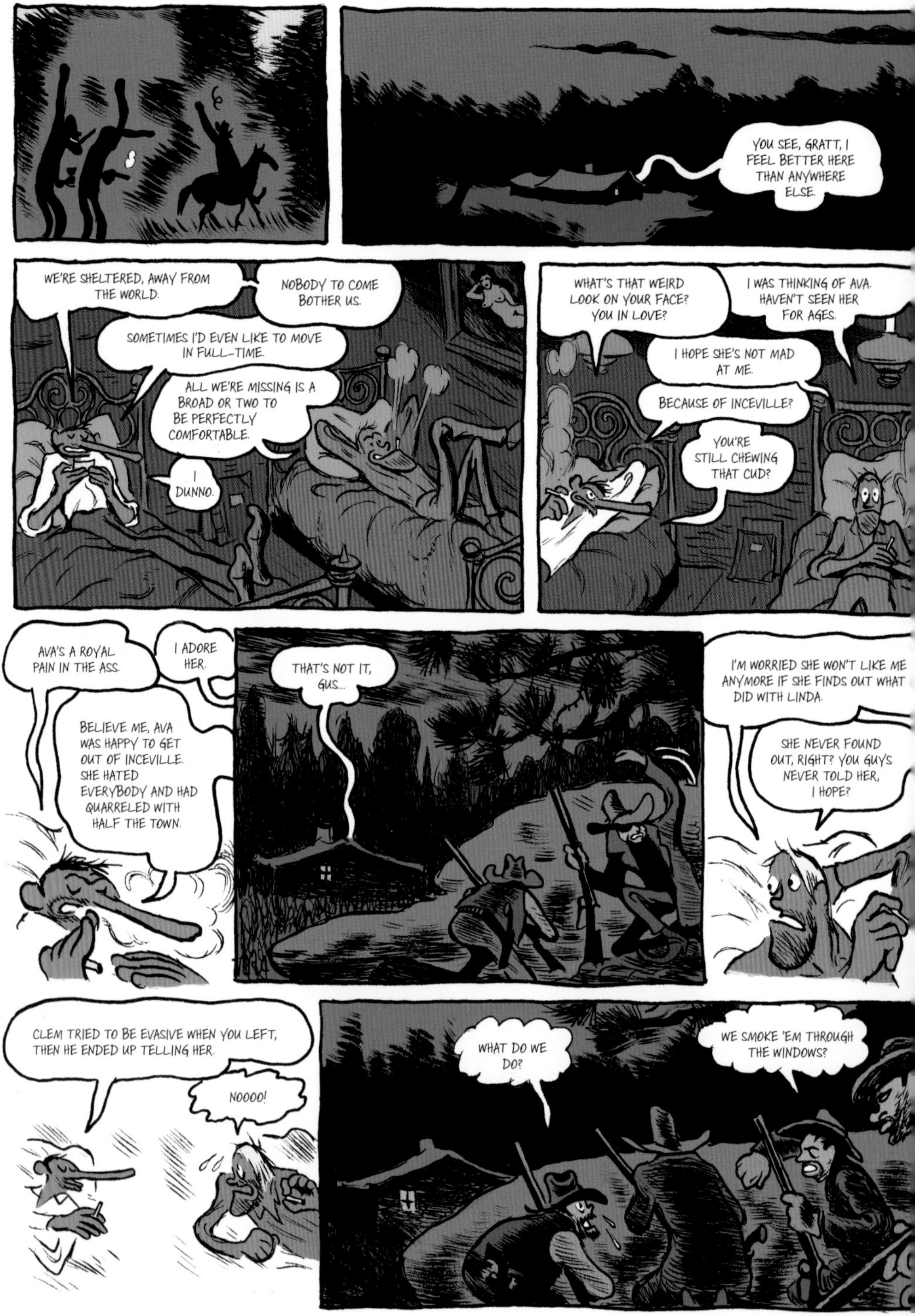
YOU SEE, GRATT, I FEEL BETTER HERE THAN ANYWHERE ELSE.
WE'RE SHELTERED, AWAY FROM THE WORLD.
NOBODY TO COME BOTHER US.
SOMETIMES I'D EVEN LIKE TO MOVE IN FULL-TIME.
ALL WE'RE MISSING IS A BROAD OR TWO TO BE PERFECTLY COMFORTABLE.
I DUNNO.
WHAT'S THAT WEIRD LOOK ON YOUR FACE? YOU IN LOVE?
I WAS THINKING OF AVA. HAVEN'T SEEN HER FOR AGES.
I HOPE SHE'S NOT MAD AT ME.
BECAUSE OF INCEVILLE?
YOU'RE STILL CHEWING THAT CUD?
AVA'S A ROYAL PAIN IN THE ASS.
I ADORE HER.
BELIEVE ME, AVA WAS HAPPY TO GET OUT OF INCEVILLE. SHE HATED EVERYBODY AND HAD QUARRELED WITH HALF THE TOWN.
THAT'S NOT IT, GUS...
I'M WORRIED SHE WON'T LIKE ME ANYMORE IF SHE FINDS OUT WHAT DID WITH LINDA.
SHE NEVER FOUND OUT, RIGHT? YOU GUYS NEVER TOLD HER, I HOPE?
CLEM TRIED TO BE EVASIVE WHEN YOU LEFT, THEN HE ENDED UP TELLING HER.
NOOOO!
WHAT DO WE DO?
WE SMOKE 'EM THROUGH THE WINDOWS?

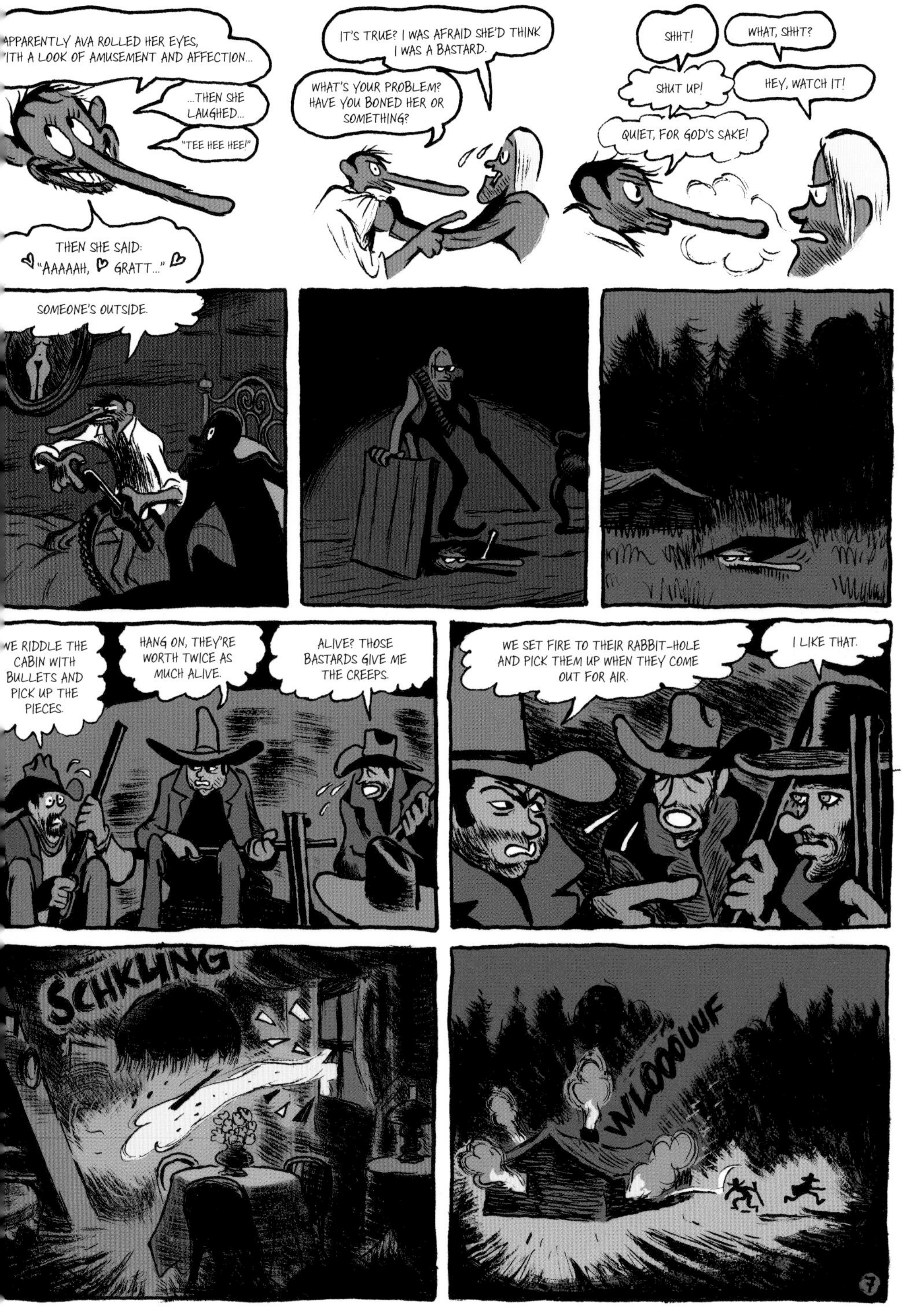

APPARENTLY AVA ROLLED HER EYES, WITH A LOOK OF AMUSEMENT AND AFFECTION...
...THEN SHE LAUGHED...
"TEE HEE HEE!"
THEN SHE SAID: "AAAAAH, GRATT..."
IT'S TRUE? I WAS AFRAID SHE'D THINK I WAS A BASTARD.
WHAT'S YOUR PROBLEM? HAVE YOU BONED HER OR SOMETHING?
SHHT!
WHAT, SHHT?
SHUT UP!
HEY, WATCH IT!
QUIET, FOR GOD'S SAKE!
SOMEONE'S OUTSIDE.
WE RIDDLE THE CABIN WITH BULLETS AND PICK UP THE PIECES.
HANG ON, THEY'RE WORTH TWICE AS MUCH ALIVE.
ALIVE? THOSE BASTARDS GIVE ME THE CREEPS.
WE SET FIRE TO THEIR RABBIT-HOLE AND PICK THEM UP WHEN THEY COME OUT FOR AIR.
I LIKE THAT.
SCHKLING
WLOOOUUF
7

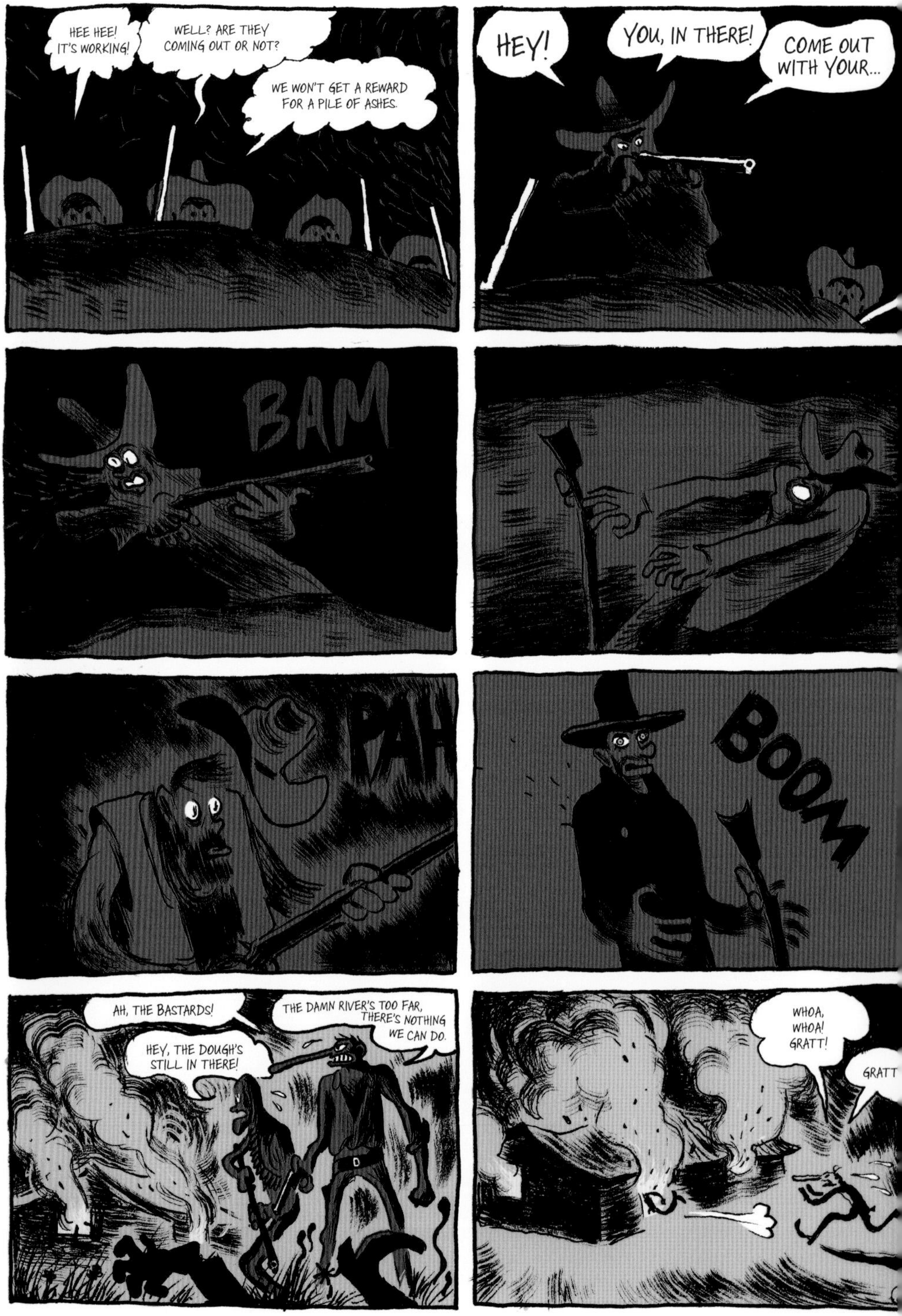
HEE HEE! IT'S WORKING!
WELL? ARE THEY COMING OUT OR NOT?
WE WON'T GET A REWARD FOR A PILE OF ASHES.
HEY!
YOU, IN THERE!
COME OUT WITH YOUR...
BAM
PAH
BOOM
AH, THE BASTARDS!
THE DAMN RIVER'S TOO FAR, THERE'S NOTHING WE CAN DO.
HEY, THE DOUGH'S STILL IN THERE!
WHOA, WHOA! GRATT!
GRATT

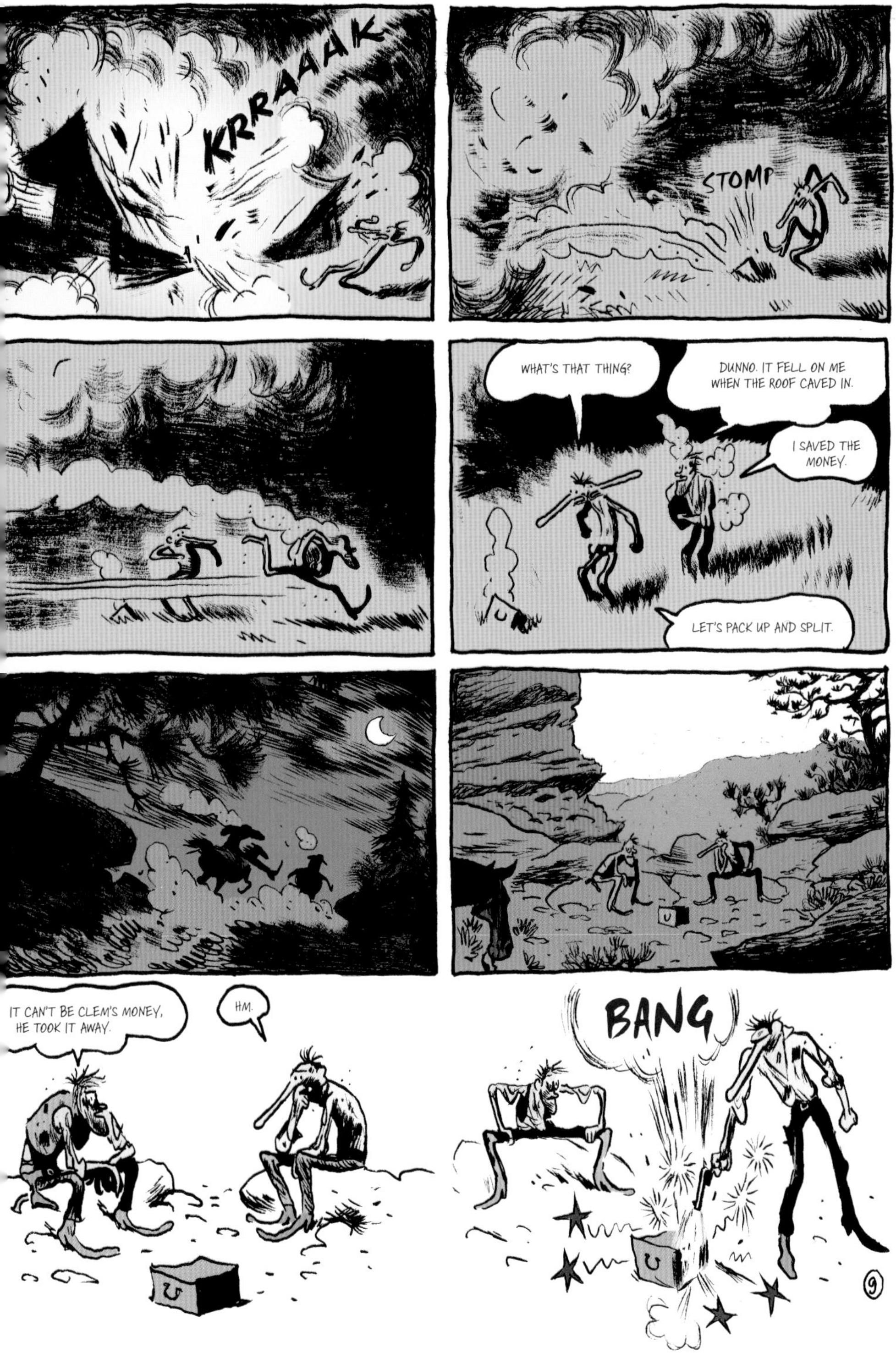
KRRAAAK
STOMP
WHAT'S THAT THING?
DUNNO. IT FELL ON ME WHEN THE ROOF CAVED IN.
I SAVED THE MONEY.
LET'S PACK UP AND SPLIT.
IT CAN'T BE CLEM'S MONEY, HE TOOK IT AWAY.
HM.
BANG
9

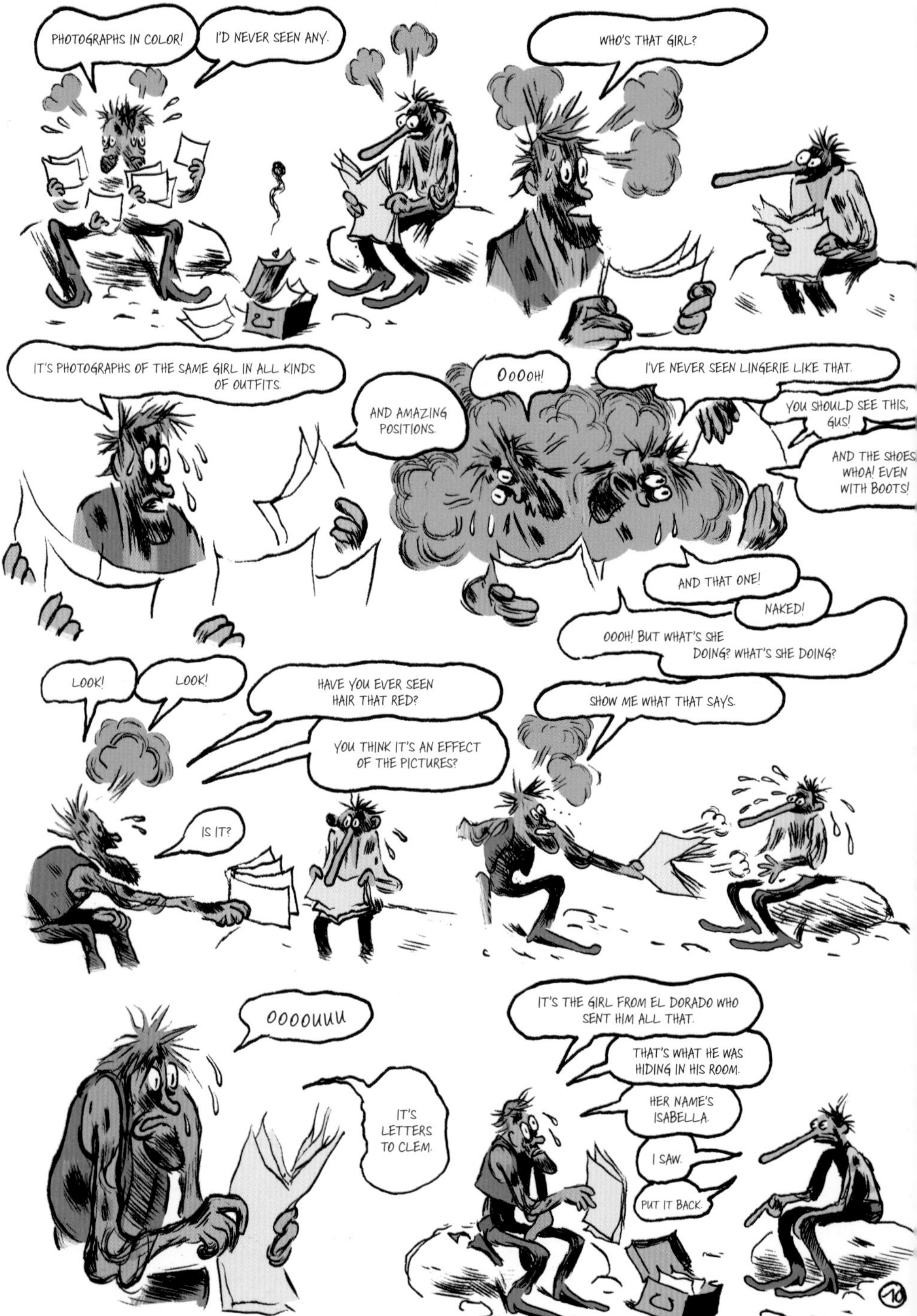
PHOTOGRAPHS IN COLOR!
I'D NEVER SEEN ANY.
WHO'S THAT GIRL?
IT'S PHOTOGRAPHS OF THE SAME GIRL IN ALL KINDS OF OUTFITS.
AND AMAZING POSITIONS.
OOOOH!
I'VE NEVER SEEN LINGERIE LIKE THAT.
YOU SHOULD SEE THIS, GUS!
AND THE SHOES WHOA! EVEN WITH BOOTS!
AND THAT ONE!
NAKED!
OOOH! BUT WHAT'S SHE DOING? WHAT'S SHE DOING?
LOOK!
LOOK!
HAVE YOU EVER SEEN HAIR THAT RED?
YOU THINK IT'S AN EFFECT OF THE PICTURES?
IS IT?
SHOW ME WHAT THAT SAYS.
OOOOUUU
IT'S LETTERS TO CLEM.
IT'S THE GIRL FROM EL DORADO WHO SENT HIM ALL THAT.
THAT'S WHAT HE WAS HIDING IN HIS ROOM.
HER NAME'S ISABELLA.
I SAW.
PUT IT BACK.
10

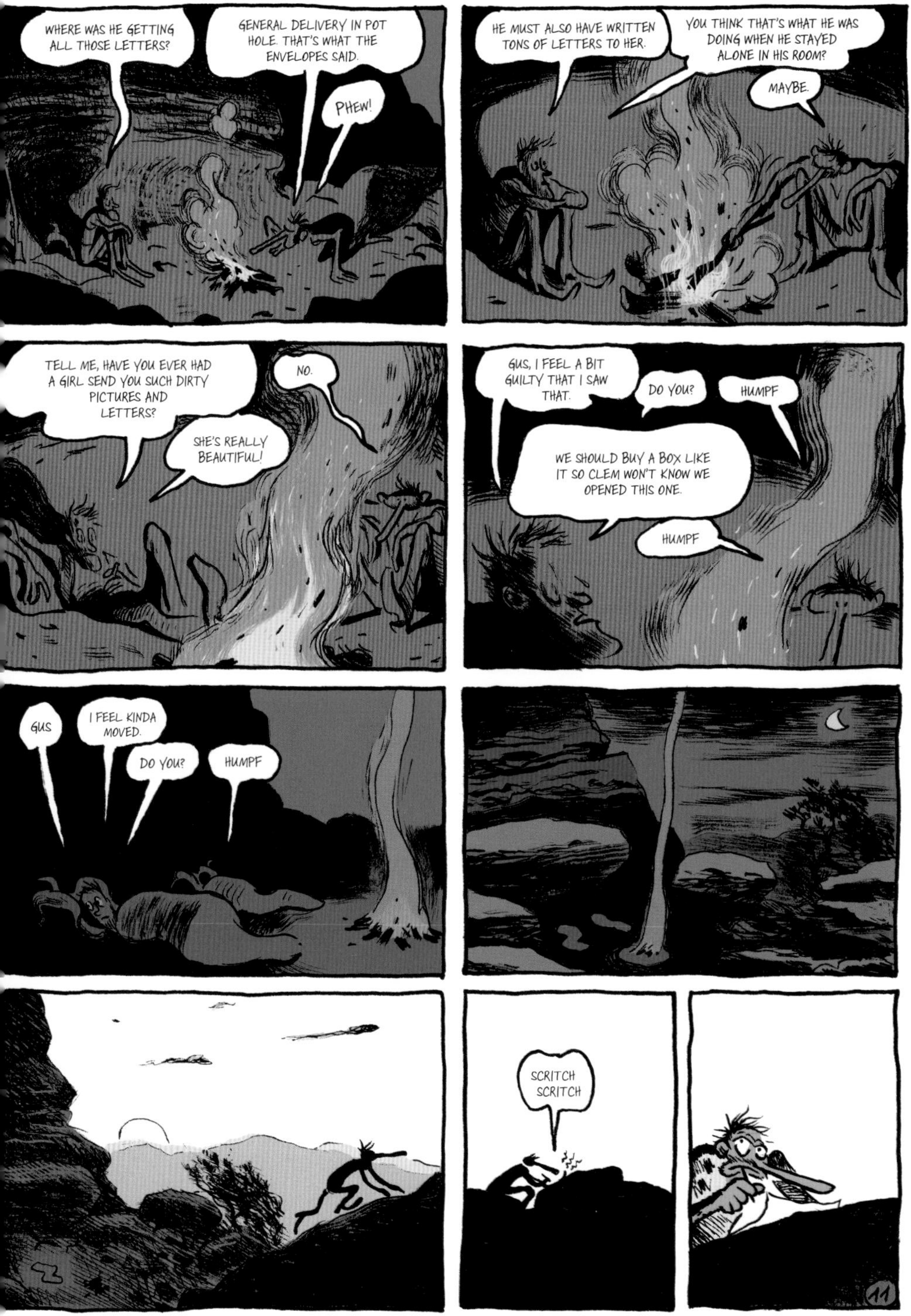
WHERE WAS HE GETTING ALL THOSE LETTERS?
GENERAL DELIVERY IN POT HOLE. THAT'S WHAT THE ENVELOPES SAID.
PHEW!
HE MUST ALSO HAVE WRITTEN TONS OF LETTERS TO HER.
YOU THINK THAT'S WHAT HE WAS DOING WHEN HE STAYED ALONE IN HIS ROOM?
MAYBE.
TELL ME, HAVE YOU EVER HAD A GIRL SEND YOU SUCH DIRTY PICTURES AND LETTERS?
NO.
SHE'S REALLY BEAUTIFUL!
GUS, I FEEL A BIT GUILTY THAT I SAW THAT.
DO YOU?
HUMPF
WE SHOULD BUY A BOX LIKE IT SO CLEM WON'T KNOW WE OPENED THIS ONE.
HUMPF
GUS
I FEEL KINDA MOVED.
DO YOU?
HUMPF
SCRITCH SCRITCH
11

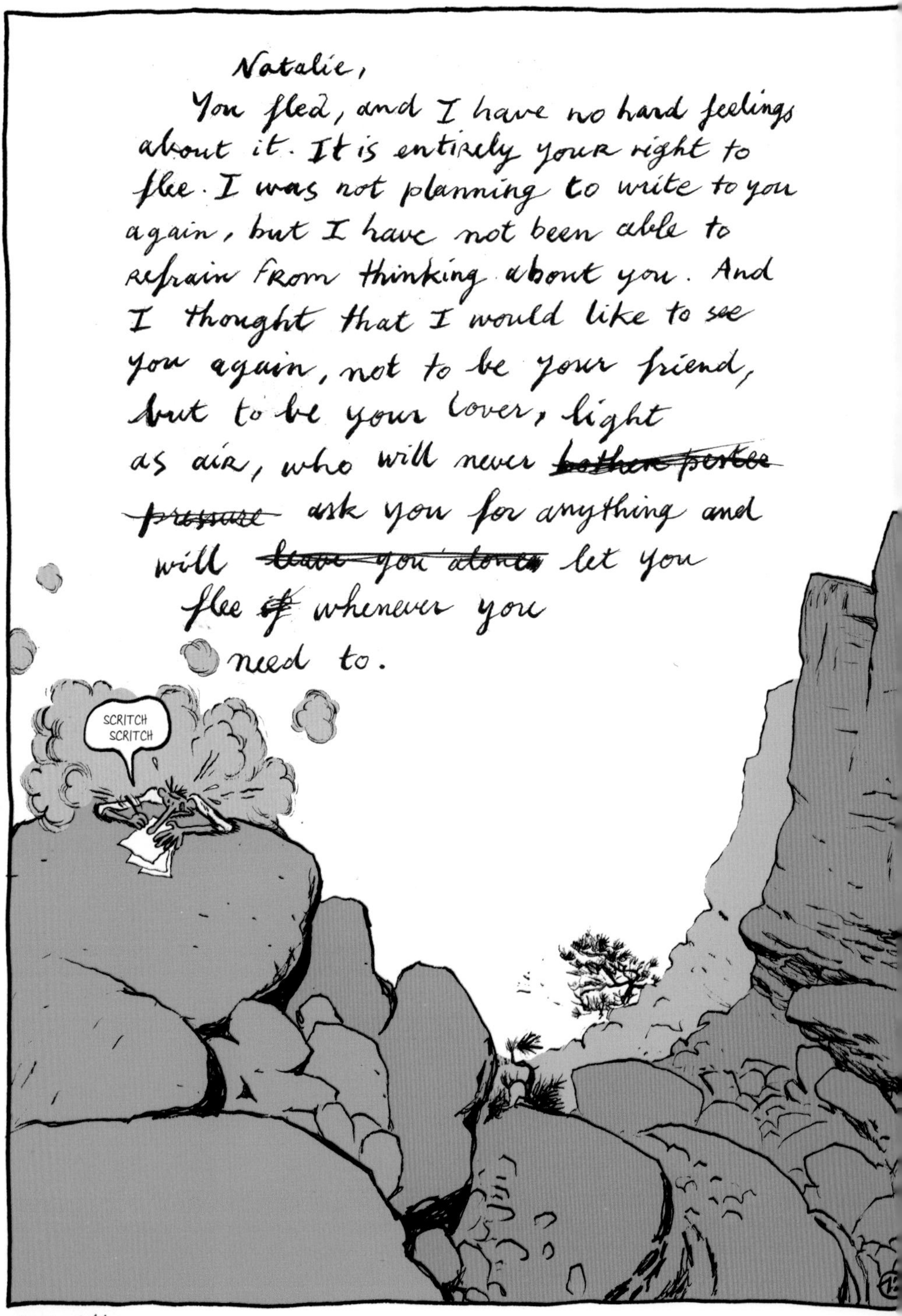
Natalie,
You fled, and I have no hard feelings about it. It is entirely your right to flee. I was not planning to write to you again, but I have not been able to refrain from thinking about you. And I thought that I would like to see you again, not to be your friend, but to be your lover, light as air, who will never ~~bother pester pressure~~ ask you for anything and will ~~leave you alone~~ let you flee ~~of~~ whenever you need to.
SCRITCH SCRITCH

Christopheblain

PEGGY

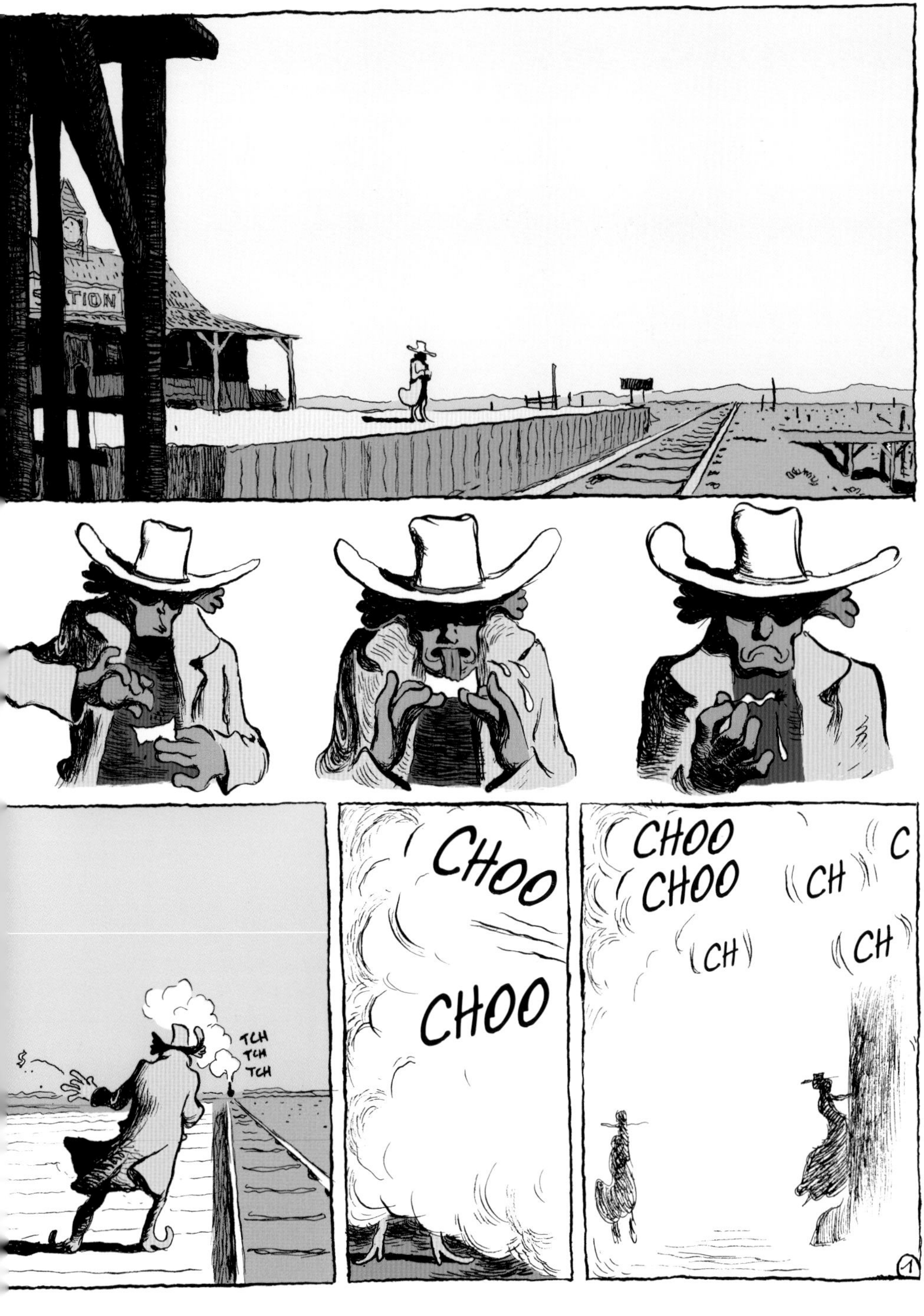
TATION
TCH
TCH
TCH
CHOO
CHOO
CHOO
CHOO
CH
C
CH
CH
1

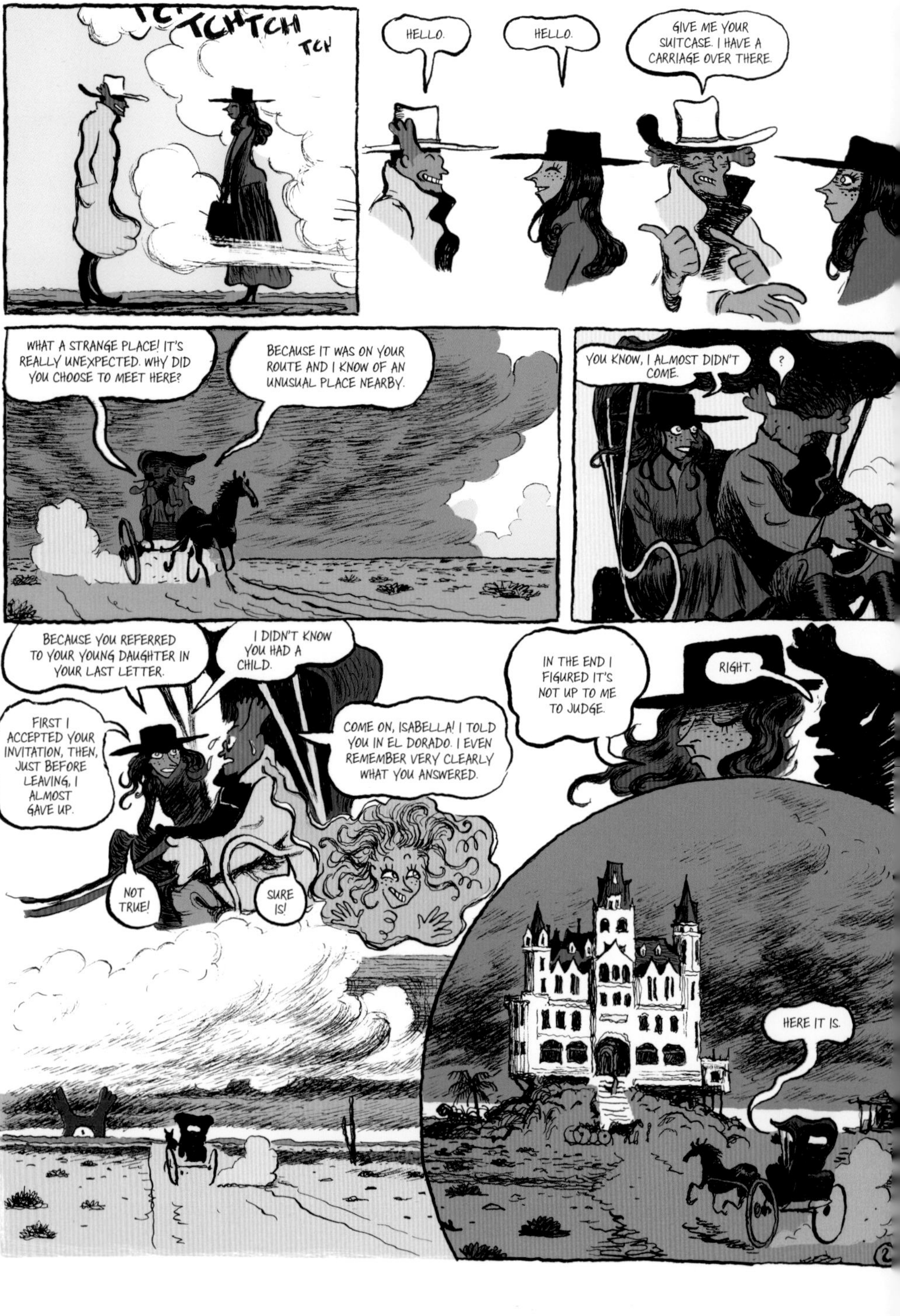
TCH TCHTCH
TCH
HELLO.
HELLO.
GIVE ME YOUR SUITCASE. I HAVE A CARRIAGE OVER THERE.
WHAT A STRANGE PLACE! IT'S REALLY UNEXPECTED. WHY DID YOU CHOOSE TO MEET HERE?
BECAUSE IT WAS ON YOUR ROUTE AND I KNOW OF AN UNUSUAL PLACE NEARBY.
YOU KNOW, I ALMOST DIDN'T COME.
?
BECAUSE YOU REFERRED TO YOUR YOUNG DAUGHTER IN YOUR LAST LETTER.
I DIDN'T KNOW YOU HAD A CHILD.
FIRST I ACCEPTED YOUR INVITATION, THEN, JUST BEFORE LEAVING, I ALMOST GAVE UP.
COME ON, ISABELLA! I TOLD YOU IN EL DORADO. I EVEN REMEMBER VERY CLEARLY WHAT YOU ANSWERED.
NOT TRUE!
SURE IS!
IN THE END I FIGURED IT'S NOT UP TO ME TO JUDGE.
RIGHT.
HERE IT IS.

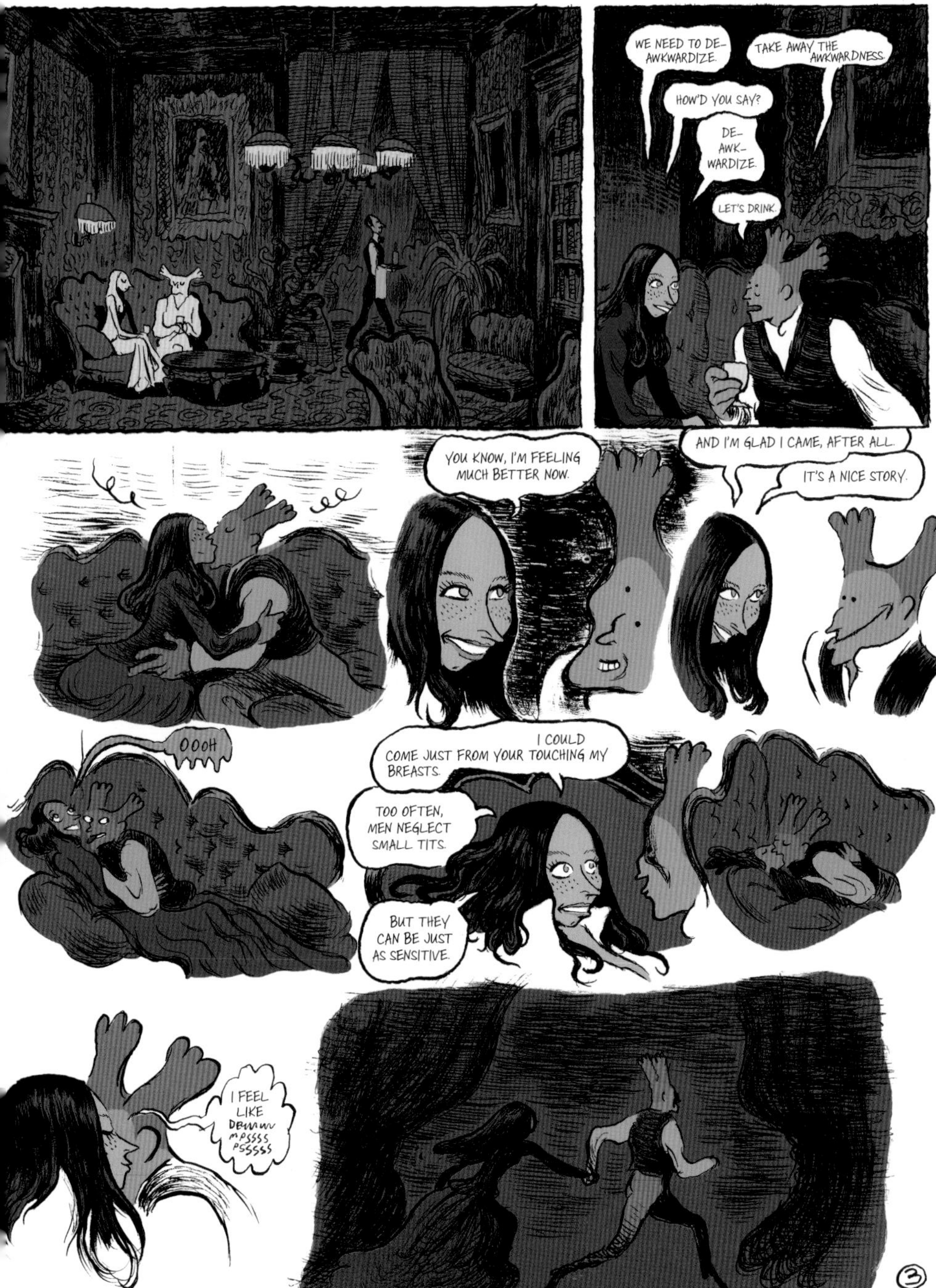

WE NEED TO DE-AWKWARDIZE.
TAKE AWAY THE AWKWARDNESS.
HOW'D YOU SAY?
DE-AWK-WARDIZE.
LET'S DRINK.
YOU KNOW, I'M FEELING MUCH BETTER NOW.
AND I'M GLAD I CAME, AFTER ALL.
IT'S A NICE STORY.
OOOH
I COULD COME JUST FROM YOUR TOUCHING MY BREASTS.
TOO OFTEN, MEN NEGLECT SMALL TITS.
BUT THEY CAN BE JUST AS SENSITIVE.
I FEEL LIKE

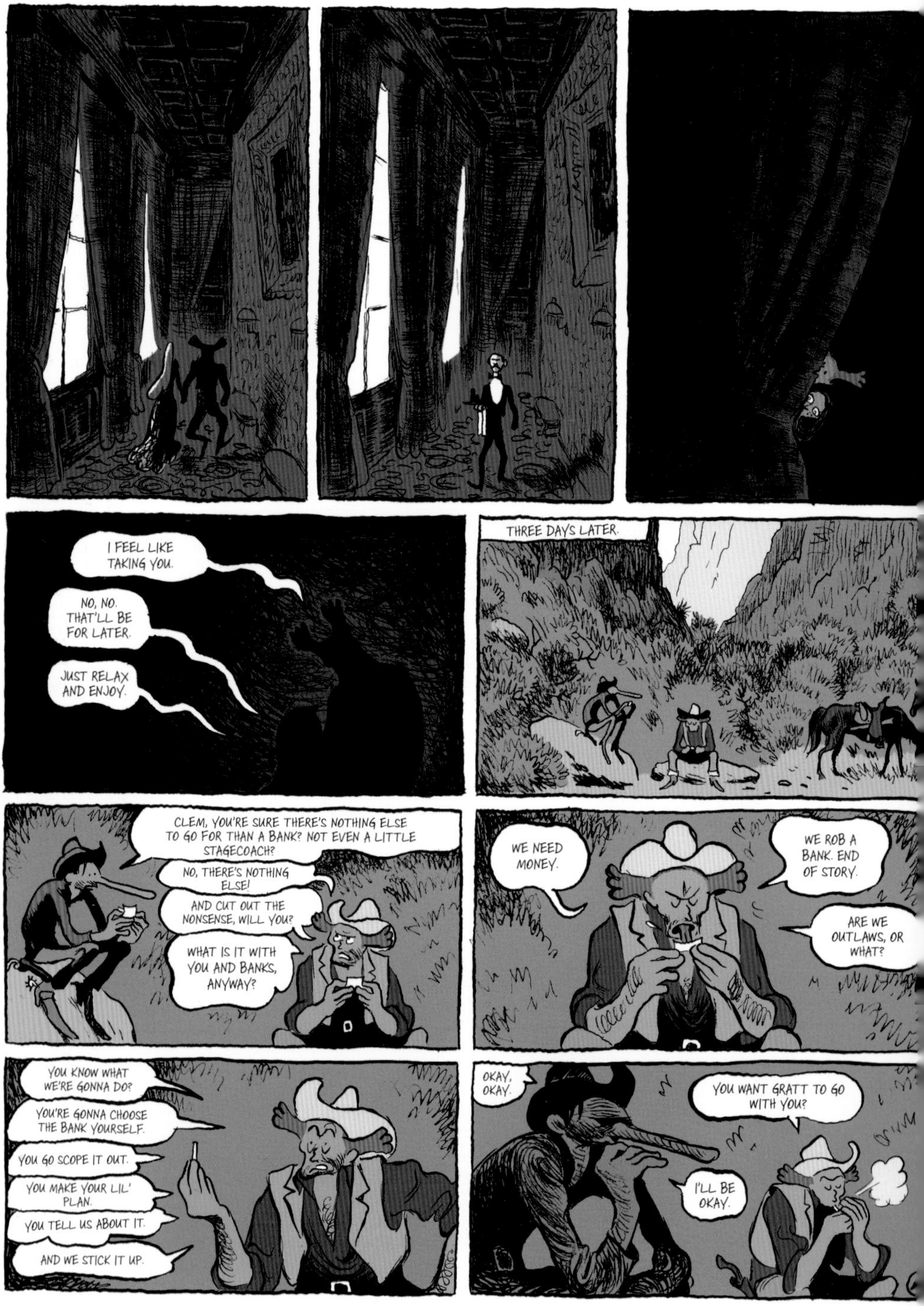
I FEEL LIKE TAKING YOU.
NO, NO. THAT'LL BE FOR LATER.
JUST RELAX AND ENJOY.
THREE DAYS LATER.
CLEM, YOU'RE SURE THERE'S NOTHING ELSE TO GO FOR THAN A BANK? NOT EVEN A LITTLE STAGECOACH?
NO, THERE'S NOTHING ELSE!
AND CUT OUT THE NONSENSE, WILL YOU?
WHAT IS IT WITH YOU AND BANKS, ANYWAY?
WE NEED MONEY.
WE ROB A BANK. END OF STORY.
ARE WE OUTLAWS, OR WHAT?
YOU KNOW WHAT WE'RE GONNA DO?
YOU'RE GONNA CHOOSE THE BANK YOURSELF.
YOU GO SCOPE IT OUT.
YOU MAKE YOUR LIL' PLAN.
YOU TELL US ABOUT IT.
AND WE STICK IT UP.
OKAY, OKAY.
YOU WANT GRATT TO GO WITH YOU?
I'LL BE OKAY.

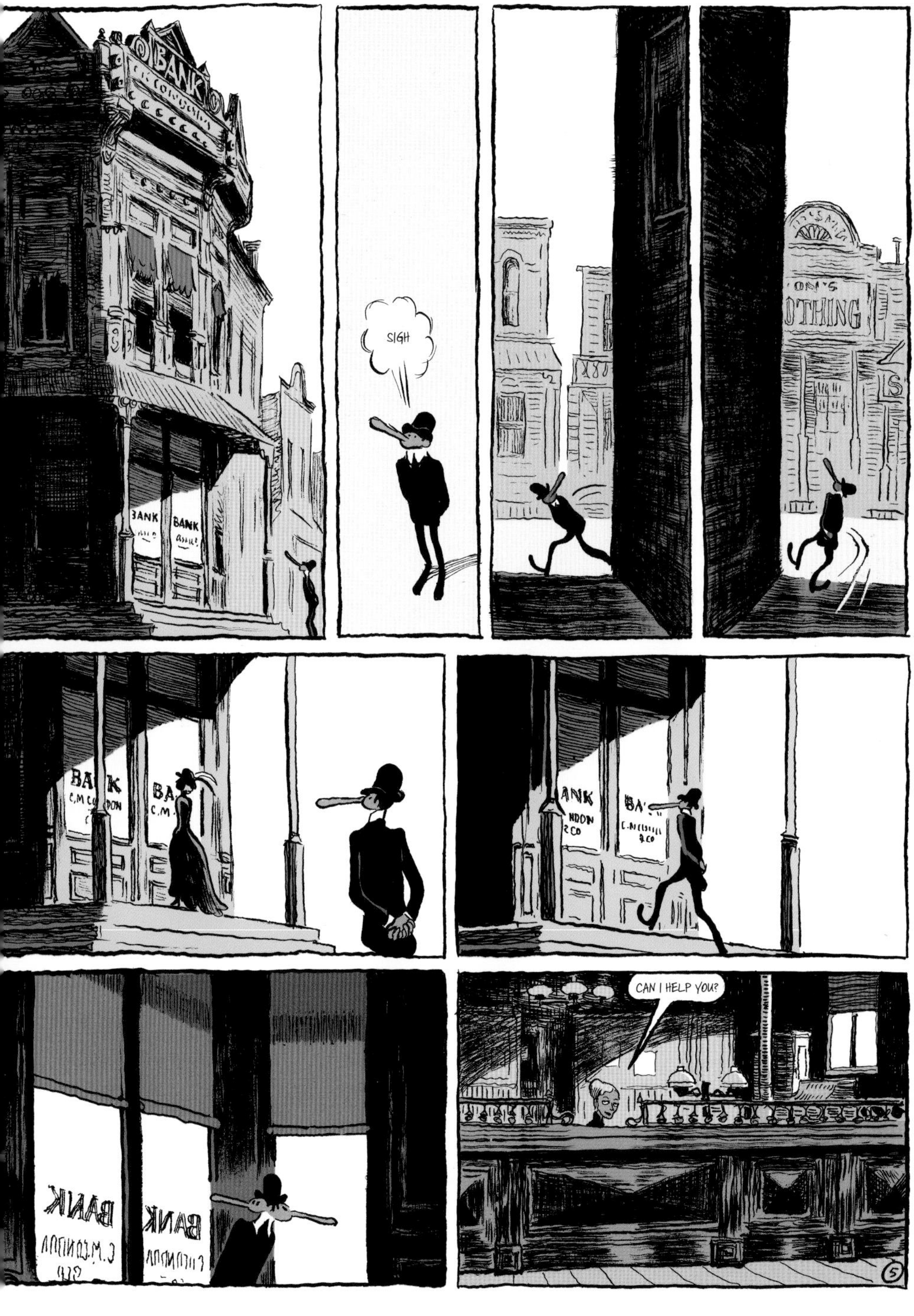
BANK
SIGH
BANK
BANK
CAN I HELP YOU?

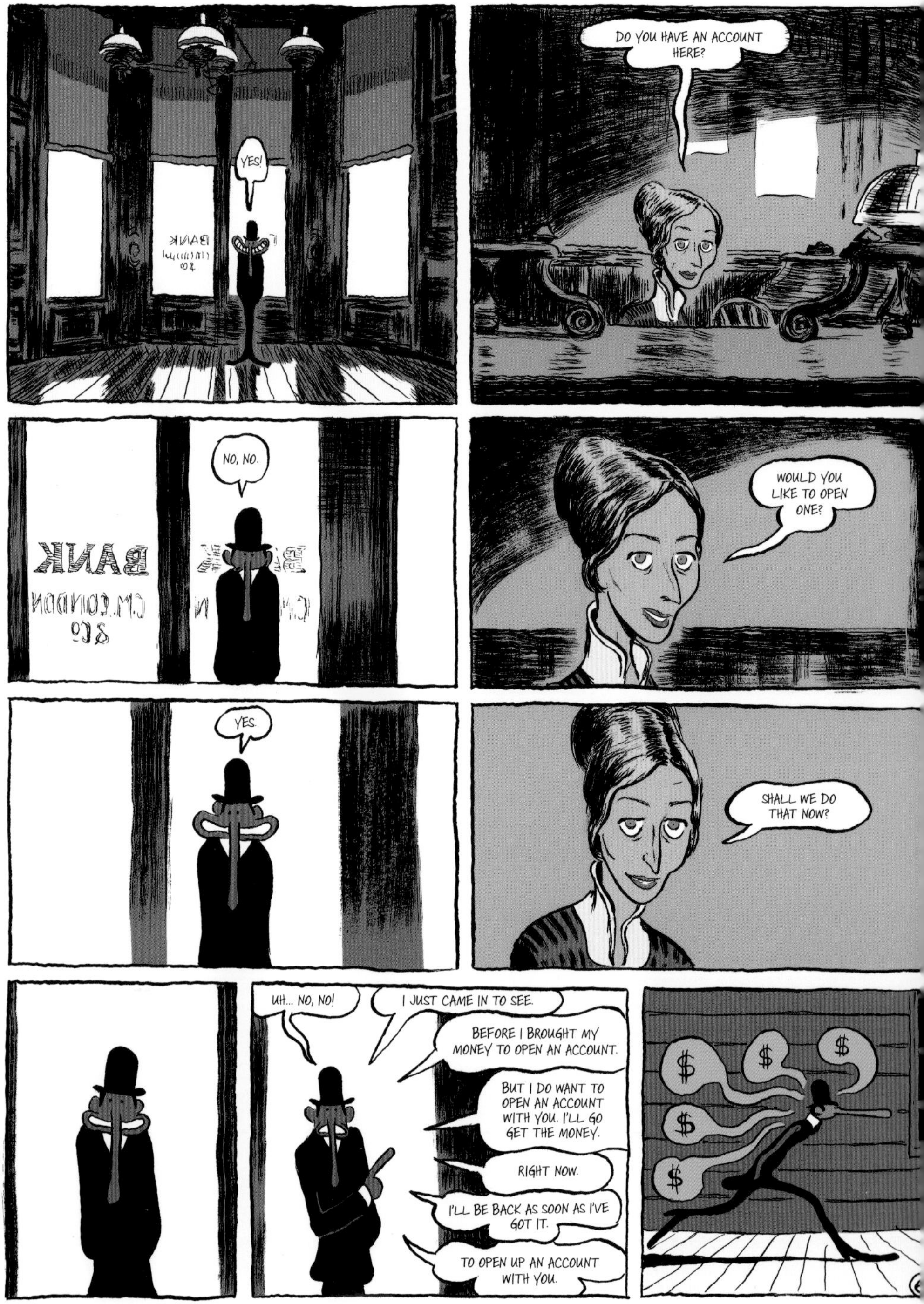
YES!
DO YOU HAVE AN ACCOUNT HERE?
NO, NO.
WOULD YOU LIKE TO OPEN ONE?
YES.
SHALL WE DO THAT NOW?
UH... NO, NO!
I JUST CAME IN TO SEE.
BEFORE I BROUGHT MY MONEY TO OPEN AN ACCOUNT.
BUT I DO WANT TO OPEN AN ACCOUNT WITH YOU. I'LL GO GET THE MONEY.
RIGHT NOW.
I'LL BE BACK AS SOON AS I'VE GOT IT.
TO OPEN UP AN ACCOUNT WITH YOU.

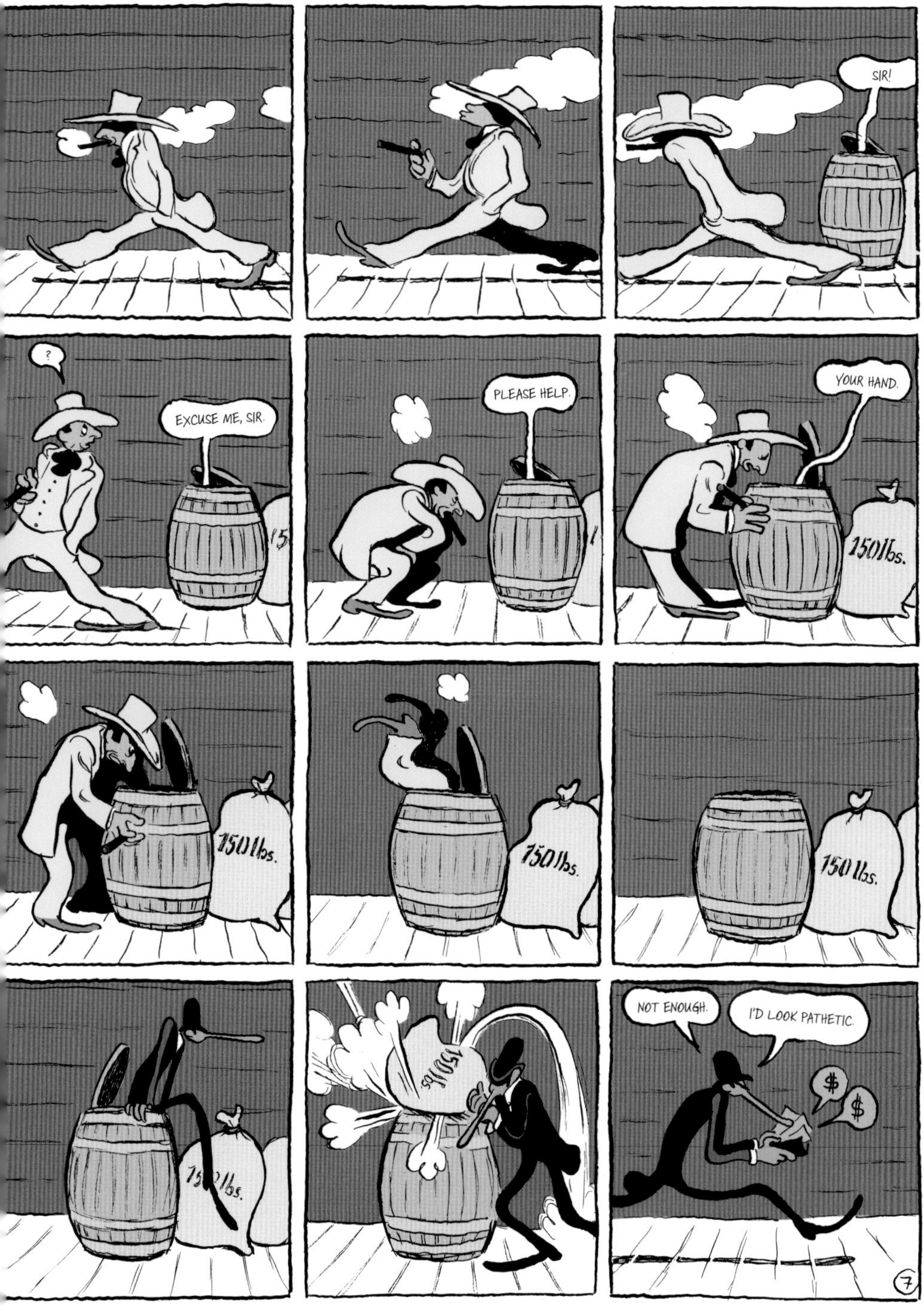
SIR!
?
EXCUSE ME, SIR.
PLEASE HELP.
YOUR HAND.
150 lbs.
150 lbs.
150 lbs.
150 lbs.
NOT ENOUGH.
I'D LOOK PATHETIC.
$
$
7

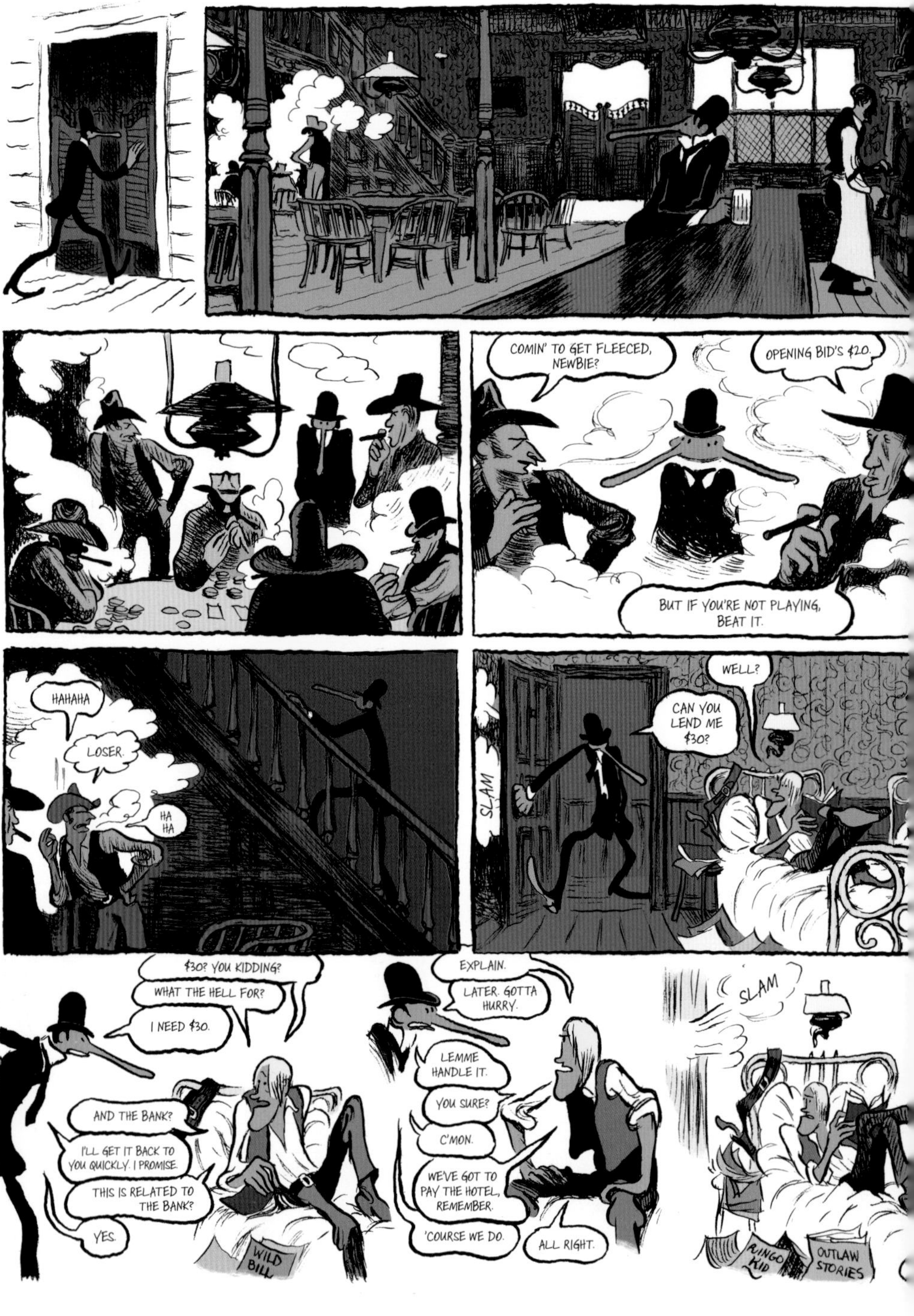
COMIN' TO GET FLEECED, NEWBIE?
OPENING BID'S $20.
BUT IF YOU'RE NOT PLAYING, BEAT IT.
HAHAHA
LOSER.
HA HA
SLAM
WELL?
CAN YOU LEND ME $30?
$30? YOU KIDDING?
WHAT THE HELL FOR?
I NEED $30.
AND THE BANK?
I'LL GET IT BACK TO YOU QUICKLY. I PROMISE.
THIS IS RELATED TO THE BANK?
YES.
WILD BILL
EXPLAIN.
LATER. GOTTA HURRY.
LEMME HANDLE IT.
YOU SURE?
C'MON.
WE'VE GOT TO PAY THE HOTEL, REMEMBER.
'COURSE WE DO.
ALL RIGHT.
SLAM
RINGO KID
OUTLAW STORIES

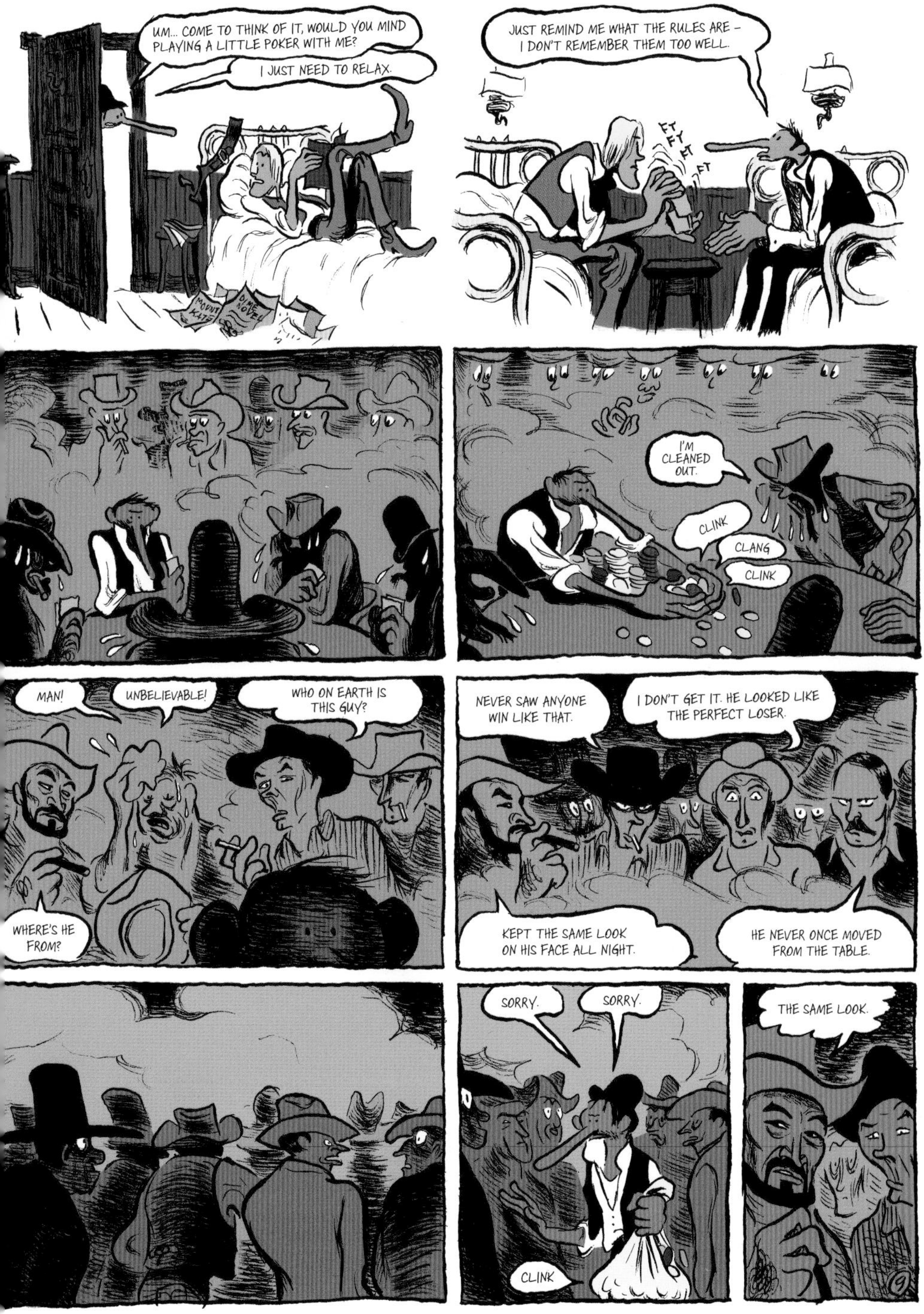
UM... COME TO THINK OF IT, WOULD YOU MIND PLAYING A LITTLE POKER WITH ME?
I JUST NEED TO RELAX.
JUST REMIND ME WHAT THE RULES ARE – I DON'T REMEMBER THEM TOO WELL.
FT FT FT FT
I'M CLEANED OUT.
CLINK
CLANG
CLINK
MAN!
UNBELIEVABLE!
WHO ON EARTH IS THIS GUY?
WHERE'S HE FROM?
NEVER SAW ANYONE WIN LIKE THAT.
I DON'T GET IT. HE LOOKED LIKE THE PERFECT LOSER.
KEPT THE SAME LOOK ON HIS FACE ALL NIGHT.
HE NEVER ONCE MOVED FROM THE TABLE.
SORRY.
SORRY.
CLINK
THE SAME LOOK.

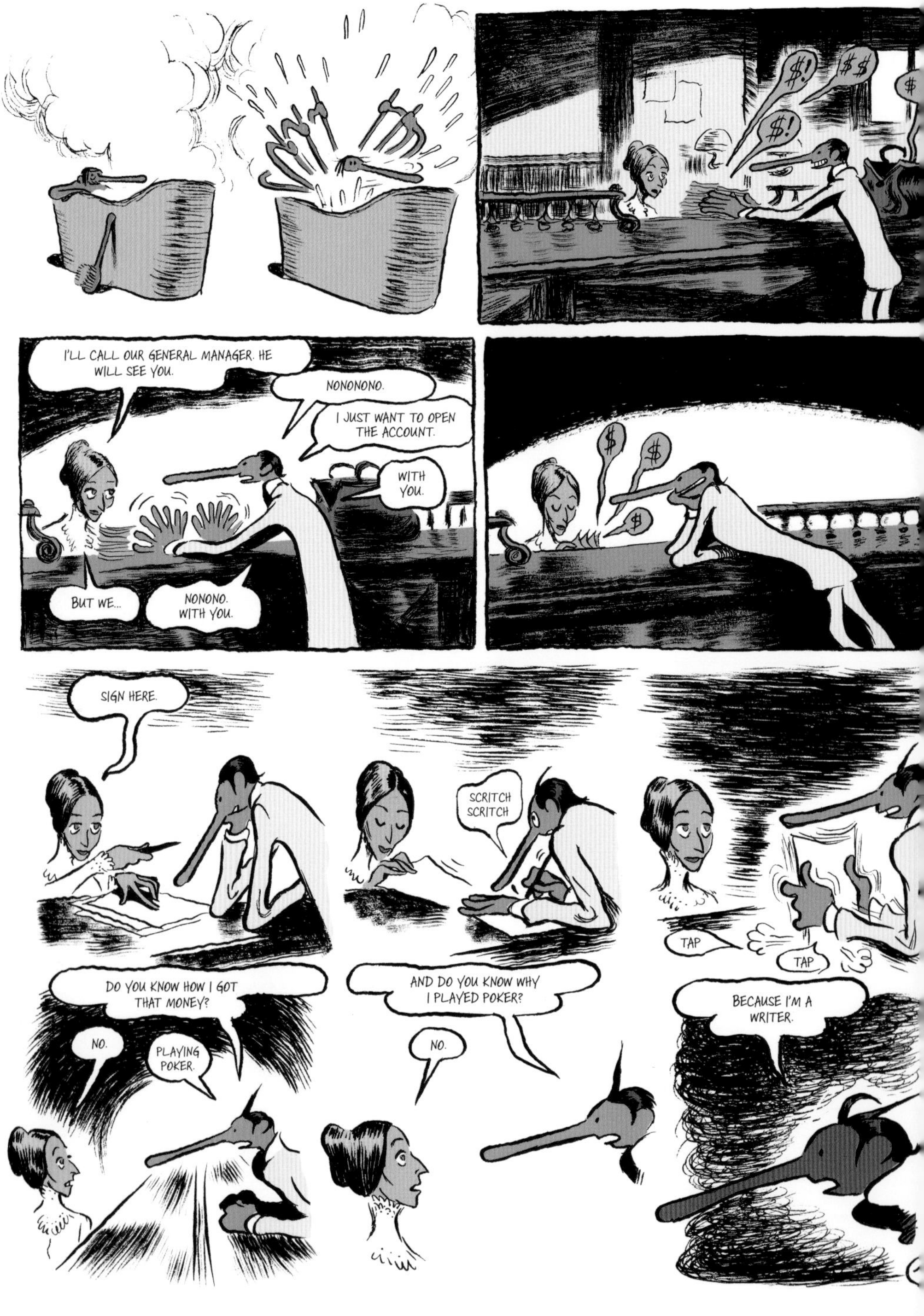
$!
$$
$!
$
I'LL CALL OUR GENERAL MANAGER. HE WILL SEE YOU.
NONONONO.
I JUST WANT TO OPEN THE ACCOUNT.
WITH YOU.
BUT WE...
NONONO. WITH YOU.
$
$
$
SIGN HERE.
SCRITCH SCRITCH
TAP
TAP
DO YOU KNOW HOW I GOT THAT MONEY?
NO.
PLAYING POKER.
AND DO YOU KNOW WHY I PLAYED POKER?
NO.
BECAUSE I'M A WRITER.

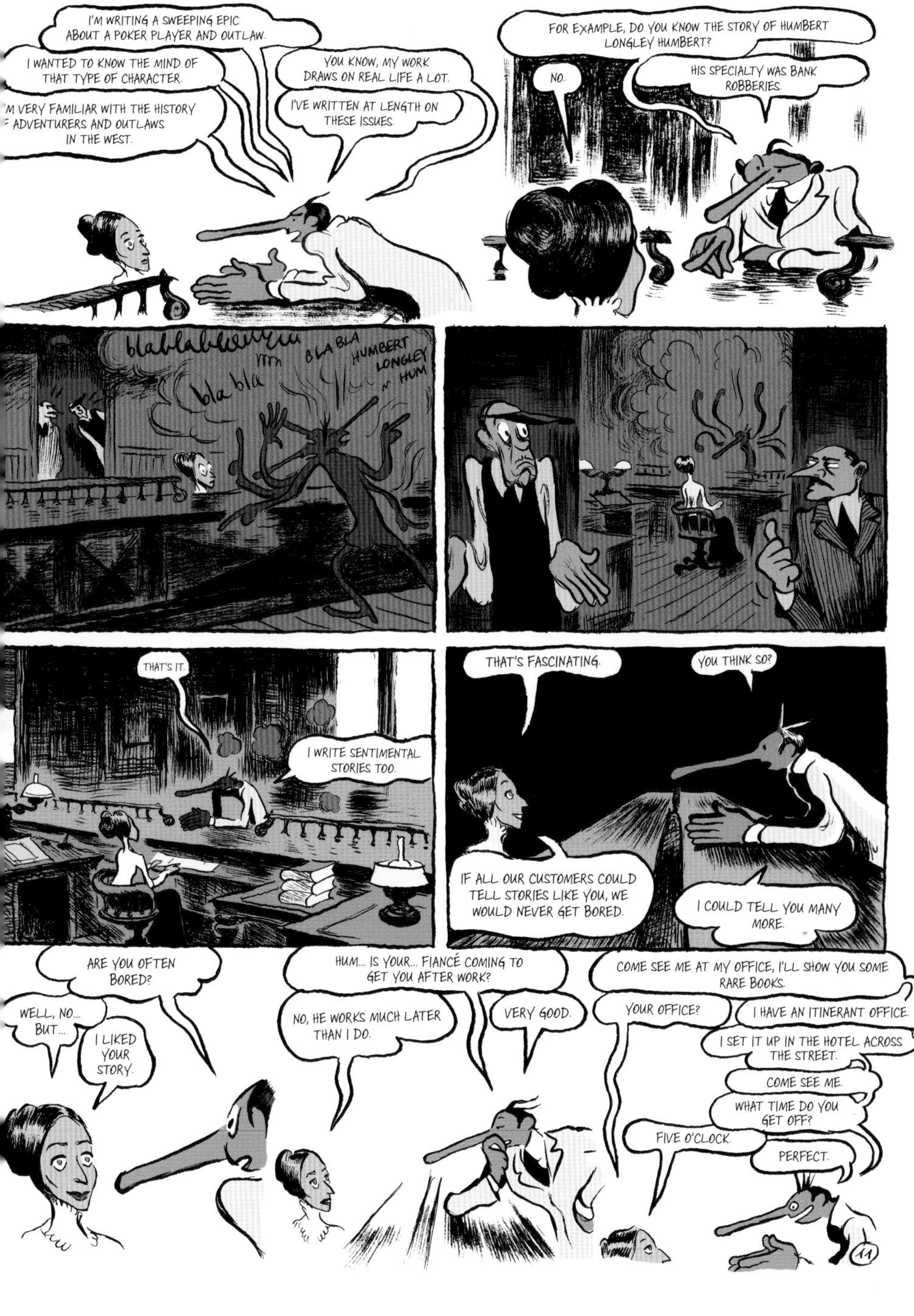
I'M WRITING A SWEEPING EPIC ABOUT A POKER PLAYER AND OUTLAW.
I WANTED TO KNOW THE MIND OF THAT TYPE OF CHARACTER.
'M VERY FAMILIAR WITH THE HISTORY
ADVENTURERS AND OUTLAWS IN THE WEST.
YOU KNOW, MY WORK DRAWS ON REAL LIFE A LOT.
I'VE WRITTEN AT LENGTH ON THESE ISSUES.
FOR EXAMPLE, DO YOU KNOW THE STORY OF HUMBERT LONGLEY HUMBERT?
NO.
HIS SPECIALTY WAS BANK ROBBERIES.
blablabla
bla bla
BLA BLA
HUMBERT LONGLEY HUM
THAT'S IT.
I WRITE SENTIMENTAL STORIES TOO.
THAT'S FASCINATING.
YOU THINK SO?
IF ALL OUR CUSTOMERS COULD TELL STORIES LIKE YOU, WE WOULD NEVER GET BORED.
I COULD TELL YOU MANY MORE.
ARE YOU OFTEN BORED?
WELL, NO... BUT...
I LIKED YOUR STORY.
HUM... IS YOUR... FIANCÉ COMING TO GET YOU AFTER WORK?
NO, HE WORKS MUCH LATER THAN I DO.
VERY GOOD.
COME SEE ME AT MY OFFICE, I'LL SHOW YOU SOME RARE BOOKS.
YOUR OFFICE?
I HAVE AN ITINERANT OFFICE.
I SET IT UP IN THE HOTEL ACROSS THE STREET.
COME SEE ME.
WHAT TIME DO YOU GET OFF?
FIVE O'CLOCK.
PERFECT.
11

KNOCK
KNOCK

WOULD YOU MIND HELPING ME GET THIS THING INSIDE.

SCRRRAPE

HEY, STOP IT! WHAT THE HELL ARE YOU DOING WITH MY BOOKS? I'M READING THEM.

LET ME REMIND YOU THAT THEY'RE *MY* BOOKS.

MAYBE, BUT I'M READING THEM.

JUST READ ONE AT A TIME.

BEADLE'S DIME NOVELS
MOUNTAIN KATE

DIME New York LIBRARY
COLD HAND JOE

THE CRAZY COLT OF ARIZON

HUMBER LONGLEY HUM

BUFFALO BILL STORIES
BILL'S STRATEGY

FANCY FRANK OF COLORADO

DEN DAN

SCRITCH SCRITCH
SCR SCRITCH
SCR SCRITCH
SCR SCRITCH

WHAT ARE YOU DOING? MAKING A PLAN?

IS HOLDING UP A BANK THAT COMPLICATED?

YES.

DIDN'T YOU SEE THE LOOK OF THE BANK?

THIS ISN'T JUST ANYTHING. IT'S A HIGH-WIR ACT. WE CAN'T IMPROVISE

YOU COULDN'T HAVE MADE IT SIMPLER?

OKAY, GRATT, DO YOU MIND?

I'M GOING FOR A WALK.

GOOD.

TWO HOURS LATER.

WHAT HAPPENED TO THE ROOM?

HEY! DON'T START MAKING A MESS, OKAY?

BUT...

AAARGH! PUT IT DOWN, WILL YOU?

YOU COPIED THE THIRD VOLUME OF THE ADVENTURES OF NEVADA BROWN. I READ IT LAST NIGHT.

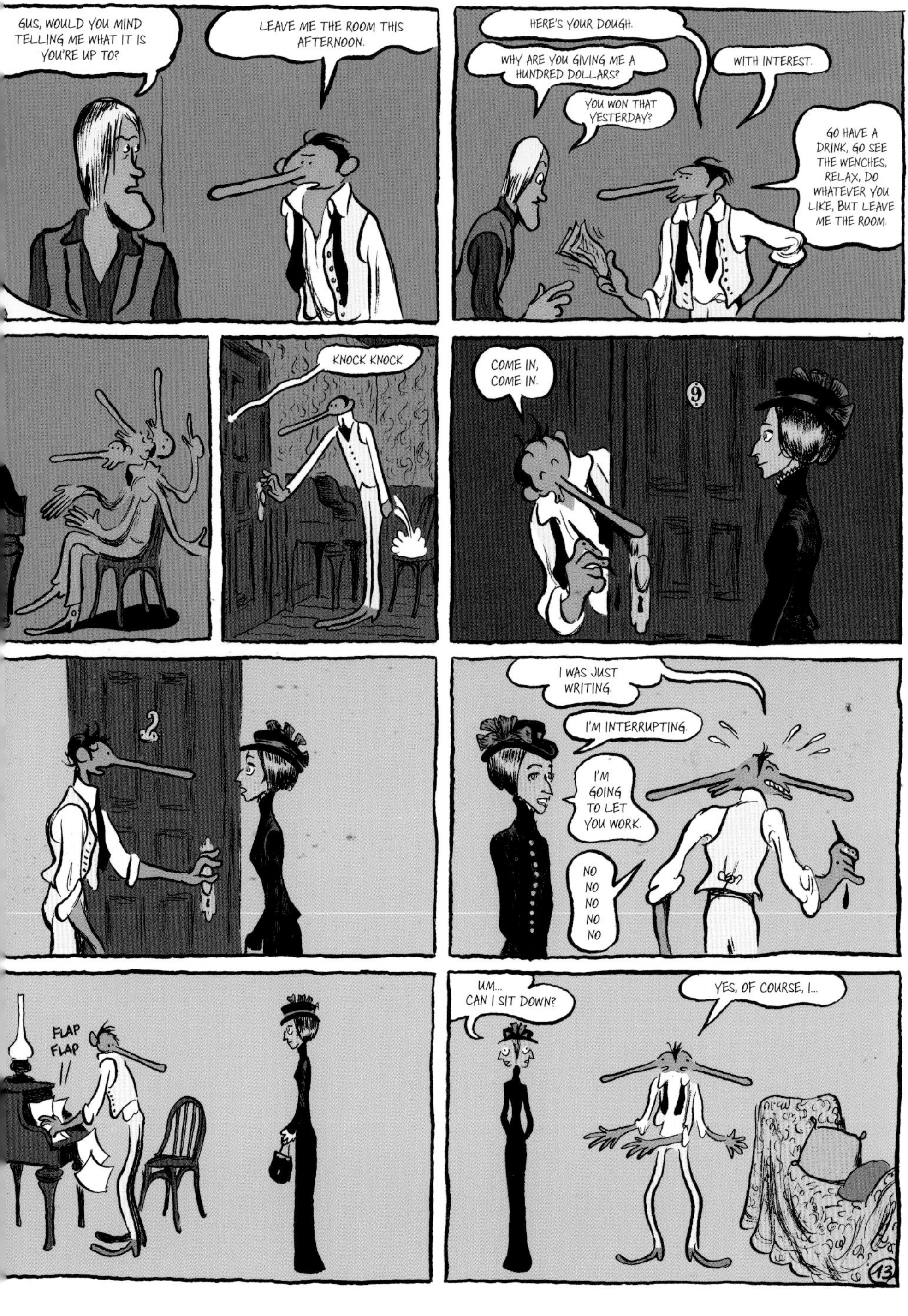
GUS, WOULD YOU MIND TELLING ME WHAT IT IS YOU'RE UP TO?
LEAVE ME THE ROOM THIS AFTERNOON.
HERE'S YOUR DOUGH.
WHY ARE YOU GIVING ME A HUNDRED DOLLARS?
WITH INTEREST.
YOU WON THAT YESTERDAY?
GO HAVE A DRINK, GO SEE THE WENCHES, RELAX, DO WHATEVER YOU LIKE, BUT LEAVE ME THE ROOM.
KNOCK KNOCK
COME IN, COME IN.
I WAS JUST WRITING.
I'M INTERRUPTING.
I'M GOING TO LET YOU WORK.
NO NO NO NO NO
FLAP FLAP
UM... CAN I SIT DOWN?
YES, OF COURSE, I...
13

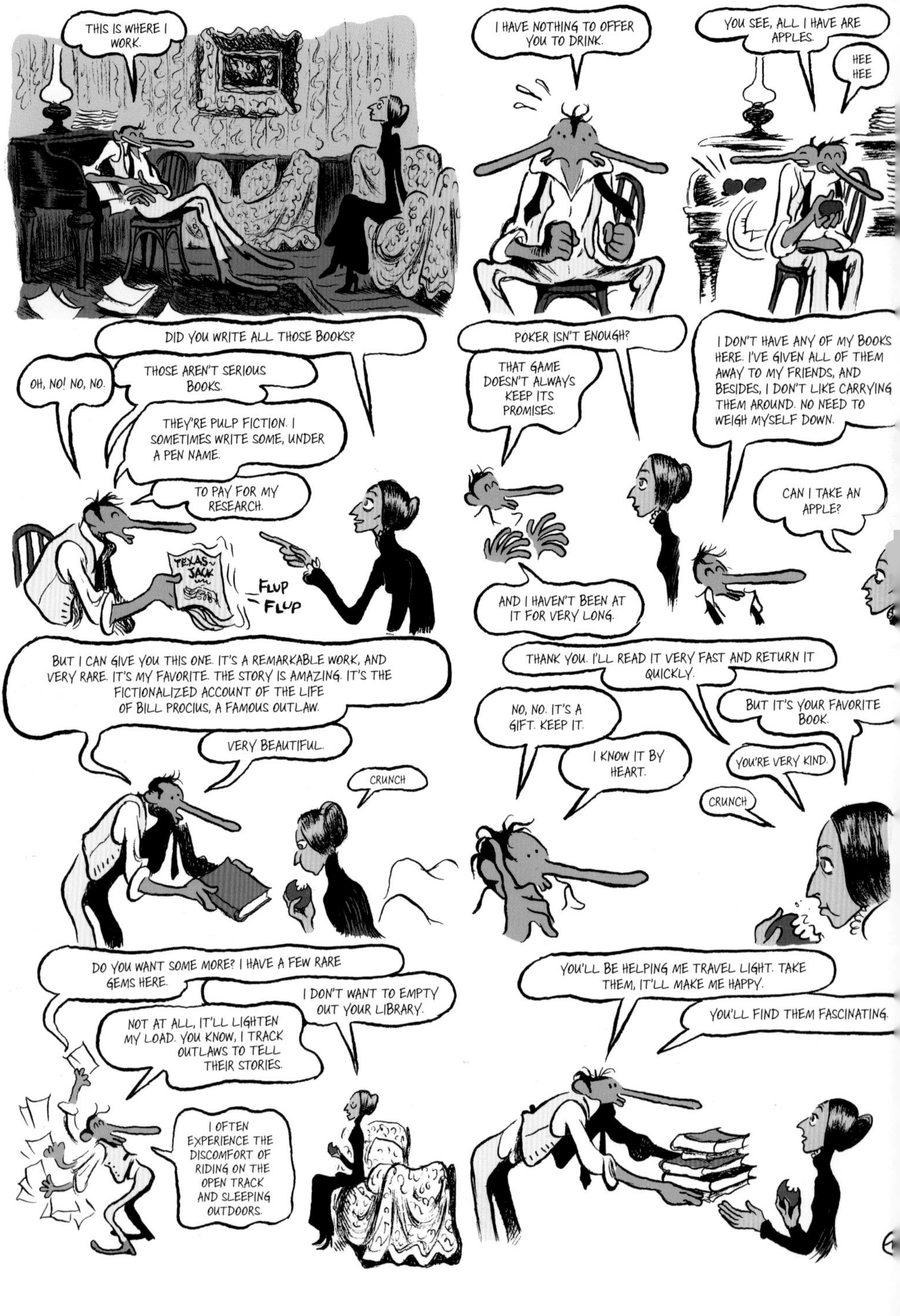

THIS IS WHERE I WORK.
I HAVE NOTHING TO OFFER YOU TO DRINK.
YOU SEE, ALL I HAVE ARE APPLES.
HEE HEE
DID YOU WRITE ALL THOSE BOOKS?
OH, NO! NO, NO.
THOSE AREN'T SERIOUS BOOKS.
THEY'RE PULP FICTION. I SOMETIMES WRITE SOME, UNDER A PEN NAME.
TO PAY FOR MY RESEARCH.
TEXAS JACK
FLUP FLUP
POKER ISN'T ENOUGH?
THAT GAME DOESN'T ALWAYS KEEP ITS PROMISES.
AND I HAVEN'T BEEN AT IT FOR VERY LONG.
I DON'T HAVE ANY OF MY BOOKS HERE. I'VE GIVEN ALL OF THEM AWAY TO MY FRIENDS, AND BESIDES, I DON'T LIKE CARRYING THEM AROUND. NO NEED TO WEIGH MYSELF DOWN.
CAN I TAKE AN APPLE?
BUT I CAN GIVE YOU THIS ONE. IT'S A REMARKABLE WORK, AND VERY RARE. IT'S MY FAVORITE. THE STORY IS AMAZING. IT'S THE FICTIONALIZED ACCOUNT OF THE LIFE OF BILL PROCIUS, A FAMOUS OUTLAW.
VERY BEAUTIFUL.
CRUNCH
THANK YOU. I'LL READ IT VERY FAST AND RETURN IT QUICKLY.
NO, NO. IT'S A GIFT. KEEP IT.
I KNOW IT BY HEART.
BUT IT'S YOUR FAVORITE BOOK.
YOU'RE VERY KIND.
CRUNCH
DO YOU WANT SOME MORE? I HAVE A FEW RARE GEMS HERE.
I DON'T WANT TO EMPTY OUT YOUR LIBRARY.
NOT AT ALL, IT'LL LIGHTEN MY LOAD. YOU KNOW, I TRACK OUTLAWS TO TELL THEIR STORIES.
I OFTEN EXPERIENCE THE DISCOMFORT OF RIDING ON THE OPEN TRACK AND SLEEPING OUTDOORS.
YOU'LL BE HELPING ME TRAVEL LIGHT. TAKE THEM, IT'LL MAKE ME HAPPY.
YOU'LL FIND THEM FASCINATING.

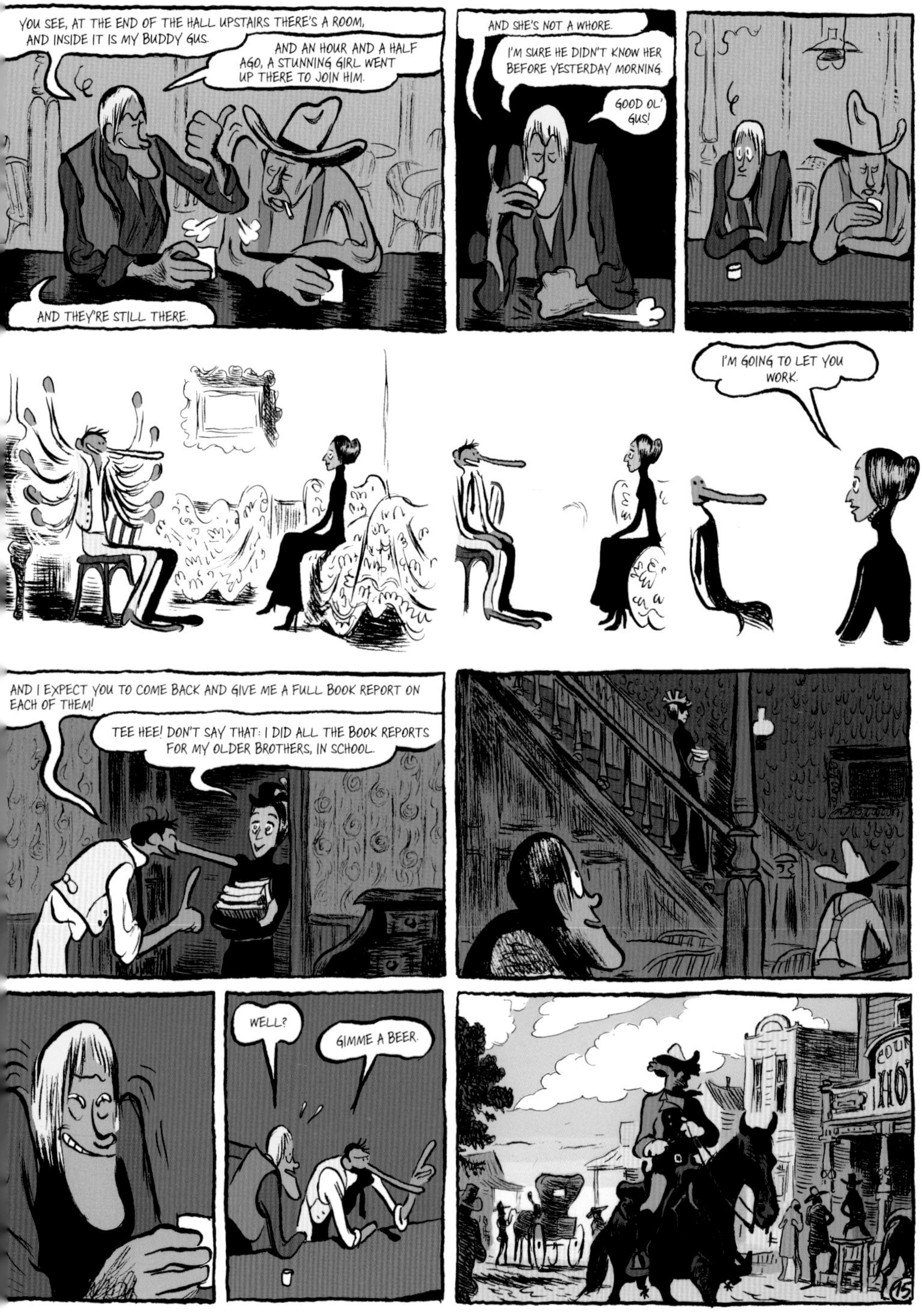
YOU SEE, AT THE END OF THE HALL UPSTAIRS THERE'S A ROOM, AND INSIDE IT IS MY BUDDY GUS.
AND AN HOUR AND A HALF AGO, A STUNNING GIRL WENT UP THERE TO JOIN HIM.
AND THEY'RE STILL THERE.
AND SHE'S NOT A WHORE.
I'M SURE HE DIDN'T KNOW HER BEFORE YESTERDAY MORNING.
GOOD OL' GUS!
I'M GOING TO LET YOU WORK.
AND I EXPECT YOU TO COME BACK AND GIVE ME A FULL BOOK REPORT ON EACH OF THEM!
TEE HEE! DON'T SAY THAT: I DID ALL THE BOOK REPORTS FOR MY OLDER BROTHERS, IN SCHOOL.
WELL?
GIMME A BEER.
15

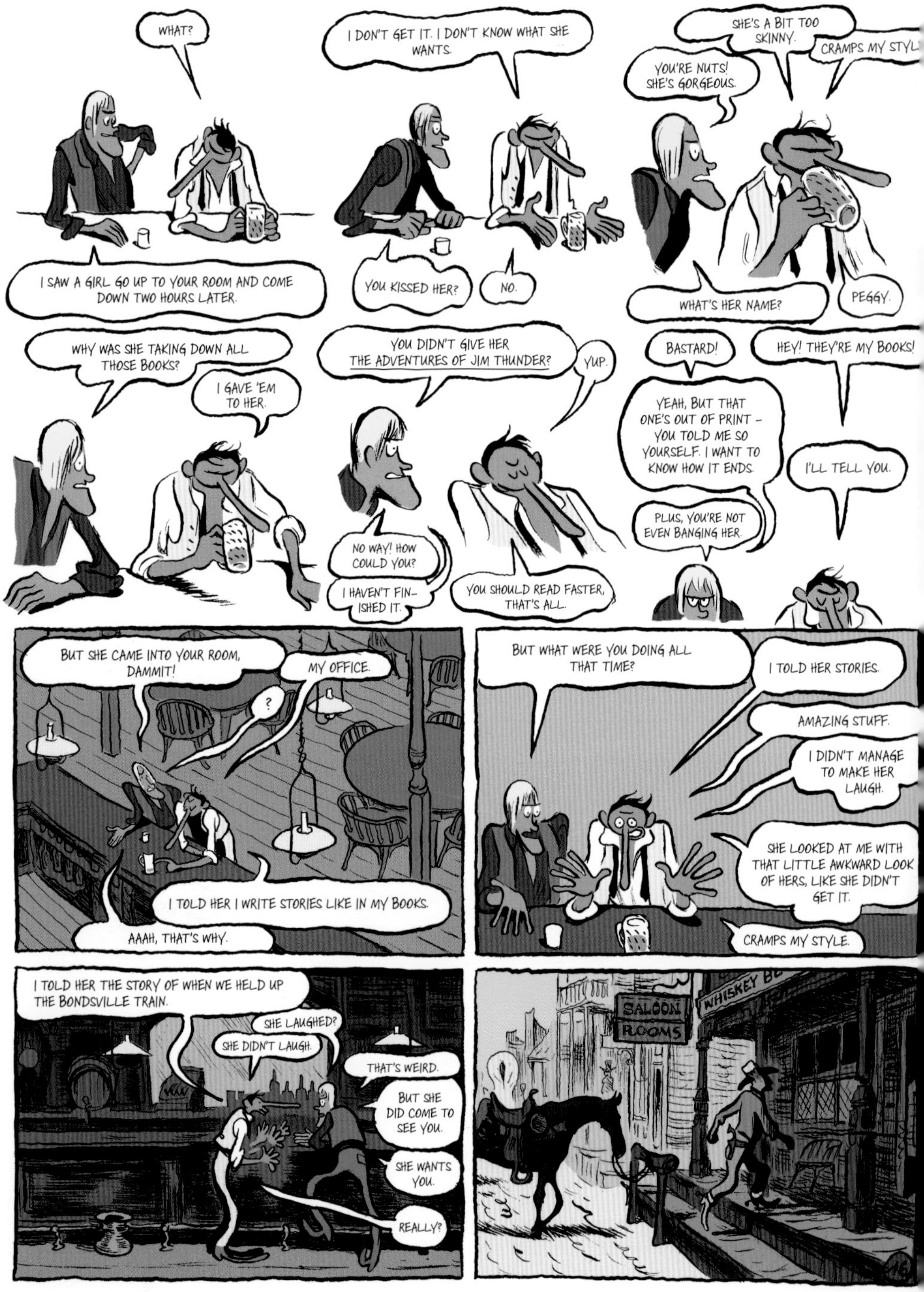
WHAT?
I SAW A GIRL GO UP TO YOUR ROOM AND COME DOWN TWO HOURS LATER.
I DON'T GET IT. I DON'T KNOW WHAT SHE WANTS.
YOU KISSED HER?
NO.
SHE'S A BIT TOO SKINNY.
CRAMPS MY STYL
YOU'RE NUTS! SHE'S GORGEOUS.
WHAT'S HER NAME?
PEGGY.
WHY WAS SHE TAKING DOWN ALL THOSE BOOKS?
I GAVE 'EM TO HER.
YOU DIDN'T GIVE HER THE ADVENTURES OF JIM THUNDER?
YUP.
NO WAY! HOW COULD YOU?
I HAVEN'T FIN-ISHED IT.
YOU SHOULD READ FASTER, THAT'S ALL.
BASTARD!
HEY! THEY'RE MY BOOKS!
YEAH, BUT THAT ONE'S OUT OF PRINT - YOU TOLD ME SO YOURSELF. I WANT TO KNOW HOW IT ENDS.
I'LL TELL YOU.
PLUS, YOU'RE NOT EVEN BANGING HER.
BUT SHE CAME INTO YOUR ROOM, DAMMIT!
MY OFFICE.
?
I TOLD HER I WRITE STORIES LIKE IN MY BOOKS.
AAAH, THAT'S WHY.
BUT WHAT WERE YOU DOING ALL THAT TIME?
I TOLD HER STORIES.
AMAZING STUFF.
I DIDN'T MANAGE TO MAKE HER LAUGH.
SHE LOOKED AT ME WITH THAT LITTLE AWKWARD LOOK OF HERS, LIKE SHE DIDN'T GET IT.
CRAMPS MY STYLE.
I TOLD HER THE STORY OF WHEN WE HELD UP THE BONDSVILLE TRAIN.
SHE LAUGHED?
SHE DIDN'T LAUGH.
THAT'S WEIRD.
BUT SHE DID COME TO SEE YOU.
SHE WANTS YOU.
REALLY?
SALOON
ROOMS
WHISKEY B
16

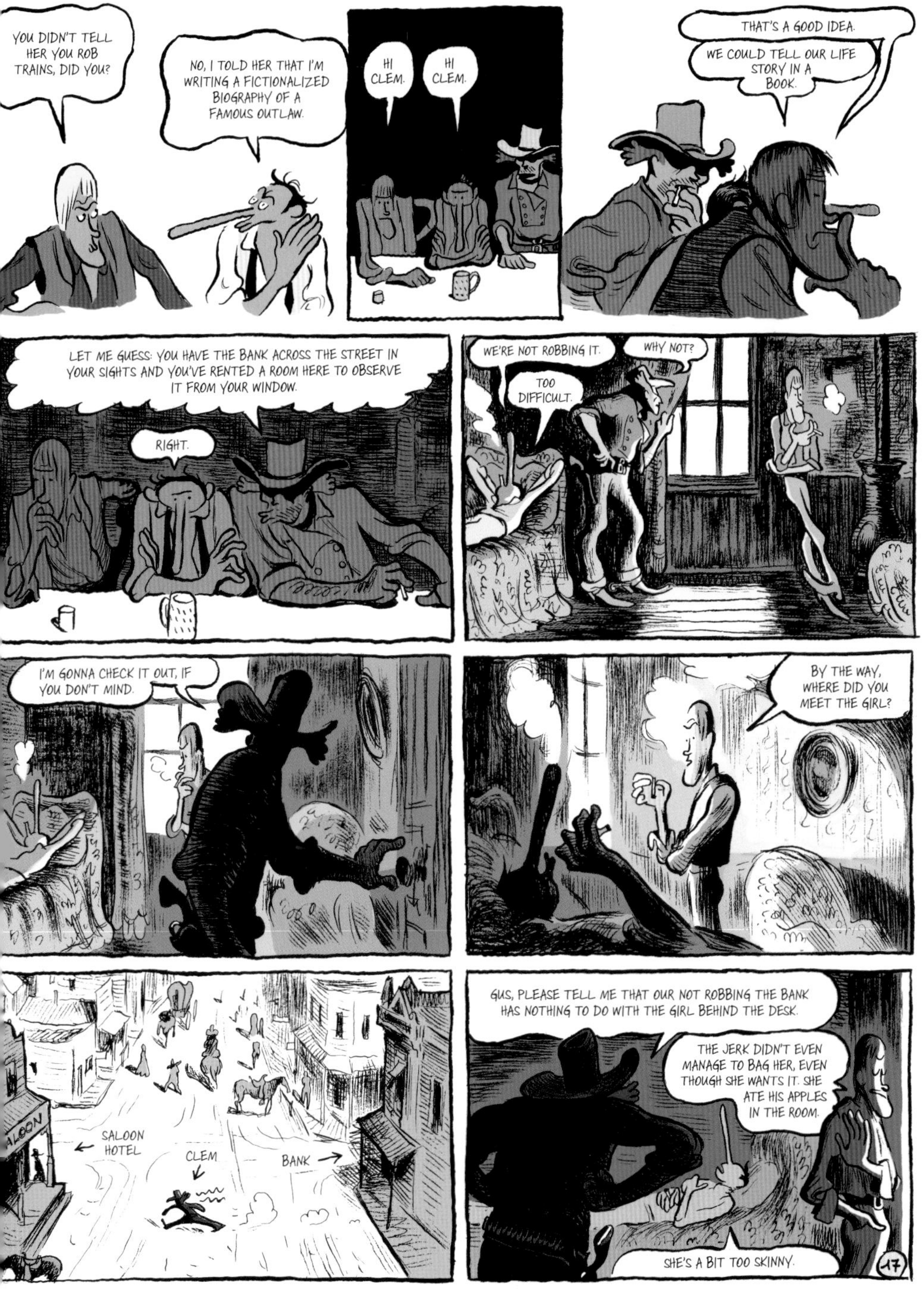
YOU DIDN'T TELL HER YOU ROB TRAINS, DID YOU?
NO, I TOLD HER THAT I'M WRITING A FICTIONALIZED BIOGRAPHY OF A FAMOUS OUTLAW.
HI CLEM.
HI CLEM.
THAT'S A GOOD IDEA.
WE COULD TELL OUR LIFE STORY IN A BOOK.
LET ME GUESS: YOU HAVE THE BANK ACROSS THE STREET IN YOUR SIGHTS AND YOU'VE RENTED A ROOM HERE TO OBSERVE IT FROM YOUR WINDOW.
RIGHT.
WE'RE NOT ROBBING IT.
WHY NOT?
TOO DIFFICULT.
I'M GONNA CHECK IT OUT, IF YOU DON'T MIND.
BY THE WAY, WHERE DID YOU MEET THE GIRL?
SALOON
SALOON HOTEL
CLEM
BANK
GUS, PLEASE TELL ME THAT OUR NOT ROBBING THE BANK HAS NOTHING TO DO WITH THE GIRL BEHIND THE DESK.
THE JERK DIDN'T EVEN MANAGE TO BAG HER, EVEN THOUGH SHE WANTS IT. SHE ATE HIS APPLES IN THE ROOM.
SHE'S A BIT TOO SKINNY.
17

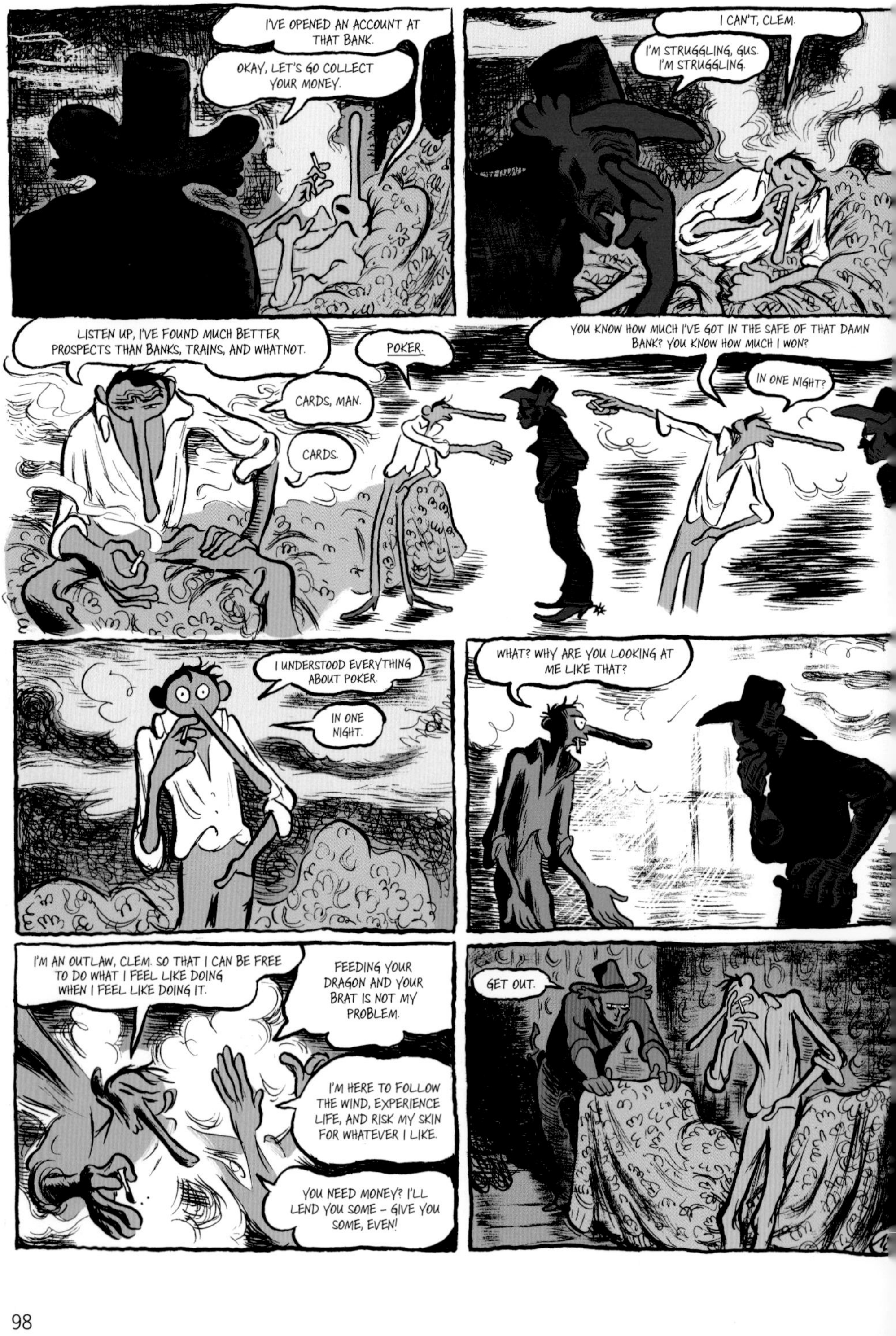
I'VE OPENED AN ACCOUNT AT THAT BANK.
OKAY, LET'S GO COLLECT YOUR MONEY.
I CAN'T, CLEM.
I'M STRUGGLING, GUS. I'M STRUGGLING.
LISTEN UP, I'VE FOUND MUCH BETTER PROSPECTS THAN BANKS, TRAINS, AND WHATNOT.
CARDS, MAN.
CARDS.
POKER.
YOU KNOW HOW MUCH I'VE GOT IN THE SAFE OF THAT DAMN BANK? YOU KNOW HOW MUCH I WON?
IN ONE NIGHT?
I UNDERSTOOD EVERYTHING ABOUT POKER.
IN ONE NIGHT.
WHAT? WHY ARE YOU LOOKING AT ME LIKE THAT?
I'M AN OUTLAW, CLEM. SO THAT I CAN BE FREE TO DO WHAT I FEEL LIKE DOING WHEN I FEEL LIKE DOING IT.
FEEDING YOUR DRAGON AND YOUR BRAT IS NOT MY PROBLEM.
I'M HERE TO FOLLOW THE WIND, EXPERIENCE LIFE, AND RISK MY SKIN FOR WHATEVER I LIKE.
YOU NEED MONEY? I'LL LEND YOU SOME - GIVE YOU SOME, EVEN!
GET OUT.

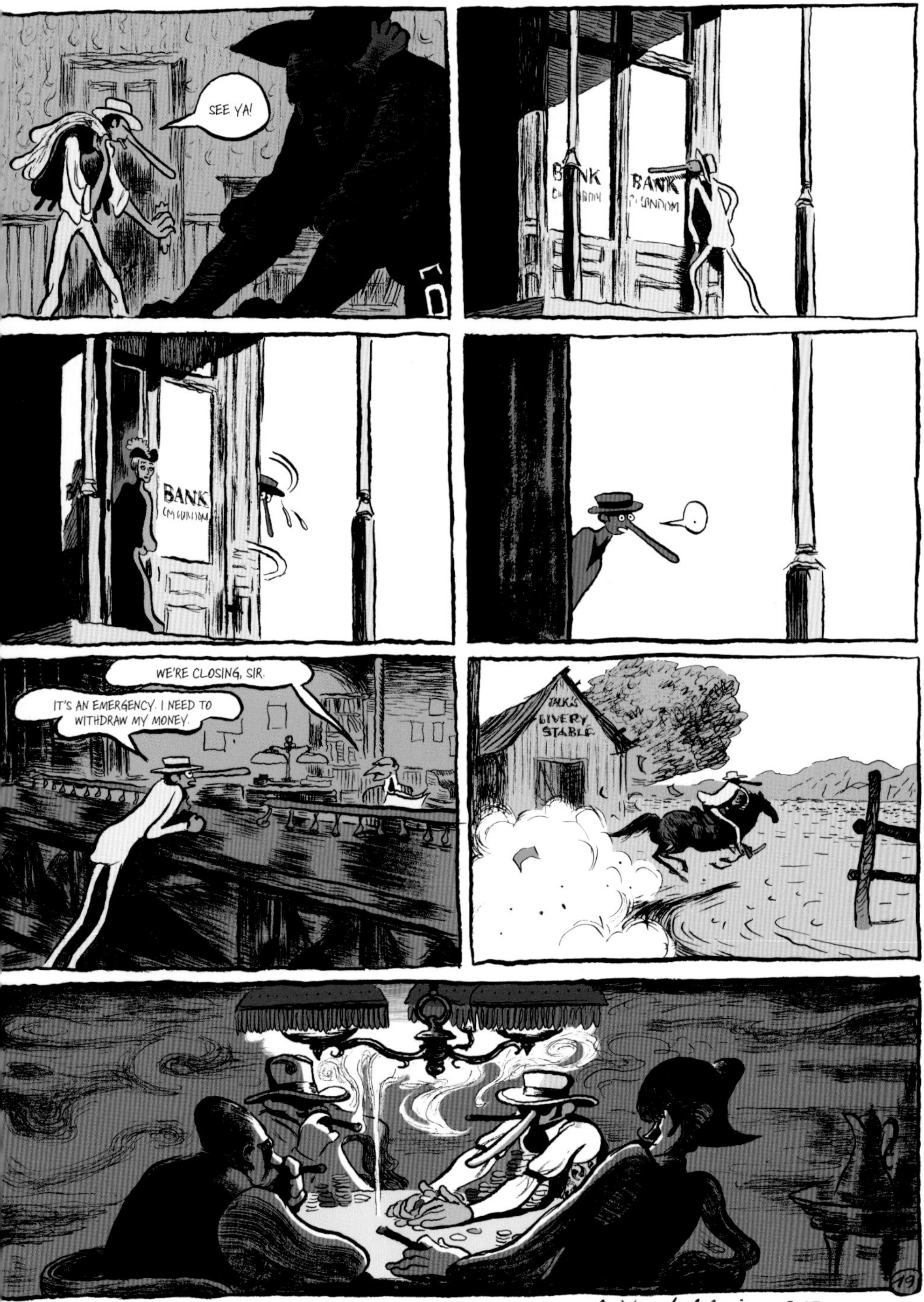
SEE YA!
BANK
BANK
BANK
WE'RE CLOSING, SIR.
IT'S AN EMERGENCY. I NEED TO WITHDRAW MY MONEY.
JACK'S LIVERY STABLE
19

Christopheblain 03.07

ADIOS

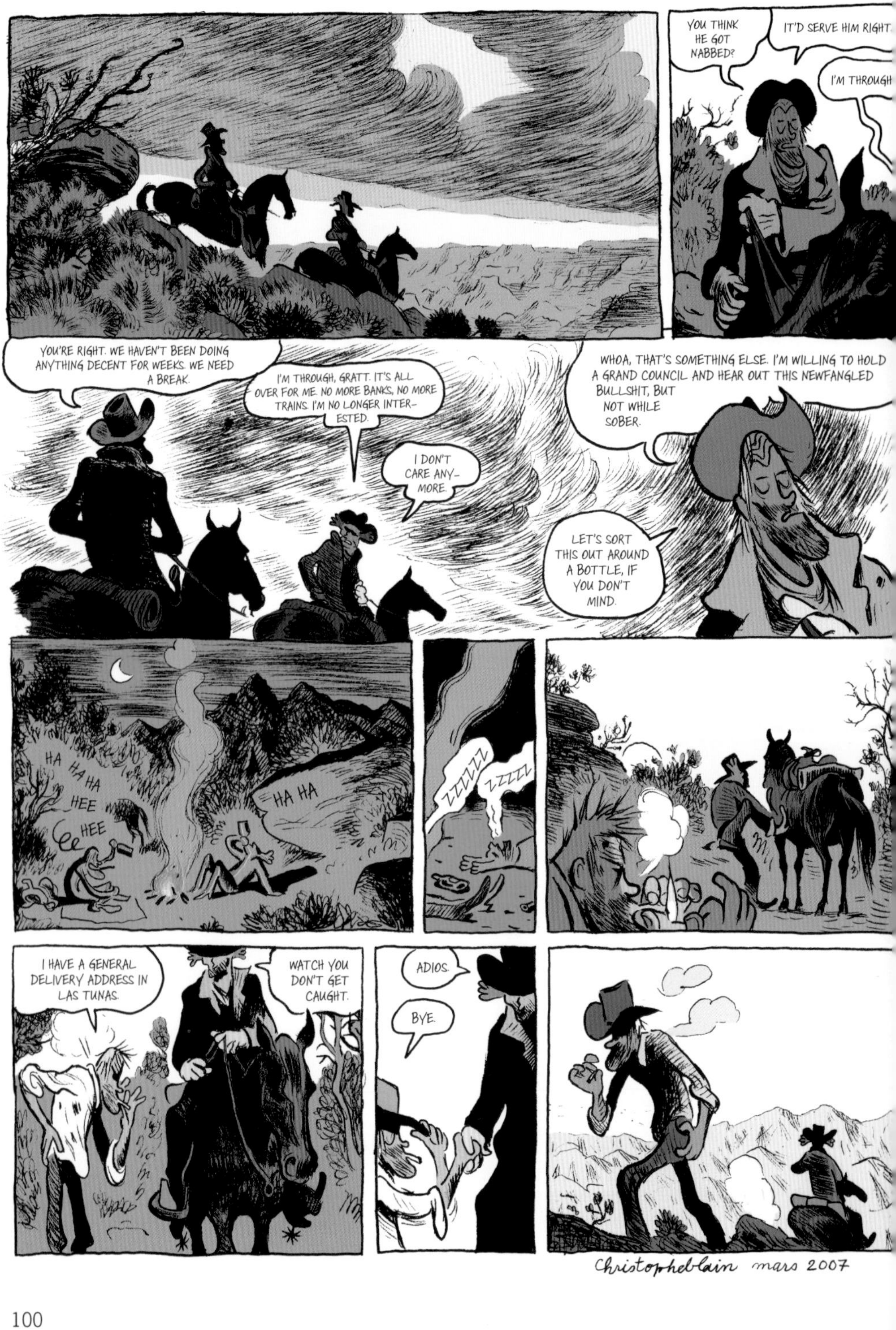
YOU THINK HE GOT NABBED?
IT'D SERVE HIM RIGHT.
I'M THROUGH
YOU'RE RIGHT. WE HAVEN'T BEEN DOING ANYTHING DECENT FOR WEEKS. WE NEED A BREAK.
I'M THROUGH, GRATT. IT'S ALL OVER FOR ME. NO MORE BANKS, NO MORE TRAINS. I'M NO LONGER INTER-ESTED.
I DON'T CARE ANY-MORE.
WHOA, THAT'S SOMETHING ELSE. I'M WILLING TO HOLD A GRAND COUNCIL AND HEAR OUT THIS NEWFANGLED BULLSHIT, BUT NOT WHILE SOBER.
LET'S SORT THIS OUT AROUND A BOTTLE, IF YOU DON'T MIND.
HA HA HA HEE HEE
HA HA
ZZZZZZ
ZZZZZ
I HAVE A GENERAL DELIVERY ADDRESS IN LAS TUNAS.
WATCH YOU DON'T GET CAUGHT.
ADIOS.
BYE.
Christophe Blain mars 2007

TRIUMPH

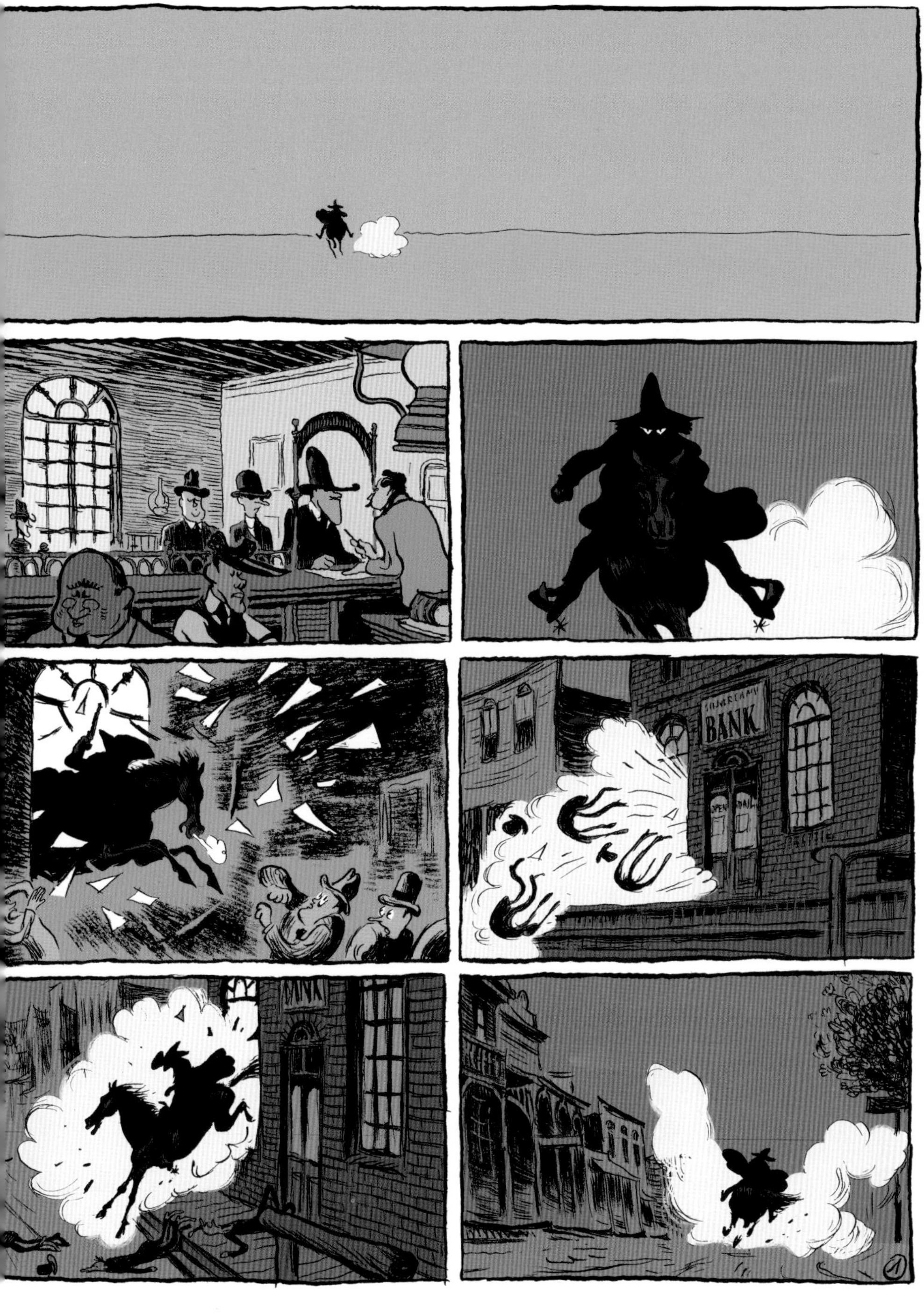
BANK
OPEN
BANK

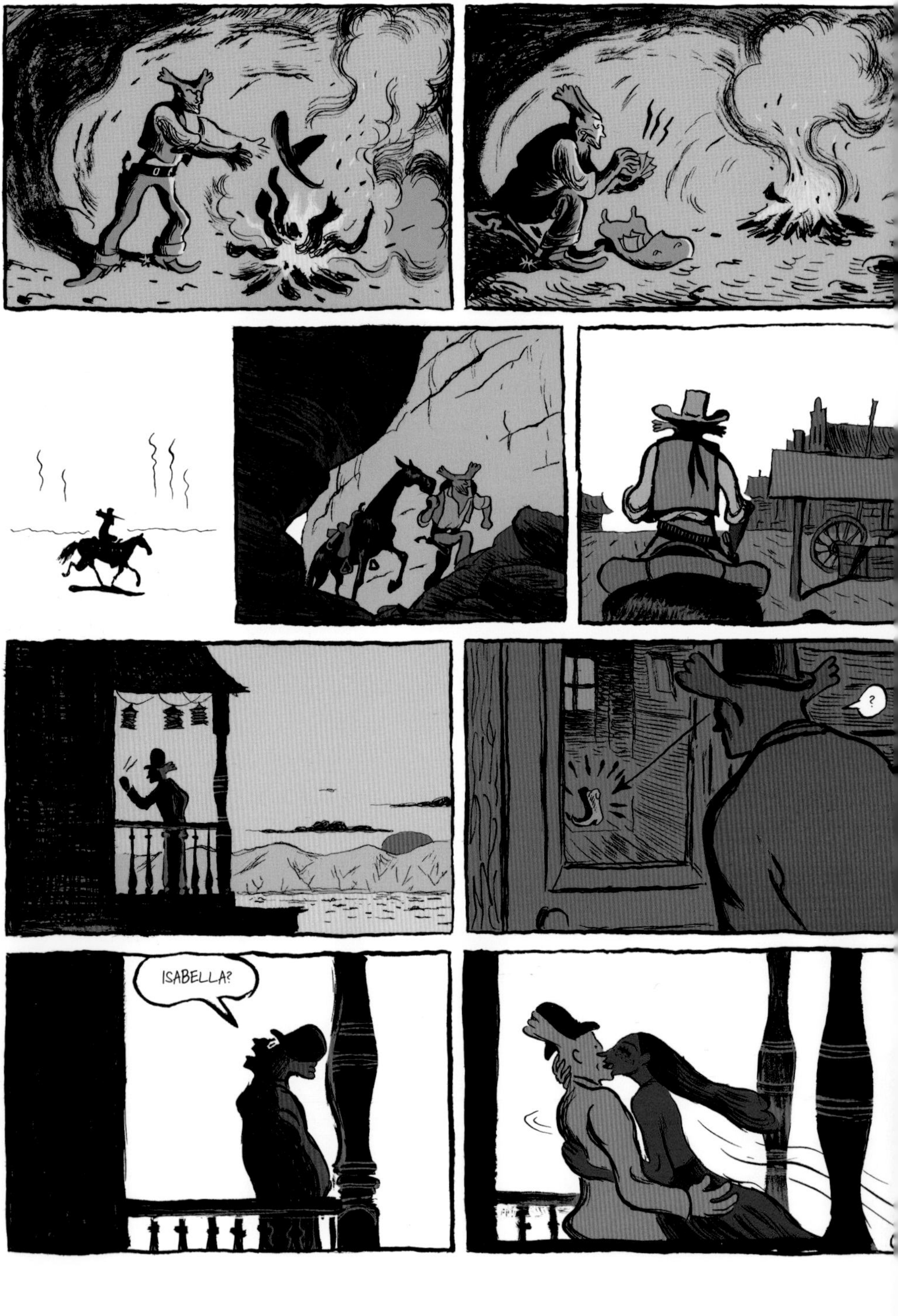
?
ISABELLA?

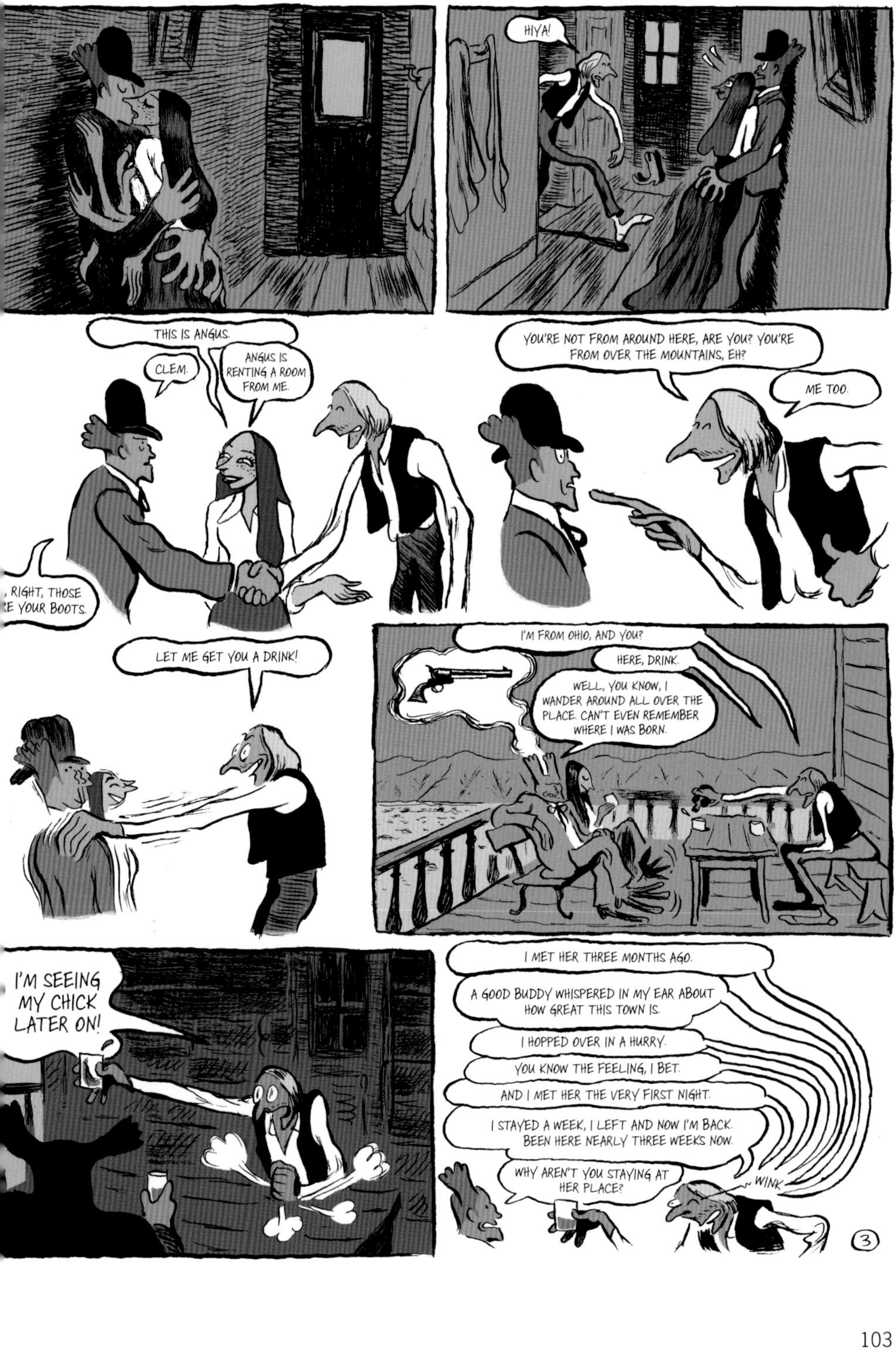
HIYA!
THIS IS ANGUS.
CLEM.
ANGUS IS RENTING A ROOM FROM ME.
, RIGHT, THOSE
E YOUR BOOTS.
YOU'RE NOT FROM AROUND HERE, ARE YOU? YOU'RE FROM OVER THE MOUNTAINS, EH?
ME TOO.
LET ME GET YOU A DRINK!
I'M FROM OHIO, AND YOU?
HERE, DRINK.
WELL, YOU KNOW, I WANDER AROUND ALL OVER THE PLACE. CAN'T EVEN REMEMBER WHERE I WAS BORN.
I'M SEEING MY CHICK LATER ON!
I MET HER THREE MONTHS AGO.
A GOOD BUDDY WHISPERED IN MY EAR ABOUT HOW GREAT THIS TOWN IS.
I HOPPED OVER IN A HURRY.
YOU KNOW THE FEELING, I BET.
AND I MET HER THE VERY FIRST NIGHT.
I STAYED A WEEK, I LEFT AND NOW I'M BACK. BEEN HERE NEARLY THREE WEEKS NOW.
WHY AREN'T YOU STAYING AT HER PLACE?
WINK
3

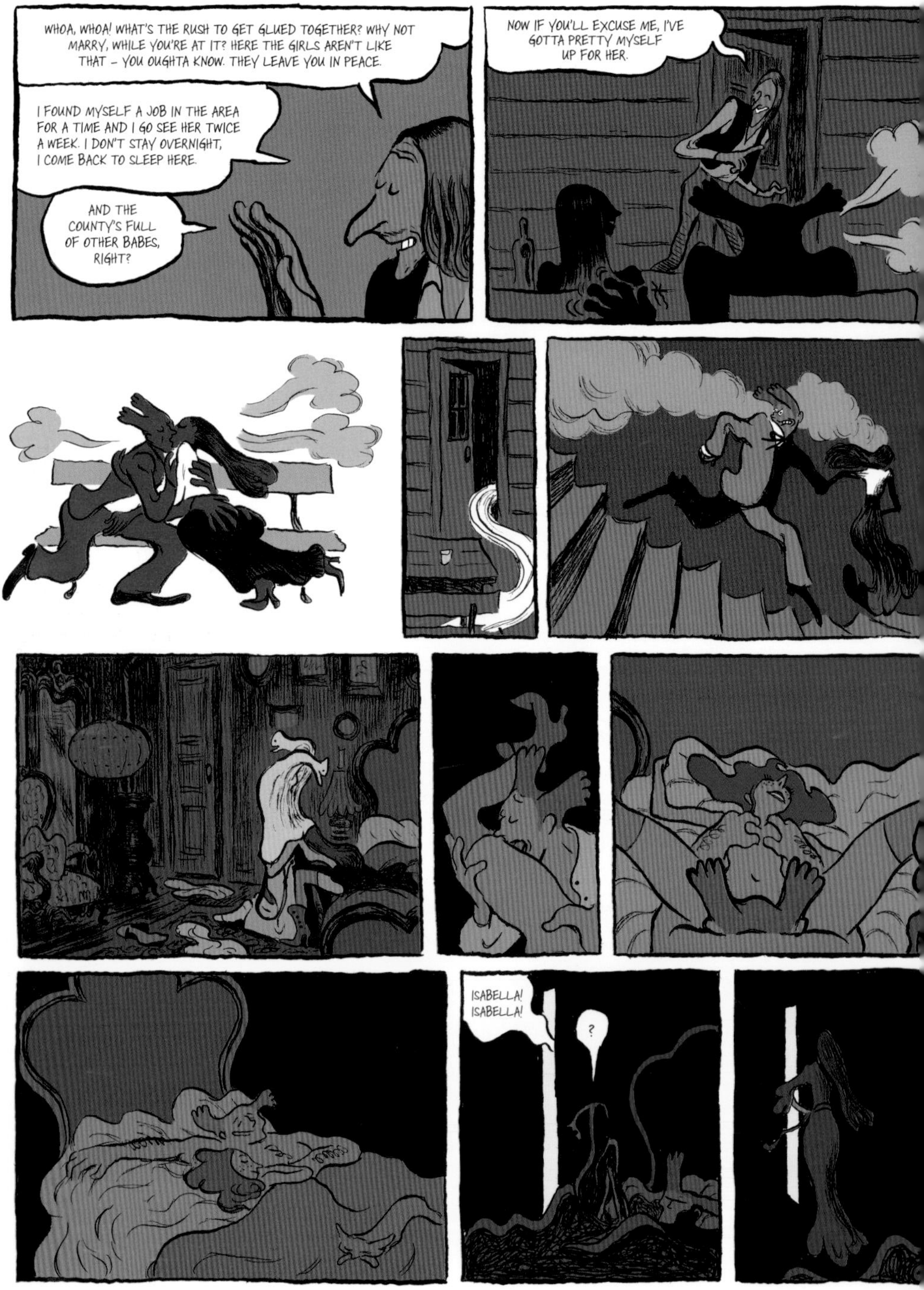
WHOA, WHOA! WHAT'S THE RUSH TO GET GLUED TOGETHER? WHY NOT MARRY, WHILE YOU'RE AT IT? HERE THE GIRLS AREN'T LIKE THAT – YOU OUGHTA KNOW. THEY LEAVE YOU IN PEACE.
I FOUND MYSELF A JOB IN THE AREA FOR A TIME AND I GO SEE HER TWICE A WEEK. I DON'T STAY OVERNIGHT, I COME BACK TO SLEEP HERE.
AND THE COUNTY'S FULL OF OTHER BABES, RIGHT?
NOW IF YOU'LL EXCUSE ME, I'VE GOTTA PRETTY MYSELF UP FOR HER.
ISABELLA! ISABELLA!
?

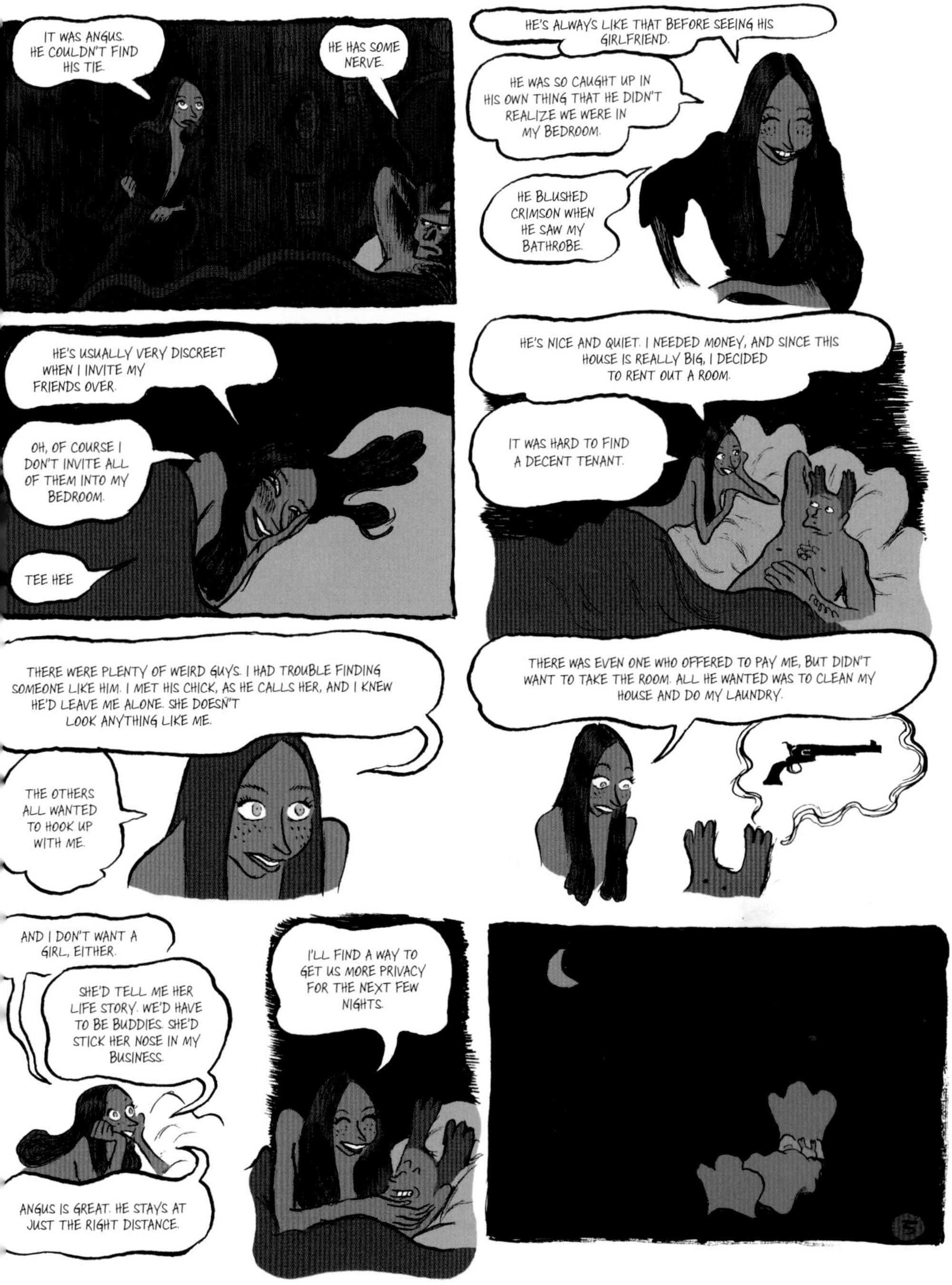
IT WAS ANGUS. HE COULDN'T FIND HIS TIE.
HE HAS SOME NERVE.
HE'S ALWAYS LIKE THAT BEFORE SEEING HIS GIRLFRIEND.
HE WAS SO CAUGHT UP IN HIS OWN THING THAT HE DIDN'T REALIZE WE WERE IN MY BEDROOM.
HE BLUSHED CRIMSON WHEN HE SAW MY BATHROBE.
HE'S USUALLY VERY DISCREET WHEN I INVITE MY FRIENDS OVER.
OH, OF COURSE I DON'T INVITE ALL OF THEM INTO MY BEDROOM.
TEE HEE
HE'S NICE AND QUIET. I NEEDED MONEY, AND SINCE THIS HOUSE IS REALLY BIG, I DECIDED TO RENT OUT A ROOM.
IT WAS HARD TO FIND A DECENT TENANT.
THERE WERE PLENTY OF WEIRD GUYS. I HAD TROUBLE FINDING SOMEONE LIKE HIM. I MET HIS CHICK, AS HE CALLS HER, AND I KNEW HE'D LEAVE ME ALONE. SHE DOESN'T LOOK ANYTHING LIKE ME.
THE OTHERS ALL WANTED TO HOOK UP WITH ME.
THERE WAS EVEN ONE WHO OFFERED TO PAY ME, BUT DIDN'T WANT TO TAKE THE ROOM. ALL HE WANTED WAS TO CLEAN MY HOUSE AND DO MY LAUNDRY.
AND I DON'T WANT A GIRL, EITHER.
SHE'D TELL ME HER LIFE STORY. WE'D HAVE TO BE BUDDIES. SHE'D STICK HER NOSE IN MY BUSINESS.
ANGUS IS GREAT. HE STAYS AT JUST THE RIGHT DISTANCE.
I'LL FIND A WAY TO GET US MORE PRIVACY FOR THE NEXT FEW NIGHTS.

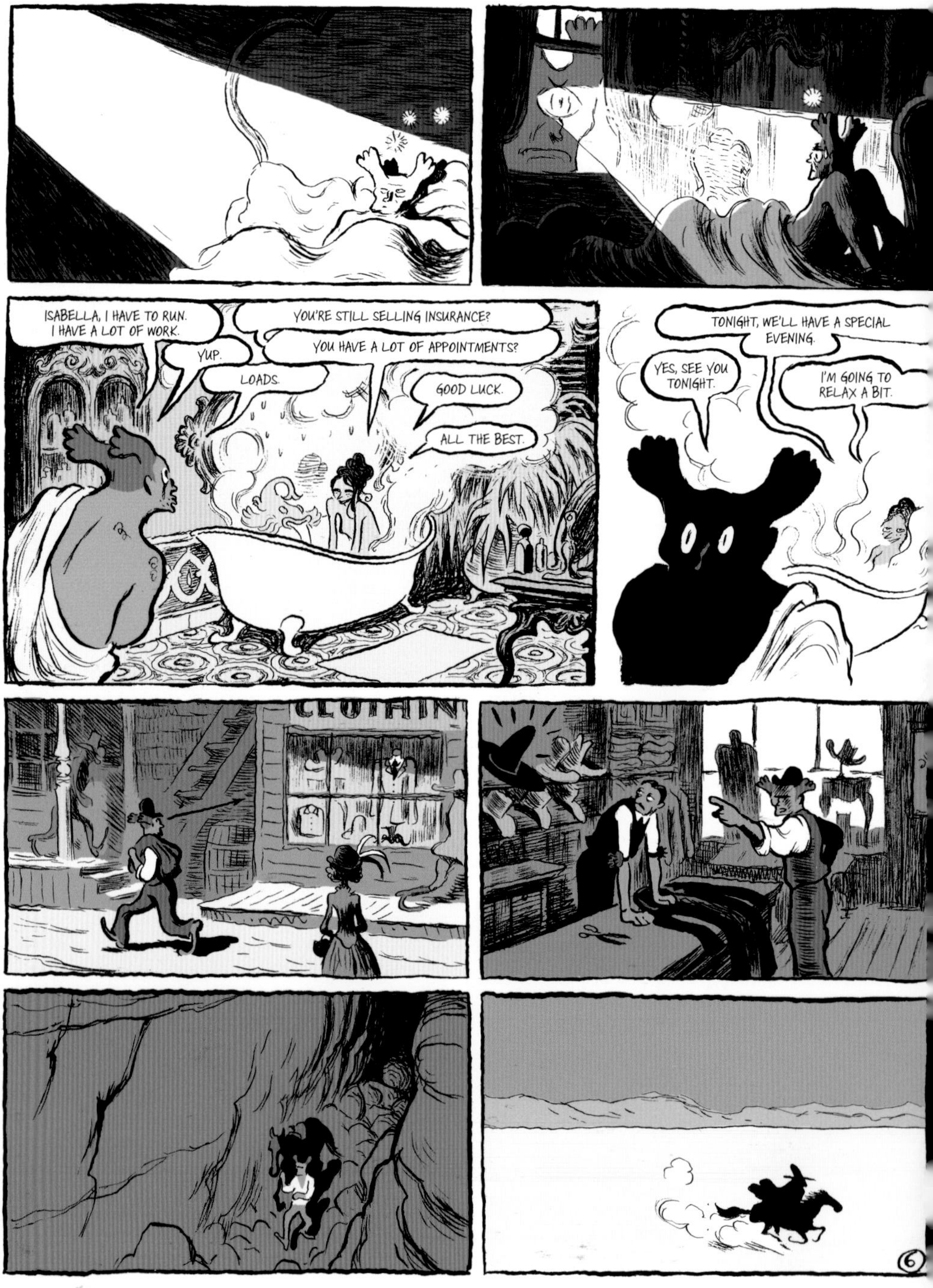
ISABELLA, I HAVE TO RUN. I HAVE A LOT OF WORK.
YOU'RE STILL SELLING INSURANCE?
YUP.
YOU HAVE A LOT OF APPOINTMENTS?
LOADS.
GOOD LUCK.
ALL THE BEST.
TONIGHT, WE'LL HAVE A SPECIAL EVENING.
YES, SEE YOU TONIGHT.
I'M GOING TO RELAX A BIT.
CLOTHIN
6

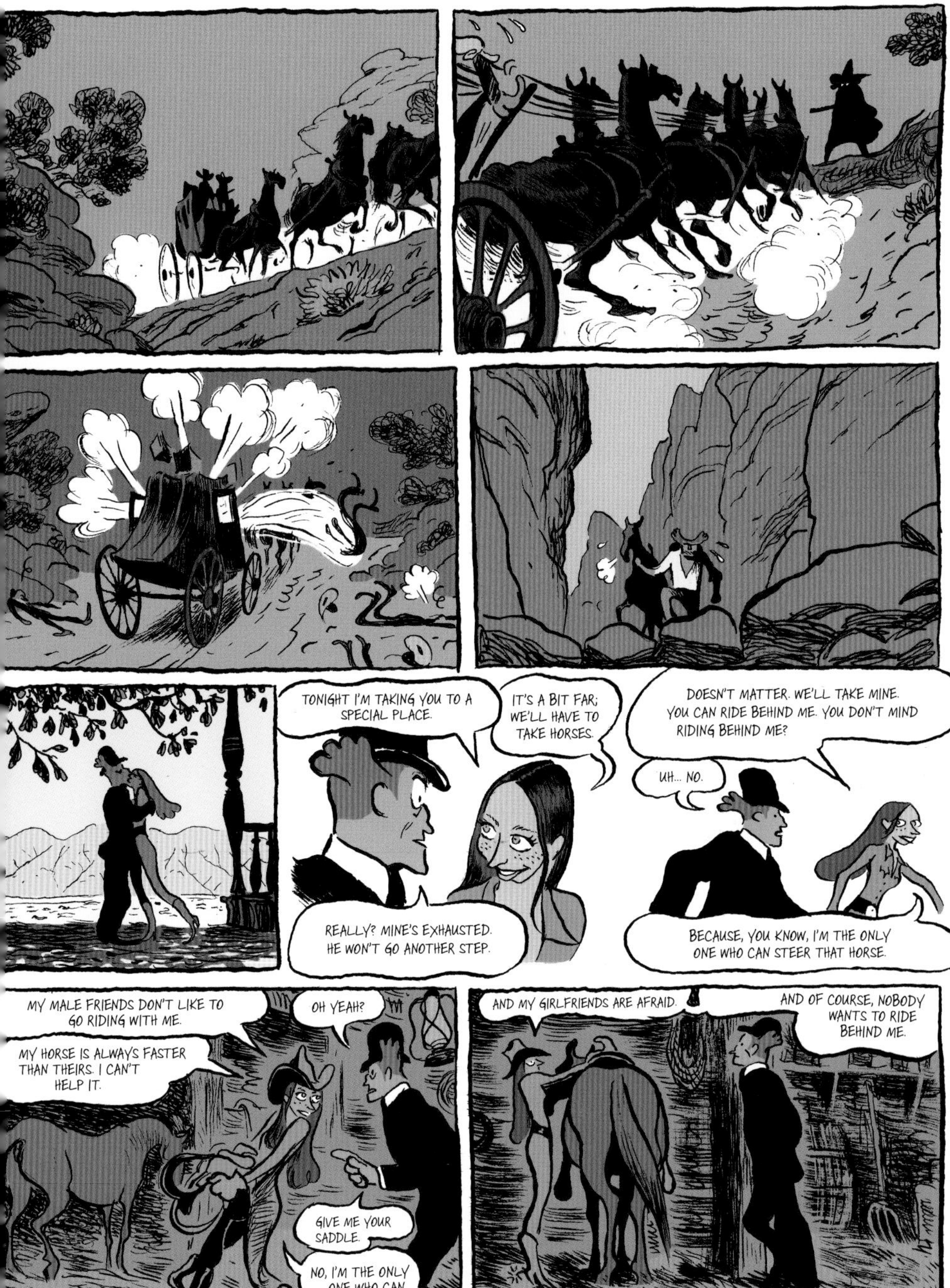
TONIGHT I'M TAKING YOU TO A SPECIAL PLACE.
IT'S A BIT FAR; WE'LL HAVE TO TAKE HORSES.
REALLY? MINE'S EXHAUSTED. HE WON'T GO ANOTHER STEP.
DOESN'T MATTER. WE'LL TAKE MINE. YOU CAN RIDE BEHIND ME. YOU DON'T MIND RIDING BEHIND ME?
UH... NO.
BECAUSE, YOU KNOW, I'M THE ONLY ONE WHO CAN STEER THAT HORSE.
MY MALE FRIENDS DON'T LIKE TO GO RIDING WITH ME.
MY HORSE IS ALWAYS FASTER THAN THEIRS. I CAN'T HELP IT.
OH YEAH?
GIVE ME YOUR SADDLE.
NO, I'M THE ONLY ONE WHO CAN SADDLE HIM.
AND MY GIRLFRIENDS ARE AFRAID.
AND OF COURSE, NOBODY WANTS TO RIDE BEHIND ME.
7

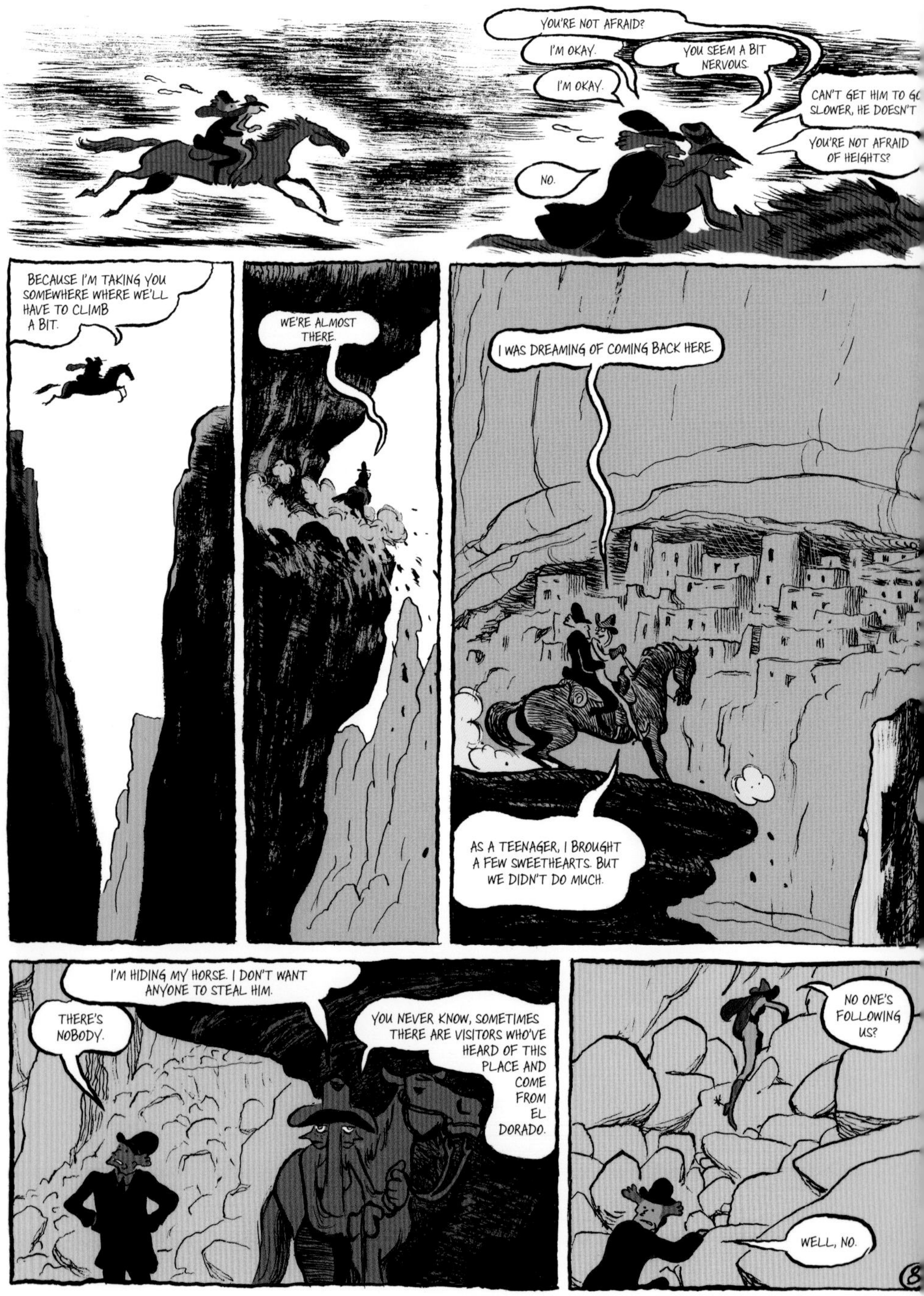
YOU'RE NOT AFRAID?
I'M OKAY.
YOU SEEM A BIT NERVOUS.
I'M OKAY.
CAN'T GET HIM TO GO SLOWER, HE DOESN'T
YOU'RE NOT AFRAID OF HEIGHTS?
NO.
BECAUSE I'M TAKING YOU SOMEWHERE WHERE WE'LL HAVE TO CLIMB A BIT.
WE'RE ALMOST THERE.
I WAS DREAMING OF COMING BACK HERE.
AS A TEENAGER, I BROUGHT A FEW SWEETHEARTS. BUT WE DIDN'T DO MUCH.
I'M HIDING MY HORSE. I DON'T WANT ANYONE TO STEAL HIM.
THERE'S NOBODY.
YOU NEVER KNOW, SOMETIMES THERE ARE VISITORS WHO'VE HEARD OF THIS PLACE AND COME FROM EL DORADO.
NO ONE'S FOLLOWING US?
WELL, NO.
8

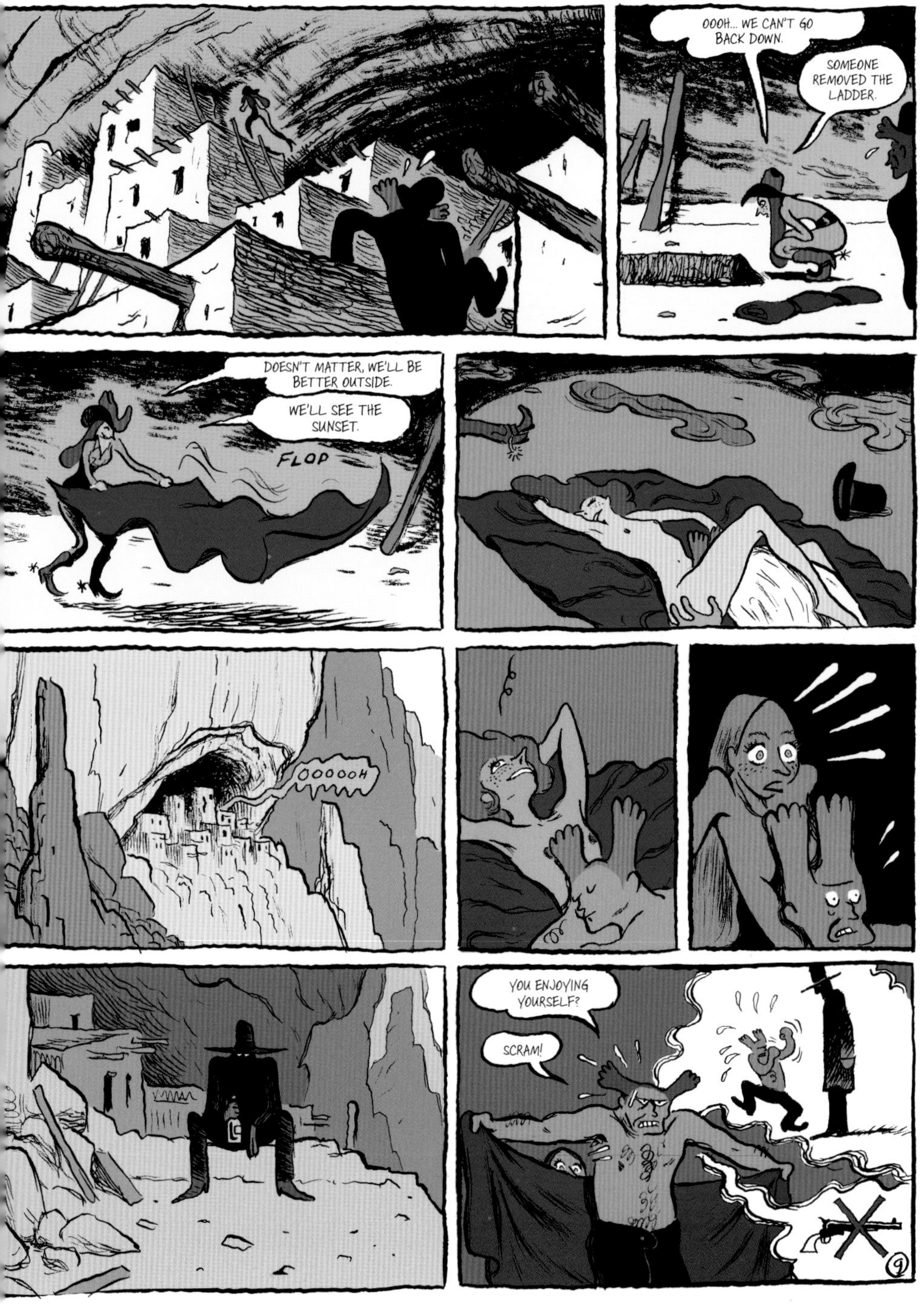
OOOH... WE CAN'T GO BACK DOWN.
SOMEONE REMOVED THE LADDER.
DOESN'T MATTER, WE'LL BE BETTER OUTSIDE.
WE'LL SEE THE SUNSET.
FLOP
OOOOOH
YOU ENJOYING YOURSELF?
SCRAM!

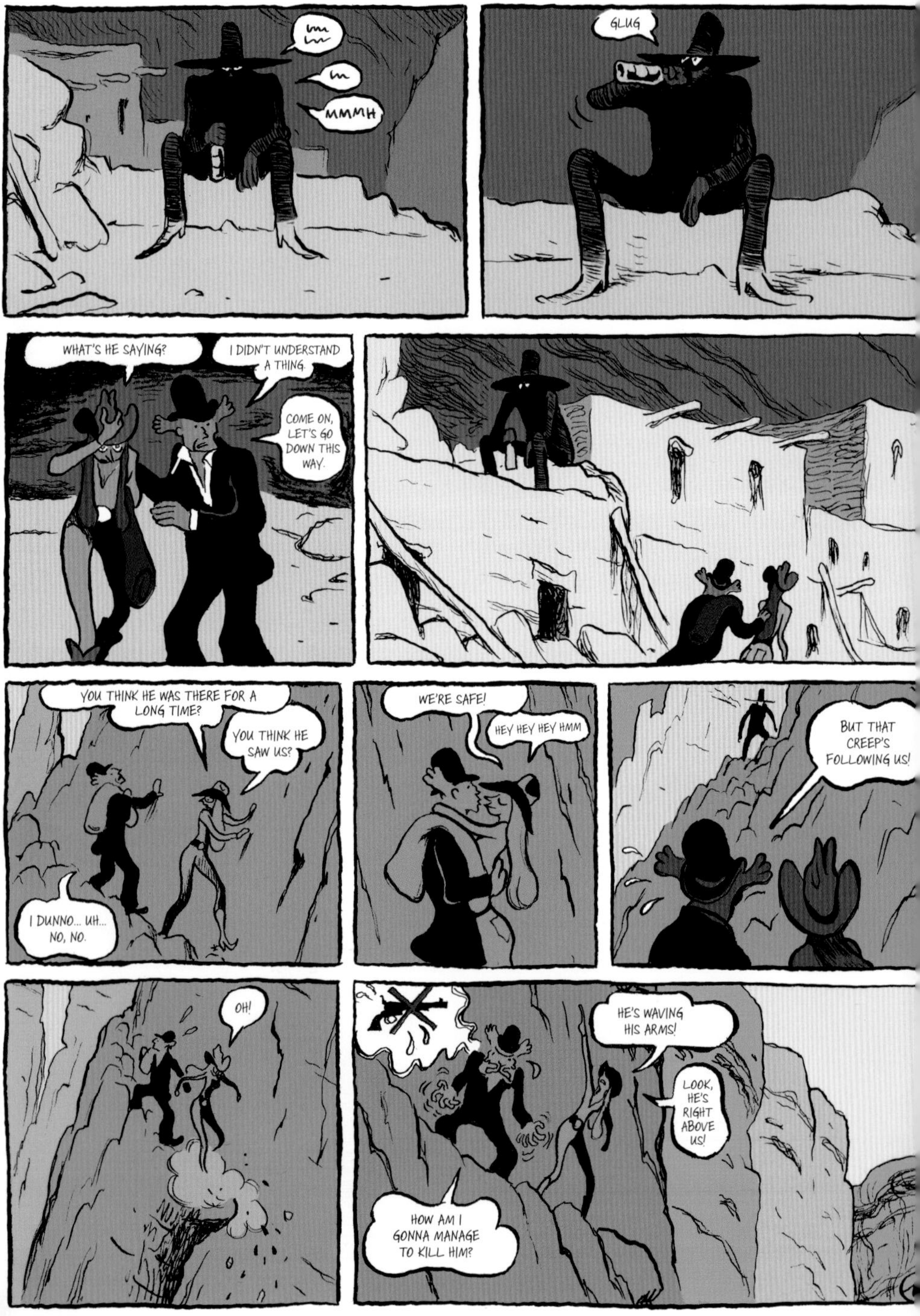

MMMH
GLUG
WHAT'S HE SAYING?
I DIDN'T UNDERSTAND A THING.
COME ON, LET'S GO DOWN THIS WAY.
YOU THINK HE WAS THERE FOR A LONG TIME?
YOU THINK HE SAW US?
I DUNNO... UH... NO, NO.
WE'RE SAFE!
HEY HEY HEY HMM
BUT THAT CREEP'S FOLLOWING US!
OH!
HE'S WAVING HIS ARMS!
LOOK, HE'S RIGHT ABOVE US!
HOW AM I GONNA MANAGE TO KILL HIM?

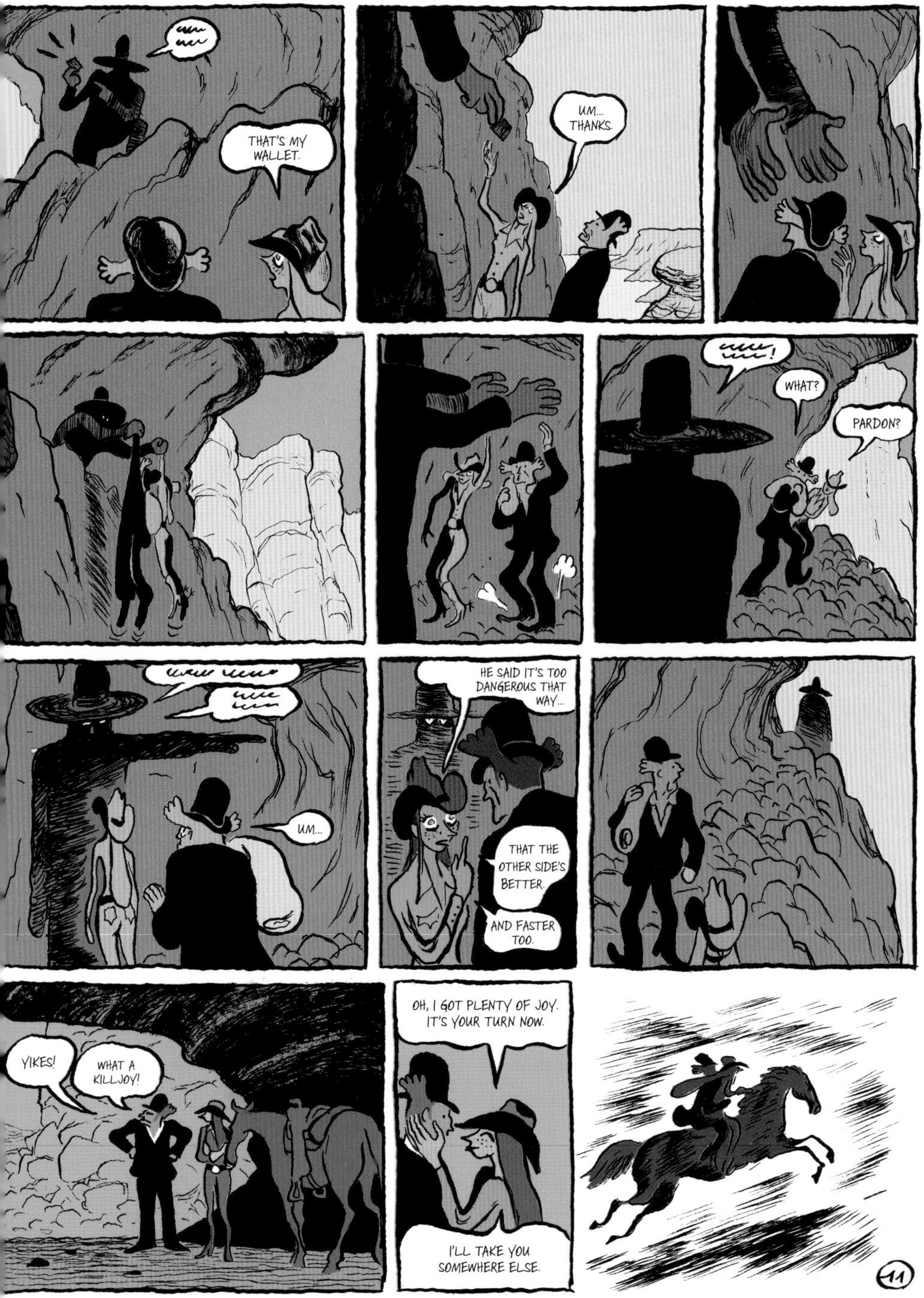
THAT'S MY WALLET.
UM... THANKS.
WHAT?
PARDON?
UM...
HE SAID IT'S TOO DANGEROUS THAT WAY...
THAT THE OTHER SIDE'S BETTER.
AND FASTER TOO.
YIKES!
WHAT A KILLJOY!
OH, I GOT PLENTY OF JOY. IT'S YOUR TURN NOW.
I'LL TAKE YOU SOMEWHERE ELSE.
11

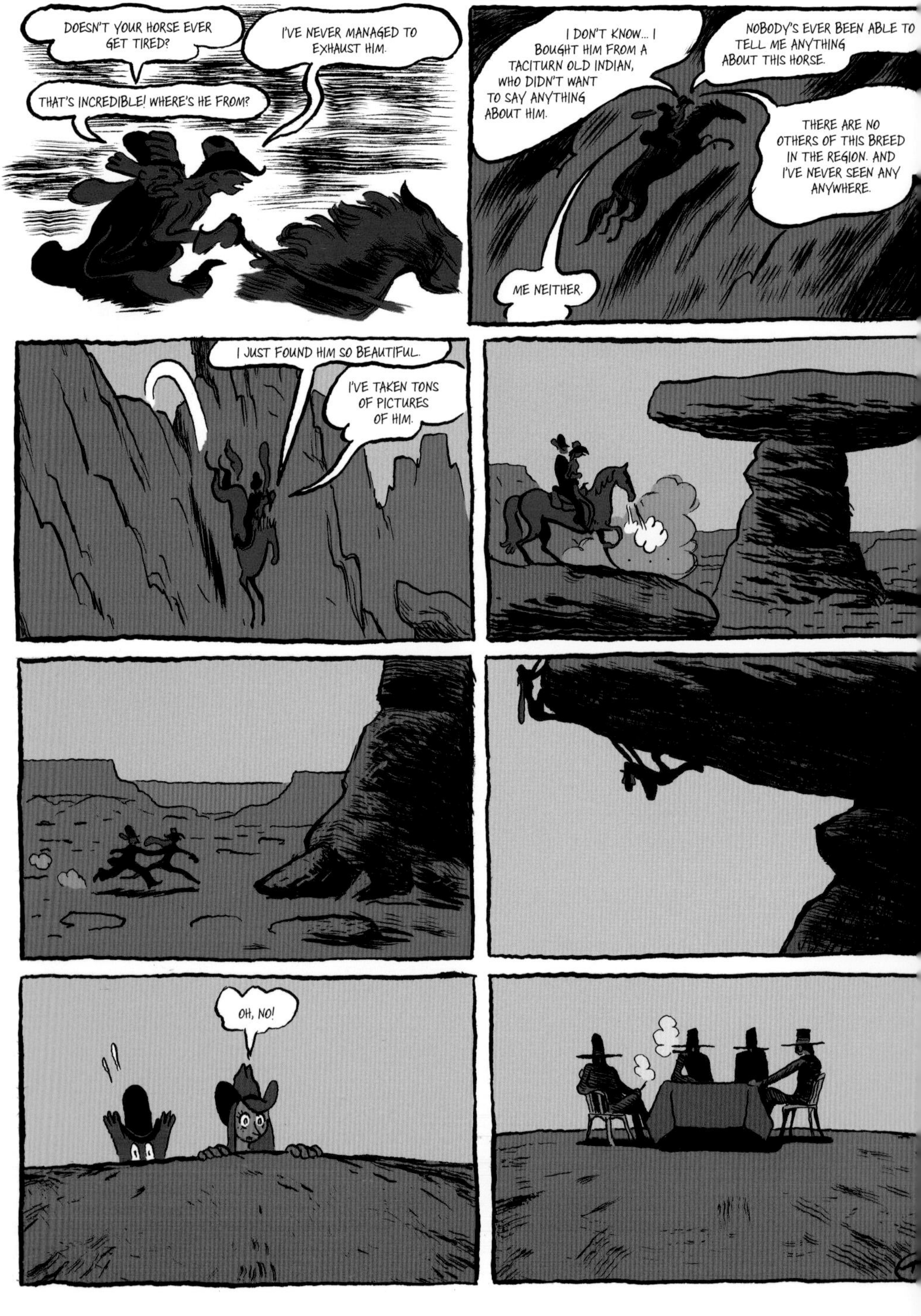
DOESN'T YOUR HORSE EVER GET TIRED?
I'VE NEVER MANAGED TO EXHAUST HIM.
THAT'S INCREDIBLE! WHERE'S HE FROM?
I DON'T KNOW... I BOUGHT HIM FROM A TACITURN OLD INDIAN, WHO DIDN'T WANT TO SAY ANYTHING ABOUT HIM.
NOBODY'S EVER BEEN ABLE TO TELL ME ANYTHING ABOUT THIS HORSE.
THERE ARE NO OTHERS OF THIS BREED IN THE REGION. AND I'VE NEVER SEEN ANY ANYWHERE.
ME NEITHER.
I JUST FOUND HIM SO BEAUTIFUL.
I'VE TAKEN TONS OF PICTURES OF HIM.
OH, NO!

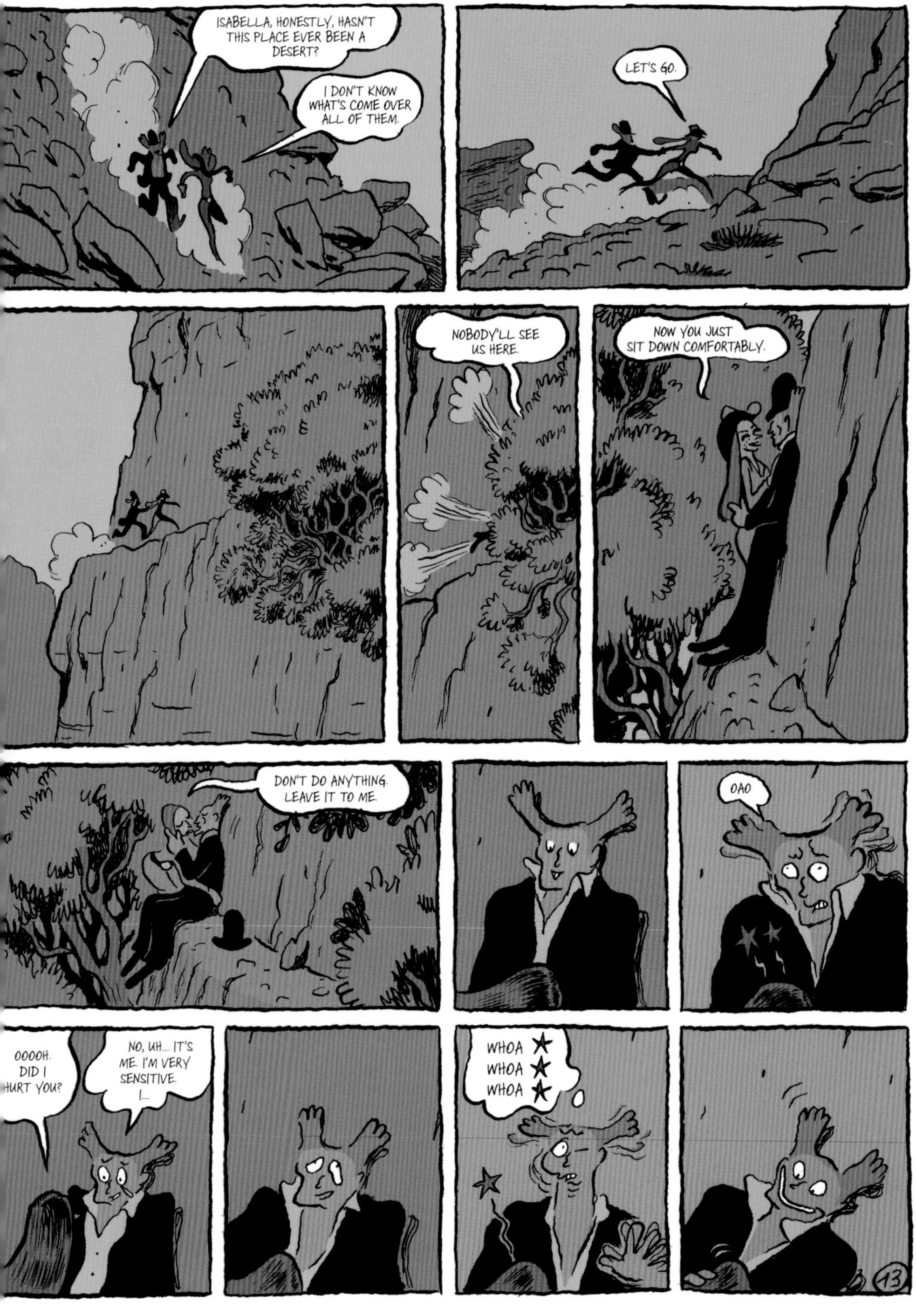
ISABELLA, HONESTLY, HASN'T THIS PLACE EVER BEEN A DESERT?
I DON'T KNOW WHAT'S COME OVER ALL OF THEM.
LET'S GO.
NOBODY'LL SEE US HERE.
NOW YOU JUST SIT DOWN COMFORTABLY.
DON'T DO ANYTHING. LEAVE IT TO ME.
OAO
OOOOH. DID I HURT YOU?
NO, UH... IT'S ME. I'M VERY SENSITIVE. I...
WHOA WHOA WHOA
13

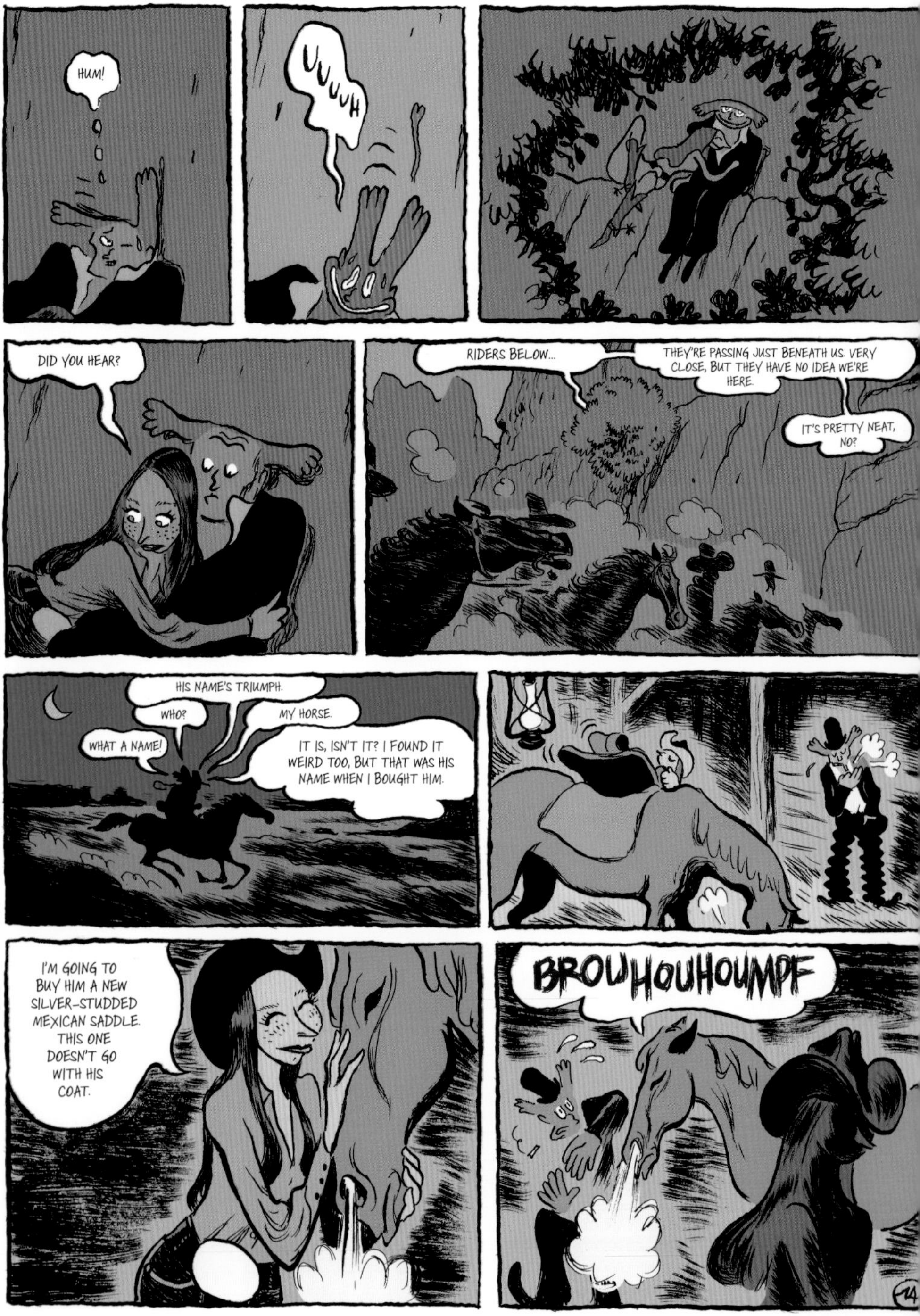
HUM!
UUUUH
DID YOU HEAR?
RIDERS BELOW...
THEY'RE PASSING JUST BENEATH US. VERY CLOSE, BUT THEY HAVE NO IDEA WE'RE HERE.
IT'S PRETTY NEAT, NO?
HIS NAME'S TRIUMPH.
WHO?
MY HORSE.
WHAT A NAME!
IT IS, ISN'T IT? I FOUND IT WEIRD TOO, BUT THAT WAS HIS NAME WHEN I BOUGHT HIM.
I'M GOING TO BUY HIM A NEW SILVER-STUDDED MEXICAN SADDLE. THIS ONE DOESN'T GO WITH HIS COAT.
BROUHOUHOUMPF

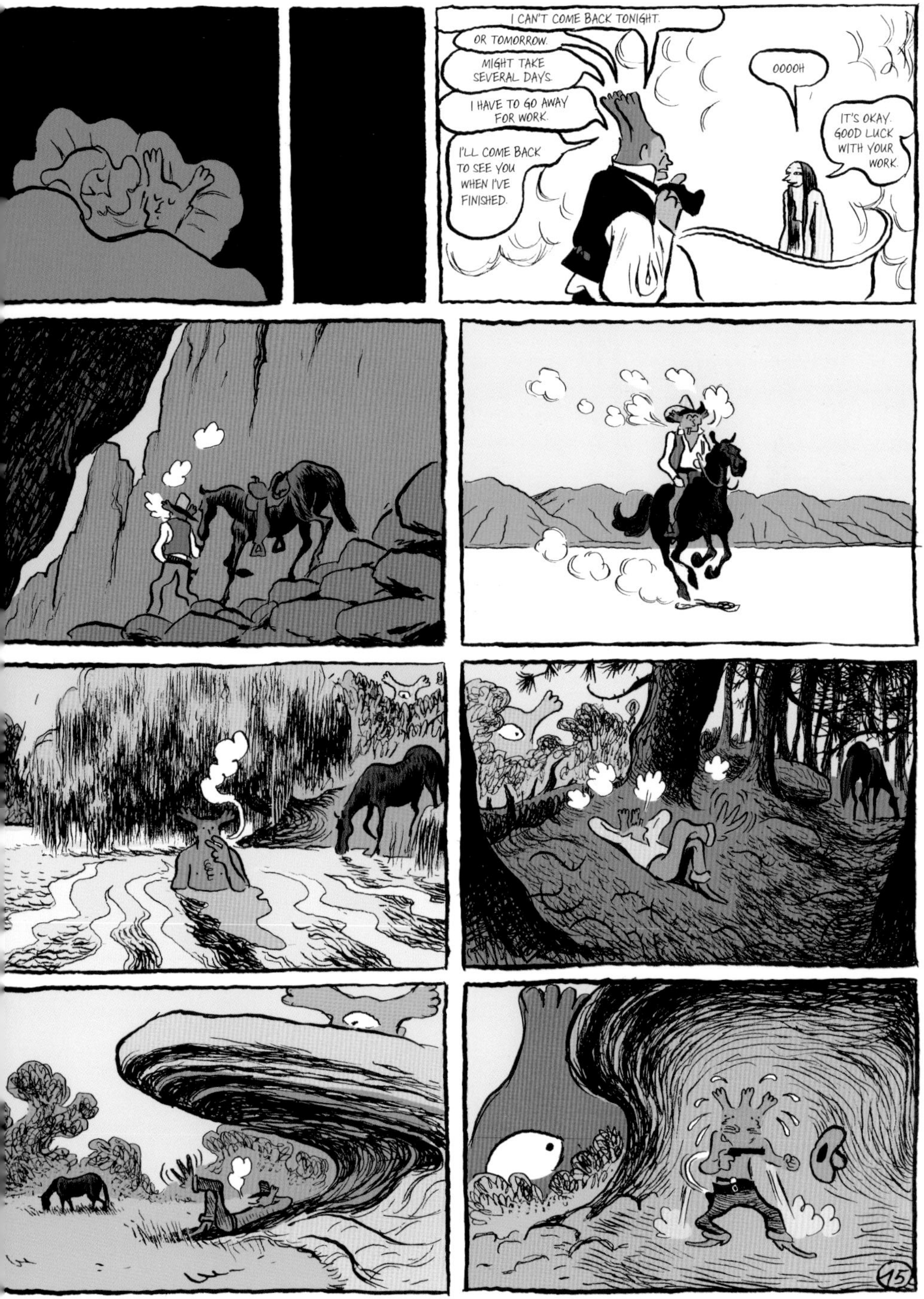
I CAN'T COME BACK TONIGHT.
OR TOMORROW.
MIGHT TAKE SEVERAL DAYS.
I HAVE TO GO AWAY FOR WORK.
I'LL COME BACK TO SEE YOU WHEN I'VE FINISHED.
OOOOH
IT'S OKAY. GOOD LUCK WITH YOUR WORK.
15

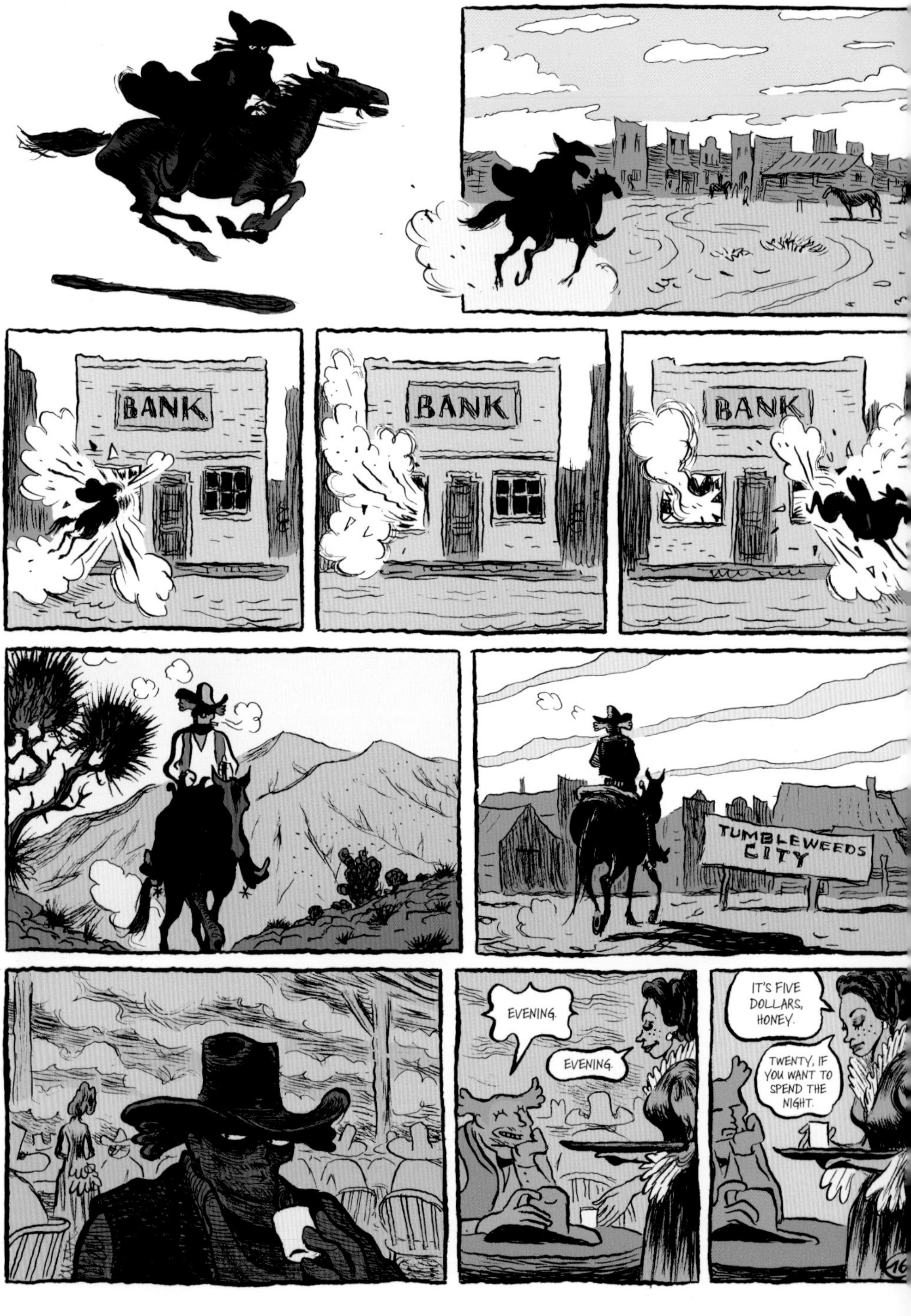
BANK
BANK
BANK
TUMBLEWEEDS CITY
EVENING.
EVENING.
IT'S FIVE DOLLARS, HONEY.
TWENTY, IF YOU WANT TO SPEND THE NIGHT.

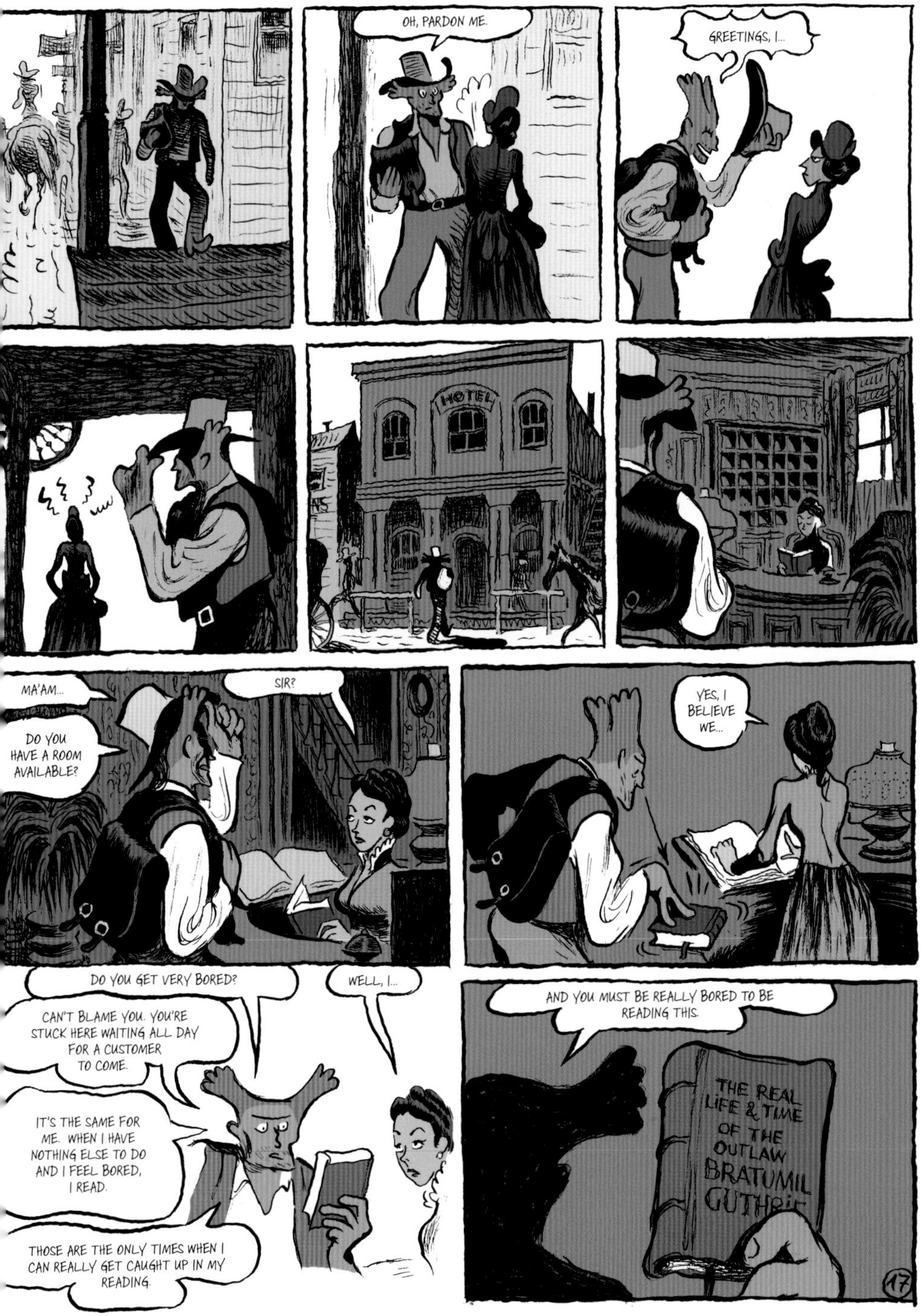

OH, PARDON ME.
GREETINGS, I...
HOTEL
MA'AM...
SIR?
DO YOU HAVE A ROOM AVAILABLE?
YES, I BELIEVE WE...
DO YOU GET VERY BORED?
WELL, I...
CAN'T BLAME YOU. YOU'RE STUCK HERE WAITING ALL DAY FOR A CUSTOMER TO COME.
IT'S THE SAME FOR ME. WHEN I HAVE NOTHING ELSE TO DO AND I FEEL BORED, I READ.
THOSE ARE THE ONLY TIMES WHEN I CAN REALLY GET CAUGHT UP IN MY READING.
AND YOU MUST BE REALLY BORED TO BE READING THIS.
THE REAL LIFE & TIME OF THE OUTLAW BRATUMIL GUTHRi
17

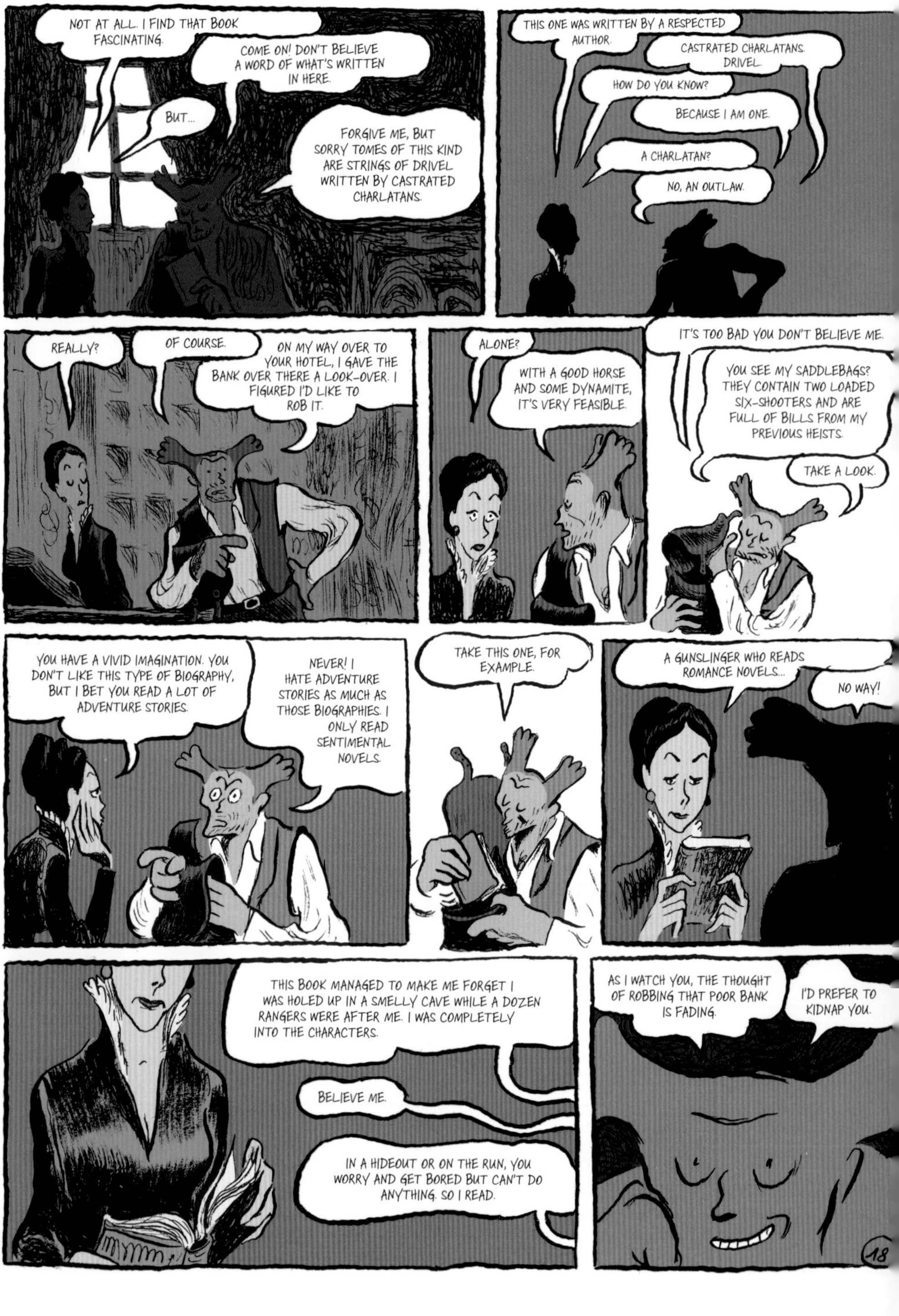
NOT AT ALL. I FIND THAT BOOK FASCINATING.
COME ON! DON'T BELIEVE A WORD OF WHAT'S WRITTEN IN HERE.
BUT...
FORGIVE ME, BUT SORRY TOMES OF THIS KIND ARE STRINGS OF DRIVEL WRITTEN BY CASTRATED CHARLATANS.
THIS ONE WAS WRITTEN BY A RESPECTED AUTHOR.
CASTRATED CHARLATANS. DRIVEL.
HOW DO YOU KNOW?
BECAUSE I AM ONE.
A CHARLATAN?
NO, AN OUTLAW.
REALLY?
OF COURSE.
ON MY WAY OVER TO YOUR HOTEL, I GAVE THE BANK OVER THERE A LOOK-OVER. I FIGURED I'D LIKE TO ROB IT.
ALONE?
WITH A GOOD HORSE AND SOME DYNAMITE, IT'S VERY FEASIBLE.
IT'S TOO BAD YOU DON'T BELIEVE ME.
YOU SEE MY SADDLEBAGS? THEY CONTAIN TWO LOADED SIX-SHOOTERS AND ARE FULL OF BILLS FROM MY PREVIOUS HEISTS.
TAKE A LOOK.
YOU HAVE A VIVID IMAGINATION. YOU DON'T LIKE THIS TYPE OF BIOGRAPHY, BUT I BET YOU READ A LOT OF ADVENTURE STORIES.
NEVER! I HATE ADVENTURE STORIES AS MUCH AS THOSE BIOGRAPHIES. I ONLY READ SENTIMENTAL NOVELS.
TAKE THIS ONE, FOR EXAMPLE.
A GUNSLINGER WHO READS ROMANCE NOVELS...
NO WAY!
THIS BOOK MANAGED TO MAKE ME FORGET I WAS HOLED UP IN A SMELLY CAVE WHILE A DOZEN RANGERS WERE AFTER ME. I WAS COMPLETELY INTO THE CHARACTERS.
BELIEVE ME.
IN A HIDEOUT OR ON THE RUN, YOU WORRY AND GET BORED BUT CAN'T DO ANYTHING. SO I READ.
AS I WATCH YOU, THE THOUGHT OF ROBBING THAT POOR BANK IS FADING.
I'D PREFER TO KIDNAP YOU.
18

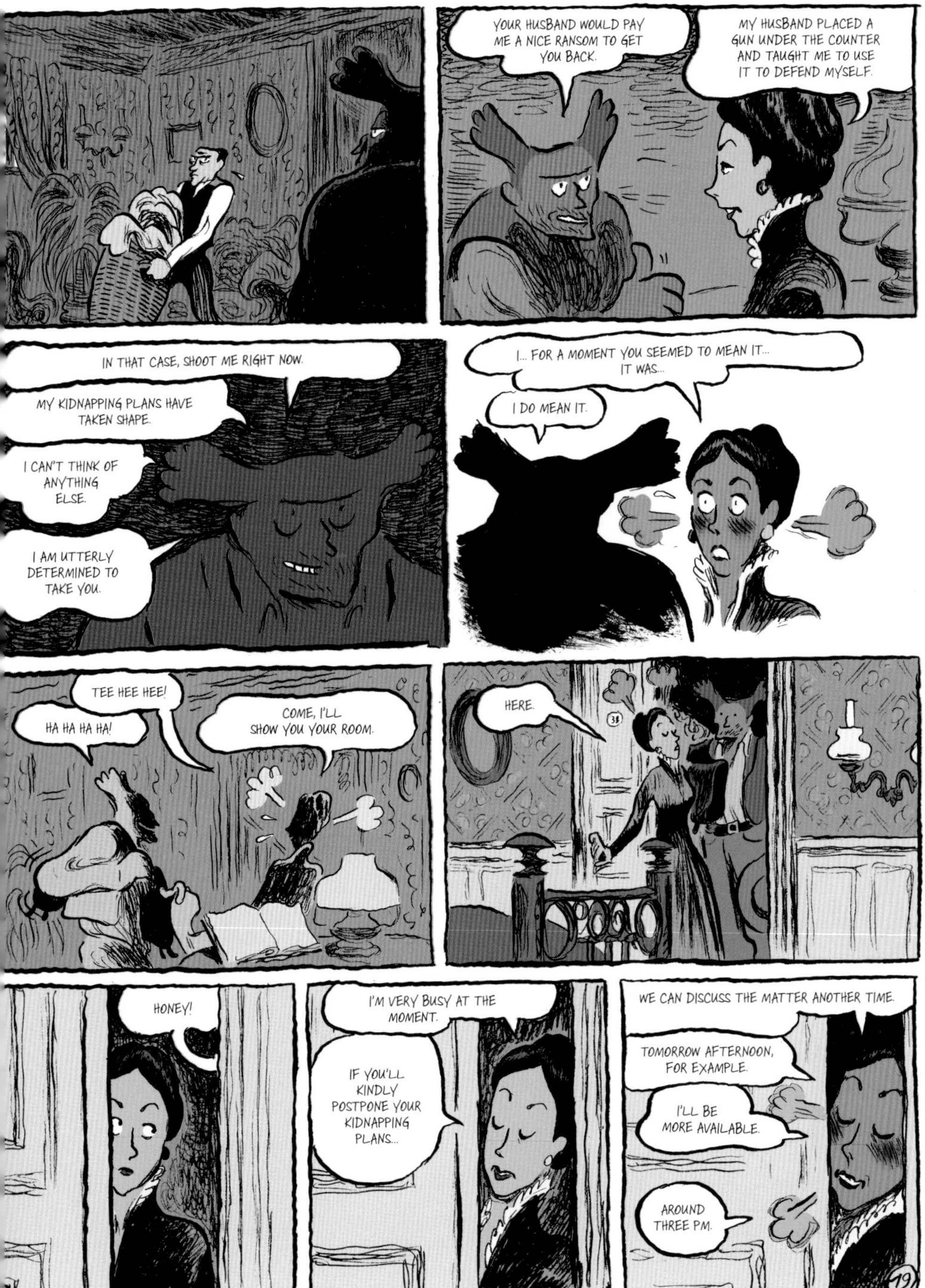

YOUR HUSBAND WOULD PAY ME A NICE RANSOM TO GET YOU BACK.
MY HUSBAND PLACED A GUN UNDER THE COUNTER AND TAUGHT ME TO USE IT TO DEFEND MYSELF.
IN THAT CASE, SHOOT ME RIGHT NOW.
MY KIDNAPPING PLANS HAVE TAKEN SHAPE.
I CAN'T THINK OF ANYTHING ELSE.
I AM UTTERLY DETERMINED TO TAKE YOU.
I... FOR A MOMENT YOU SEEMED TO MEAN IT... IT WAS...
I DO MEAN IT.
TEE HEE HEE!
HA HA HA HA!
COME, I'LL SHOW YOU YOUR ROOM.
HERE.
HONEY!
I'M VERY BUSY AT THE MOMENT.
IF YOU'LL KINDLY POSTPONE YOUR KIDNAPPING PLANS...
WE CAN DISCUSS THE MATTER ANOTHER TIME.
TOMORROW AFTERNOON, FOR EXAMPLE.
I'LL BE MORE AVAILABLE.
AROUND THREE P.M.
19

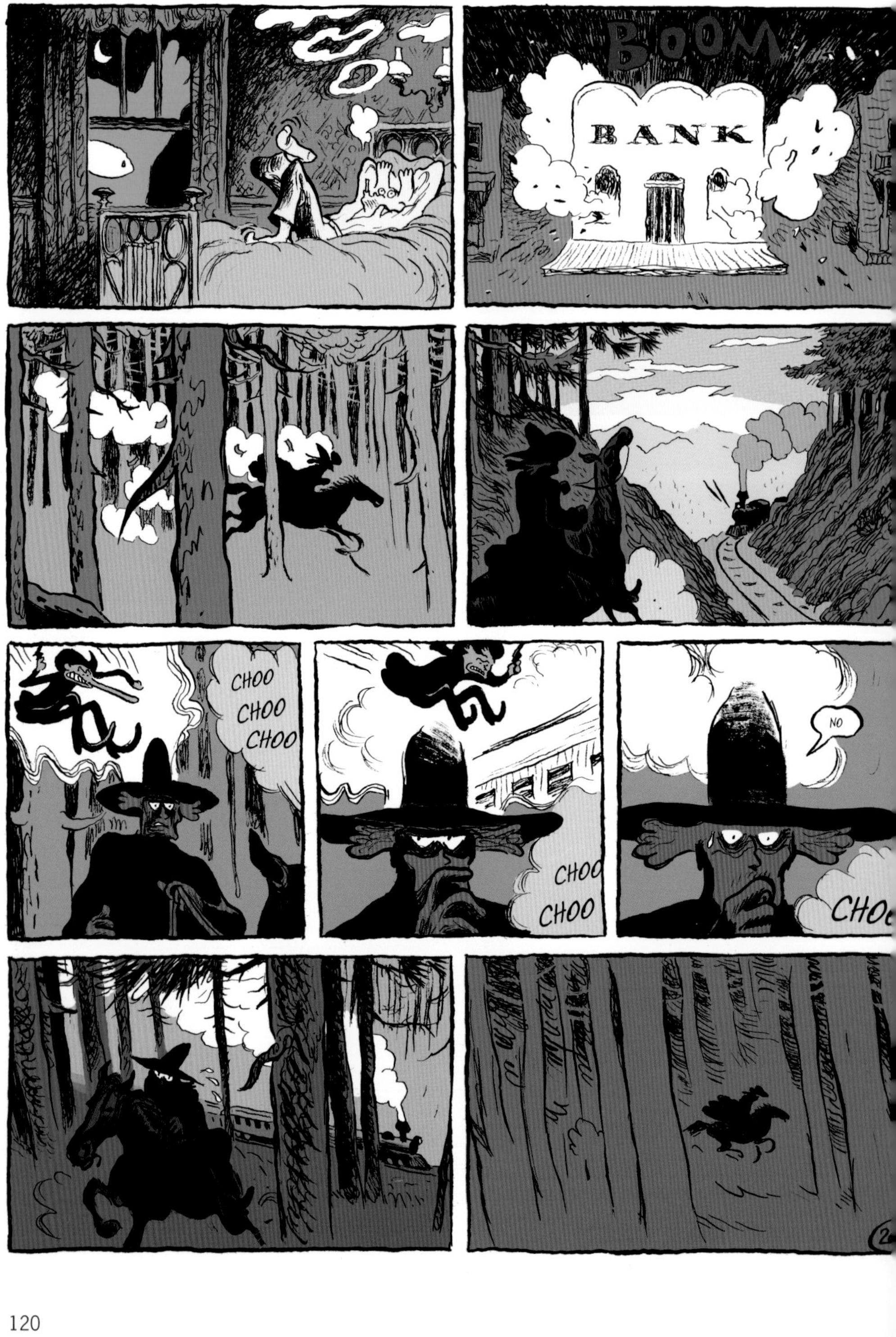
BOOM
BANK
CHOO
CHOO
CHOO
CHOO
CHOO
NO

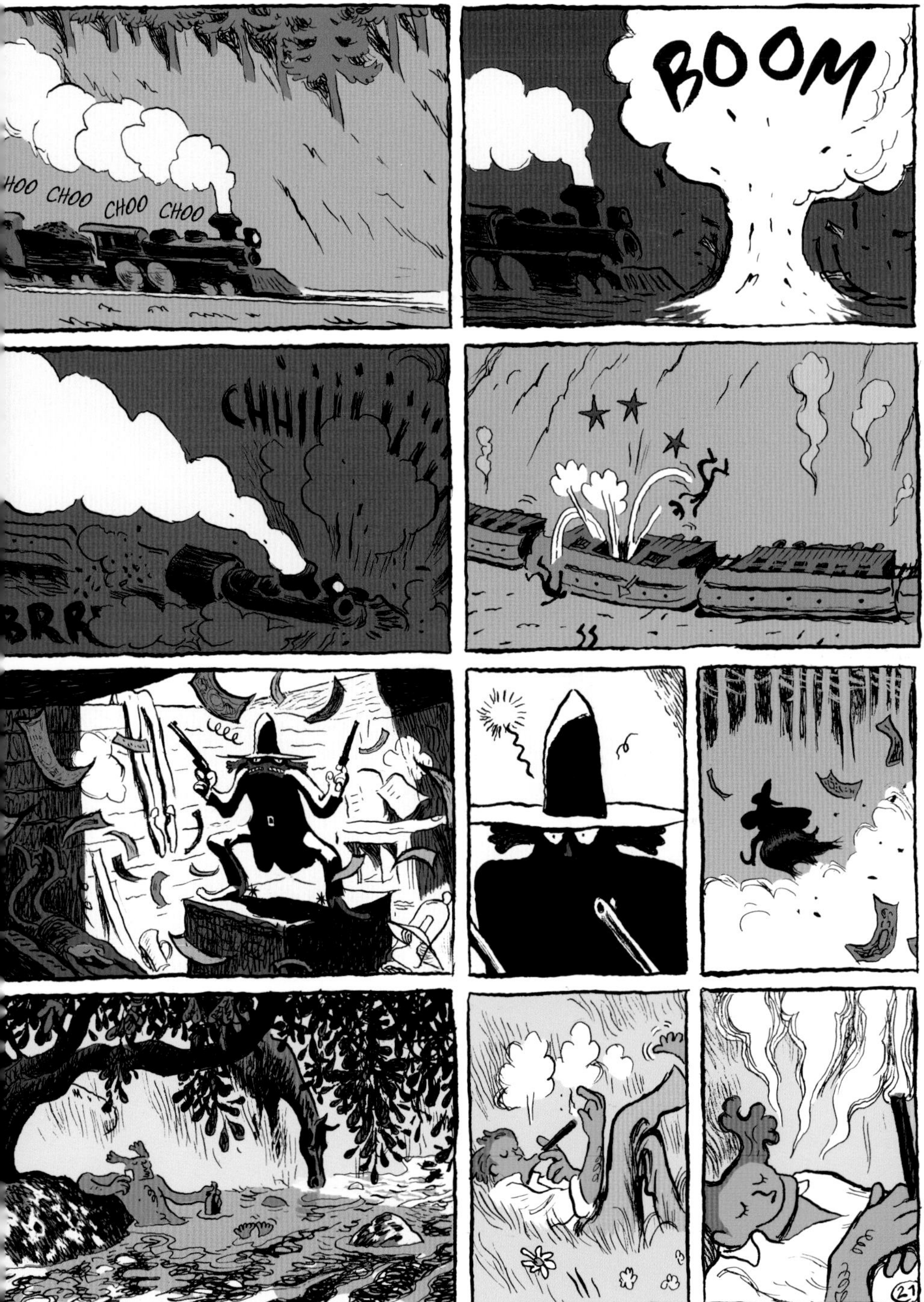
HOO CHOO CHOO CHOO
BOOM
CHHI
BRR
21

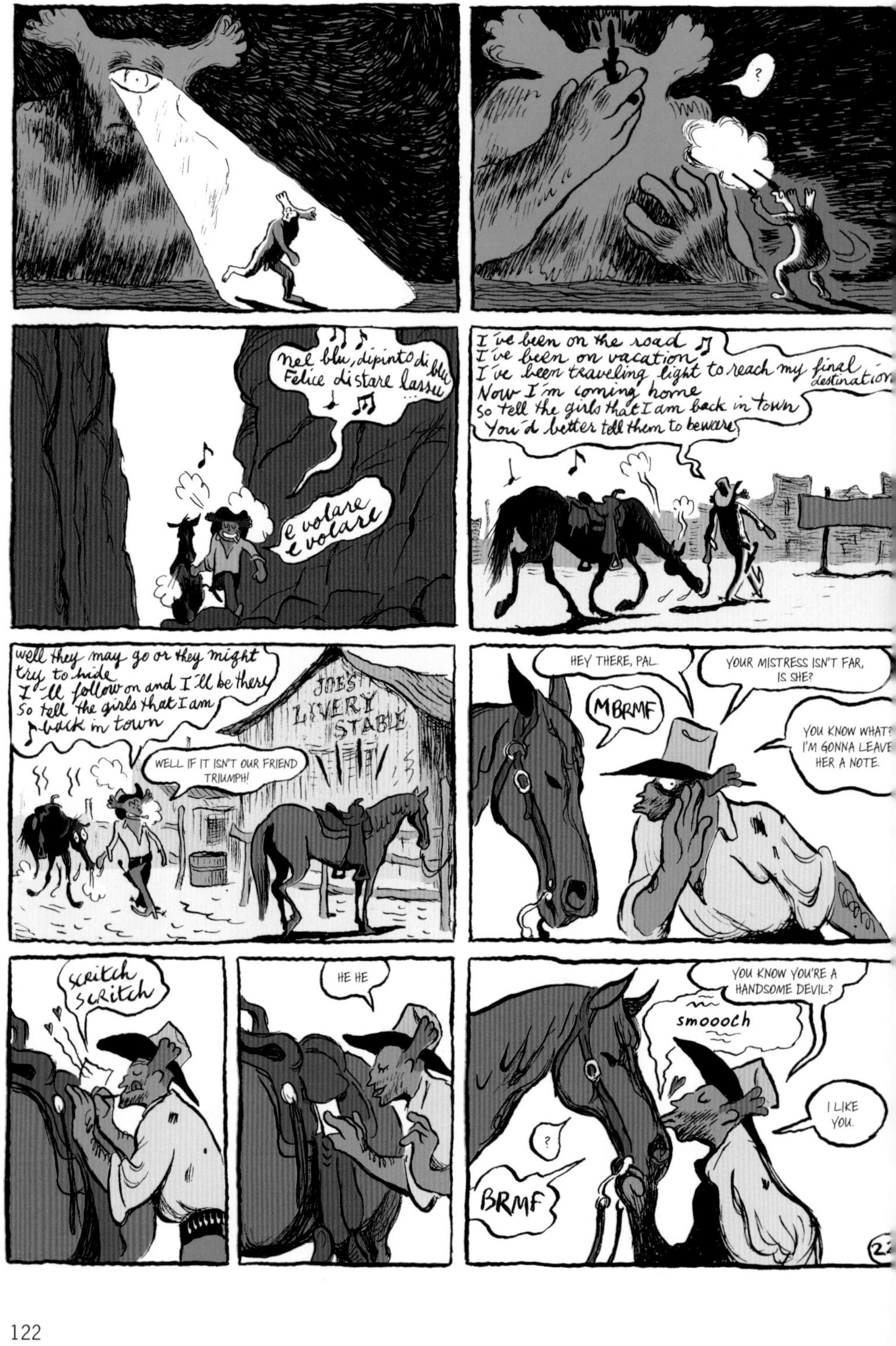
?
nel blu, dipinto di blu
Felice di stare lassù
e volare
e volare
I've been on the road
I've been on vacation
I've been traveling light to reach my final destination
Now I'm coming home
so tell the girls that I am back in town
You'd better tell them to beware
well they may go or they might try to hide
I'll follow on and I'll be there
so tell the girls that I am back in town
JOE'S LIVERY STABLE
WELL IF IT ISN'T OUR FRIEND TRIUMPH!
HEY THERE, PAL.
MBRMF
YOUR MISTRESS ISN'T FAR, IS SHE?
YOU KNOW WHAT? I'M GONNA LEAVE HER A NOTE.
scritch scritch
HE HE
YOU KNOW YOU'RE A HANDSOME DEVIL?
smoooch
I LIKE YOU.
?
BRMF

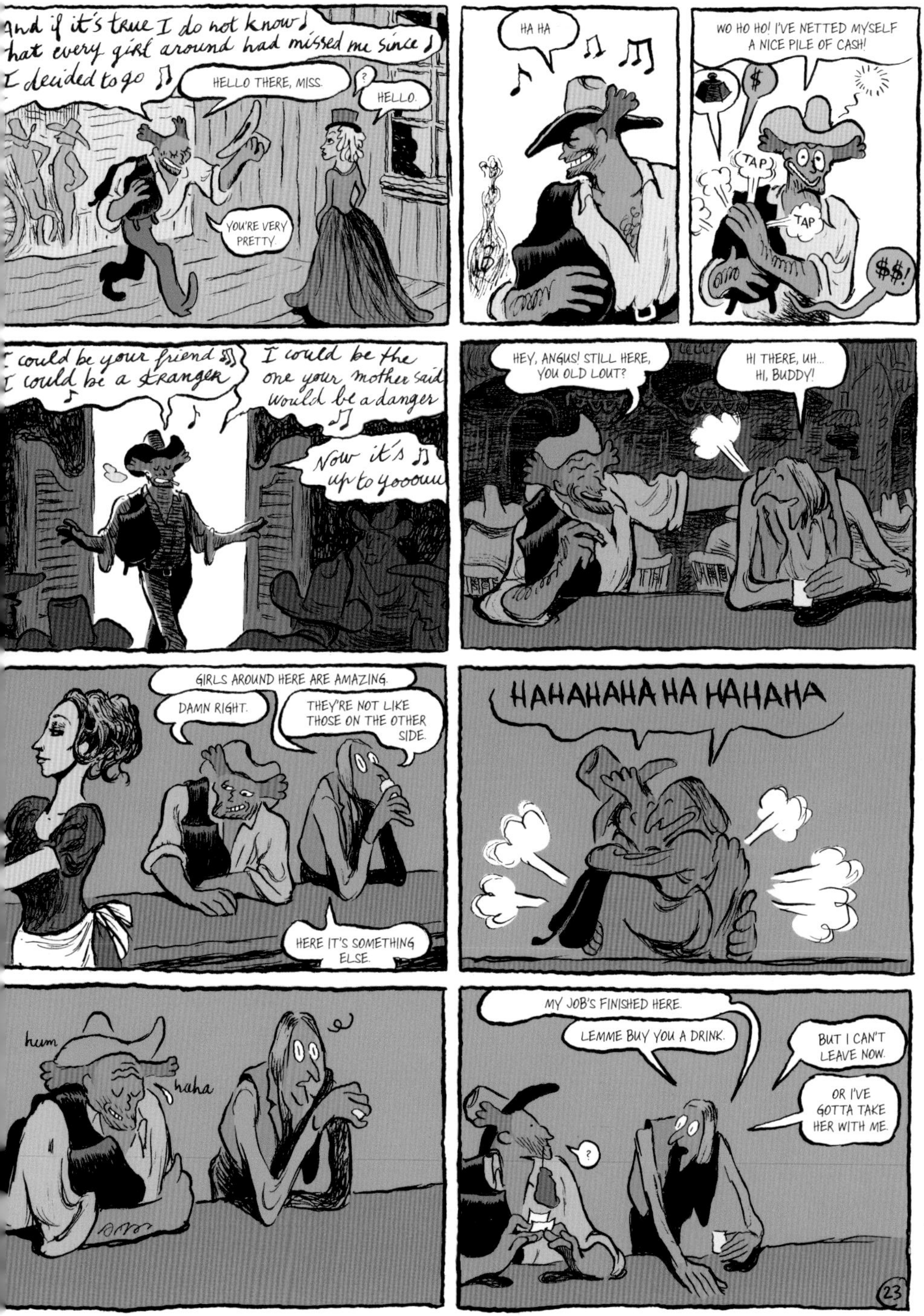

and if it's true I do not know
hat every girl around had missed me since
I decided to go
HELLO THERE, MISS.
?
HELLO.
YOU'RE VERY PRETTY.
HA HA
WO HO HO! I'VE NETTED MYSELF A NICE PILE OF CASH!
$
TAP
TAP
$$!
I could be your friend
I could be a stranger
I could be the one your mother said would be a danger
Now it's up to yooouu
HEY, ANGUS! STILL HERE, YOU OLD LOUT?
HI THERE, UH... HI, BUDDY!
GIRLS AROUND HERE ARE AMAZING.
DAMN RIGHT.
THEY'RE NOT LIKE THOSE ON THE OTHER SIDE.
HERE IT'S SOMETHING ELSE.
HAHAHAHA HA HAHAHA
hum
haha
MY JOB'S FINISHED HERE.
LEMME BUY YOU A DRINK.
BUT I CAN'T LEAVE NOW.
OR I'VE GOTTA TAKE HER WITH ME.
?
23

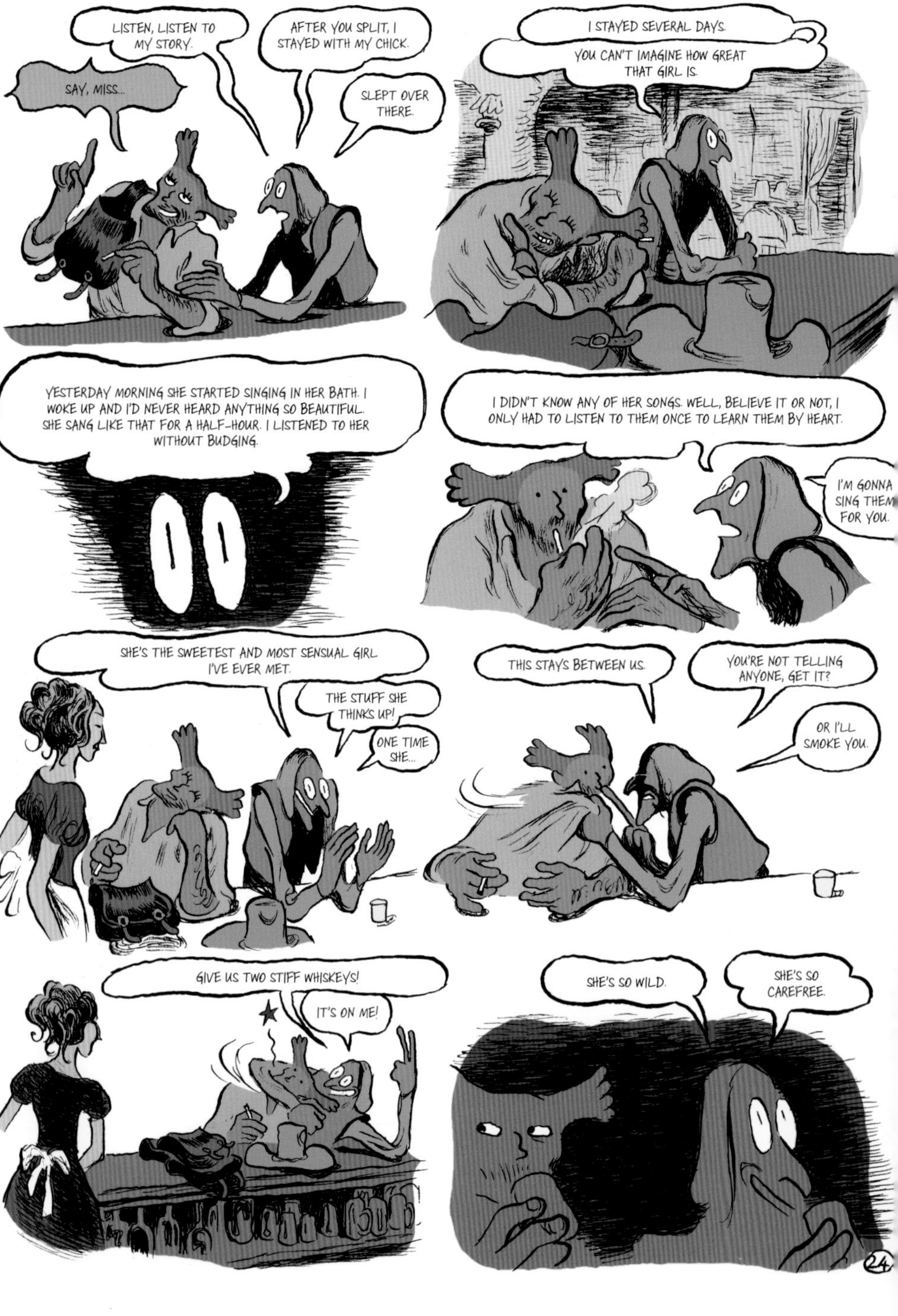

SAY, MISS...
LISTEN, LISTEN TO MY STORY.
AFTER YOU SPLIT, I STAYED WITH MY CHICK.
SLEPT OVER THERE.
I STAYED SEVERAL DAYS.
YOU CAN'T IMAGINE HOW GREAT THAT GIRL IS.
YESTERDAY MORNING SHE STARTED SINGING IN HER BATH. I WOKE UP AND I'D NEVER HEARD ANYTHING SO BEAUTIFUL. SHE SANG LIKE THAT FOR A HALF-HOUR. I LISTENED TO HER WITHOUT BUDGING.
I DIDN'T KNOW ANY OF HER SONGS. WELL, BELIEVE IT OR NOT, I ONLY HAD TO LISTEN TO THEM ONCE TO LEARN THEM BY HEART.
I'M GONNA SING THEM FOR YOU.
SHE'S THE SWEETEST AND MOST SENSUAL GIRL I'VE EVER MET.
THE STUFF SHE THINKS UP!
ONE TIME SHE...
THIS STAYS BETWEEN US.
YOU'RE NOT TELLING ANYONE, GET IT?
OR I'LL SMOKE YOU.
GIVE US TWO STIFF WHISKEYS!
IT'S ON ME!
SHE'S SO WILD.
SHE'S SO CAREFREE.
24

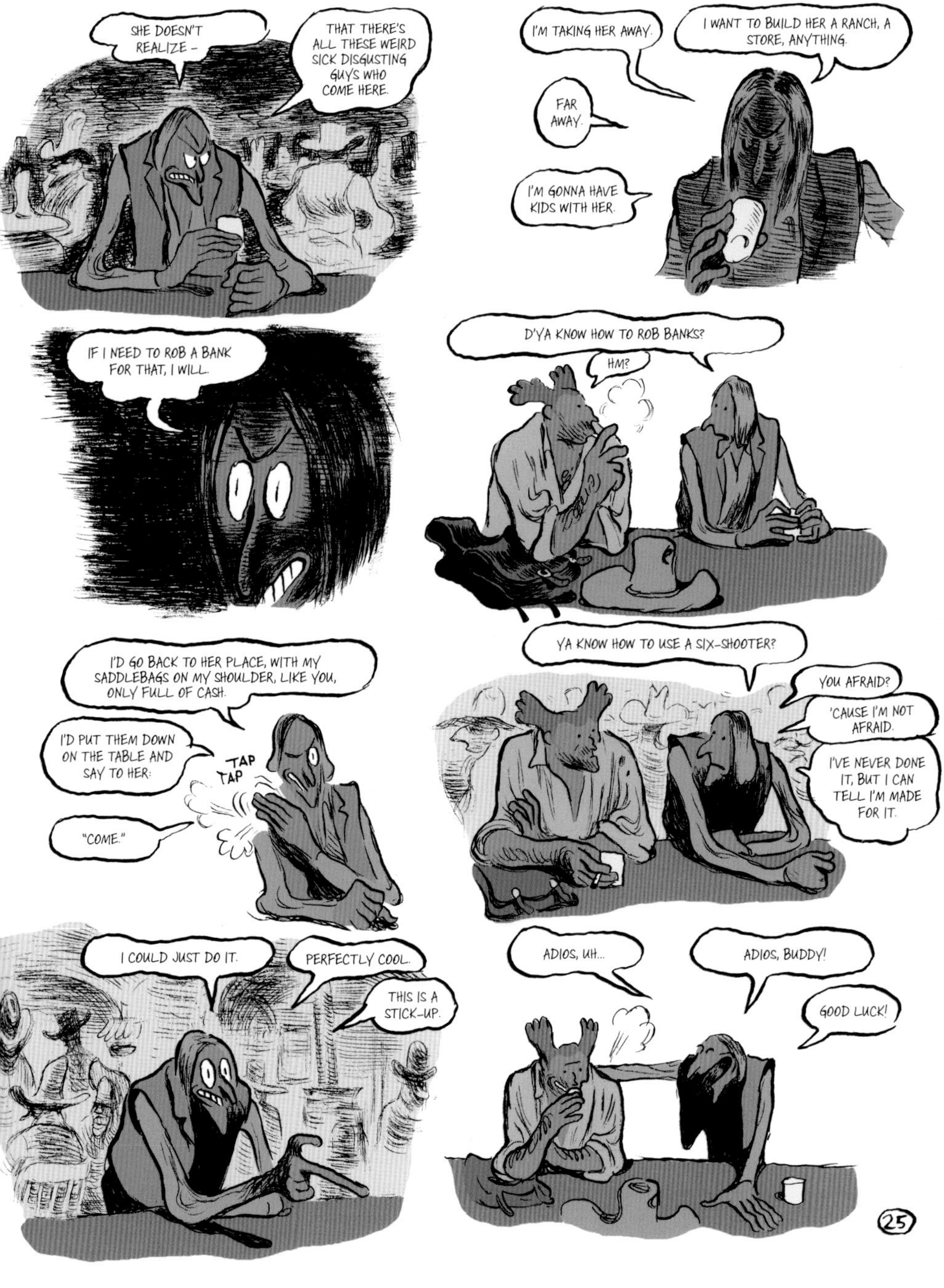
SHE DOESN'T REALIZE -
THAT THERE'S ALL THESE WEIRD SICK DISGUSTING GUYS WHO COME HERE.
I'M TAKING HER AWAY.
FAR AWAY.
I WANT TO BUILD HER A RANCH, A STORE, ANYTHING.
I'M GONNA HAVE KIDS WITH HER.
IF I NEED TO ROB A BANK FOR THAT, I WILL.
D'YA KNOW HOW TO ROB BANKS?
HM?
I'D GO BACK TO HER PLACE, WITH MY SADDLEBAGS ON MY SHOULDER, LIKE YOU, ONLY FULL OF CASH.
I'D PUT THEM DOWN ON THE TABLE AND SAY TO HER:
TAP TAP
"COME."
YA KNOW HOW TO USE A SIX-SHOOTER?
YOU AFRAID?
'CAUSE I'M NOT AFRAID.
I'VE NEVER DONE IT, BUT I CAN TELL I'M MADE FOR IT.
I COULD JUST DO IT.
PERFECTLY COOL.
THIS IS A STICK-UP.
ADIOS, UH...
ADIOS, BUDDY!
GOOD LUCK!
25

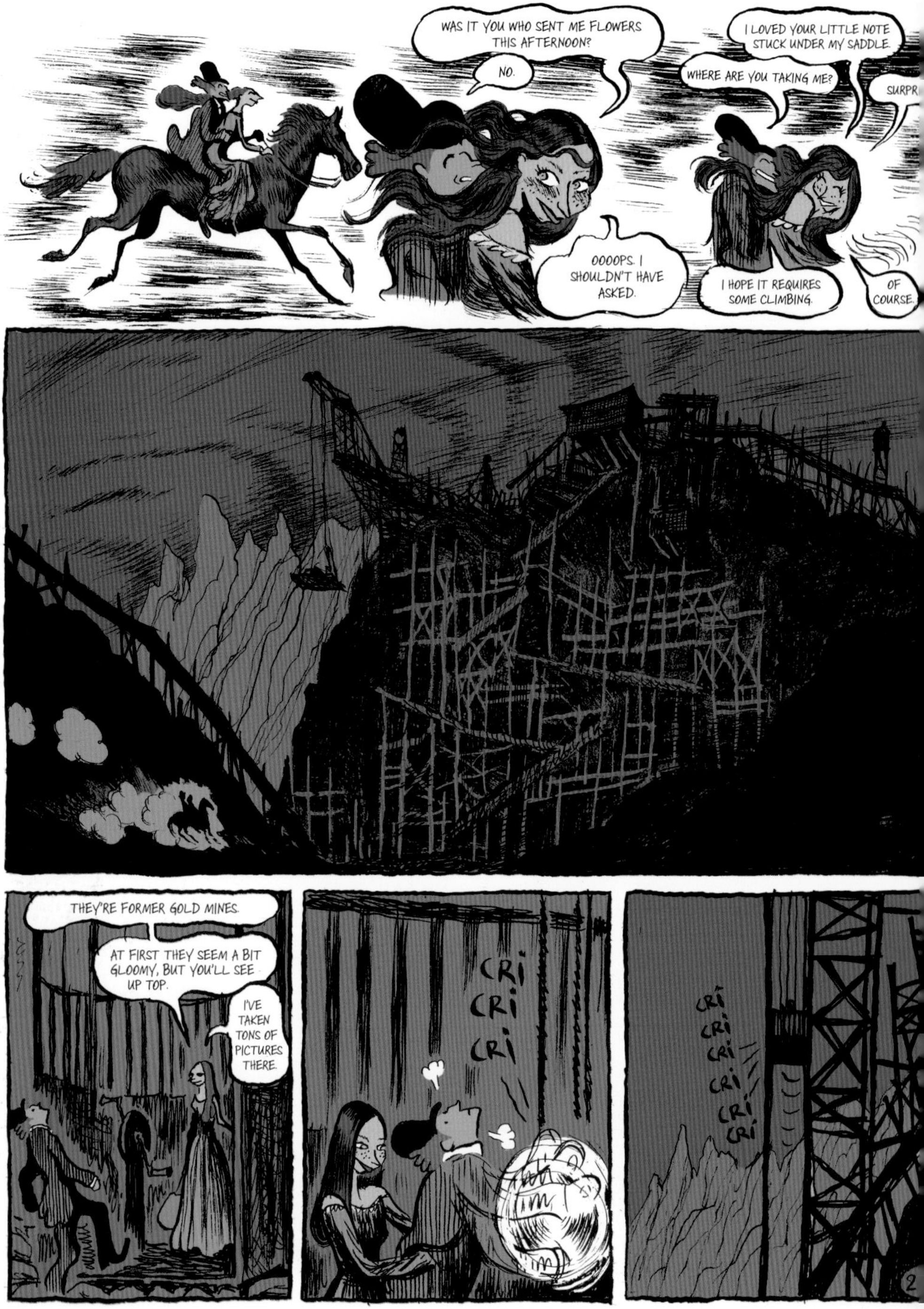
WAS IT YOU WHO SENT ME FLOWERS THIS AFTERNOON?
NO.
OOOOPS. I SHOULDN'T HAVE ASKED.
I LOVED YOUR LITTLE NOTE STUCK UNDER MY SADDLE.
WHERE ARE YOU TAKING ME?
SURPR
I HOPE IT REQUIRES SOME CLIMBING.
OF COURSE.
THEY'RE FORMER GOLD MINES.
AT FIRST THEY SEEM A BIT GLOOMY, BUT YOU'LL SEE UP TOP.
I'VE TAKEN TONS OF PICTURES THERE.
CRI CRI CRI
CRI CRI CRI CRI CRI CRI

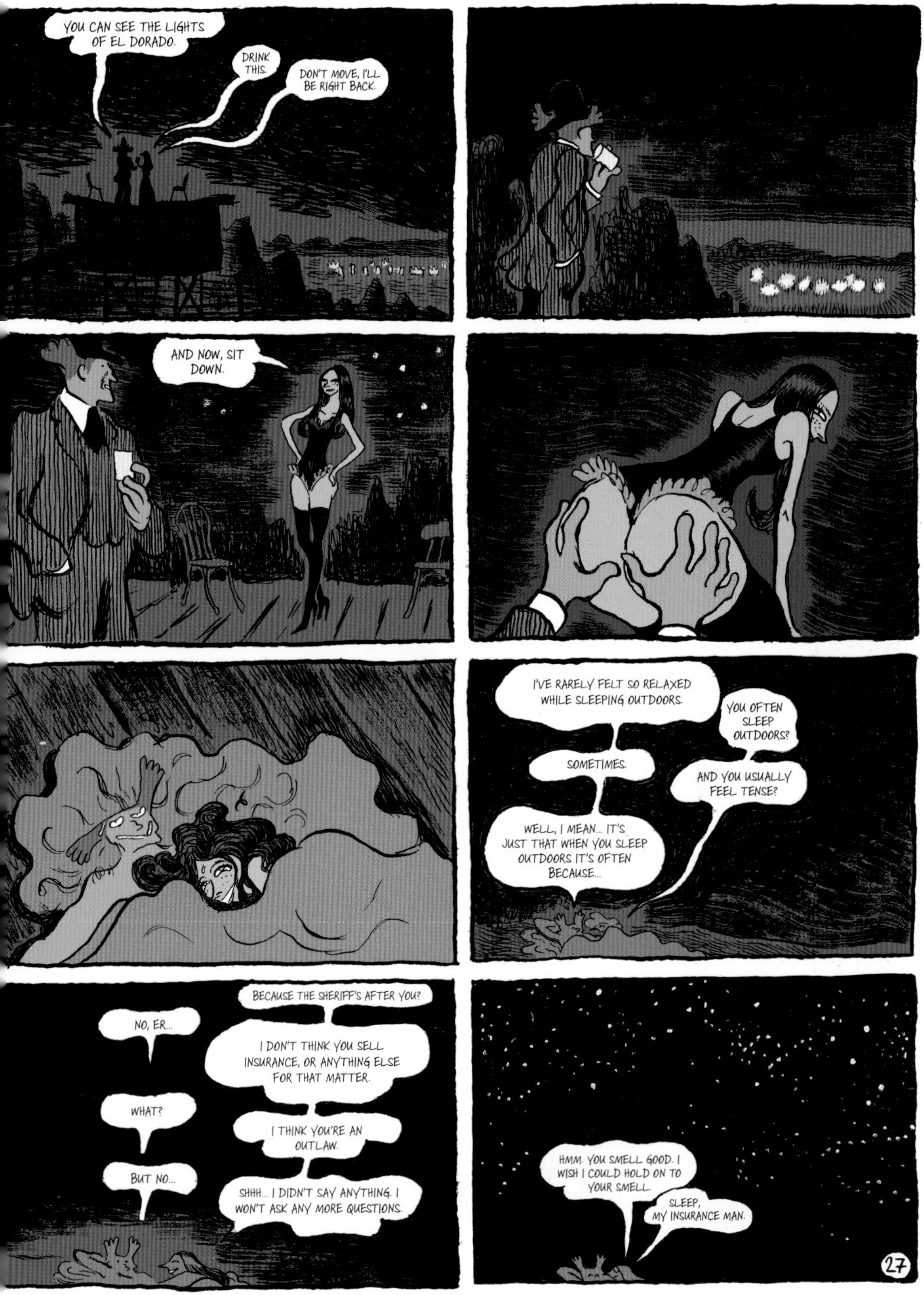
YOU CAN SEE THE LIGHTS OF EL DORADO.
DRINK THIS.
DON'T MOVE, I'LL BE RIGHT BACK.
AND NOW, SIT DOWN.
I'VE RARELY FELT SO RELAXED WHILE SLEEPING OUTDOORS.
YOU OFTEN SLEEP OUTDOORS?
SOMETIMES.
AND YOU USUALLY FEEL TENSE?
WELL, I MEAN... IT'S JUST THAT WHEN YOU SLEEP OUTDOORS IT'S OFTEN BECAUSE...
BECAUSE THE SHERIFF'S AFTER YOU?
NO, ER...
I DON'T THINK YOU SELL INSURANCE, OR ANYTHING ELSE FOR THAT MATTER.
WHAT?
I THINK YOU'RE AN OUTLAW.
BUT NO...
SHHH... I DIDN'T SAY ANYTHING. I WON'T ASK ANY MORE QUESTIONS.
HMM. YOU SMELL GOOD. I WISH I COULD HOLD ON TO YOUR SMELL.
SLEEP, MY INSURANCE MAN.
27

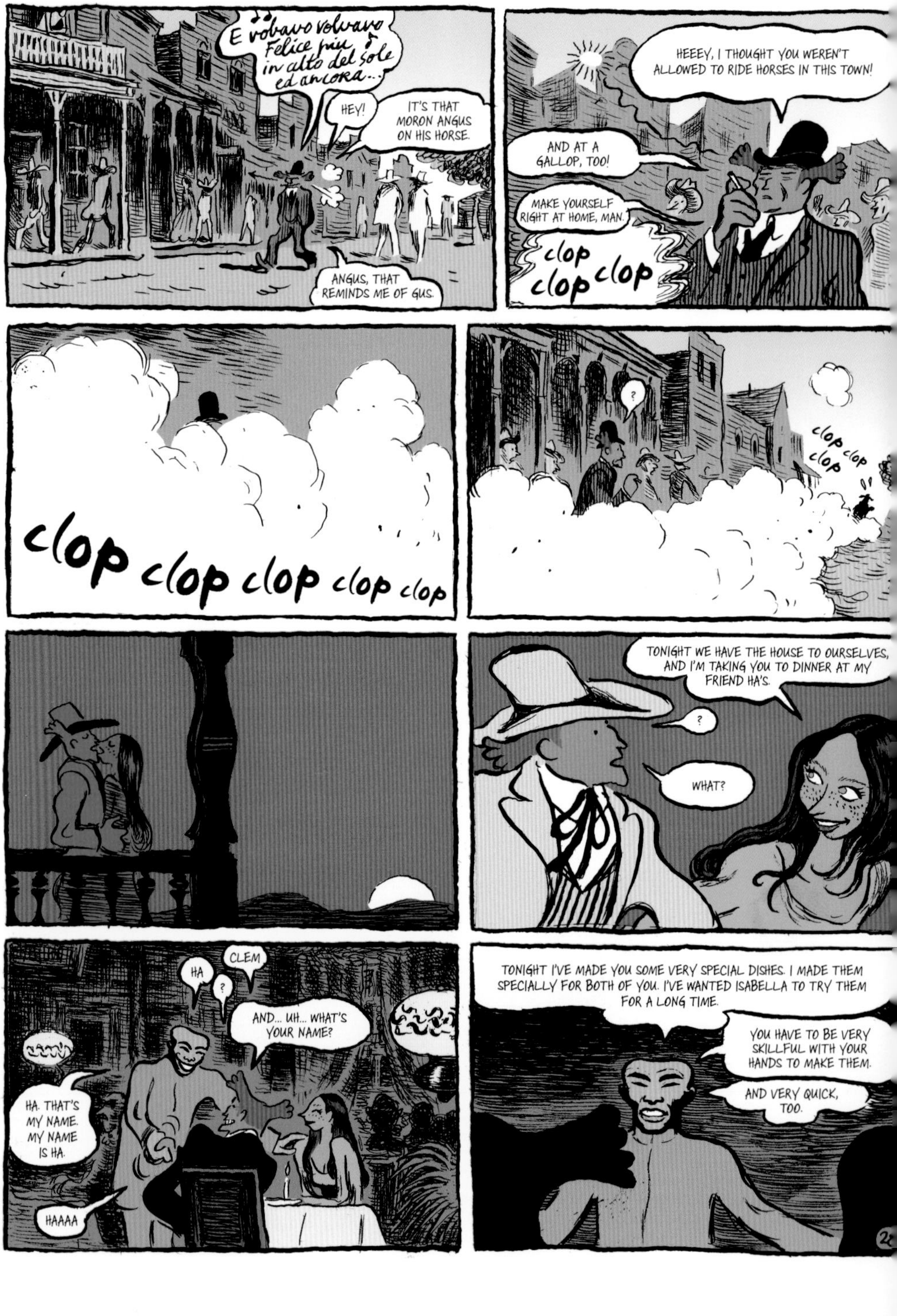

E volavo volavo Felice piu in alto del sole ed ancora...
HEY!
IT'S THAT MORON ANGUS ON HIS HORSE.
ANGUS, THAT REMINDS ME OF GUS.
HEEEY, I THOUGHT YOU WEREN'T ALLOWED TO RIDE HORSES IN THIS TOWN!
AND AT A GALLOP, TOO!
MAKE YOURSELF RIGHT AT HOME, MAN.
clop clop clop
clop clop clop clop clop
?
clop clop clop
TONIGHT WE HAVE THE HOUSE TO OURSELVES, AND I'M TAKING YOU TO DINNER AT MY FRIEND HA'S.
?
WHAT?
HA
?
CLEM
AND... UH... WHAT'S YOUR NAME?
HA. THAT'S MY NAME. MY NAME IS HA.
HAAAA
TONIGHT I'VE MADE YOU SOME VERY SPECIAL DISHES. I MADE THEM SPECIALLY FOR BOTH OF YOU. I'VE WANTED ISABELLA TO TRY THEM FOR A LONG TIME.
YOU HAVE TO BE VERY SKILLFUL WITH YOUR HANDS TO MAKE THEM.
AND VERY QUICK, TOO.

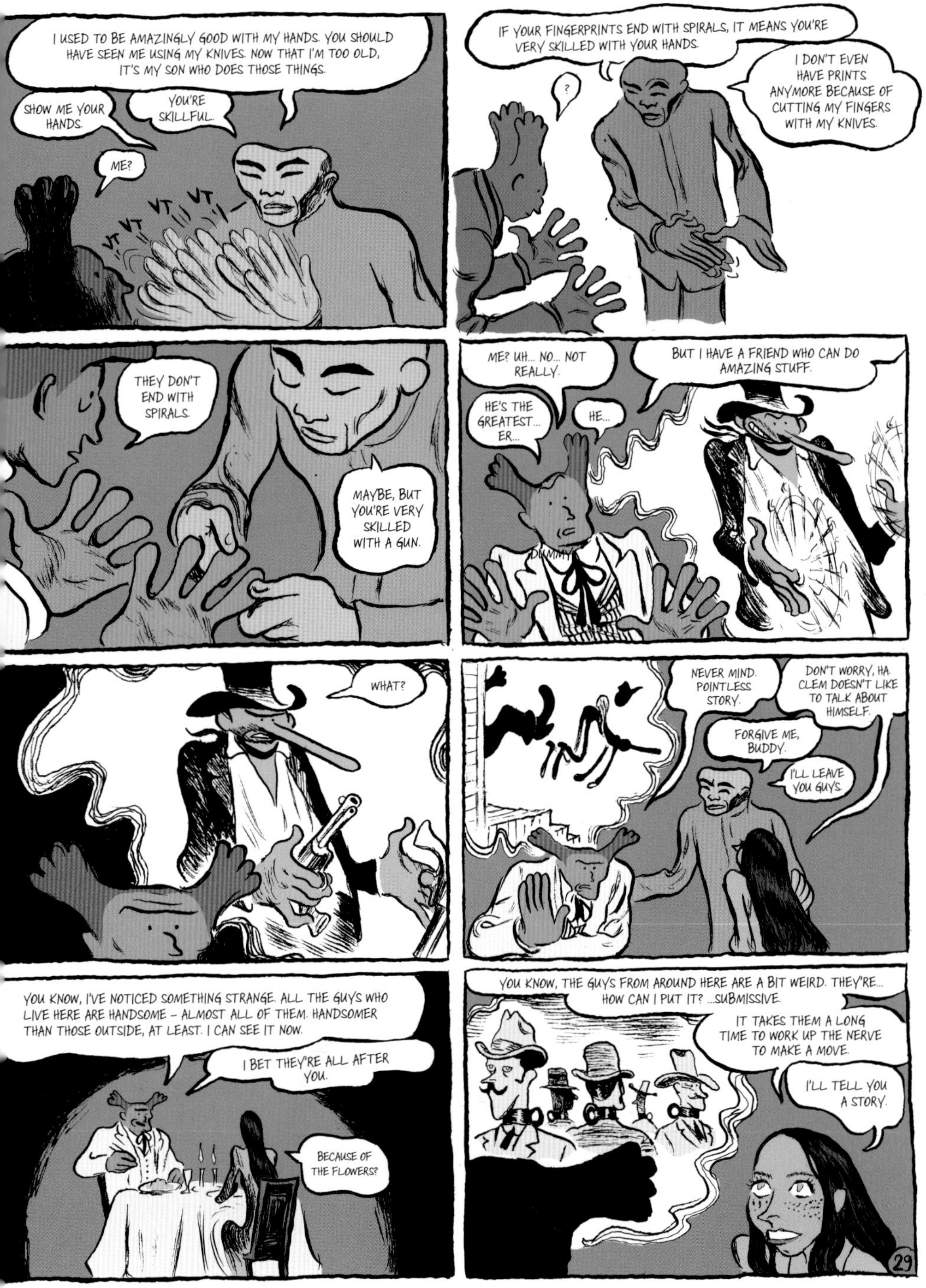
I USED TO BE AMAZINGLY GOOD WITH MY HANDS. YOU SHOULD HAVE SEEN ME USING MY KNIVES. NOW THAT I'M TOO OLD, IT'S MY SON WHO DOES THOSE THINGS.
SHOW ME YOUR HANDS.
YOU'RE SKILLFUL.
ME?
VT VT VT VT
IF YOUR FINGERPRINTS END WITH SPIRALS, IT MEANS YOU'RE VERY SKILLED WITH YOUR HANDS.
?
I DON'T EVEN HAVE PRINTS ANYMORE BECAUSE OF CUTTING MY FINGERS WITH MY KNIVES.
THEY DON'T END WITH SPIRALS.
MAYBE, BUT YOU'RE VERY SKILLED WITH A GUN.
ME? UH... NO... NOT REALLY.
BUT I HAVE A FRIEND WHO CAN DO AMAZING STUFF.
HE'S THE GREATEST... ER...
HE...
DUMMY
WHAT?
NEVER MIND. POINTLESS STORY.
DON'T WORRY, HA. CLEM DOESN'T LIKE TO TALK ABOUT HIMSELF.
FORGIVE ME, BUDDY.
I'LL LEAVE YOU GUYS.
YOU KNOW, I'VE NOTICED SOMETHING STRANGE. ALL THE GUYS WHO LIVE HERE ARE HANDSOME – ALMOST ALL OF THEM. HANDSOMER THAN THOSE OUTSIDE, AT LEAST. I CAN SEE IT NOW.
I BET THEY'RE ALL AFTER YOU.
BECAUSE OF THE FLOWERS?
YOU KNOW, THE GUYS FROM AROUND HERE ARE A BIT WEIRD. THEY'RE... HOW CAN I PUT IT? ...SUBMISSIVE.
IT TAKES THEM A LONG TIME TO WORK UP THE NERVE TO MAKE A MOVE.
I'LL TELL YOU A STORY.
29

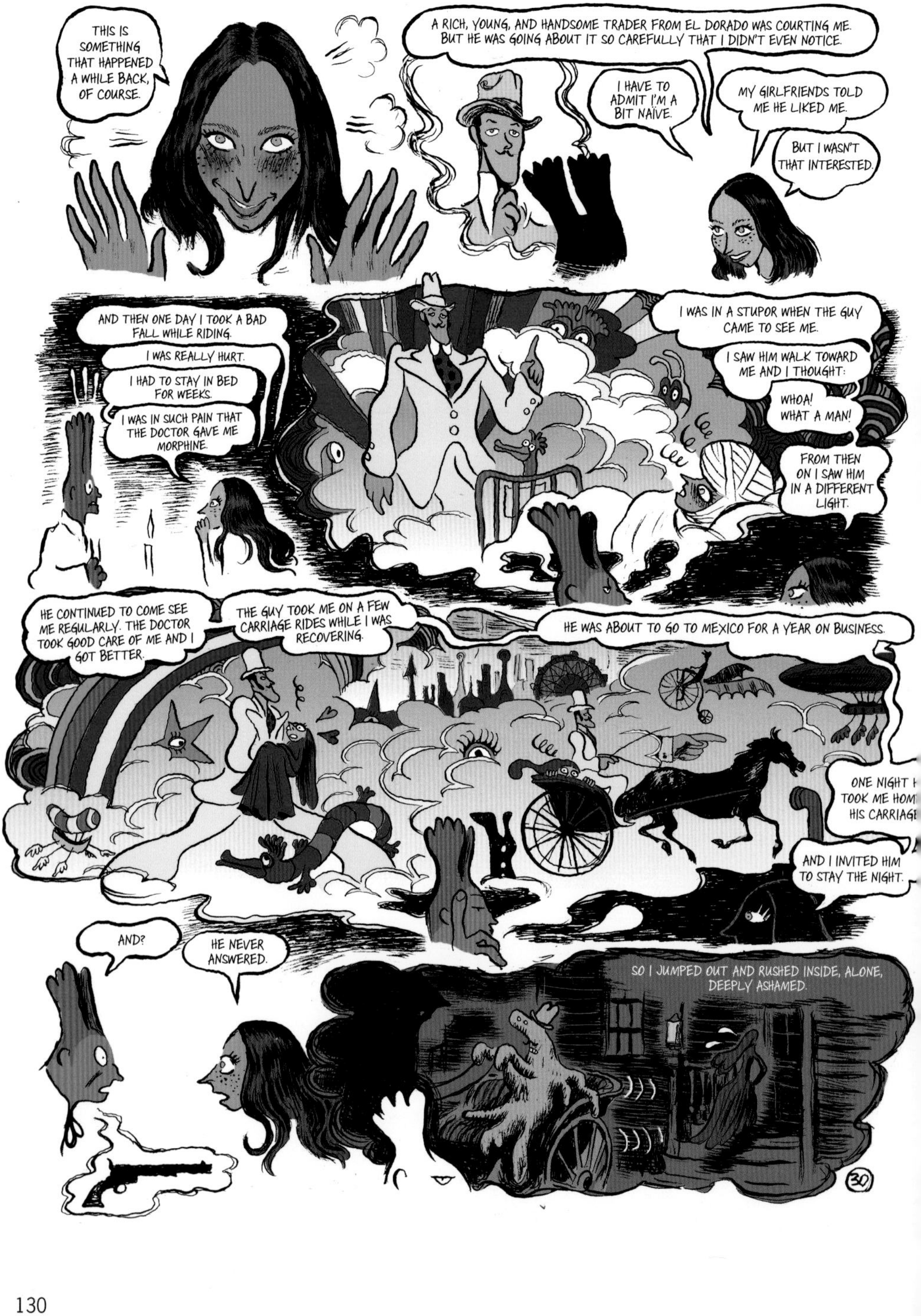

THIS IS SOMETHING THAT HAPPENED A WHILE BACK, OF COURSE.
A RICH, YOUNG, AND HANDSOME TRADER FROM EL DORADO WAS COURTING ME. BUT HE WAS GOING ABOUT IT SO CAREFULLY THAT I DIDN'T EVEN NOTICE.
I HAVE TO ADMIT I'M A BIT NAÏVE.
MY GIRLFRIENDS TOLD ME HE LIKED ME.
BUT I WASN'T THAT INTERESTED.
AND THEN ONE DAY I TOOK A BAD FALL WHILE RIDING.
I WAS REALLY HURT.
I HAD TO STAY IN BED FOR WEEKS.
I WAS IN SUCH PAIN THAT THE DOCTOR GAVE ME MORPHINE.
I WAS IN A STUPOR WHEN THE GUY CAME TO SEE ME.
I SAW HIM WALK TOWARD ME AND I THOUGHT:
WHOA! WHAT A MAN!
FROM THEN ON I SAW HIM IN A DIFFERENT LIGHT.
HE CONTINUED TO COME SEE ME REGULARLY. THE DOCTOR TOOK GOOD CARE OF ME AND I GOT BETTER.
THE GUY TOOK ME ON A FEW CARRIAGE RIDES WHILE I WAS RECOVERING.
HE WAS ABOUT TO GO TO MEXICO FOR A YEAR ON BUSINESS.
AND I INVITED HIM TO STAY THE NIGHT.
AND?
HE NEVER ANSWERED.
SO I JUMPED OUT AND RUSHED INSIDE, ALONE, DEEPLY ASHAMED.
30

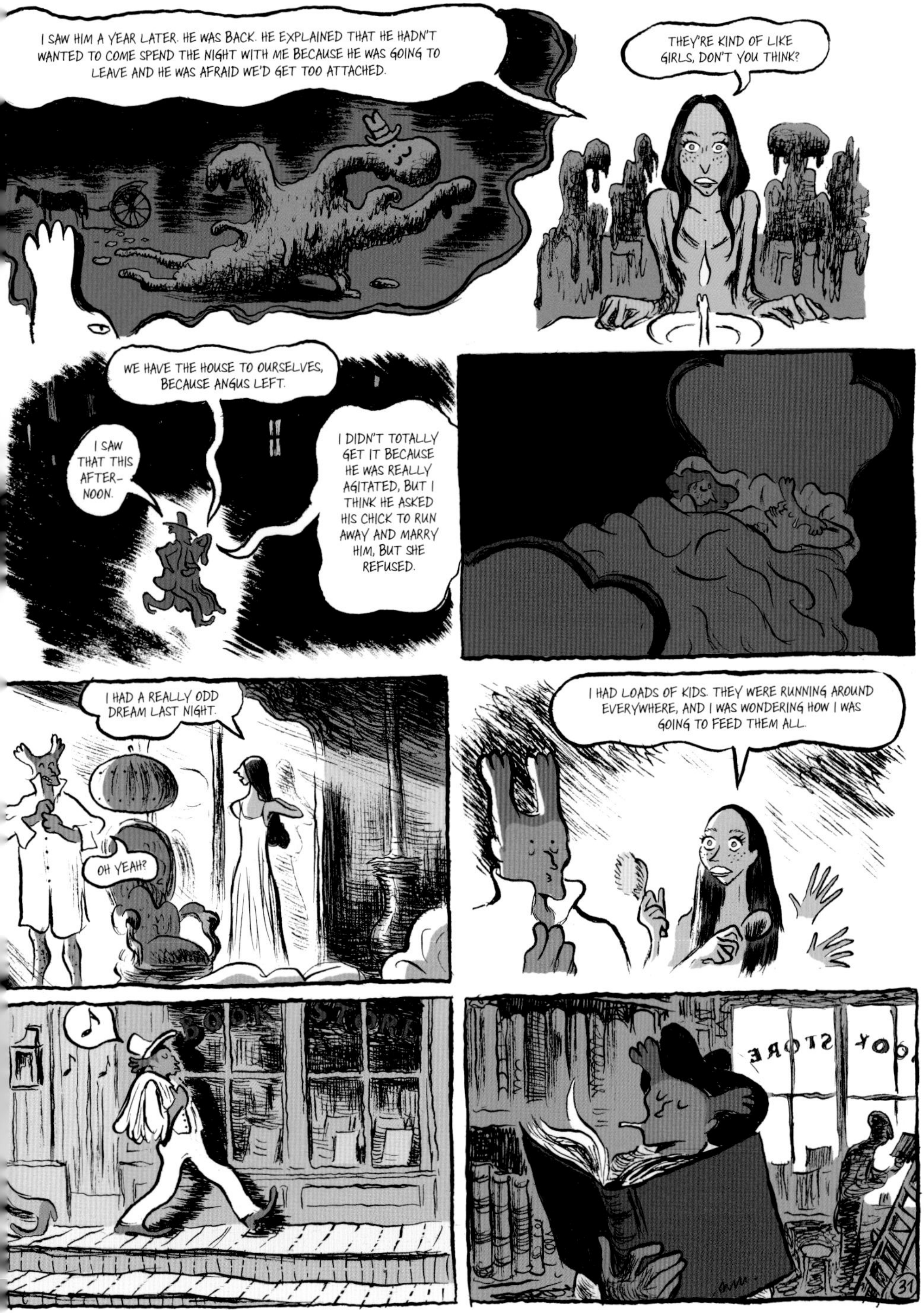
I SAW HIM A YEAR LATER. HE WAS BACK. HE EXPLAINED THAT HE HADN'T WANTED TO COME SPEND THE NIGHT WITH ME BECAUSE HE WAS GOING TO LEAVE AND HE WAS AFRAID WE'D GET TOO ATTACHED.
THEY'RE KIND OF LIKE GIRLS, DON'T YOU THINK?
WE HAVE THE HOUSE TO OURSELVES, BECAUSE ANGUS LEFT.
I SAW THAT THIS AFTER-NOON.
I DIDN'T TOTALLY GET IT BECAUSE HE WAS REALLY AGITATED, BUT I THINK HE ASKED HIS CHICK TO RUN AWAY AND MARRY HIM, BUT SHE REFUSED.
I HAD A REALLY ODD DREAM LAST NIGHT.
OH YEAH?
I HAD LOADS OF KIDS. THEY WERE RUNNING AROUND EVERYWHERE, AND I WAS WONDERING HOW I WAS GOING TO FEED THEM ALL.
BOOK STORE
STORE
31

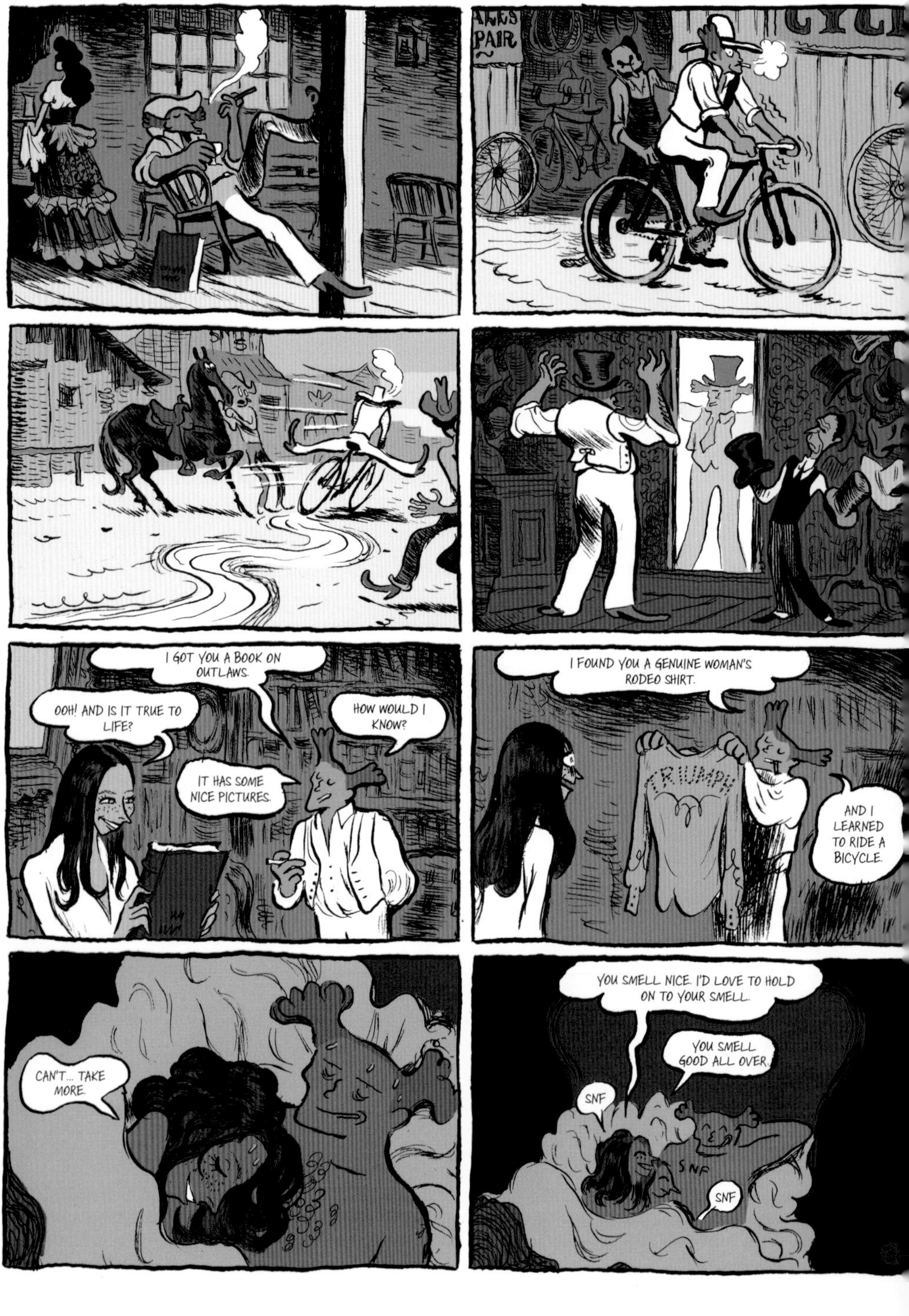
I GOT YOU A BOOK ON OUTLAWS.
OOH! AND IS IT TRUE TO LIFE?
HOW WOULD I KNOW?
IT HAS SOME NICE PICTURES.
I FOUND YOU A GENUINE WOMAN'S RODEO SHIRT.
TRIUMPH
AND I LEARNED TO RIDE A BICYCLE.
CAN'T... TAKE MORE.
YOU SMELL NICE. I'D LOVE TO HOLD ON TO YOUR SMELL.
YOU SMELL GOOD ALL OVER.
SNF
SNF
SNF

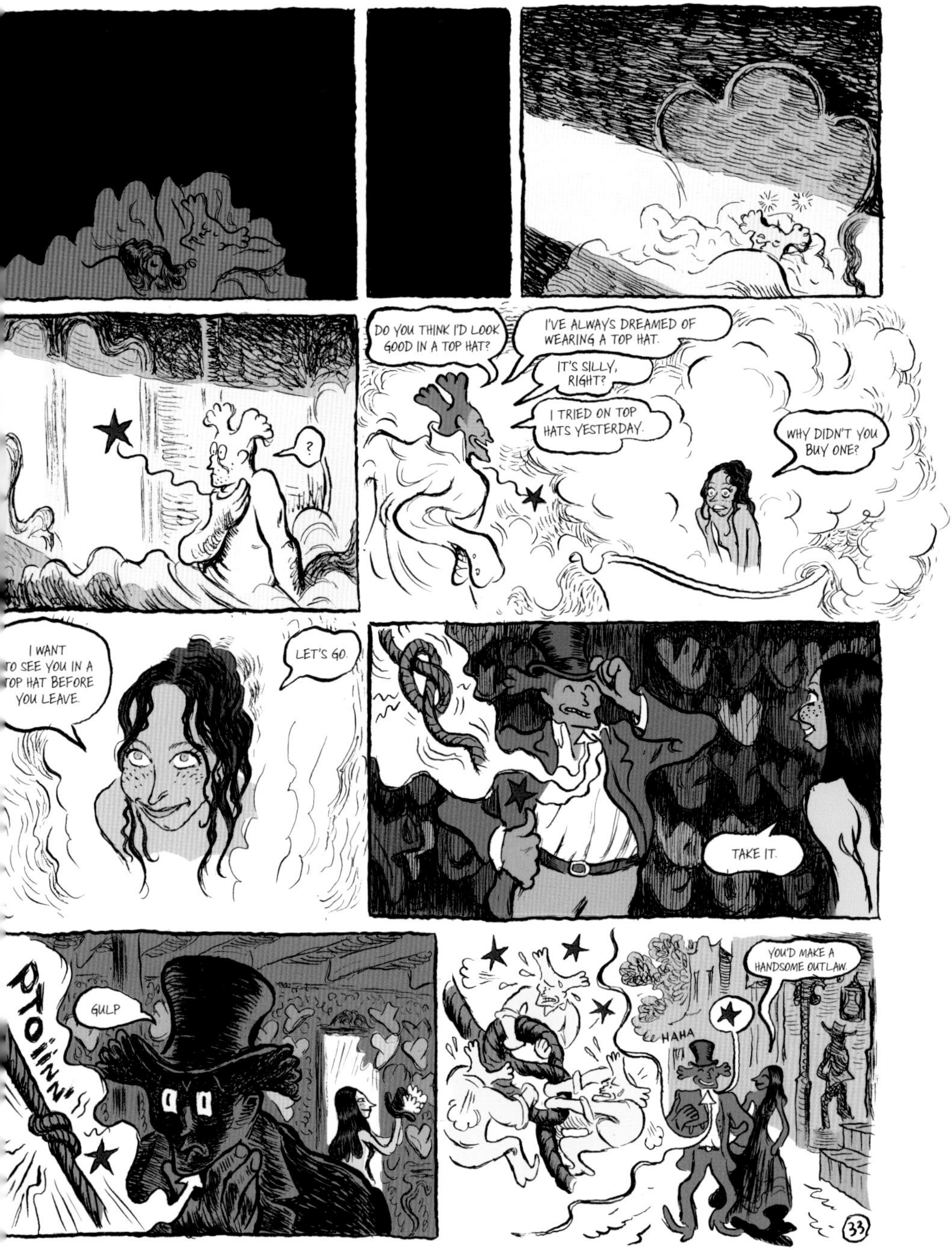
?
DO YOU THINK I'D LOOK GOOD IN A TOP HAT?
I'VE ALWAYS DREAMED OF WEARING A TOP HAT.
IT'S SILLY, RIGHT?
I TRIED ON TOP HATS YESTERDAY.
WHY DIDN'T YOU BUY ONE?
I WANT TO SEE YOU IN A TOP HAT BEFORE YOU LEAVE.
LET'S GO.
TAKE IT.
PTOïïNN'
GULP
HAHA
YOU'D MAKE A HANDSOME OUTLAW.
33

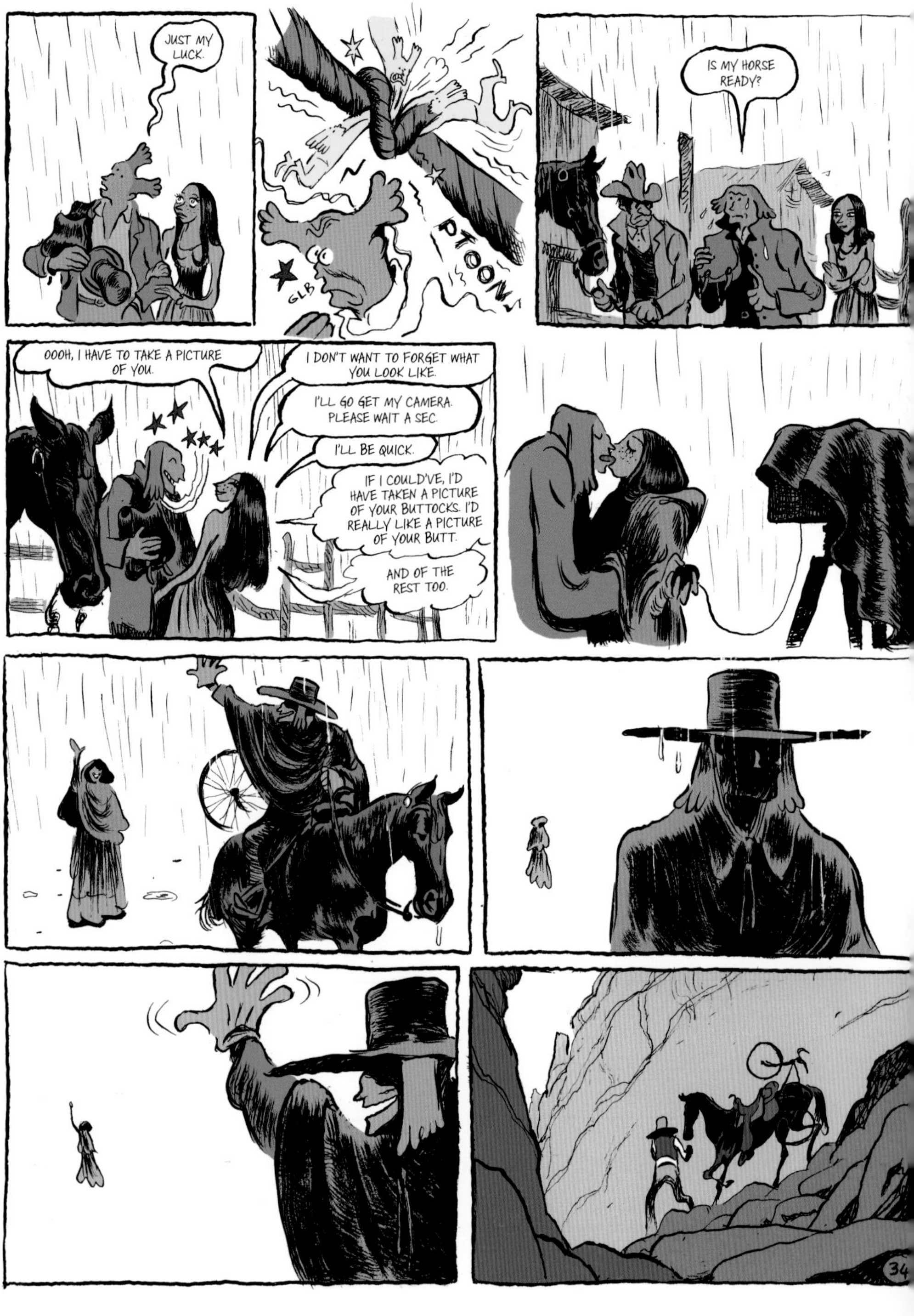
JUST MY LUCK.
GLB
PTOOM!
IS MY HORSE READY?
OOOH, I HAVE TO TAKE A PICTURE OF YOU.
I DON'T WANT TO FORGET WHAT YOU LOOK LIKE.
I'LL GO GET MY CAMERA. PLEASE WAIT A SEC.
I'LL BE QUICK.
IF I COULD'VE, I'D HAVE TAKEN A PICTURE OF YOUR BUTTOCKS. I'D REALLY LIKE A PICTURE OF YOUR BUTT.
AND OF THE REST TOO.
34

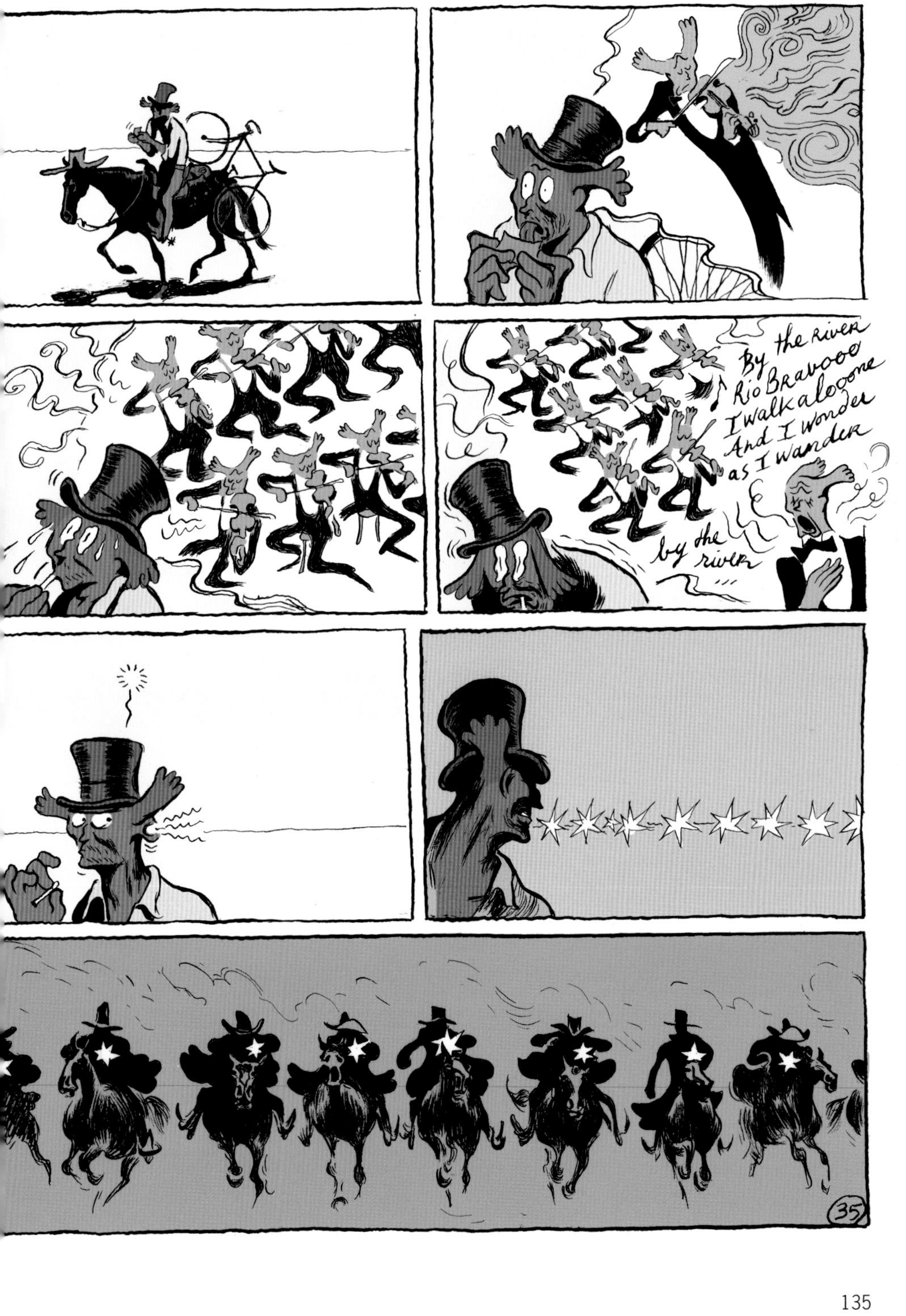
By the river
Rio Bravooo
I walk alooone
And I wonder
as I wander
by the river
35

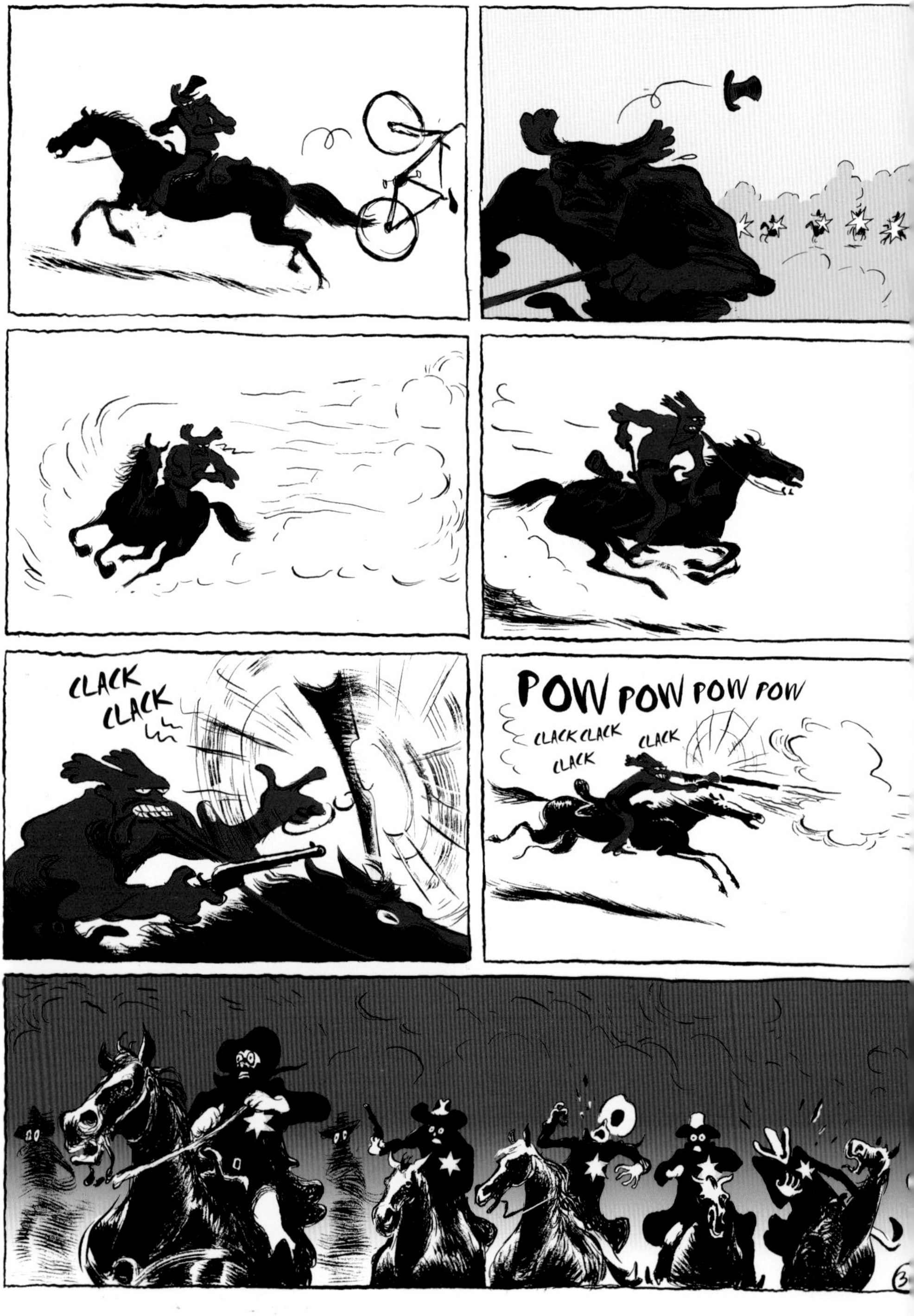
CLACK
CLACK
POW POW POW POW
CLACK CLACK
CLACK
CLACK

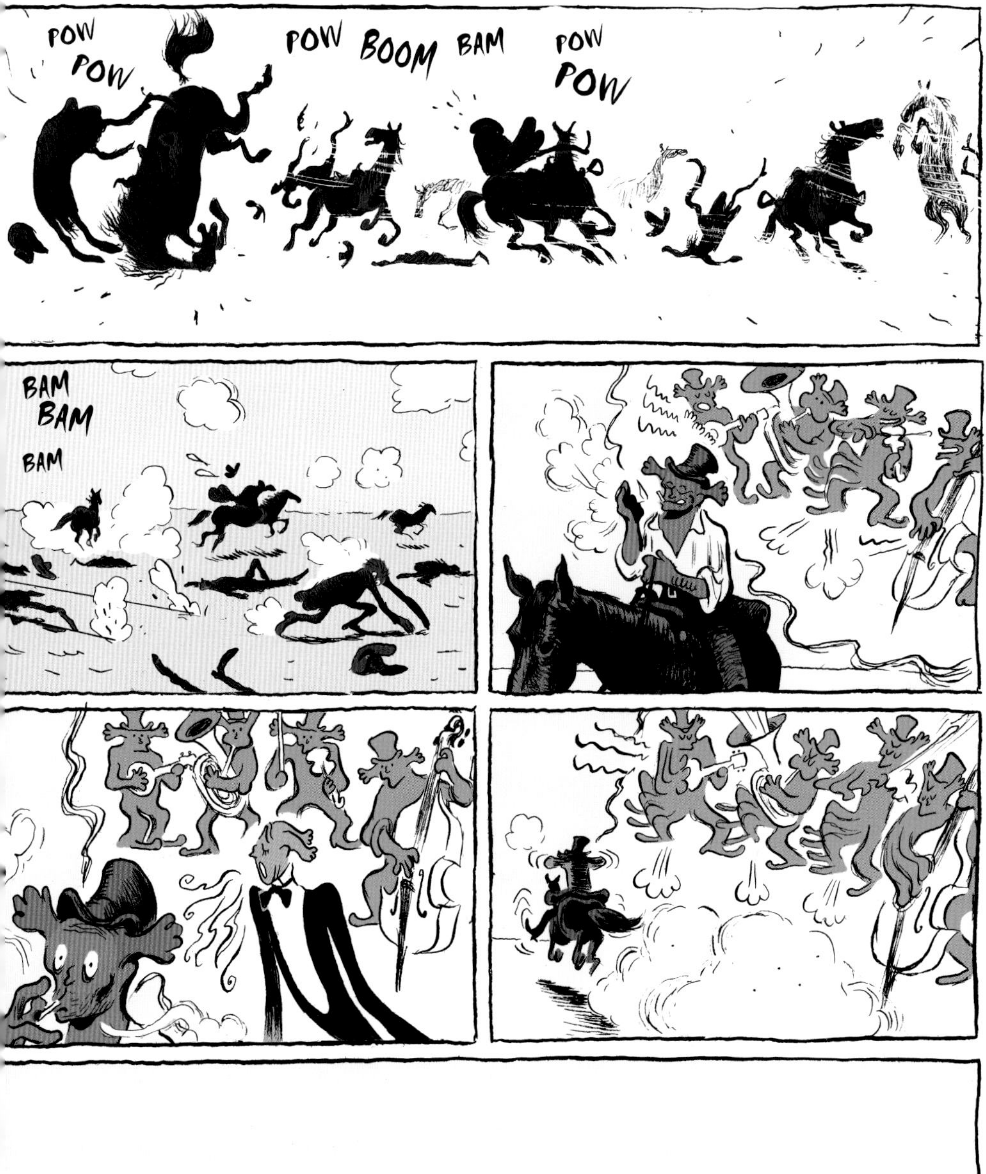
POW
POW
POW
BOOM
BAM
POW
POW
BAM
BAM
BAM
37

Christopheblain dec. 06

INGER LUTZ

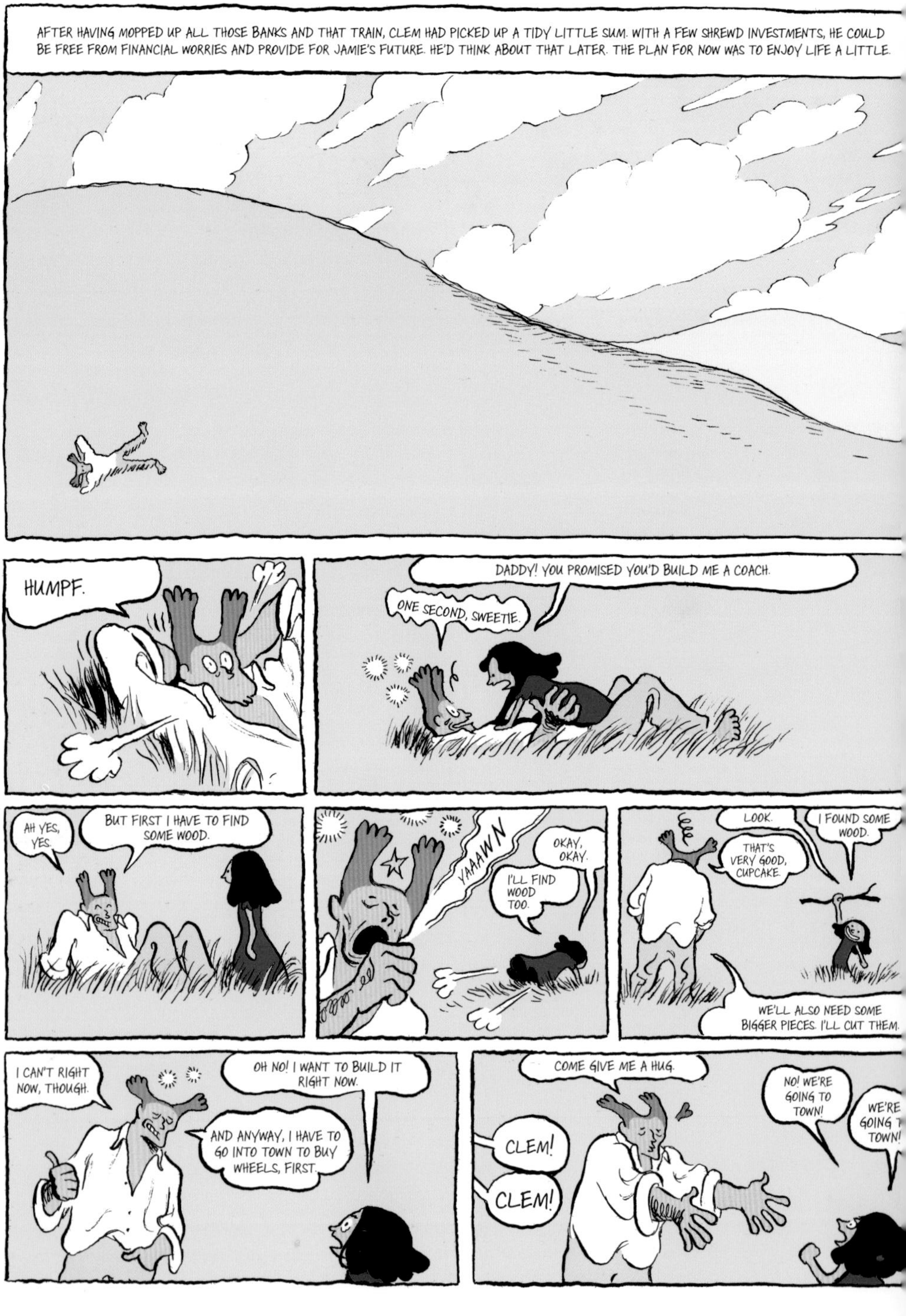

AFTER HAVING MOPPED UP ALL THOSE BANKS AND THAT TRAIN, CLEM HAD PICKED UP A TIDY LITTLE SUM. WITH A FEW SHREWD INVESTMENTS, HE COULD BE FREE FROM FINANCIAL WORRIES AND PROVIDE FOR JAMIE'S FUTURE. HE'D THINK ABOUT THAT LATER. THE PLAN FOR NOW WAS TO ENJOY LIFE A LITTLE.
HUMPF.
DADDY! YOU PROMISED YOU'D BUILD ME A COACH.
ONE SECOND, SWEETIE.
AH YES, YES.
BUT FIRST I HAVE TO FIND SOME WOOD.
YAAAWN
OKAY, OKAY.
I'LL FIND WOOD TOO.
LOOK.
I FOUND SOME WOOD.
THAT'S VERY GOOD, CUPCAKE.
WE'LL ALSO NEED SOME BIGGER PIECES. I'LL CUT THEM.
I CAN'T RIGHT NOW, THOUGH.
OH NO! I WANT TO BUILD IT RIGHT NOW.
AND ANYWAY, I HAVE TO GO INTO TOWN TO BUY WHEELS, FIRST.
COME GIVE ME A HUG.
CLEM!
CLEM!
NO! WE'RE GOING TO TOWN!
WE'RE GOING T TOWN!

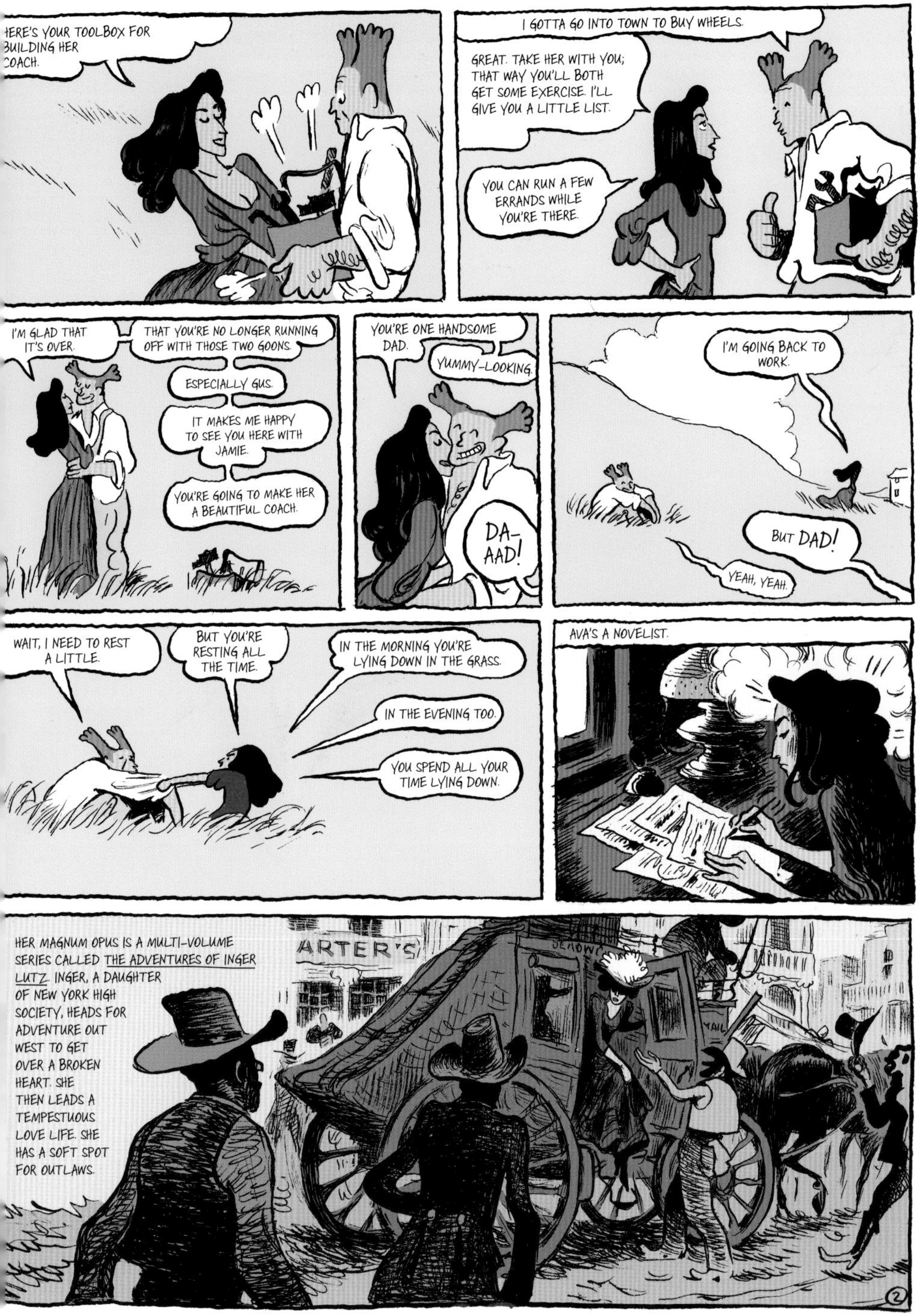
HERE'S YOUR TOOLBOX FOR BUILDING HER COACH.
I GOTTA GO INTO TOWN TO BUY WHEELS.
GREAT. TAKE HER WITH YOU; THAT WAY YOU'LL BOTH GET SOME EXERCISE. I'LL GIVE YOU A LITTLE LIST.
YOU CAN RUN A FEW ERRANDS WHILE YOU'RE THERE.
I'M GLAD THAT IT'S OVER.
THAT YOU'RE NO LONGER RUNNING OFF WITH THOSE TWO GOONS.
ESPECIALLY GUS.
IT MAKES ME HAPPY TO SEE YOU HERE WITH JAMIE.
YOU'RE GOING TO MAKE HER A BEAUTIFUL COACH.
YOU'RE ONE HANDSOME DAD.
YUMMY-LOOKING.
DA-AAD!
I'M GOING BACK TO WORK.
BUT DAD!
YEAH, YEAH.
WAIT, I NEED TO REST A LITTLE.
BUT YOU'RE RESTING ALL THE TIME.
IN THE MORNING YOU'RE LYING DOWN IN THE GRASS.
IN THE EVENING TOO.
YOU SPEND ALL YOUR TIME LYING DOWN.
AVA'S A NOVELIST.
HER MAGNUM OPUS IS A MULTI-VOLUME SERIES CALLED THE ADVENTURES OF INGER LUTZ. INGER, A DAUGHTER OF NEW YORK HIGH SOCIETY, HEADS FOR ADVENTURE OUT WEST TO GET OVER A BROKEN HEART. SHE THEN LEADS A TEMPESTUOUS LOVE LIFE. SHE HAS A SOFT SPOT FOR OUTLAWS.
ARTER'S
2

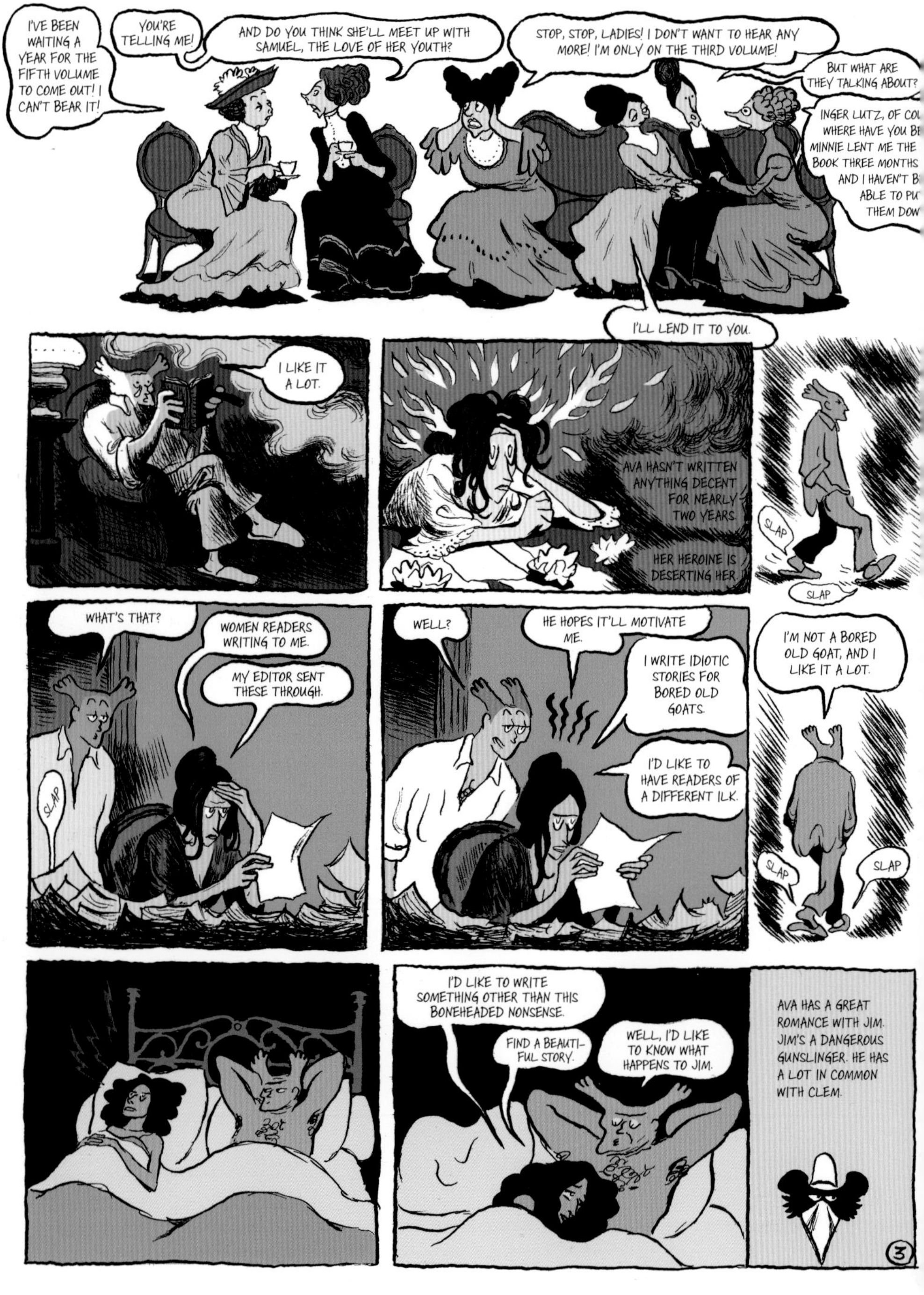
I'VE BEEN WAITING A YEAR FOR THE FIFTH VOLUME TO COME OUT! I CAN'T BEAR IT!
YOU'RE TELLING ME!
AND DO YOU THINK SHE'LL MEET UP WITH SAMUEL, THE LOVE OF HER YOUTH?
STOP, STOP, LADIES! I DON'T WANT TO HEAR ANY MORE! I'M ONLY ON THE THIRD VOLUME!
BUT WHAT ARE THEY TALKING ABOUT?
INGER LUTZ, OF CO
WHERE HAVE YOU B
MINNIE LENT ME THE BOOK THREE MONTHS AND I HAVEN'T B ABLE TO PU THEM DOW
I'LL LEND IT TO YOU.
I LIKE IT A LOT.
AVA HASN'T WRITTEN ANYTHING DECENT FOR NEARLY TWO YEARS.
HER HEROINE IS DESERTING HER.
SLAP
SLAP
WHAT'S THAT?
WOMEN READERS WRITING TO ME.
MY EDITOR SENT THESE THROUGH.
SLAP
WELL?
HE HOPES IT'LL MOTIVATE ME.
I WRITE IDIOTIC STORIES FOR BORED OLD GOATS.
I'D LIKE TO HAVE READERS OF A DIFFERENT ILK.
I'M NOT A BORED OLD GOAT, AND I LIKE IT A LOT.
SLAP
SLAP
I'D LIKE TO WRITE SOMETHING OTHER THAN THIS BONEHEADED NONSENSE.
FIND A BEAUTI-FUL STORY.
WELL, I'D LIKE TO KNOW WHAT HAPPENS TO JIM.
AVA HAS A GREAT ROMANCE WITH JIM. JIM'S A DANGEROUS GUNSLINGER. HE HAS A LOT IN COMMON WITH CLEM.
3

WHAT'S WITH THE HAT?

MY PUBLISHER'S INVITING ME TO NEW YORK.

HE'S PRODUCING A ONE-VOLUME EDITION OF INGER'S STORIES.

HE SURE SEEMS TO CARE ABOUT YOU.

HE'S GOING TO ORGANIZE MAJOR SIGNINGS WITH MY READERS.

APPARENTLY, I'M REALLY IN DEMAND.

WHAT AM I GOING TO TELL THEM?

TAKE OFF THAT HAT, WOULD YOU?

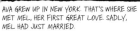

AVA GREW UP IN NEW YORK. THAT'S WHERE SHE MET MEL, HER FIRST GREAT LOVE. SADLY, MEL HAD JUST MARRIED.

AVA FLED AND SOUGHT REFUGE IN SAN BERNARDINO, CALIFORNIA, WITH HER AUNT KATIE, TO THE DISMAY OF HER PARENTS.

THAT'S WHERE SHE WROTE HER FIRST NOVEL (A FORGETTABLE TOME).

CLEM KNOWS ABOUT MEL'S EXISTENCE. HE'S NOT AFRAID OF HIM.

WANT A DRINK?

WHAT ARE YOU LAUGHING ABOUT?

IT'S MEL, RIGHT?

HEE HEE... HE MIGHT COME SEE ME.

OO

OO

FFFRRRR RLLLT♫

CH

?

FFFRRRRLLLLT♫

FFFRRRRLLLT♫

141

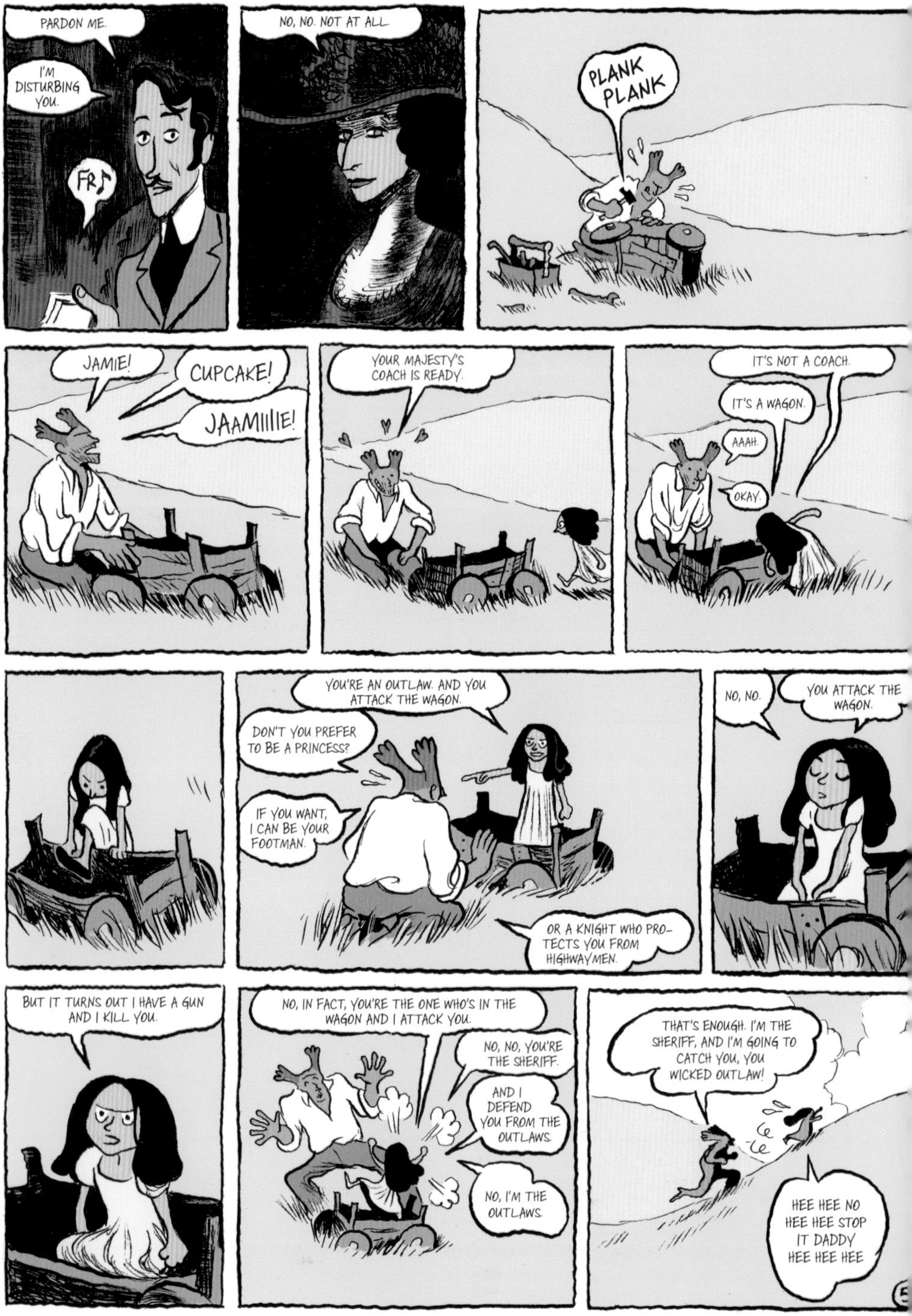
PARDON ME.
I'M DISTURBING YOU.
FR♪
NO, NO. NOT AT ALL.
PLANK PLANK
JAMIE!
CUPCAKE!
JAAMIIIIE!
YOUR MAJESTY'S COACH IS READY.
IT'S NOT A COACH.
IT'S A WAGON.
AAAH.
OKAY.
YOU'RE AN OUTLAW. AND YOU ATTACK THE WAGON.
DON'T YOU PREFER TO BE A PRINCESS?
IF YOU WANT, I CAN BE YOUR FOOTMAN.
OR A KNIGHT WHO PROTECTS YOU FROM HIGHWAYMEN.
NO, NO.
YOU ATTACK THE WAGON.
BUT IT TURNS OUT I HAVE A GUN AND I KILL YOU.
NO, IN FACT, YOU'RE THE ONE WHO'S IN THE WAGON AND I ATTACK YOU.
NO, NO, YOU'RE THE SHERIFF.
AND I DEFEND YOU FROM THE OUTLAWS.
NO, I'M THE OUTLAWS.
THAT'S ENOUGH. I'M THE SHERIFF, AND I'M GOING TO CATCH YOU, YOU WICKED OUTLAW!
HEE HEE NO HEE HEE STOP IT DADDY HEE HEE HEE

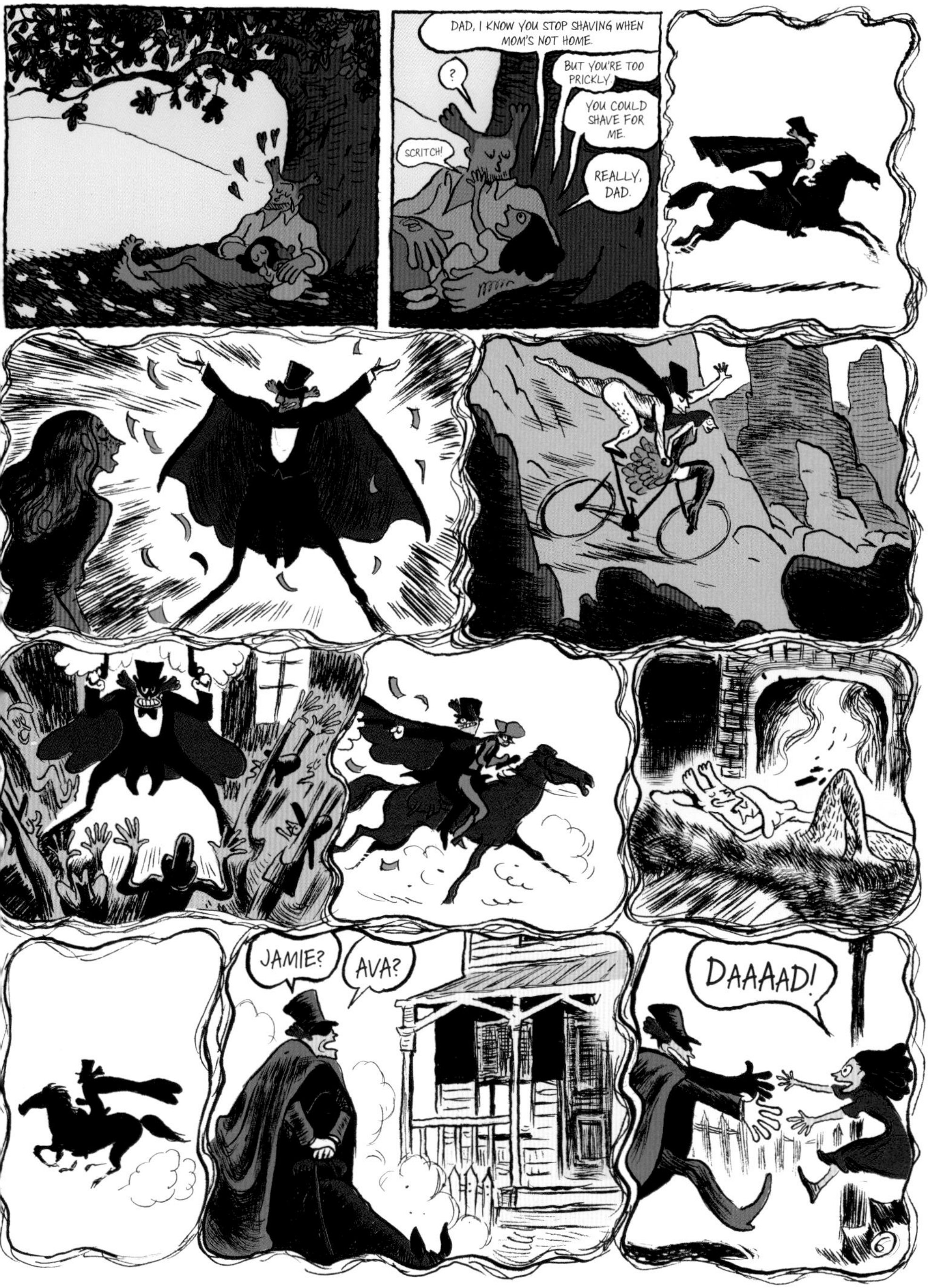
DAD, I KNOW YOU STOP SHAVING WHEN MOM'S NOT HOME.
?
BUT YOU'RE TOO PRICKLY.
YOU COULD SHAVE FOR ME.
SCRITCH!
REALLY, DAD.
JAMIE?
AVA?
DAAAAD!

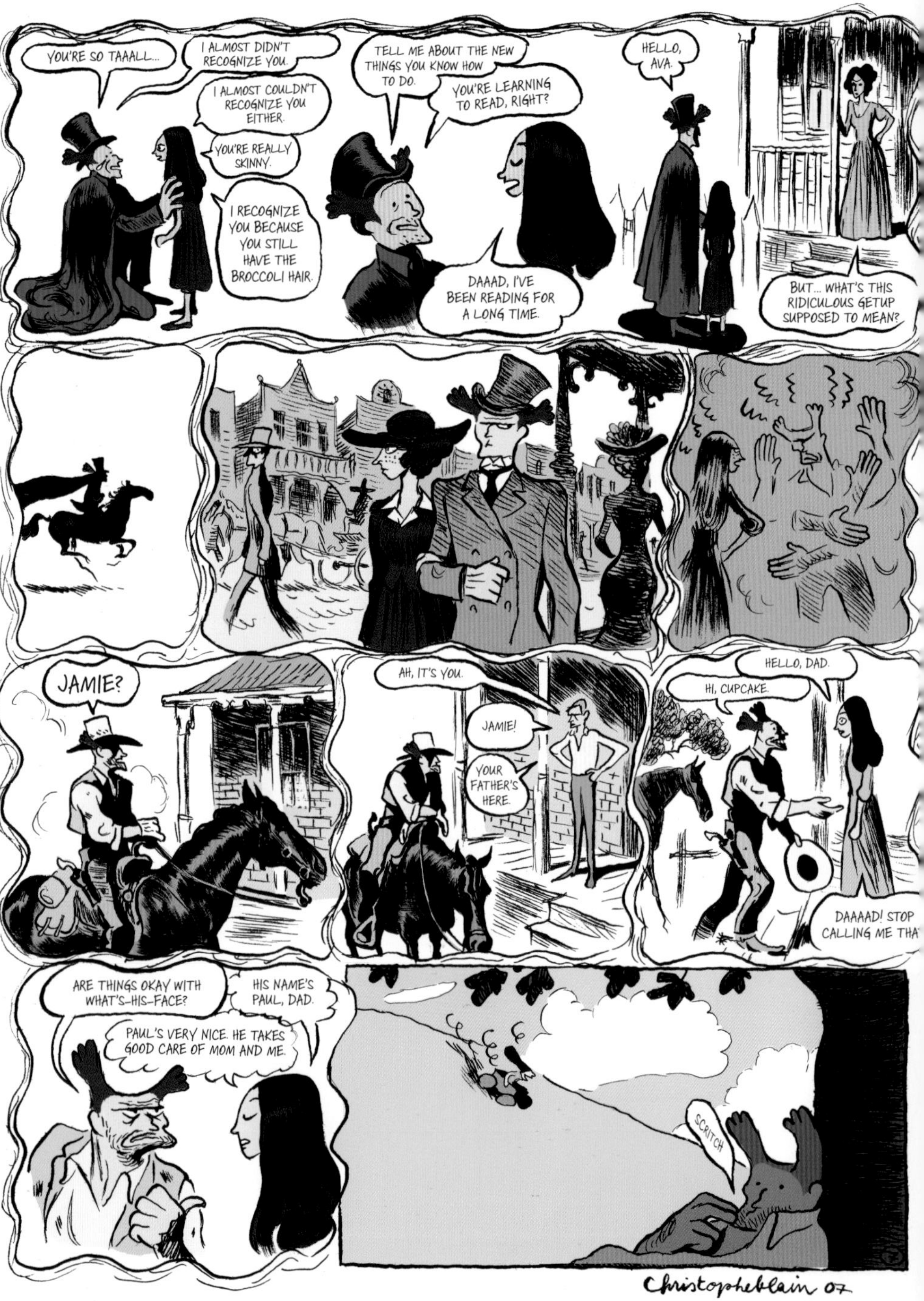
YOU'RE SO TAAALL...
I ALMOST DIDN'T RECOGNIZE YOU.
I ALMOST COULDN'T RECOGNIZE YOU EITHER.
YOU'RE REALLY SKINNY.
I RECOGNIZE YOU BECAUSE YOU STILL HAVE THE BROCCOLI HAIR.
TELL ME ABOUT THE NEW THINGS YOU KNOW HOW TO DO.
YOU'RE LEARNING TO READ, RIGHT?
DAAAD, I'VE BEEN READING FOR A LONG TIME.
HELLO, AVA.
BUT... WHAT'S THIS RIDICULOUS GETUP SUPPOSED TO MEAN?
JAMIE?
AH, IT'S YOU.
JAMIE!
YOUR FATHER'S HERE.
HI, CUPCAKE.
HELLO, DAD.
DAAAAD! STOP CALLING ME THA
ARE THINGS OKAY WITH WHAT'S-HIS-FACE?
HIS NAME'S PAUL, DAD.
PAUL'S VERY NICE. HE TAKES GOOD CARE OF MOM AND ME.
SCRITCH
Christopheblain 07

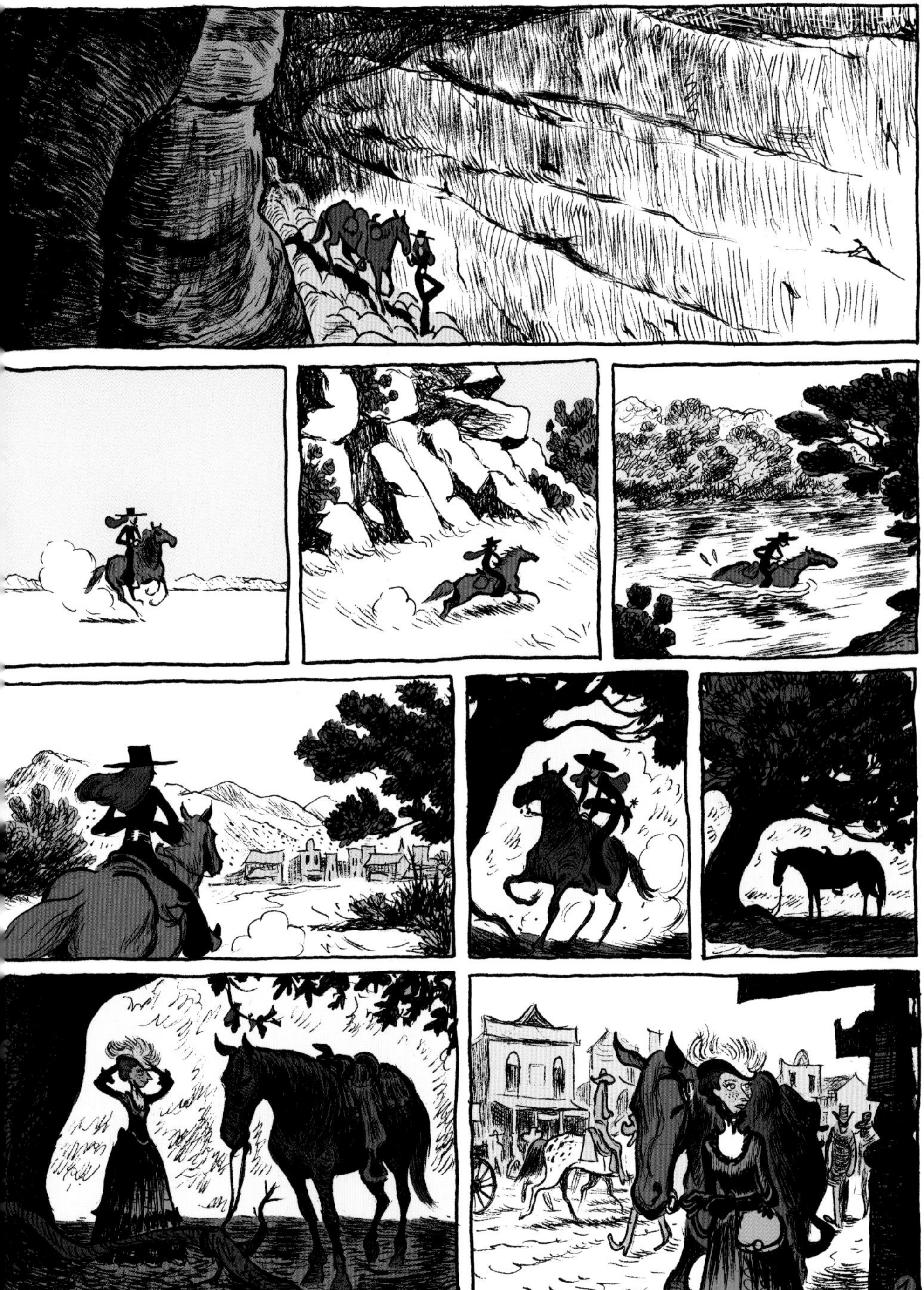

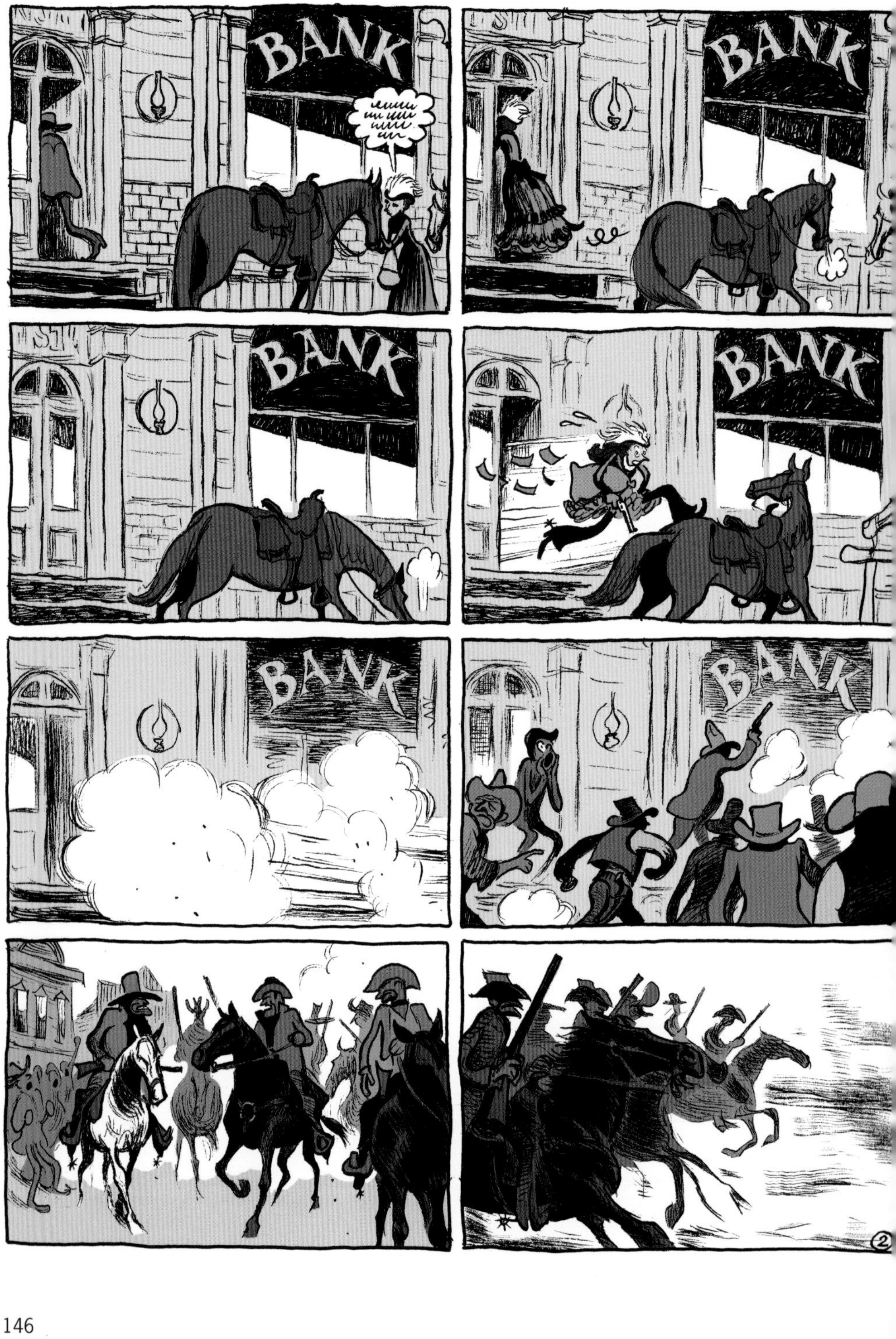
BANK
BANK
BANK
BANK
BANK
BANK
2

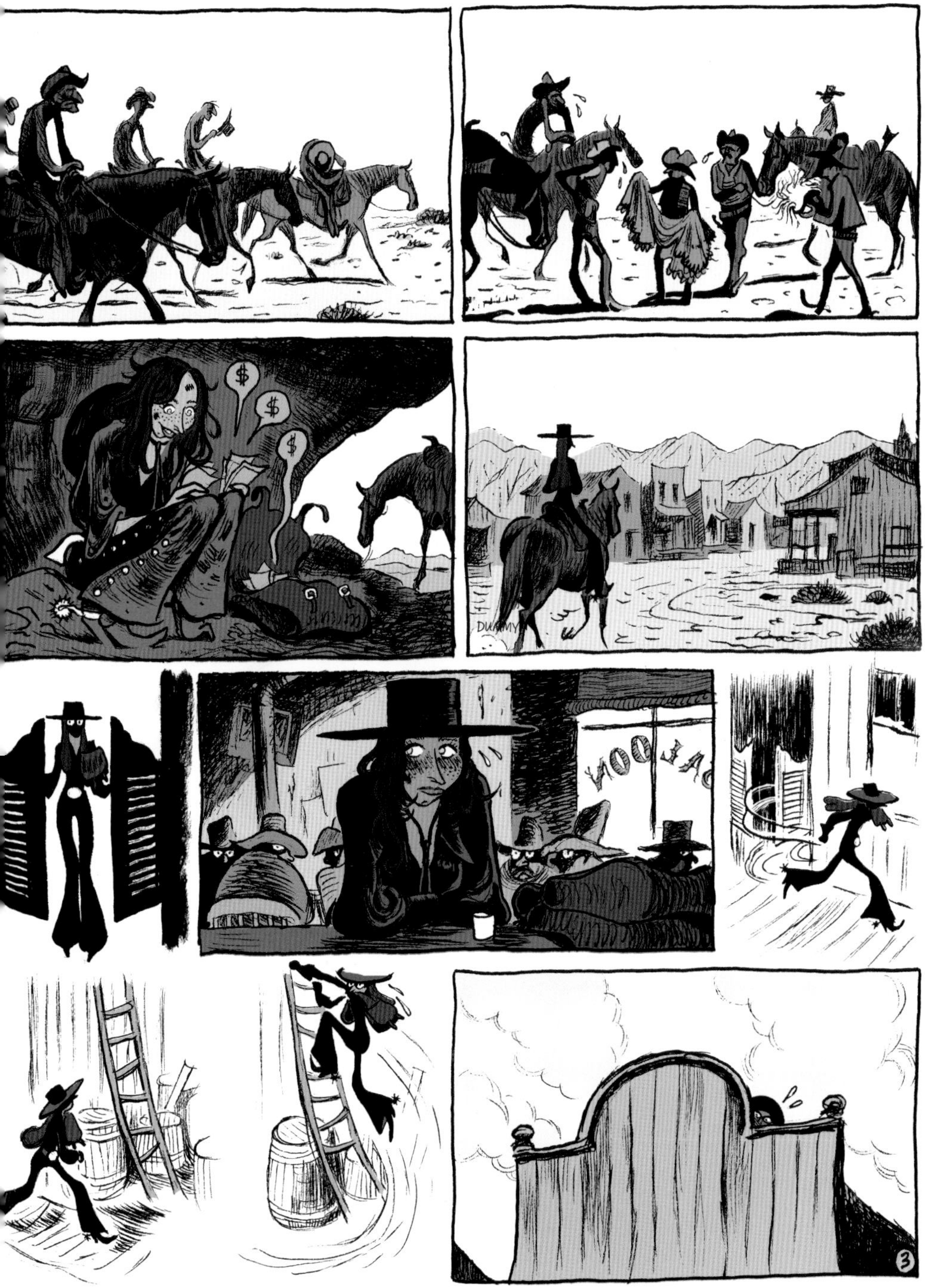
$
$
$
DUMMY

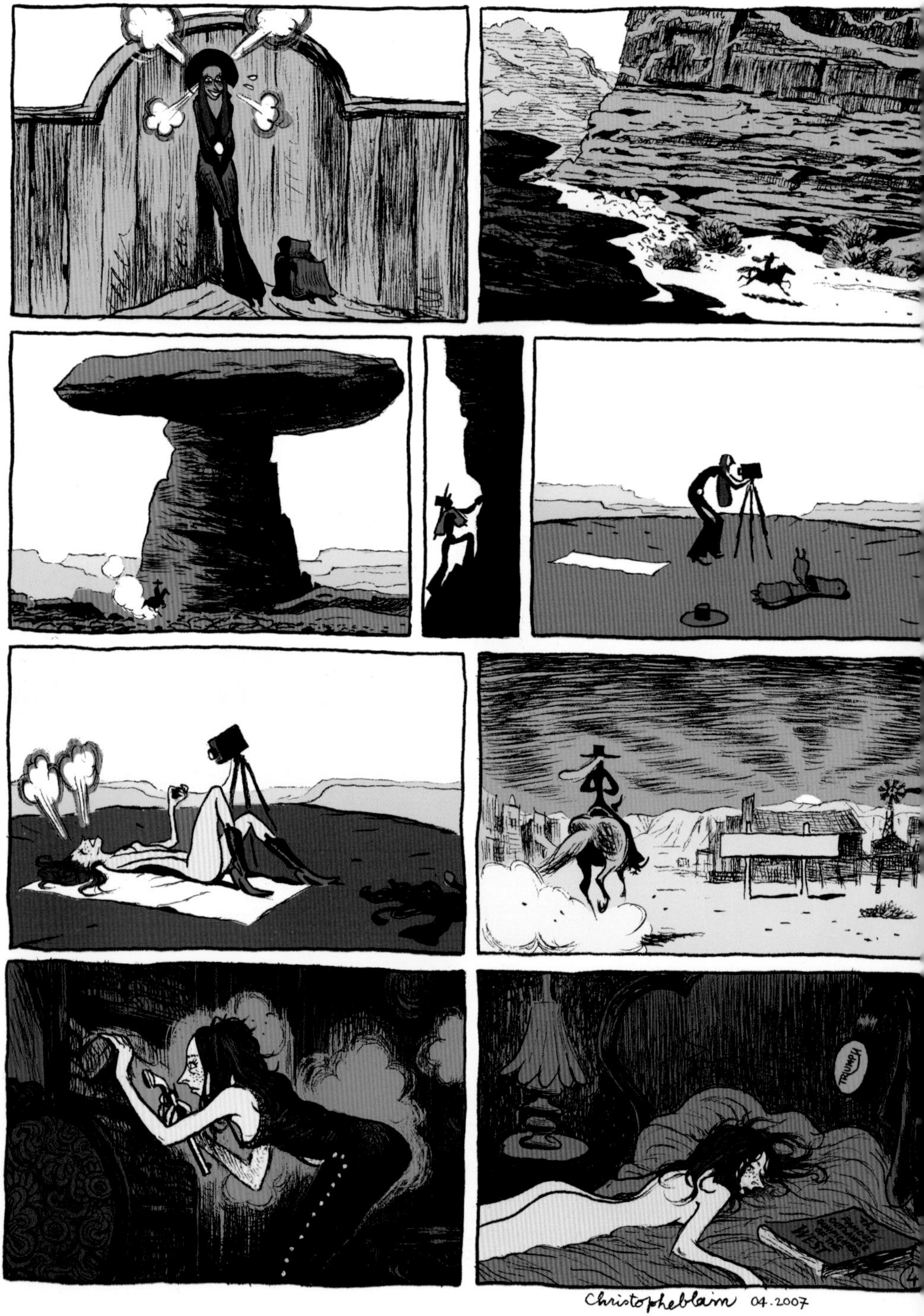
TRIUMPH

Christopheblain 04.2007

FRISCO

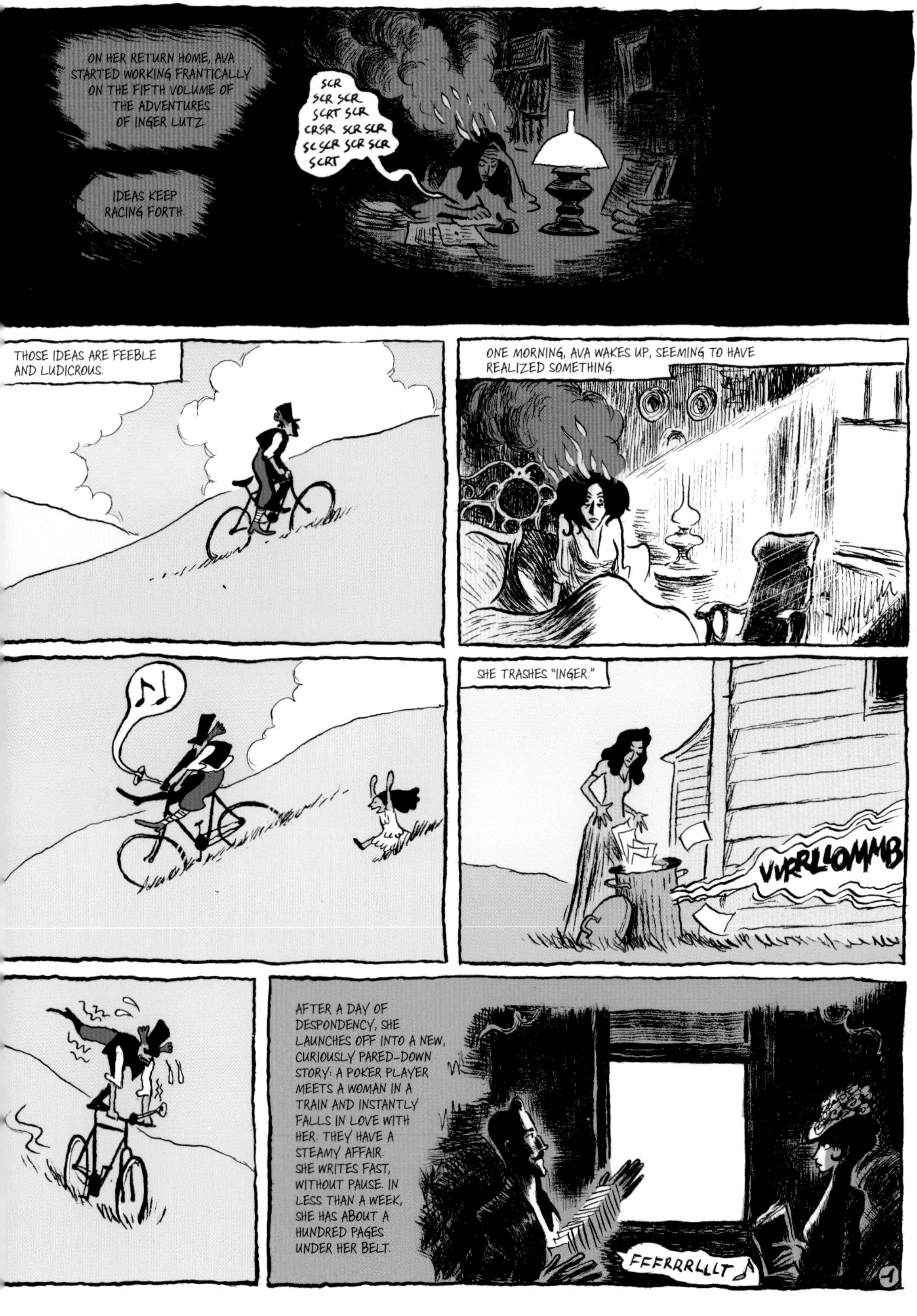

ON HER RETURN HOME, AVA STARTED WORKING FRANTICALLY ON THE FIFTH VOLUME OF THE ADVENTURES OF INGER LUTZ.
IDEAS KEEP RACING FORTH.
SCR SCR SCR SCRT SCR CRSR SCR SCR SC SCR SCR SCR SCRT
THOSE IDEAS ARE FEEBLE AND LUDICROUS.
ONE MORNING, AVA WAKES UP, SEEMING TO HAVE REALIZED SOMETHING.
SHE TRASHES "INGER."
VVRRLLOMMB
AFTER A DAY OF DESPONDENCY, SHE LAUNCHES OFF INTO A NEW, CURIOUSLY PARED-DOWN STORY: A POKER PLAYER MEETS A WOMAN IN A TRAIN AND INSTANTLY FALLS IN LOVE WITH HER. THEY HAVE A STEAMY AFFAIR. SHE WRITES FAST, WITHOUT PAUSE. IN LESS THAN A WEEK, SHE HAS ABOUT A HUNDRED PAGES UNDER HER BELT.
FFFRRRLLLT

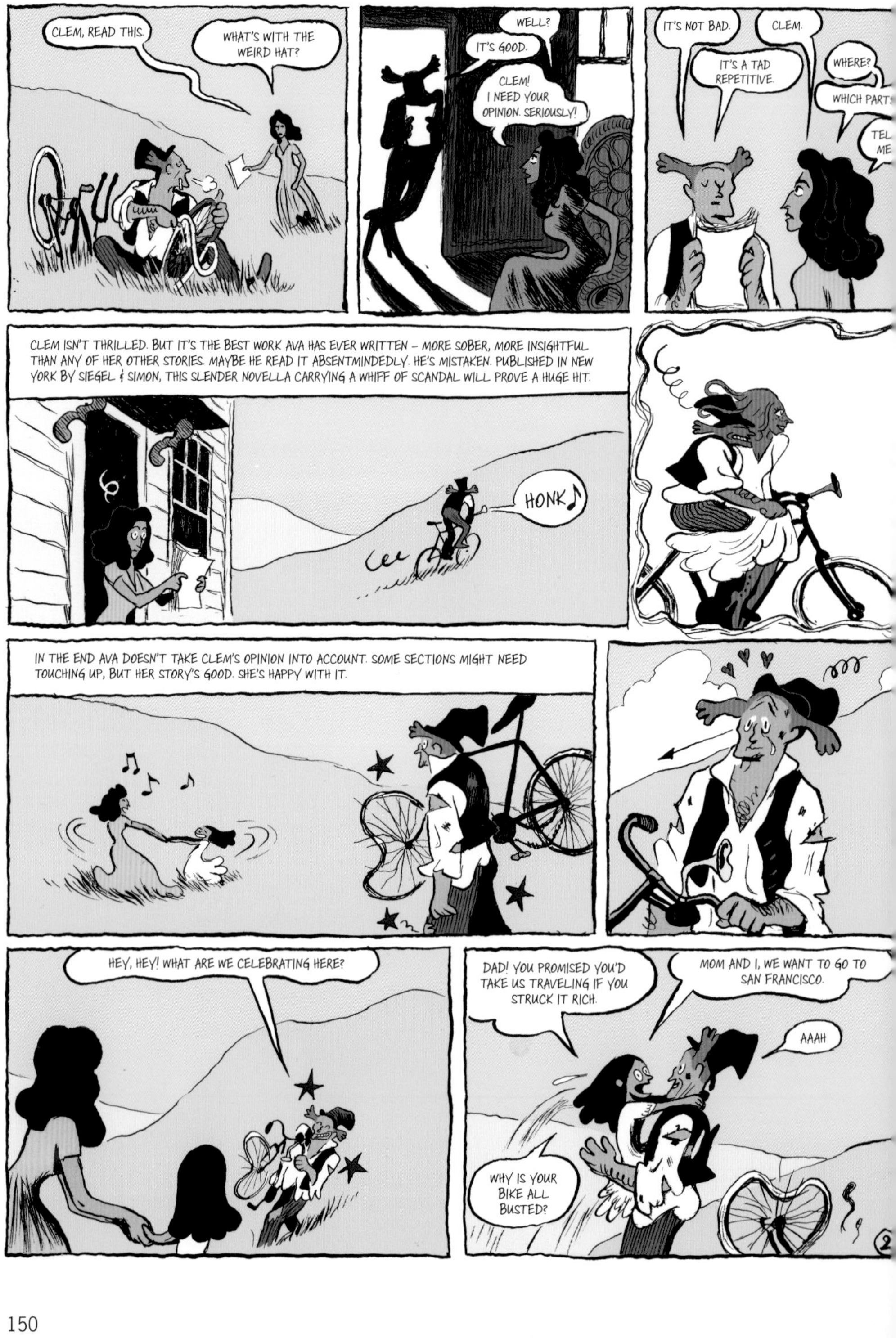
CLEM, READ THIS.
WHAT'S WITH THE WEIRD HAT?
WELL?
IT'S GOOD.
CLEM! I NEED YOUR OPINION. SERIOUSLY!
IT'S NOT BAD.
IT'S A TAD REPETITIVE.
CLEM.
WHERE?
WHICH PART
CLEM ISN'T THRILLED. BUT IT'S THE BEST WORK AVA HAS EVER WRITTEN – MORE SOBER, MORE INSIGHTFUL THAN ANY OF HER OTHER STORIES. MAYBE HE READ IT ABSENTMINDEDLY. HE'S MISTAKEN. PUBLISHED IN NEW YORK BY SIEGEL & SIMON, THIS SLENDER NOVELLA CARRYING A WHIFF OF SCANDAL WILL PROVE A HUGE HIT.
HONK♪
IN THE END AVA DOESN'T TAKE CLEM'S OPINION INTO ACCOUNT. SOME SECTIONS MIGHT NEED TOUCHING UP, BUT HER STORY'S GOOD. SHE'S HAPPY WITH IT.
HEY, HEY! WHAT ARE WE CELEBRATING HERE?
DAD! YOU PROMISED YOU'D TAKE US TRAVELING IF YOU STRUCK IT RICH.
MOM AND I, WE WANT TO GO TO SAN FRANCISCO.
AAAH
WHY IS YOUR BIKE ALL BUSTED?

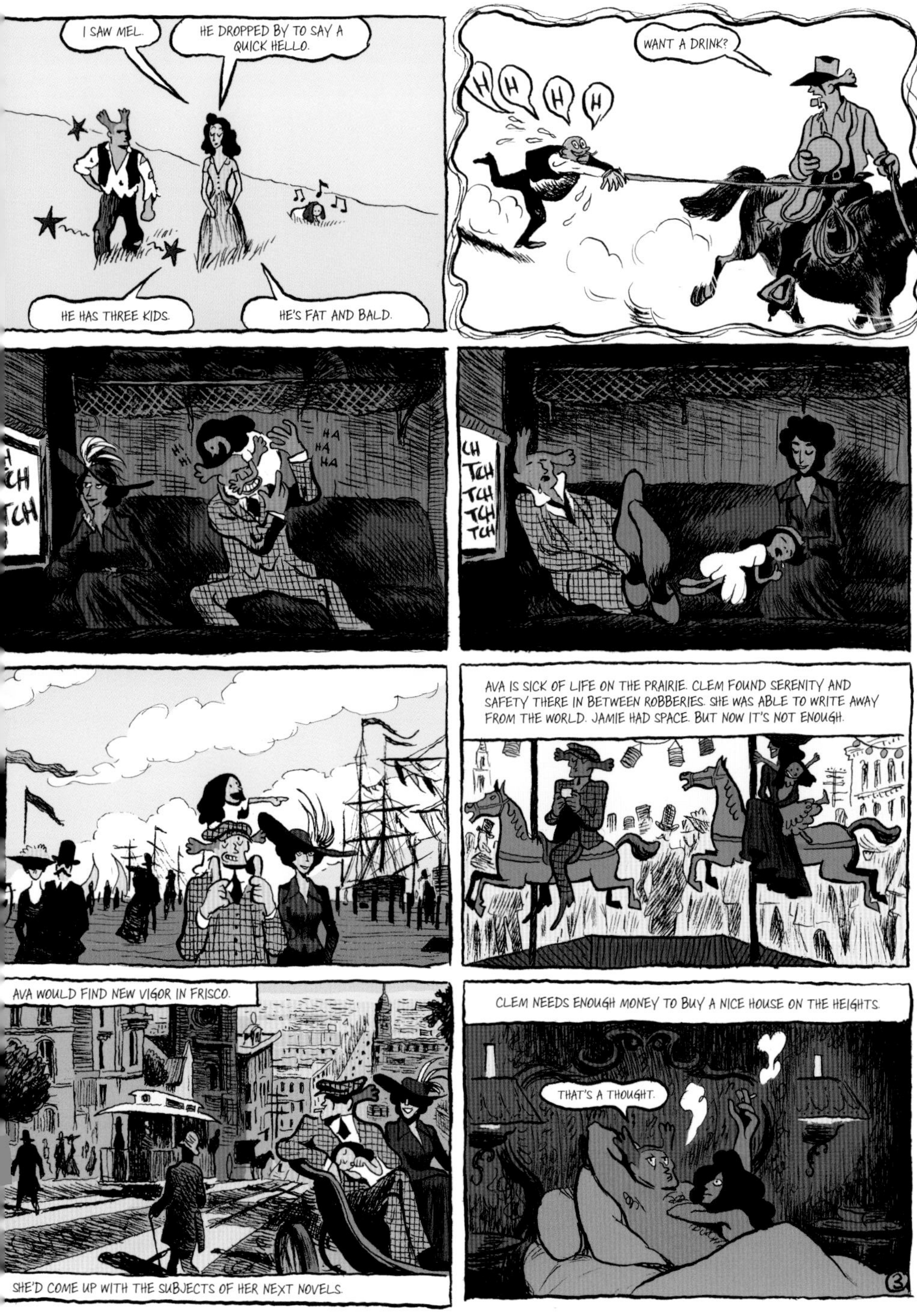
I SAW MEL.
HE DROPPED BY TO SAY A QUICK HELLO.
HE HAS THREE KIDS.
HE'S FAT AND BALD.
H H H H
WANT A DRINK?
HI HI
HA HA HA
CH TCH TCH
CH TCH TCH TCH TCH
AVA IS SICK OF LIFE ON THE PRAIRIE. CLEM FOUND SERENITY AND SAFETY THERE IN BETWEEN ROBBERIES. SHE WAS ABLE TO WRITE AWAY FROM THE WORLD. JAMIE HAD SPACE. BUT NOW IT'S NOT ENOUGH.
AVA WOULD FIND NEW VIGOR IN FRISCO.
SHE'D COME UP WITH THE SUBJECTS OF HER NEXT NOVELS.
CLEM NEEDS ENOUGH MONEY TO BUY A NICE HOUSE ON THE HEIGHTS.
THAT'S A THOUGHT.
3

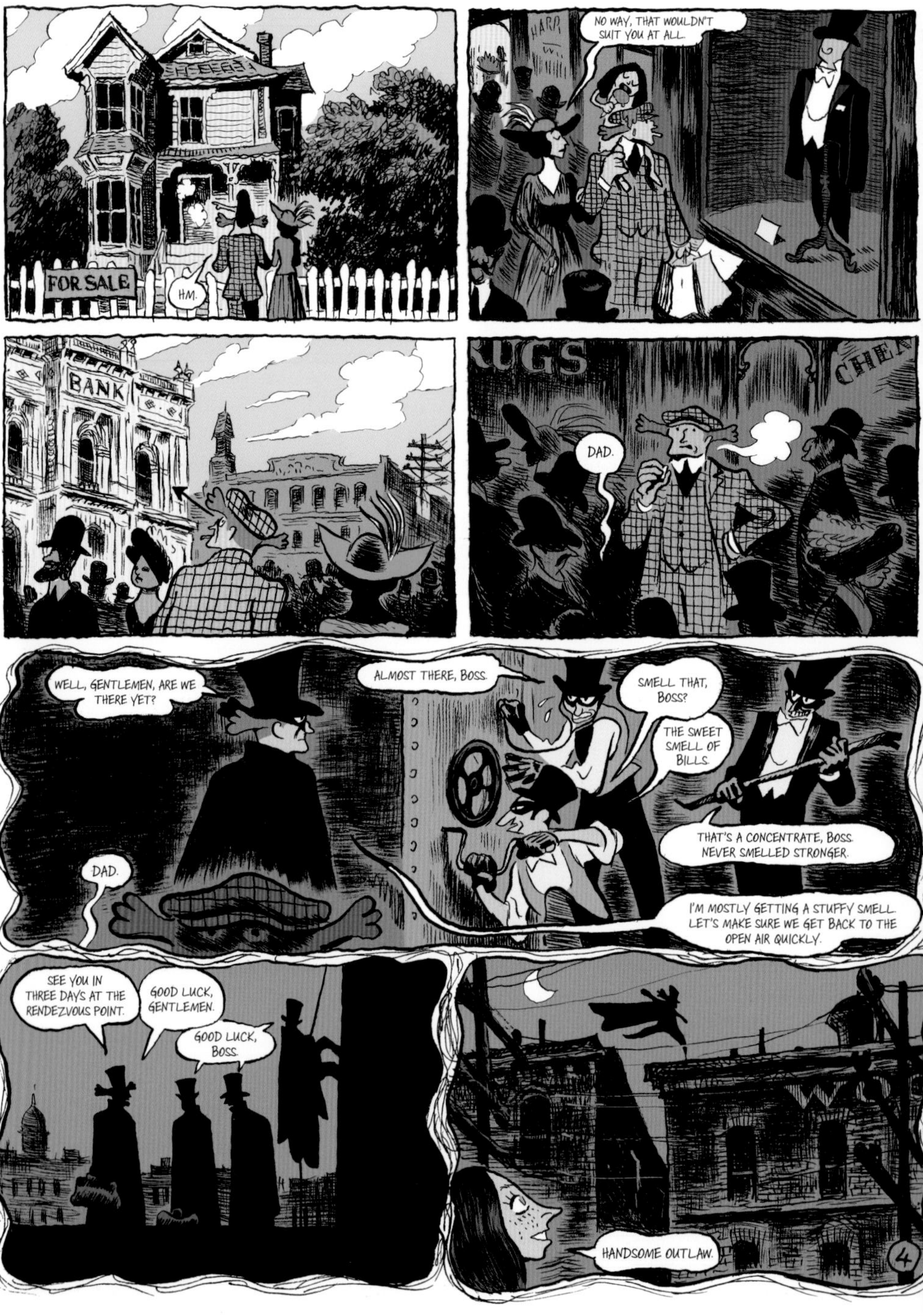
FOR SALE
HM.
HARP
NO WAY, THAT WOULDN'T SUIT YOU AT ALL.
BANK
UGS
CHEN
DAD.
WELL, GENTLEMEN, ARE WE THERE YET?
ALMOST THERE, BOSS.
SMELL THAT, BOSS?
THE SWEET SMELL OF BILLS.
THAT'S A CONCENTRATE, BOSS. NEVER SMELLED STRONGER.
DAD.
I'M MOSTLY GETTING A STUFFY SMELL. LET'S MAKE SURE WE GET BACK TO THE OPEN AIR QUICKLY.
SEE YOU IN THREE DAYS AT THE RENDEZVOUS POINT.
GOOD LUCK, GENTLEMEN.
GOOD LUCK, BOSS.
HANDSOME OUTLAW.
4

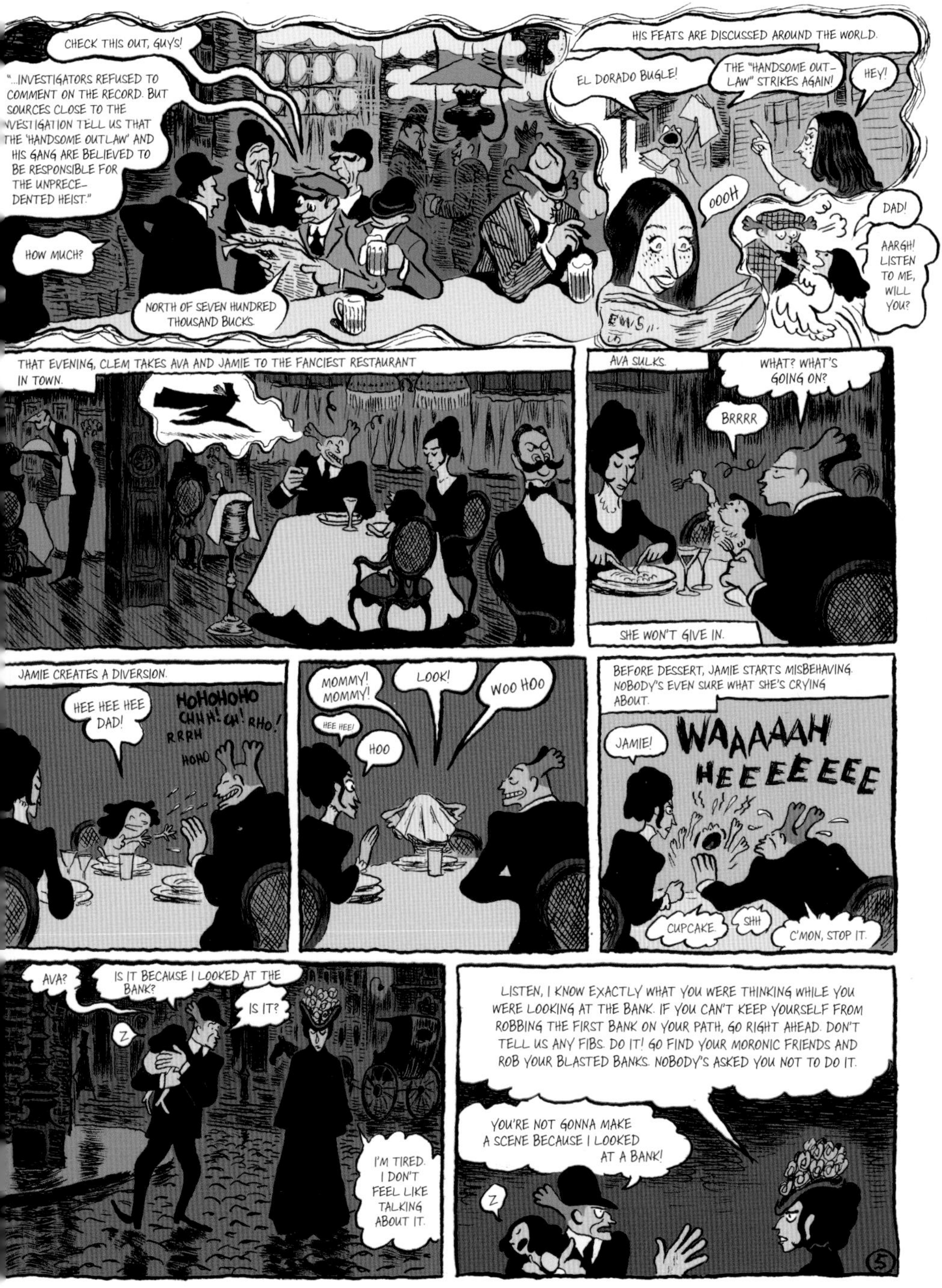
CHECK THIS OUT, GUYS!
"...INVESTIGATORS REFUSED TO COMMENT ON THE RECORD. BUT SOURCES CLOSE TO THE INVESTIGATION TELL US THAT THE 'HANDSOME OUTLAW' AND HIS GANG ARE BELIEVED TO BE RESPONSIBLE FOR THE UNPRECE-DENTED HEIST."
HOW MUCH?
NORTH OF SEVEN HUNDRED THOUSAND BUCKS.
HIS FEATS ARE DISCUSSED AROUND THE WORLD.
EL DORADO BUGLE!
THE "HANDSOME OUT-LAW" STRIKES AGAIN!
HEY!
OOOH
DAD!
AARGH! LISTEN TO ME, WILL YOU?
THAT EVENING, CLEM TAKES AVA AND JAMIE TO THE FANCIEST RESTAURANT IN TOWN.
AVA SULKS.
WHAT? WHAT'S GOING ON?
BRRRR
SHE WON'T GIVE IN.
JAMIE CREATES A DIVERSION.
HEE HEE HEE DAD!
HOHOHOHO CHHH! CH! RHO! RRRH HOHO
MOMMY! MOMMY!
LOOK!
WOO HOO
HEE HEE!
HOO
BEFORE DESSERT, JAMIE STARTS MISBEHAVING. NOBODY'S EVEN SURE WHAT SHE'S CRYING ABOUT.
JAMIE!
WAAAAAH HEEEEEEEE
CUPCAKE.
SHH
C'MON, STOP IT.
AVA?
IS IT BECAUSE I LOOKED AT THE BANK?
IS IT?
Z
I'M TIRED. I DON'T FEEL LIKE TALKING ABOUT IT.
LISTEN, I KNOW EXACTLY WHAT YOU WERE THINKING WHILE YOU WERE LOOKING AT THE BANK. IF YOU CAN'T KEEP YOURSELF FROM ROBBING THE FIRST BANK ON YOUR PATH, GO RIGHT AHEAD. DON'T TELL US ANY FIBS. DO IT! GO FIND YOUR MORONIC FRIENDS AND ROB YOUR BLASTED BANKS. NOBODY'S ASKED YOU NOT TO DO IT.
YOU'RE NOT GONNA MAKE A SCENE BECAUSE I LOOKED AT A BANK!
Z
5

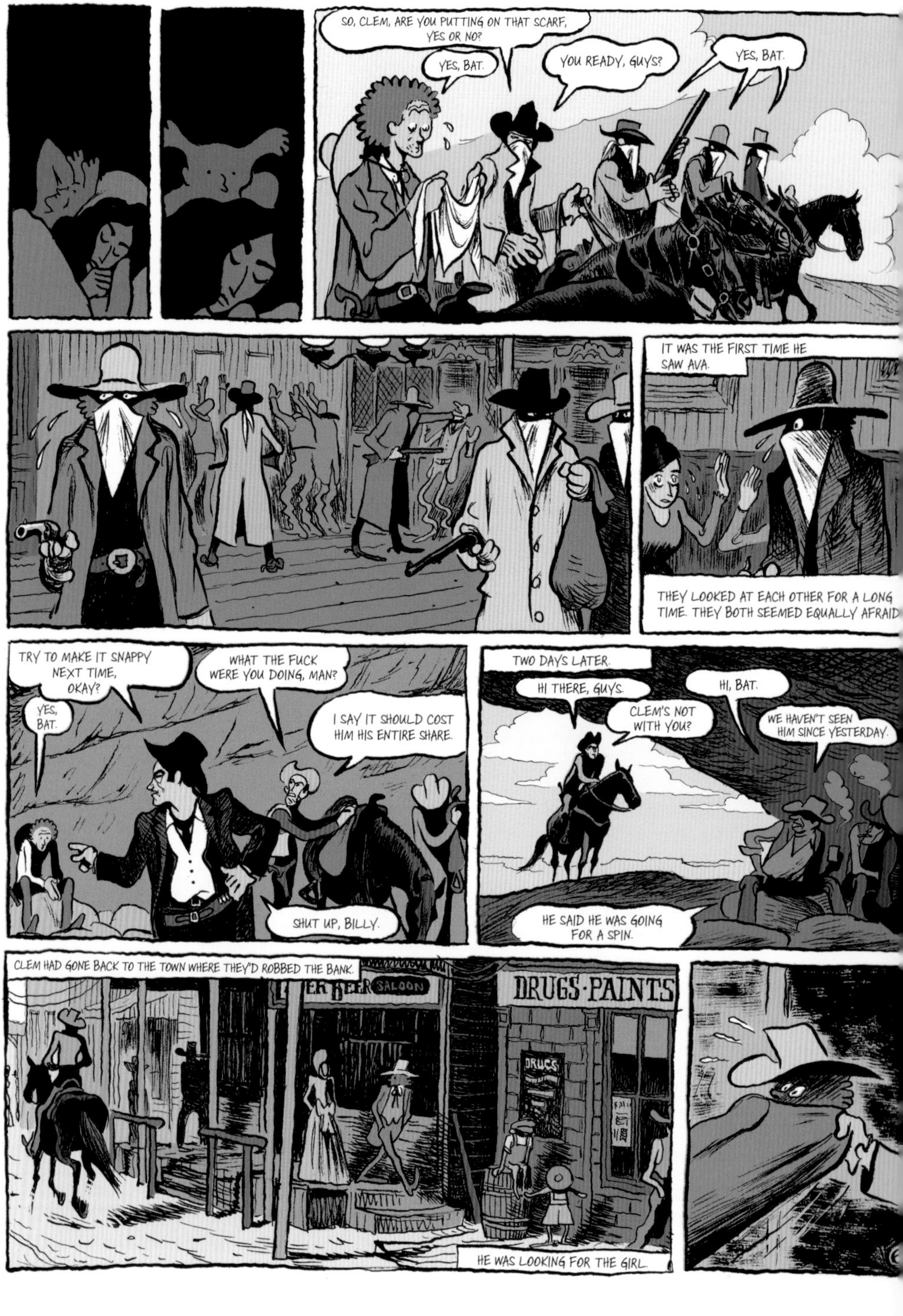
SO, CLEM, ARE YOU PUTTING ON THAT SCARF, YES OR NO?
YES, BAT.
YOU READY, GUYS?
YES, BAT.
IT WAS THE FIRST TIME HE SAW AVA.
THEY LOOKED AT EACH OTHER FOR A LONG TIME. THEY BOTH SEEMED EQUALLY AFRAID
TRY TO MAKE IT SNAPPY NEXT TIME, OKAY?
YES, BAT.
WHAT THE FUCK WERE YOU DOING, MAN?
I SAY IT SHOULD COST HIM HIS ENTIRE SHARE.
SHUT UP, BILLY.
TWO DAYS LATER.
HI THERE, GUYS.
CLEM'S NOT WITH YOU?
HI, BAT.
WE HAVEN'T SEEN HIM SINCE YESTERDAY.
HE SAID HE WAS GOING FOR A SPIN.
CLEM HAD GONE BACK TO THE TOWN WHERE THEY'D ROBBED THE BANK.
SALOON
DRUGS·PAINTS
DRUGS
HE WAS LOOKING FOR THE GIRL.

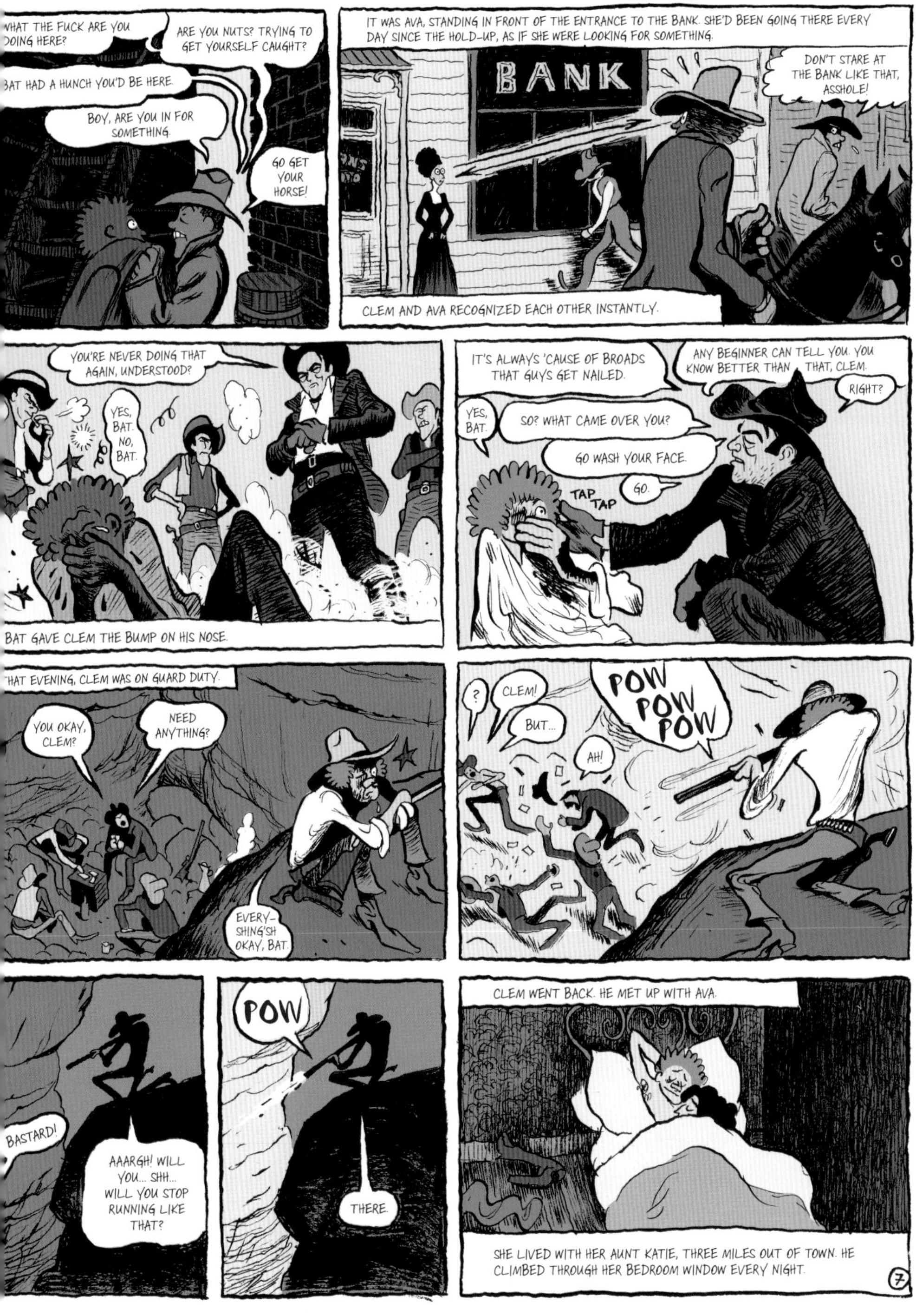
WHAT THE FUCK ARE YOU DOING HERE?
ARE YOU NUTS? TRYING TO GET YOURSELF CAUGHT?
BAT HAD A HUNCH YOU'D BE HERE.
BOY, ARE YOU IN FOR SOMETHING.
GO GET YOUR HORSE!
IT WAS AVA, STANDING IN FRONT OF THE ENTRANCE TO THE BANK. SHE'D BEEN GOING THERE EVERY DAY SINCE THE HOLD-UP, AS IF SHE WERE LOOKING FOR SOMETHING.
BANK
DON'T STARE AT THE BANK LIKE THAT, ASSHOLE!
CLEM AND AVA RECOGNIZED EACH OTHER INSTANTLY.
YOU'RE NEVER DOING THAT AGAIN, UNDERSTOOD?
YES, BAT. NO, BAT.
BAT GAVE CLEM THE BUMP ON HIS NOSE.
IT'S ALWAYS 'CAUSE OF BROADS THAT GUYS GET NAILED.
ANY BEGINNER CAN TELL YOU. YOU KNOW BETTER THAN THAT, CLEM.
RIGHT?
YES, BAT.
SO? WHAT CAME OVER YOU?
GO WASH YOUR FACE.
GO.
TAP TAP
THAT EVENING, CLEM WAS ON GUARD DUTY.
YOU OKAY, CLEM?
NEED ANYTHING?
EVERY-SHING'SH OKAY, BAT.
?
CLEM!
BUT...
POW POW POW
AH!
BASTARD!
AAARGH! WILL YOU... SHH... WILL YOU STOP RUNNING LIKE THAT?
POW
THERE.
CLEM WENT BACK. HE MET UP WITH AVA.
SHE LIVED WITH HER AUNT KATIE, THREE MILES OUT OF TOWN. HE CLIMBED THROUGH HER BEDROOM WINDOW EVERY NIGHT.
7

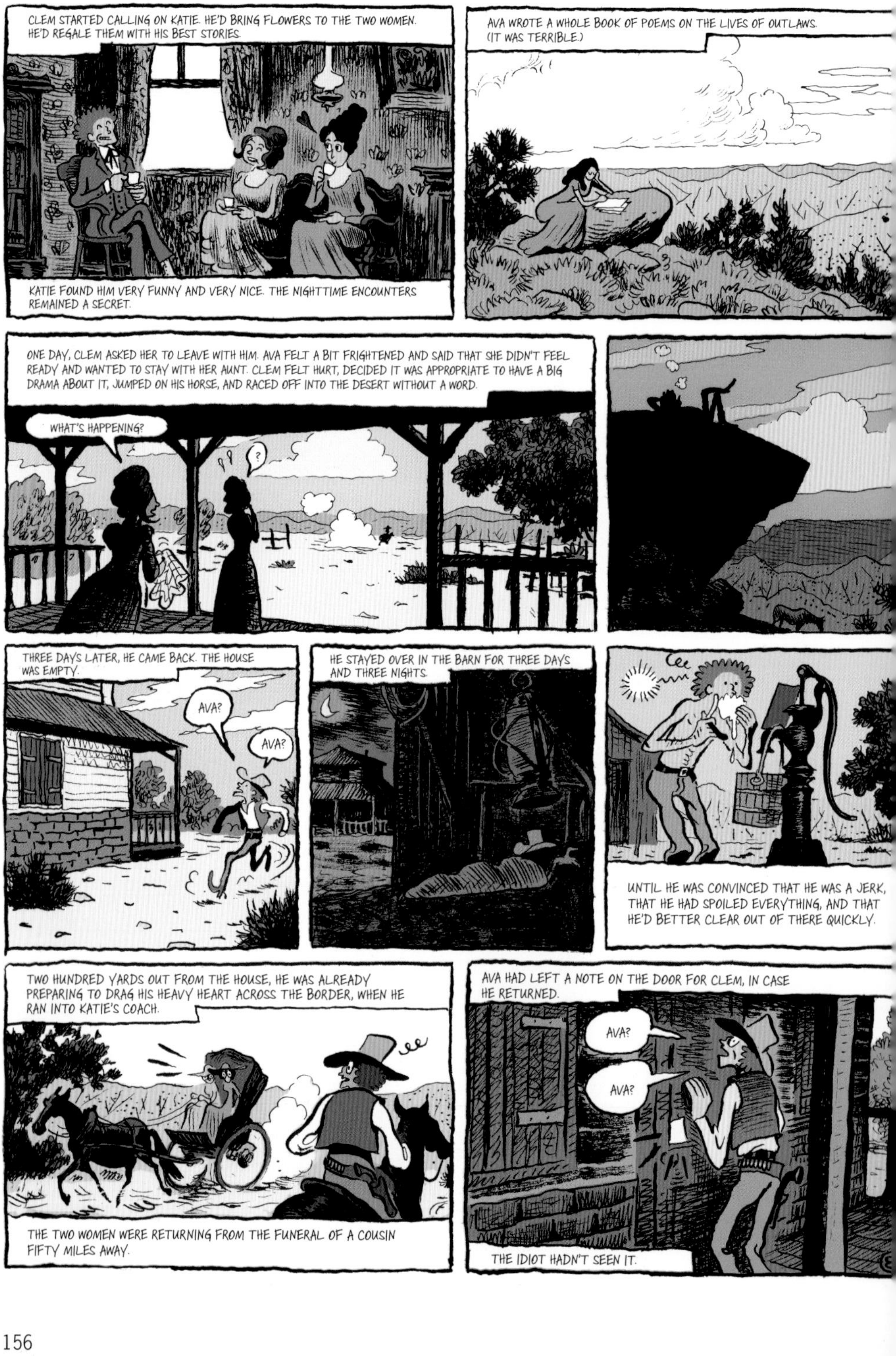
CLEM STARTED CALLING ON KATIE. HE'D BRING FLOWERS TO THE TWO WOMEN. HE'D REGALE THEM WITH HIS BEST STORIES.
KATIE FOUND HIM VERY FUNNY AND VERY NICE. THE NIGHTTIME ENCOUNTERS REMAINED A SECRET.
AVA WROTE A WHOLE BOOK OF POEMS ON THE LIVES OF OUTLAWS. (IT WAS TERRIBLE.)
ONE DAY, CLEM ASKED HER TO LEAVE WITH HIM. AVA FELT A BIT FRIGHTENED AND SAID THAT SHE DIDN'T FEEL READY AND WANTED TO STAY WITH HER AUNT. CLEM FELT HURT, DECIDED IT WAS APPROPRIATE TO HAVE A BIG DRAMA ABOUT IT, JUMPED ON HIS HORSE, AND RACED OFF INTO THE DESERT WITHOUT A WORD.
WHAT'S HAPPENING?
?
THREE DAYS LATER, HE CAME BACK. THE HOUSE WAS EMPTY.
AVA?
AVA?
HE STAYED OVER IN THE BARN FOR THREE DAYS AND THREE NIGHTS.
UNTIL HE WAS CONVINCED THAT HE WAS A JERK, THAT HE HAD SPOILED EVERYTHING, AND THAT HE'D BETTER CLEAR OUT OF THERE QUICKLY.
TWO HUNDRED YARDS OUT FROM THE HOUSE, HE WAS ALREADY PREPARING TO DRAG HIS HEAVY HEART ACROSS THE BORDER, WHEN HE RAN INTO KATIE'S COACH.
THE TWO WOMEN WERE RETURNING FROM THE FUNERAL OF A COUSIN FIFTY MILES AWAY.
AVA HAD LEFT A NOTE ON THE DOOR FOR CLEM, IN CASE HE RETURNED.
AVA?
AVA?
THE IDIOT HADN'T SEEN IT.

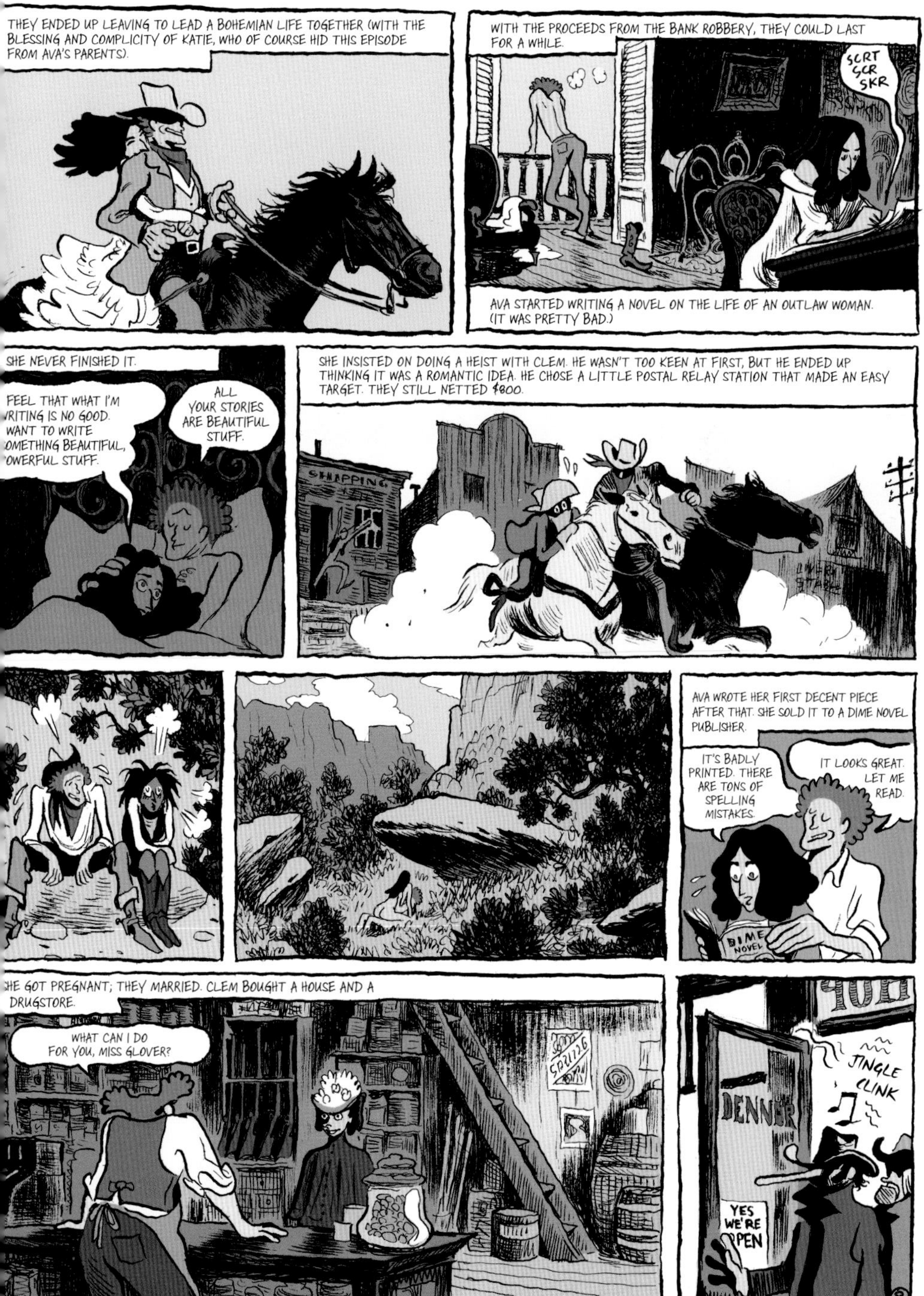
THEY ENDED UP LEAVING TO LEAD A BOHEMIAN LIFE TOGETHER (WITH THE BLESSING AND COMPLICITY OF KATIE, WHO OF COURSE HID THIS EPISODE FROM AVA'S PARENTS).
WITH THE PROCEEDS FROM THE BANK ROBBERY, THEY COULD LAST FOR A WHILE.
SCRT SCR SKR
AVA STARTED WRITING A NOVEL ON THE LIFE OF AN OUTLAW WOMAN. (IT WAS PRETTY BAD.)
SHE NEVER FINISHED IT.
FEEL THAT WHAT I'M WRITING IS NO GOOD. WANT TO WRITE SOMETHING BEAUTIFUL, POWERFUL STUFF.
ALL YOUR STORIES ARE BEAUTIFUL STUFF.
SHE INSISTED ON DOING A HEIST WITH CLEM. HE WASN'T TOO KEEN AT FIRST, BUT HE ENDED UP THINKING IT WAS A ROMANTIC IDEA. HE CHOSE A LITTLE POSTAL RELAY STATION THAT MADE AN EASY TARGET. THEY STILL NETTED $800.
SHIPPING
AVA WROTE HER FIRST DECENT PIECE AFTER THAT. SHE SOLD IT TO A DIME NOVEL PUBLISHER.
IT'S BADLY PRINTED. THERE ARE TONS OF SPELLING MISTAKES.
IT LOOKS GREAT. LET ME READ.
DIME NOVEL
SHE GOT PREGNANT; THEY MARRIED. CLEM BOUGHT A HOUSE AND A DRUGSTORE.
WHAT CAN I DO FOR YOU, MISS GLOVER?
JINGLE CLINK
DENNER
YES WE'RE OPEN

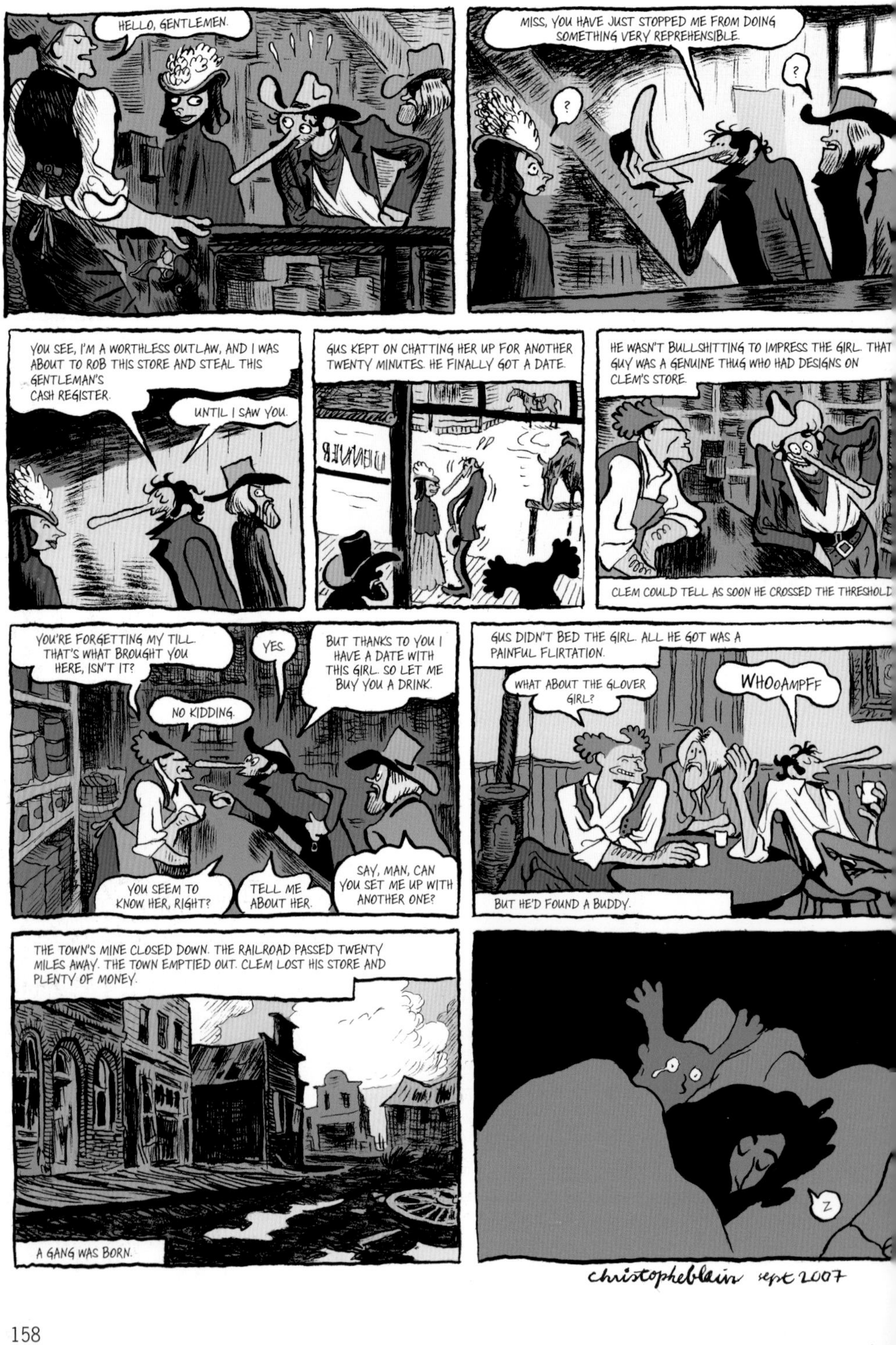
HELLO, GENTLEMEN.
MISS, YOU HAVE JUST STOPPED ME FROM DOING SOMETHING VERY REPREHENSIBLE.
?
?
YOU SEE, I'M A WORTHLESS OUTLAW, AND I WAS ABOUT TO ROB THIS STORE AND STEAL THIS GENTLEMAN'S CASH REGISTER.
UNTIL I SAW YOU.
GUS KEPT ON CHATTING HER UP FOR ANOTHER TWENTY MINUTES. HE FINALLY GOT A DATE.
HE WASN'T BULLSHITTING TO IMPRESS THE GIRL. THAT GUY WAS A GENUINE THUG WHO HAD DESIGNS ON CLEM'S STORE.
CLEM COULD TELL AS SOON HE CROSSED THE THRESHOLD.
YOU'RE FORGETTING MY TILL. THAT'S WHAT BROUGHT YOU HERE, ISN'T IT?
YES.
BUT THANKS TO YOU I HAVE A DATE WITH THIS GIRL. SO LET ME BUY YOU A DRINK.
NO KIDDING.
YOU SEEM TO KNOW HER, RIGHT?
TELL ME ABOUT HER.
SAY, MAN, CAN YOU SET ME UP WITH ANOTHER ONE?
GUS DIDN'T BED THE GIRL. ALL HE GOT WAS A PAINFUL FLIRTATION.
WHAT ABOUT THE GLOVER GIRL?
WHOoAMPFF
BUT HE'D FOUND A BUDDY.
THE TOWN'S MINE CLOSED DOWN. THE RAILROAD PASSED TWENTY MILES AWAY. THE TOWN EMPTIED OUT. CLEM LOST HIS STORE AND PLENTY OF MONEY.
A GANG WAS BORN.
Z
christopheblain sept 2007

BANK OF CALIFORNIA

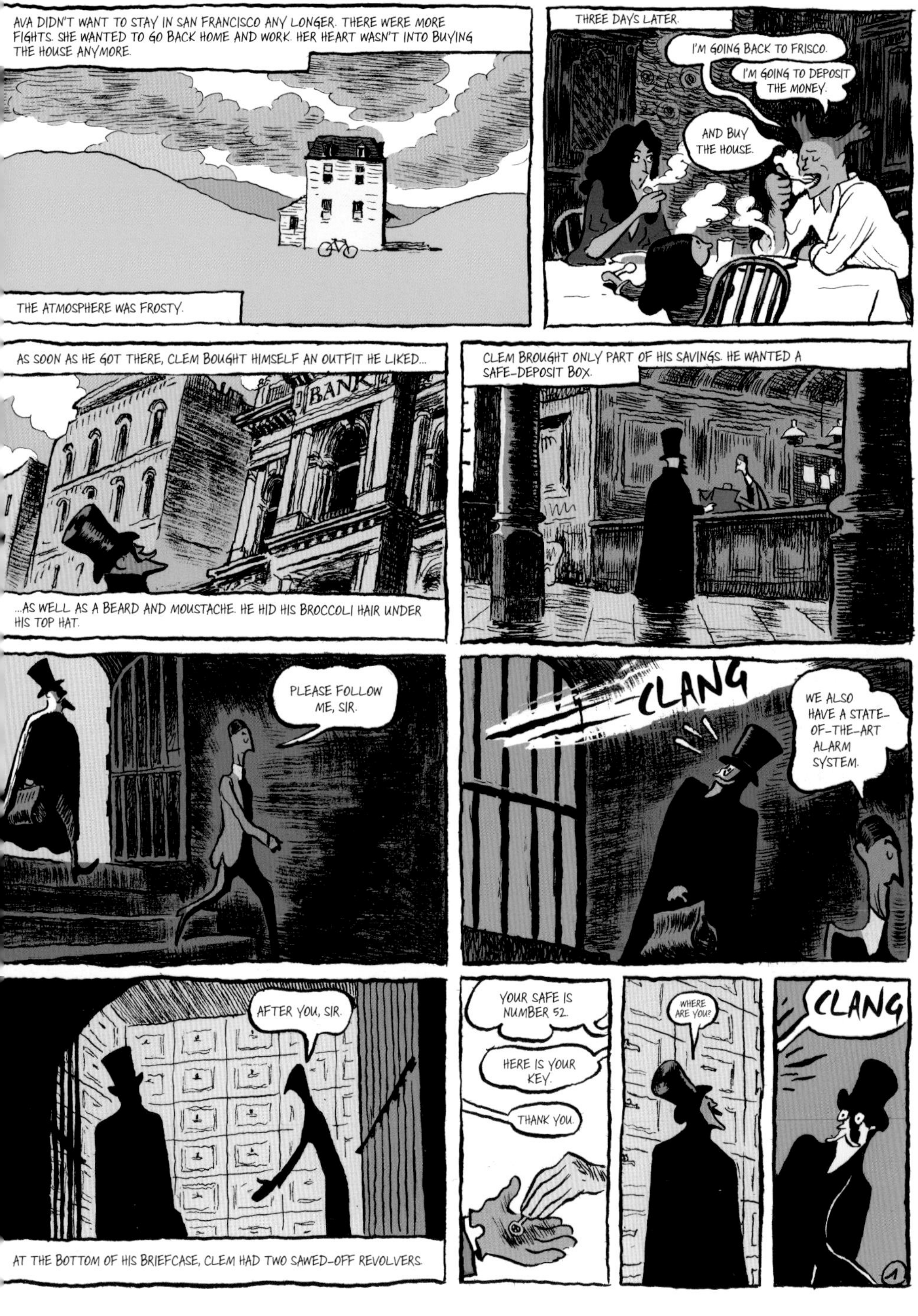
AVA DIDN'T WANT TO STAY IN SAN FRANCISCO ANY LONGER. THERE WERE MORE FIGHTS. SHE WANTED TO GO BACK HOME AND WORK. HER HEART WASN'T INTO BUYING THE HOUSE ANYMORE.
THE ATMOSPHERE WAS FROSTY.
THREE DAYS LATER.
I'M GOING BACK TO FRISCO.
I'M GOING TO DEPOSIT THE MONEY.
AND BUY THE HOUSE.
AS SOON AS HE GOT THERE, CLEM BOUGHT HIMSELF AN OUTFIT HE LIKED...
BANK
...AS WELL AS A BEARD AND MOUSTACHE. HE HID HIS BROCCOLI HAIR UNDER HIS TOP HAT.
CLEM BROUGHT ONLY PART OF HIS SAVINGS. HE WANTED A SAFE-DEPOSIT BOX.
PLEASE FOLLOW ME, SIR.
CLANG
WE ALSO HAVE A STATE-OF-THE-ART ALARM SYSTEM.
AFTER YOU, SIR.
AT THE BOTTOM OF HIS BRIEFCASE, CLEM HAD TWO SAWED-OFF REVOLVERS.
YOUR SAFE IS NUMBER 52.
HERE IS YOUR KEY.
THANK YOU.
WHERE ARE YOU?
CLANG

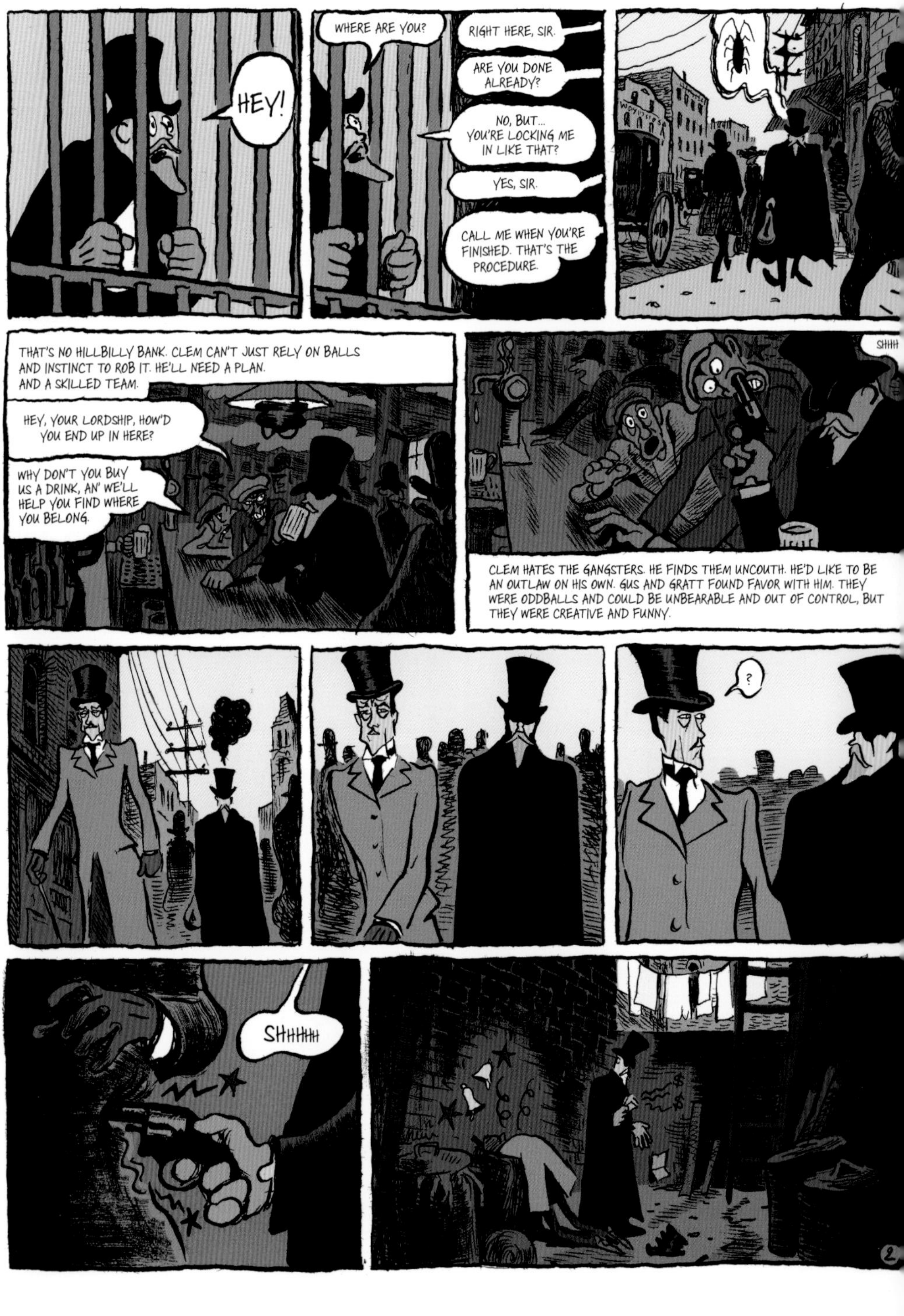
HEY!
WHERE ARE YOU?
RIGHT HERE, SIR.
ARE YOU DONE ALREADY?
NO, BUT... YOU'RE LOCKING ME IN LIKE THAT?
YES, SIR.
CALL ME WHEN YOU'RE FINISHED. THAT'S THE PROCEDURE.
THAT'S NO HILLBILLY BANK. CLEM CAN'T JUST RELY ON BALLS AND INSTINCT TO ROB IT. HE'LL NEED A PLAN. AND A SKILLED TEAM.
HEY, YOUR LORDSHIP, HOW'D YOU END UP IN HERE?
WHY DON'T YOU BUY US A DRINK, AN' WE'LL HELP YOU FIND WHERE YOU BELONG.
SHHH
CLEM HATES THE GANGSTERS. HE FINDS THEM UNCOUTH. HE'D LIKE TO BE AN OUTLAW ON HIS OWN. GUS AND GRATT FOUND FAVOR WITH HIM. THEY WERE ODDBALLS AND COULD BE UNBEARABLE AND OUT OF CONTROL, BUT THEY WERE CREATIVE AND FUNNY.
?
SHHHHH

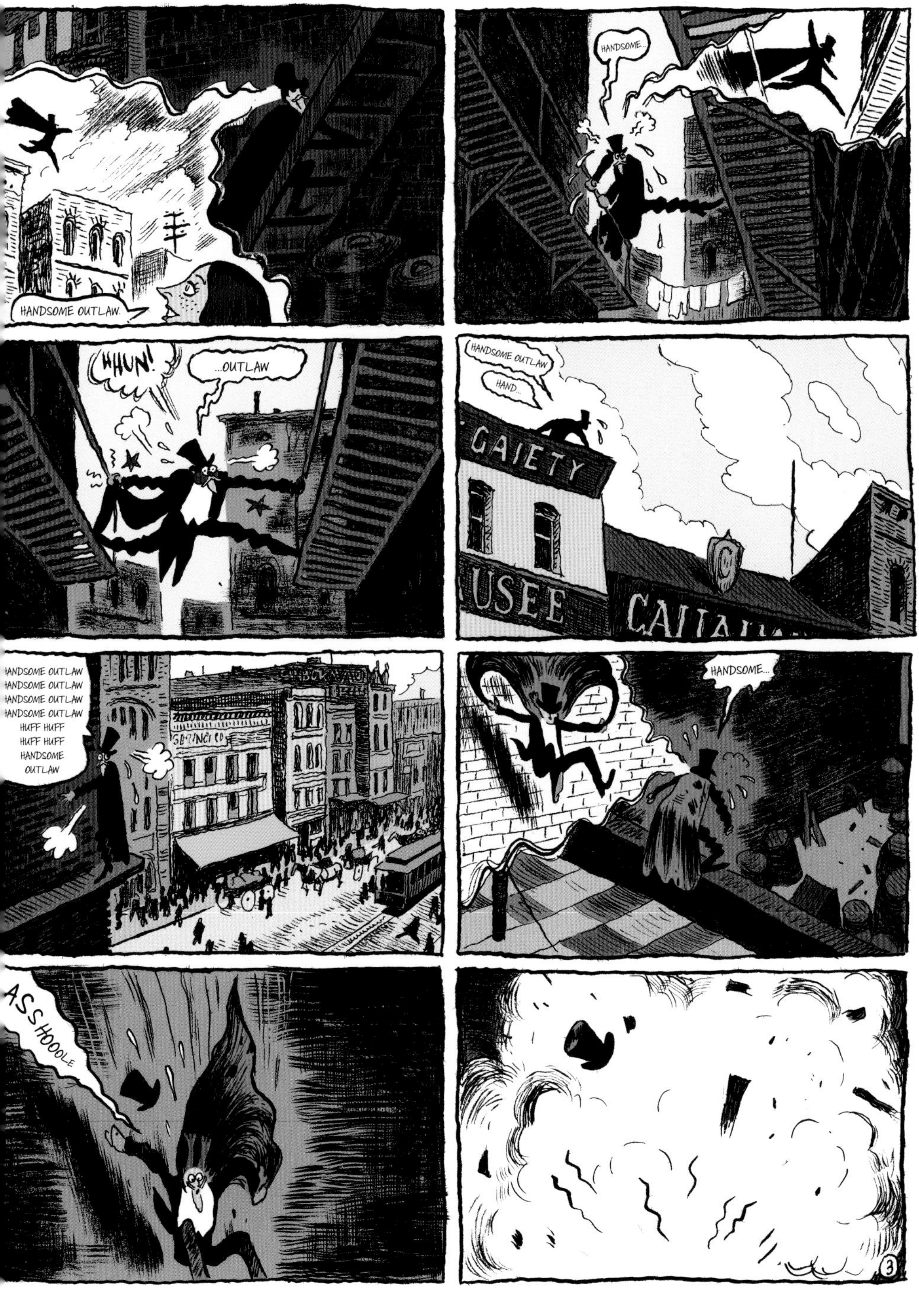
HANDSOME OUTLAW.
HANDSOME...
WHUN!
...OUTLAW
HANDSOME OUTLAW
HAND...
GAIETY
USEE
HANDSOME OUTLAW
HANDSOME OUTLAW
HANDSOME OUTLAW
HANDSOME OUTLAW
HUFF HUFF
HUFF HUFF
HANDSOME
OUTLAW
HANDSOME...
ASSHOOOLE
3

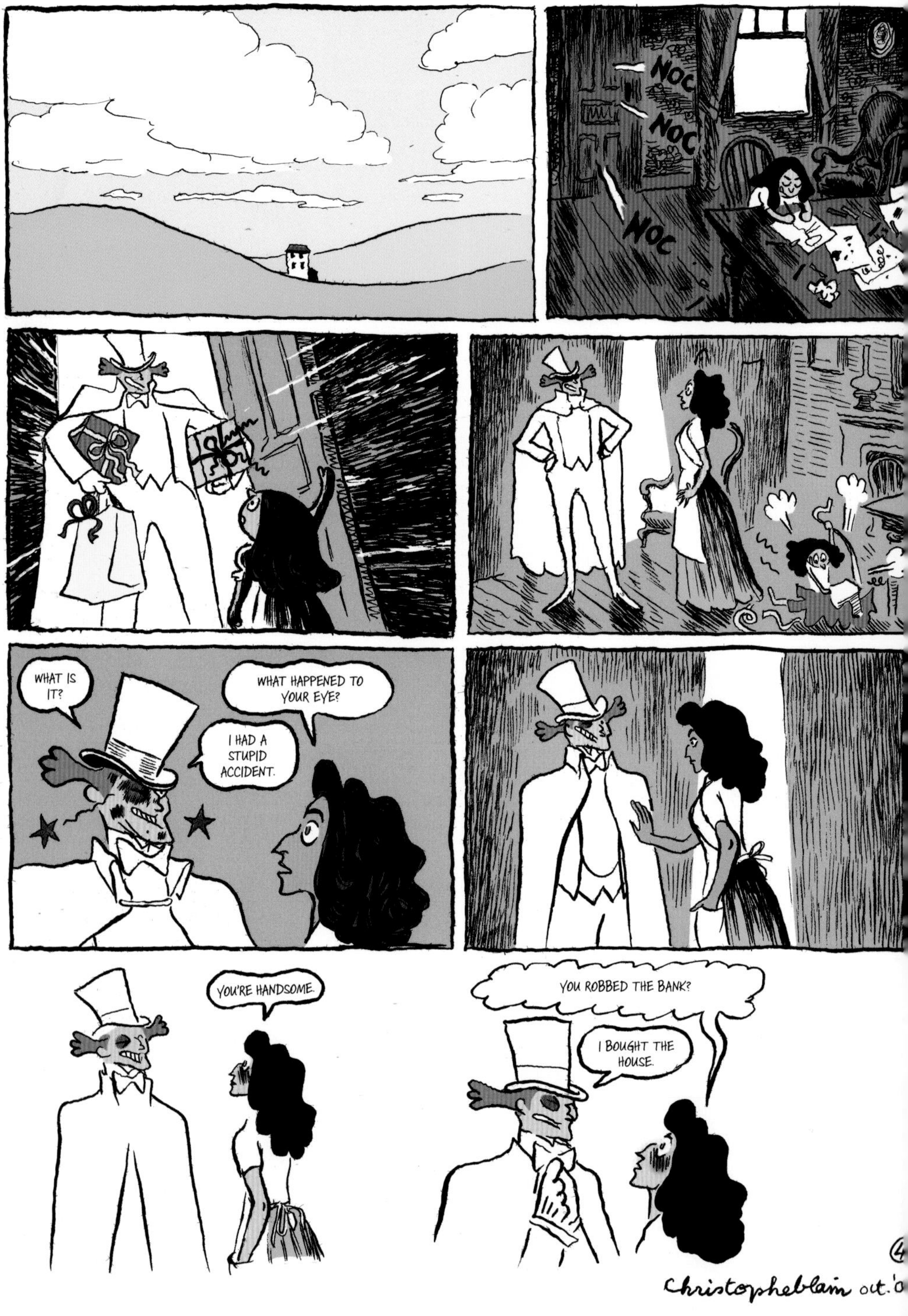
NOC
NOC
NOC
WHAT IS IT?
WHAT HAPPENED TO YOUR EYE?
I HAD A STUPID ACCIDENT.
YOU'RE HANDSOME.
YOU ROBBED THE BANK?
I BOUGHT THE HOUSE.
Christopheblain oct.'0

HANDSOME OUTLAW

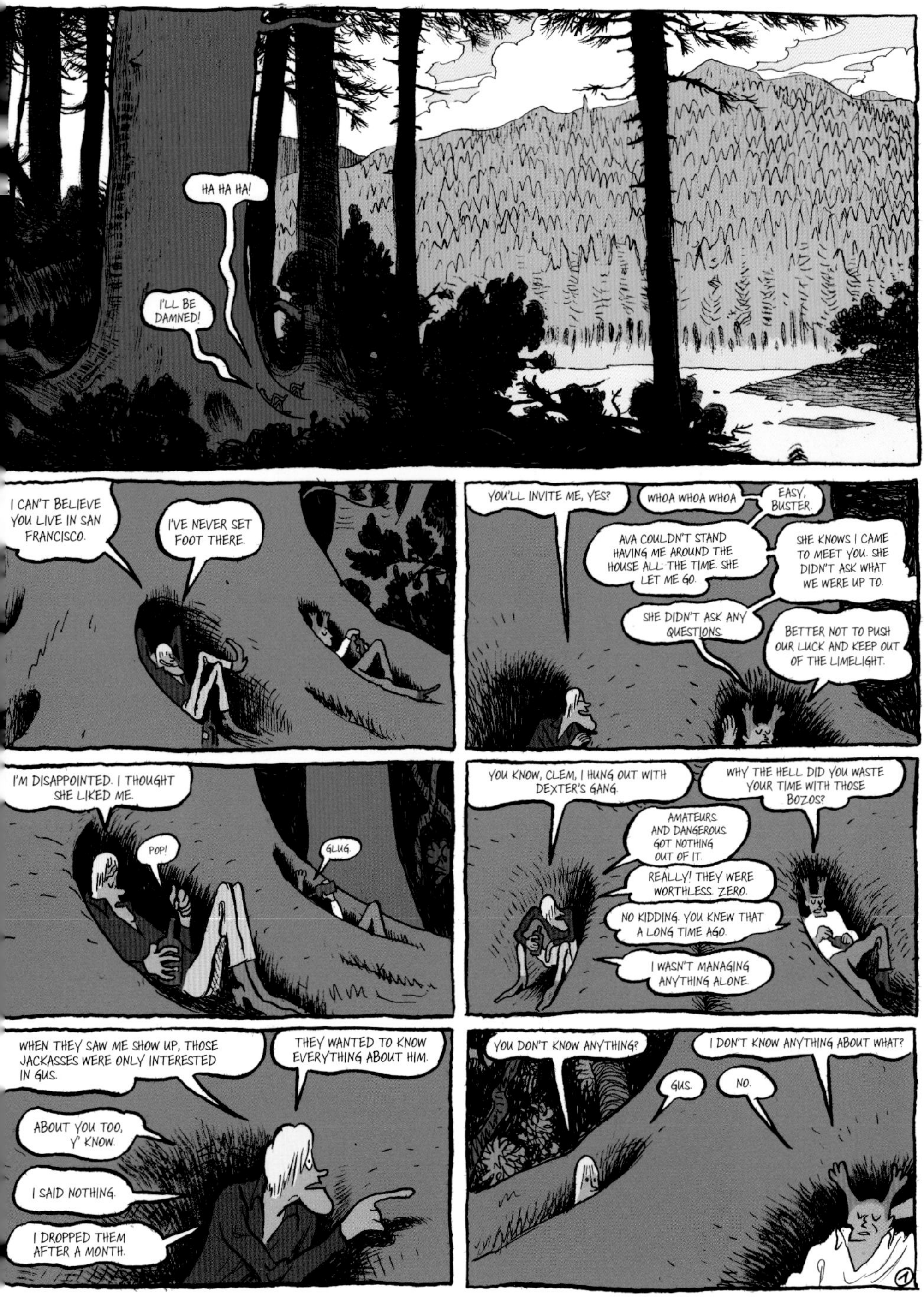
HA HA HA!
I'LL BE DAMNED!
I CAN'T BELIEVE YOU LIVE IN SAN FRANCISCO.
I'VE NEVER SET FOOT THERE.
YOU'LL INVITE ME, YES?
WHOA WHOA WHOA
EASY, BUSTER.
AVA COULDN'T STAND HAVING ME AROUND THE HOUSE ALL THE TIME. SHE LET ME GO.
SHE KNOWS I CAME TO MEET YOU. SHE DIDN'T ASK WHAT WE WERE UP TO.
SHE DIDN'T ASK ANY QUESTIONS.
BETTER NOT TO PUSH OUR LUCK AND KEEP OUT OF THE LIMELIGHT.
I'M DISAPPOINTED. I THOUGHT SHE LIKED ME.
POP!
GLUG.
YOU KNOW, CLEM, I HUNG OUT WITH DEXTER'S GANG.
WHY THE HELL DID YOU WASTE YOUR TIME WITH THOSE BOZOS?
AMATEURS AND DANGEROUS. GOT NOTHING OUT OF IT.
REALLY! THEY WERE WORTHLESS. ZERO.
NO KIDDING. YOU KNEW THAT A LONG TIME AGO.
I WASN'T MANAGING ANYTHING ALONE.
WHEN THEY SAW ME SHOW UP, THOSE JACKASSES WERE ONLY INTERESTED IN GUS.
THEY WANTED TO KNOW EVERYTHING ABOUT HIM.
ABOUT YOU TOO, Y' KNOW.
I SAID NOTHING.
I DROPPED THEM AFTER A MONTH.
YOU DON'T KNOW ANYTHING?
I DON'T KNOW ANYTHING ABOUT WHAT?
GUS.
NO.
1

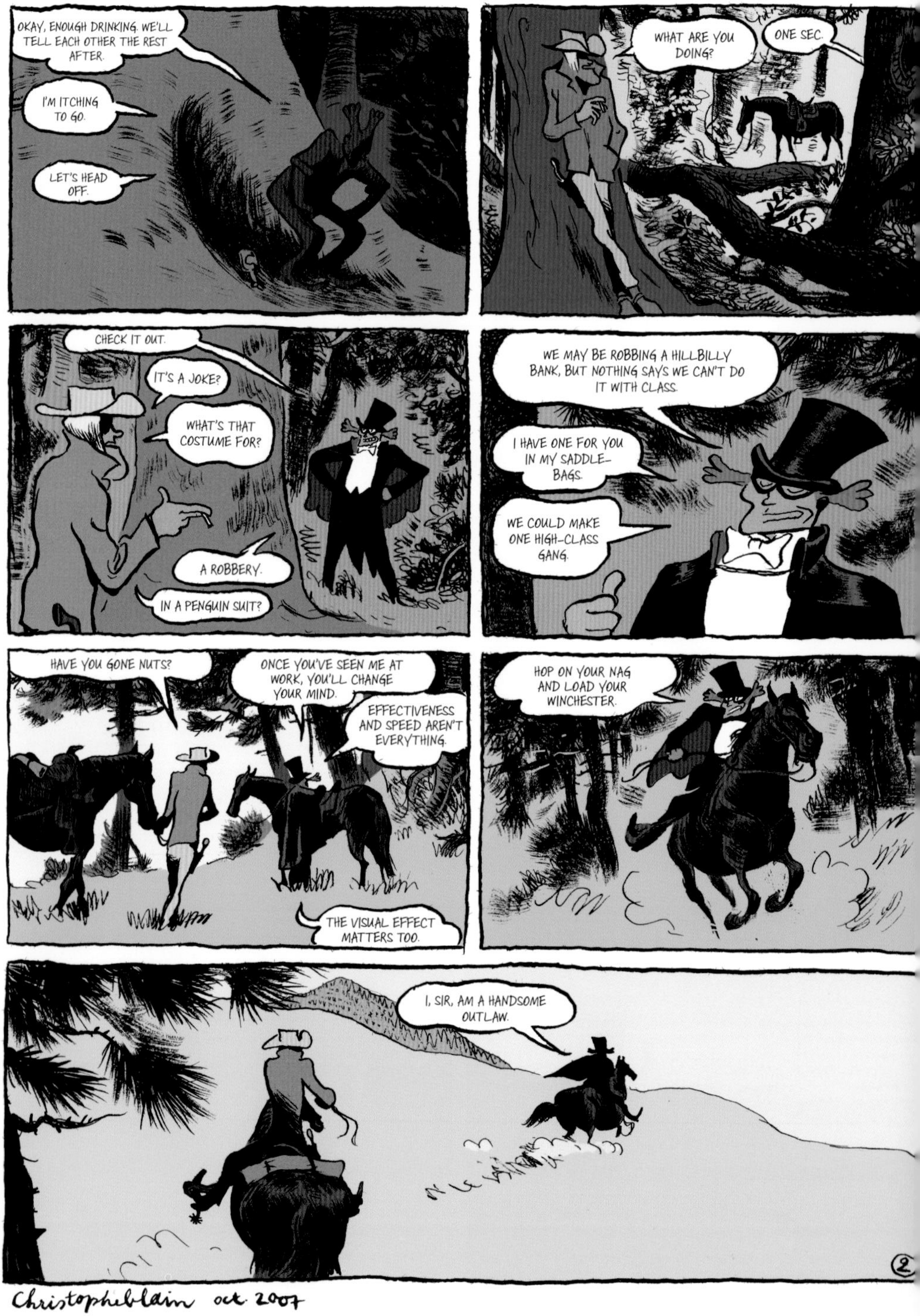
OKAY, ENOUGH DRINKING. WE'LL TELL EACH OTHER THE REST AFTER.
I'M ITCHING TO GO.
LET'S HEAD OFF.
WHAT ARE YOU DOING?
ONE SEC.
CHECK IT OUT.
IT'S A JOKE?
WHAT'S THAT COSTUME FOR?
A ROBBERY.
IN A PENGUIN SUIT?
WE MAY BE ROBBING A HILLBILLY BANK, BUT NOTHING SAYS WE CAN'T DO IT WITH CLASS.
I HAVE ONE FOR YOU IN MY SADDLE-BAGS.
WE COULD MAKE ONE HIGH-CLASS GANG.
HAVE YOU GONE NUTS?
ONCE YOU'VE SEEN ME AT WORK, YOU'LL CHANGE YOUR MIND.
EFFECTIVENESS AND SPEED AREN'T EVERYTHING.
THE VISUAL EFFECT MATTERS TOO.
HOP ON YOUR NAG AND LOAD YOUR WINCHESTER.
I, SIR, AM A HANDSOME OUTLAW.
2
Christopheblain oct. 2007

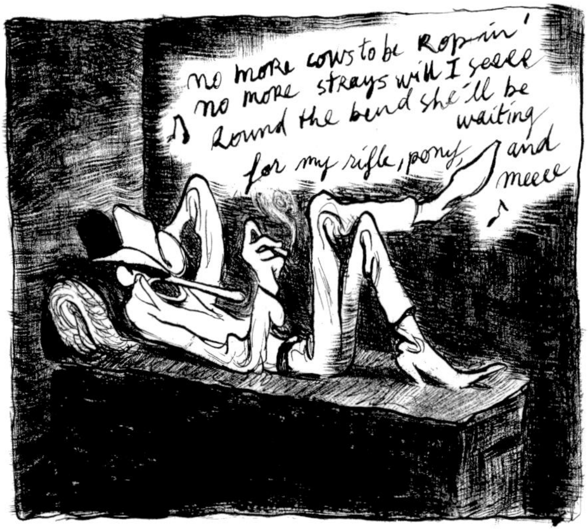
no more cows to be Ropin'
no more strays will I seeee
Round the bend she'll be waiting
for my rifle, pony, and meeee

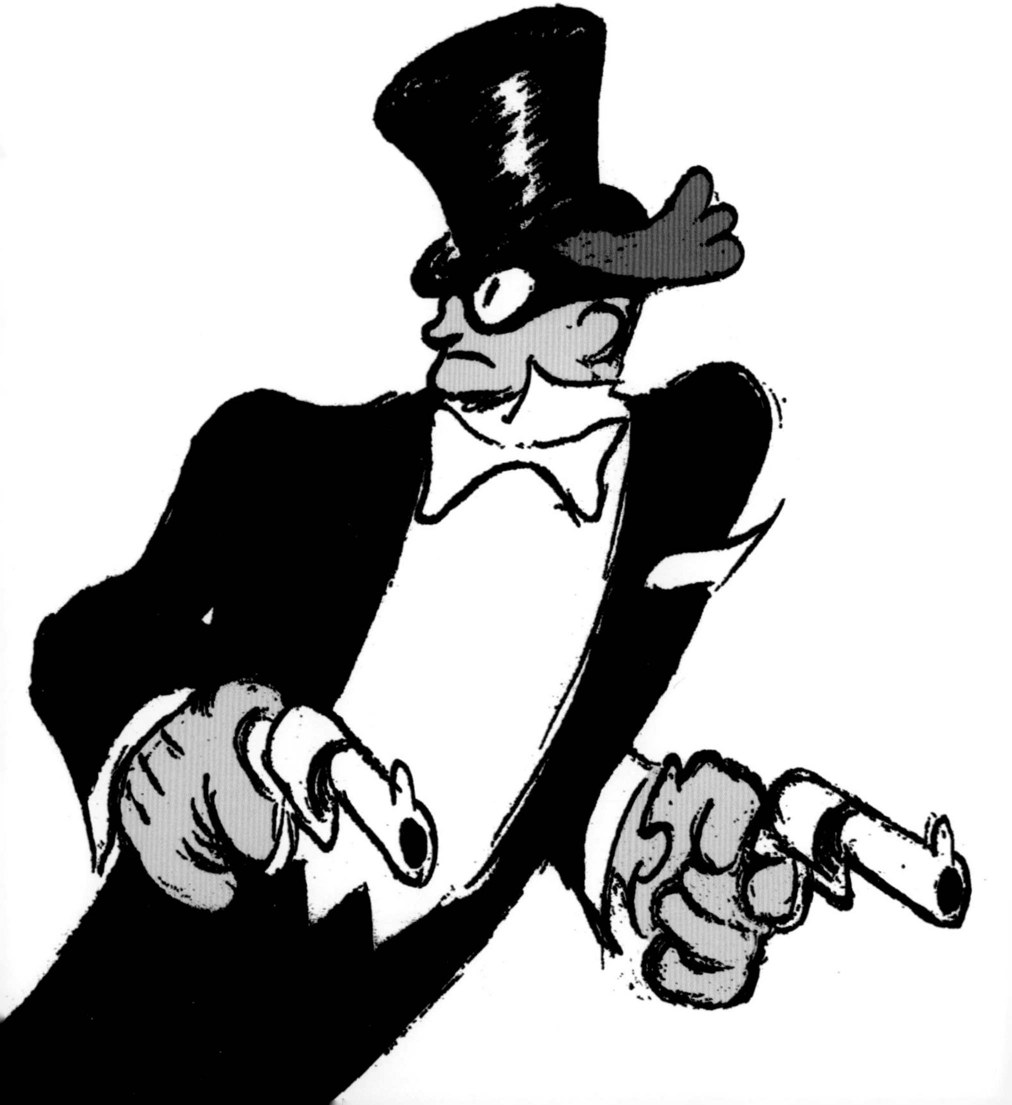

First Second
NEW YORK & LONDON

Copyright © 2008 by Chris Blain
Translation by Alexis Siegel © 2008 by First Second

Published by First Second
First Second is an imprint of Roaring Brook Press,
a division of Holtzbrinck Publishing Holdings Limited Partnership
175 Fifth Avenue, New York, NY 10010

Distributed in Canada by H. B. Fenn and Company Ltd.
Distributed in the United Kingdom by Macmillan Children's Books, a division of
Pan Macmillan.

Design by Tanja Geis

Cataloging-in-Publication Data is on file at the Library of Congress.

ISBN-13: 978-1-59643-170-6
ISBN-10: 1-59643-170-9

First Second books are available for special promotions and premiums.
For details, contact: Director of Special Markets, Holtzbrinck Publishers.

First Edition October 2008
Printed in China

1 3 5 7 9 10 8 6 4 2

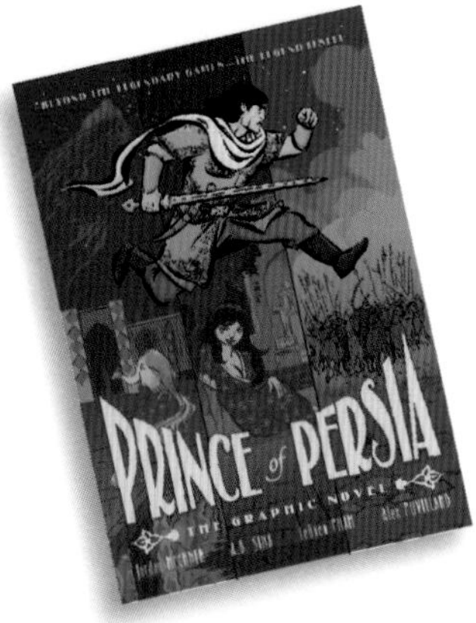
PRINCE of PERSIA
THE GRAPHIC NOVEL

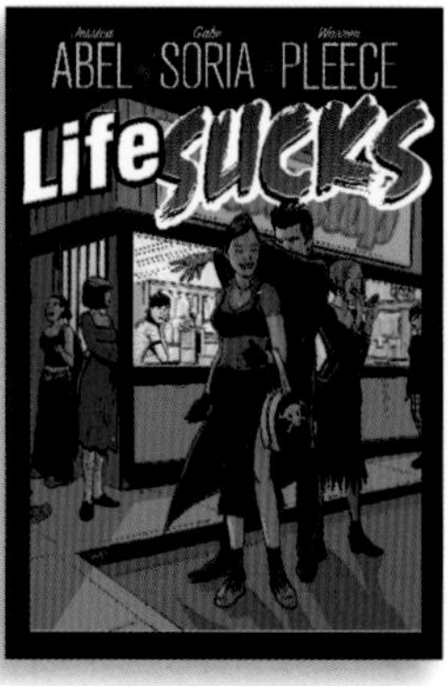
ABEL SORIA PLEECE
Life SUCKS

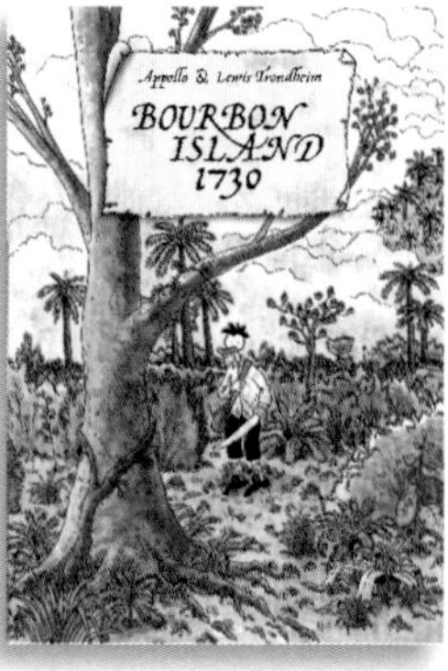
Appollo & Lewis Trondheim
BOURBON ISLAND 1730

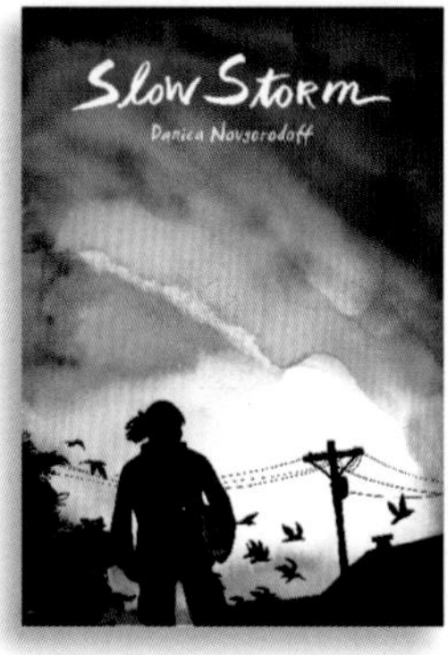
Slow Storm
Danica Novgorodoff

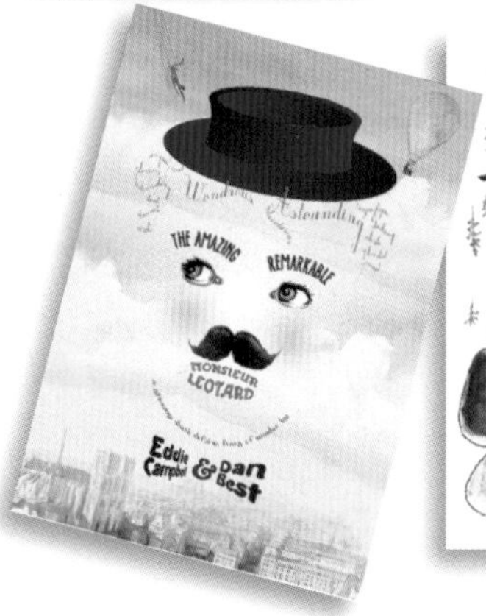
THE AMAZING
REMARKABLE
MONSIEUR LEOTARD
Eddie Campbell & Dan Best

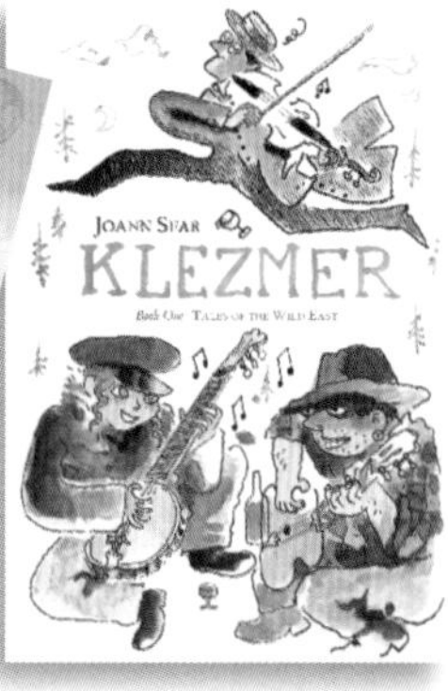
JOANN SFAR
KLEZMER
Book One: TALES OF THE WILD EAST

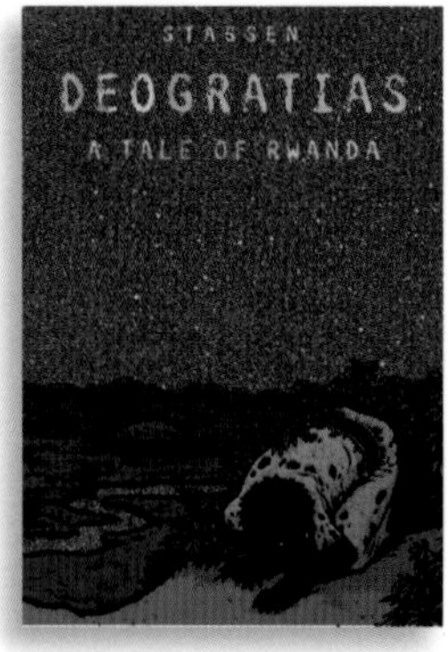
STASSEN
DEOGRATIAS
A TALE OF RWANDA

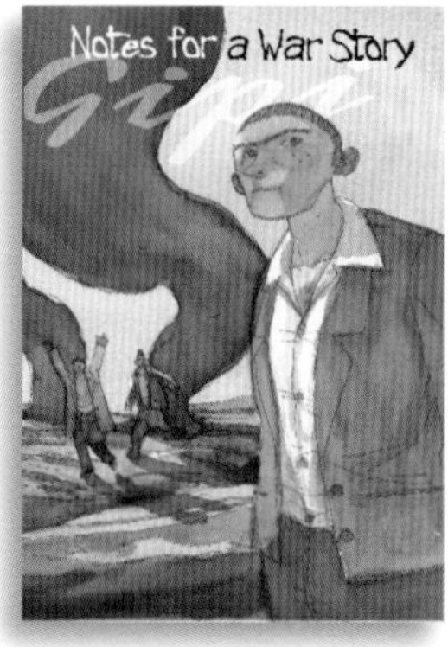
Notes for a War Story
Gipi

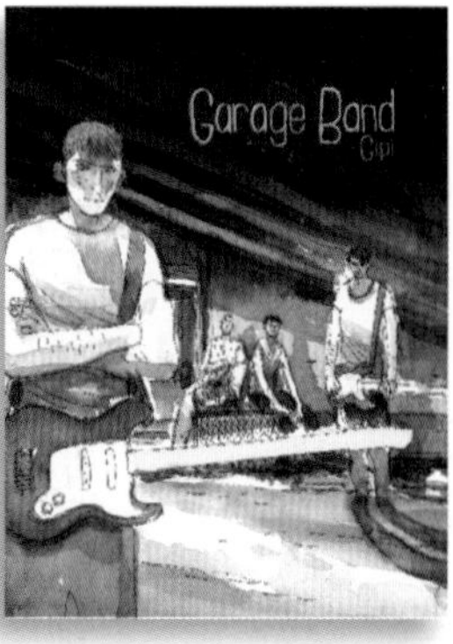
Garage Band

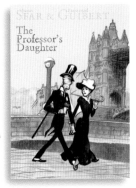

... and more at **www.firstsecondbooks.com**